HERAKLION BLUE

HERAKLION BLUE

Mike Lunnon-Wood

1 5221 8 9 21

This first world edition published in Great Britain 2001 by
SEVERN HOUSE PUBLISHERS LTD of
9–15 High Street, Sutton, Surrey SM1 1DF.
This first world edition published in the USA 2002 by
SEVERN HOUSE PUBLISHERS INC of
595 Madison Avenue, New York, N.Y. 10022.

British Library Cataloguing in Publication Data

Lunnon-Wood, Mike
  Heraklion blue
  1. Great Britain. Royal Marines Commandos –
Search and rescue operations
  2. Suspense fiction
  I. Title
  823.9'14 [F]

ISBN 0-7278-5792-4

Typeset by Palimpsest Book Production Ltd.,
Polmont, Stirlingshire, Scotland.
Printed and bound in Great Britain by
MPG Books Ltd., Bodmin, Cornwall.

For Tom Clay,
a journalist killed covering the Congo in the sixties –
our next-door neighbour at the time –
and for Joe and Wendy Whaley, my oldest friends.
Next year at Chirundu.

Preface

The people of what we now know as Angola, have been crossing into what is now the Democratic Republic of Congo in one guise or another for hundreds of years before the borders were defined as we now know them – to raid, to plunder, to take slaves, to wage war. The last forty years have been violent times in this part of Africa. Katanga, in the south-east of the old Belgian Congo, now Shaba province, was the scene of horrific violence in the sixties when Katangan secessionists known as Simbas tried to take control of that mineral-rich province, and a last-second, guns-blazing rescue of mission staff by mercenary John Peters really did take place in 1964. By this time Mike Hoare's 5 Commando had relieved huge tracts of Katanga from the Simbas, saving many lives in the process, while the UN peacekeepers, without Hoare's free-ranging mandate or, to be honest, his tactical skills or his drive, simply tried to keep the warring factions apart.

Missions and their staff have always been soft targets for anyone wanting to strike at something soft that won't fight back, or for any disaffected individual wanting a high-profile target, or wanting to hit out at Christianity, Western influences or the establishment. There is, as far as I know, no mission at Tenta. But there are still people there who remember the horror of the Simbas and the later violence around Kolwesi in the seventies and there are still people there – non-combatants, foreign civilians – at risk the next time it explodes. This is a work of fiction, but could it happen? All too easily. In fact, the Royal Marines were in Brazzaville in the Congo, awaiting

vii

orders to assist repatriating EU nationals from escalating risk in the neighbouring Democratic Republic of Congo twice recently, in 1997 and 1999.

M L-W, Chirundu – August 2001

Acknowledgements

Getting it 'about right' in a military story is difficult for a civilian, and no book like this can be done without the help and cooperation of those who do it in real life, those who know it, live it, breathe it. My gratitude firstly to the Royal Navy in the form of Commander Adrian Bell – then Captain of HMS *Birmingham* – the wardroom and various messes aboard HMS *Birmingham*. A Type 42 destroyer, by the time this book is published she will have been decommissioned, much to the dismay of many who served on her over the years. The wonderful people on 'Brum' gave up many hours to help me understand their ship and their jobs. I am indebted to them all.

I am also indebted to Major Andy Maynard, at the time of writing commander of the real OC Alpha Company 40 Commando, Royal Marines – and his 'Saints'. I was privileged to spend time with them. They were kind, hospitable beyond belief and endlessly patient helping me understand what they do. If anyone ever wonders what our defence budget is spent on, then try and see these people at work. Their sheer professionalism is awesome. I hope I have done them justice. Any mistakes are mine, not theirs.

One

T he jungle was hot, dark and loomed each side of the track. Henri Lefage settled back in the driver's seat of the jeep, wiped the sweat from his face, took a packet of cigarettes from his pocket and lit one, inhaling deeply. His hand was shaking slightly. It always did after an action. For 5 Commando this hadn't been much of a fight, a short skirmish after an ambush, but a bullet had struck the windscreen of the jeep and passed inches from his head. Another close one. He smiled. They didn't call him 'Lucky' for nothing. He looked down at his kit. Filthy. They wore khakis – creased when they could get them washed – and on his shoulder above the Wild Goose patch he wore sergeant's stripes. He disliked dirty kit. It was unprofessional. He might be a mercenary but that didn't mean he was not a professional soldier.

A patrol was moving forward on foot to the bridge, always the safest way after a halt, and as Captain Peters slid into his seat on the other side, Lefage started the engine. Behind them on the jeep, manning a pedestal-mounted Belgian MAG machine gun, was another volunteer, James Egan, a wayward public-school dropout and a close friend.

Henri Lefage was a soldier, just out of the Foreign Legion; his parents were Corsicans, but he had been born in Italy. At twenty-four, a trained soldier speaking French, English and Italian, he had been snapped up by Major Hoare's recruiters in the small flat in the avenues of Salisbury in Rhodesia.

John Peters was a lithe, green-eyed, quick-witted Yorkshireman who had served time with the SAS. Hard as nails, he was in

1

Hoare's view an outstanding officer, and his men – later to be called Force John-John – would do anything for him. In addition to his uniform he sometimes wore a cravat-like neckscarf, and as an officer he had a Browning 9-mill. pistol, but not hanging off his wide, brown, canvas issue belt, but off a narrower leather job.

Recruited to put down the Communist-backed Katangan seccession movement and restore control to the government, this was a fight that to Hoare's Wild Geese was righteous. The shocking brutality of the Simbas was almost unthinkable, with atrocities, ritual torture, rape, forced amputation and even cannibalism commonplace. And in all this, not only a local population being brutalised, but Europeans, missionaries, settlers, miners and traders.

Hoare's 5 Commando campaigned across the country relieving one Simba-held town after another, and invariably it was Peters and his command at the head of the column.

As a sergeant there was no way Lefage should have been driving the vehicle but he did anyway, enjoying his time with Peters. Henri liked Hoare and he liked Peters, liked working for them. Peters and he became quite close friends, comrades, and Peters liked to listen to Henri sing Legion songs, the Legion way, in slow time.

'Let's go,' Peters called, putting his radio handset down.

'*Oui.*' Henri let the clutch out and moved the vehicle slowly forward. As leader in the column they were following the foot patrol across the bridge, and then would speed up as they cleared the area and as the track allowed.

They had to get to Isangi by dawn and there was the river to cross first. Lives depended on it. The speaking drums were thumping out their message in the jungle to the right, and with another twenty kilometres to the river they were still in very dangerous country.

The jungle was thick, close, brooding, and they could feel they were being watched every inch of the way. Half an hour later as the lead vehicle rounded a bend several shots rang out from the right and Henri saw a thrown spear pass overhead as he slewed the vehicle to a halt and they baled out. Above him James put a heavy burst into the trees, covering fire as the men in the truck behind them jumped out and deployed. More fire was hitting the column now, and as the men returned fire into the heavy undergrowth, a couple of arrows landed among them. As James jumped down with the MAG, a stand gun went off. Made from a hollow pipe – a sawn-off propshaft was popular – it was stuffed with explosives and filled with shrapel, stones, whatever they could find. Roughly pointed at something or someone it was then detonated.

Things hit the vehicles and smoke rolled out of the trees; the mercenaries were returning fire at a furious rate and suddenly Peters was calling for a ceasefire. The Simbas never stayed round long.

'Henri, take care of him. He's hit,' Captain Peters snapped, and darted back down the column. Henri looked round quickly to where James was lying on his side on the muddy ground, his face bleeding in a dozen places, breathing roughly. Henri, one hand still holding his rifle, and looking back up at the trees every few seconds, gently rolled him over, so he could establish the extent of his wounds. 'Easy, *mon ami*,' he said gently, 'Don't move. Let me look, eh?'

The wounds in his face were messy, bloody, but superficial, caused, Henri knew, by whatever was in the stand gun. He looked further down. He was bleeding badly below, his trousers and lower shirt red with bright arterial blood. He put down his rifle and quickly undid James's belt and trousers and was appalled. There was a big exit wound, big enough to put his fist into, just below his navel. He pulled a dressing from his pocket, and someone behind him called for the medic. There was no doctor with the column, just a man who had done time as a nurse. Then he was there, and Peters was standing over them with the radio from the jeep in his hands, talking to Major Hoare down in the centre of the column.

'Sorry about this. Hate to be any trouble,' the wounded man muttered weakly through bloody lips. Well, he was English.

'Don't talk, eh?' Henri replied. 'We get you fixed up.'

3

'I'll start here. Get a dressing on the entry wound,' the medic said to Henri. 'Lower back somewhere.'

He nodded. Beneath the blood on his face his skin was pale, waxy.

'Entry wound!' the medic snapped.

'*Oui.*' Henri got on with it, found the small entry hole and staunched the flow of blood with a big dressing already muddy on the outside from his hands.

A driver back in the column had taken a bullet through the thigh, and when the fighting patrol returned to the column they reported three enemy dead in the trees and three wounded. The wounded were too far gone for interrogation and when the column moved on they were left where they had fallen. Some of the men wanted to shoot them but Hoare said no. They were no further threat.

James died that evening in the back of the sickbay truck, having never regained consciousness. It had been a costly engagement – one dead and one wounded for six enemy – and the column arrived at the river chastened and saddened. He had been a popular man. One of them.

The advance elements had got the ferry running and under the cover of darkness Hoare pushed across the river into Isangi. The mission, where they were expecting to find fifty Belgian priests and nuns, was deserted, and with mounting anxiety Hoare interrogated the village chief. 'Where are the whites?' Pale with anger he explained just what he would do if the truth was not forthcoming.

Eventually it came out. They were at Yangambi. The column recrossed the river and advanced on Yangambi at all speed fearing the worst. The atrocities committed on missionaries were almost unthinkable. Just short of Yangambi a Belgian man in his fifties ran out of hiding into the road. Terrified he had been in the bush for four days dodging anyone he saw. He confirmed the headman's story. The priests and nuns were at Yangambi, but there were five or so others up at the clinic, four kilometres up the river.

Hoare, torn between rescuing everyone and not splitting his

4

force, agreed to John Peters' suggestion, and while the main column raced down the road towards Yangambi, Peters peeled of with ten men in two jeeps. They had insufficient firepower to fight off a major attack or ambush so would rely on speed and surprise.

Lefage drove the lead vehicle and when they rolled into the tiny mission clinic Simbas ran like chickens in a farmyard, some shooting back, some so drugged up they stood with spears. The men opened fire from moving vehicles, the two MAGs hammering out, then jumped down and engaged on foot. Several Simbas, drugged or full of *muti*, and screaming *'meule'*, ran at Lefage as he dismounted. He fired a burst from his FN, then aimed shots, and they went down, the last close enough that as he moved forward he caught the falling Simba's head with his rifle butt, every ounce of strength in the swing. It made a wet meaty sound and if the bullet hadn't killed the man the blow would have.

It was all over very quickly and the scene was horrifying.

A white man – a priest, or what was left of him – was lying on the ground. His arms and legs had been hacked off, his penis and testicles were cut away, and they had penetrated his anus with a maize cob.

'Jesus!' Someone muttered, looking down at him.

'Sergeant Lefage. Find the others,' Peters called. 'You men secure a perimeter. Let's go!'

Henri swept through the small building, his weapon to the fore. In one room he found a Simba wearing a monkey skin as a hat, drunk out of his skull on medical alcohol, staggering about. Any mercy in him squeezed out by the scene outside, he shot him and moved on. In another room there were two more dead priests, tortured to death, a severed penis pinned to the notice board, and dried blood and gore down the wall.

A few rooms down there was a locked door and he put a boot straight through the lock.

Inside were two naked, bruised and bloodied women, filthy-dirty and in a terrible state. Both stood up from the floor where they had been cowering and weeping, covering their nakedness. One – young, with thick black hair, and beautiful even through the evidence of her ordeal – threw her arms round his neck. The older one sat back down on the floor holding her knees and rocking back and forth muttering to herself.

'Is OK,' he said gently to the one who was holding him. 'You are safe now.' He pushed her back and smiled. He was a very good-looking young man and his smile showed white teeth and flashing eyes. 'My name is Henri. Come, let me find your clothing.' He turned and called, '*Mon Capitain!*'

Lefage took his shirt off, draped it over her nakedness and took the red bandanna from round his neck and gently wiped her face with it and then wrapped it round her cut hand.

Peters arrived, his expression bleak. They had found another nun dead on the riverbank by the little jetty. She had been raped, tortured and beaten, her body horribly bruised. Their final indignity was to impale her on one of the uprights that formed the jetty, the five-inch-diameter pole up between her legs and into her body holding her now dead form upright.

Peters came into the room, took in the sight and swung a salute up to his beret. 'John Peters, marm. At your service.'

They found the nun's clothes, the young nun shrieking in joy at finding her little gold cross where she had left it, in the pocket of her habit. Her resilience was astonishing. After three days and nights of ongoing abuse, she was bouncing back. It was the little cross that did it. Something personal, something treasured, and something the Simbas had not found, sullied or abused.

They put them into the vehicle with Captain Peters, Lefage and a young South African who was now manning the machine gun. She chattered all the way, euphoric with life, her arm round the older nun, who just sat and stared out ahead, her ordeal all too much.

They made their way back to the main road and on to Yangambi, where a delighted column of 5 Commando had found and rescued about fifty Belgian nuns and priests.

Over the course of the day Henri kept finding reason to return to where the young nun he now knew as Mary was.

He was captivated. Smitten. Cleaned up, back in her habit, and with her community, she had an air of wonderful serenity. They talked haltingly in English. She was Greek, with huge, dark eyes and full lips and could have been Sophia Loren. When he walked over before they mounted the trucks to take everyone back to Stanleyville the look in her eye said the same as his. Another place, another time, another life. *C'est la vie* he thought.

At Stanleyville they handed the Belgians over to their consul and Henri sought out Mary one last time, hurrying. Truck engines were revving. The column was on the move again.

'We must go now.'

'Thank you. From the bottom of our hearts, thank you. The Lord sent you. Henri, you are . . . you are . . .' She faded away.

'I will never forget you.'

'Nor I you.' He paused, nervous. 'Maybe we will meet again one day?'

She nodded and took the tiny gold cross from round her neck and pressed it into his hand. 'Take this and remember me.'

'I could not,' he replied.

'Do. Take it. Go safely now.' She smiled at him and his whole world lit up. 'And come back one day.'

He took the cross, flashed her a smile and ran for the jeep, a man hopelessly in love. It was the last time he ever saw her.

Atlantic Coast, West Africa
14 November 1998, 1200 hrs

Marston looked across the bridge. Out of the starboard side over the bridge wing the lukewarm waters were shades of green under the baking sun. The bridge was closed up, the doors out on to the bridge wings either side shut to try and keep the heat at bay. But each time someone went in or out the hot, humid air blasted in, and even with the ship's air conditioning running flat-out, it was still hot. He wiped some sweat from his brow. Frigging place. He looked out through a powerful pair of binoculars and crossed back into the centre of the bridge, stepped round Lt Wallace, the officer of the watch, who was watching a tanker coming down the coast towards them, and bending down, looked through the gyroscopic compass repeater and took a bearing.

This was the WADS, the West Africa Deployment Ship. The British government's visible commitment to peace in West Africa. The ship's role in her long patrols up and down the coast of West Africa was to be there to support British interests, in particular the safety and well-being of British and EU nationals in that part of the world. Sierra Leone was on the watch list, as was Liberia.

There were peaceful places – Gabon, Ghana, the Gambia – but they were all overshadowed in every way by the Democratic Republic of Congo. The size of Western Europe, it was the old Zaire, and for all its size it was as vulnerable to influences as anywhere, maybe more so. In the last couple of months the Democratic Republic of Congo had been moved to the top of the watch list.The Foreign and Commonwealth Office had issued travel advisories against travel to the region, but that was academic. There were no meaningful numbers of tourists in the Democratic Republic of Congo, just like there were none in Congo. A few backpackers and Trans-Africa four-wheel-drive groups, but that was all. It just wasn't that kind of place. But there were diplomats, engineers, a few travelling business people, some medical types, quite a lot of aid workers, and members of various religious orders.

For the time being they were to patrol a box-shaped stretch of water up and down the Congo coast, although what good they could do was yet to be determined. Most of the Republic of Congo was well inland, beyond even the reach of the ship's helicopter.

Don Marston was the navigator, a lieutenant in HMS *Winchester*, and as she ploughed her way north-east on her patrol, he stepped into his nav station at the back of the bridge and wiped his brow again before bending over the chart on the table. Sweat left big salty marks on the chart paper. On the horizon abeam of the starboard side the bulks of oil platforms rose up from the sea. He quickly worked the plot. He didn't need to. Unlike the newer warships where underneath the chart table a set of little electric motors drove a light beam that shone upwards through the perspex top of the table illuminating the ship's position on the chart, they just had the old hard-ply surface and the GPS, the Global Positioning System. They still had old-fashioned satnav, and they even had a sextant. Occasionally Lt Marston, a very thorough individual, would drag it out at noon and do a sighting. His job was to navigate the ship and therefore he made sure he knew exactly where they were at any given moment. Not approximately where they were. *Exactly.*

Marston stepped up and stood beside Lt Wallace, who had the watch, the forenoon 0800 to 1200. She had her binoculars up and was looking out at the tanker.

'That's a big bugger,' Marston said. The supertanker was a crude carrier, passage-making, he suspected, down to round the Cape of Good Hope.

'She is,' Sally said. 'Two-fifty thousand tons. She'll pass a mile of our starboard side.'

He grinned. She wasn't a bad officer, Marston thought. A lot of women, much to the Navy's chagrin, who genuinely wanted them aboard ships, had a spatial-awareness problem. The basis of many jokes about women parking cars, too close or too far away from the other car, it was for the Navy a liability when you were responsible for driving a ship through areas where there were other ships. In many it wasn't drastic, they would simply be unable to look out at the sea ahead of them, see two other ships and be able to accurately visualise their headings and positions in their own mind. They seemed closer than they were, or further away, or on a course that might suggest they would possibly collide, where in reality the vessels were a good distance apart, were on diverging courses and in no danger. The problem, when bad, was an embuggerance, because the person with the spatial awareness problem then wanted to take action, call for a course change which was unnecessary, and a junior watch-keeper couldn't arbitrarily change course without consulting the captain, unless the ship was in danger. They would call up the navigator, or as standing orders required, advise the XO or the captain if the ship was entering any sort of higher-risk environment. On his last ship, Marston had worked with a female midshipman who eventually left the service, her spatial awareness was so bad. But Marston knew Lt Sally Wallace had no such problem. She had a hunter's eye, could judge distance with incredible accuracy, and had better spatial awareness than any man on the ship. If she reckoned the tanker would pass a mile away then it would. No course change required. But an advice to the Captain was, and Lt Wallace lifted the bridge phone to her lips.

A figure came through the bridge-wing door and another blast of hot, humid air rolled through the bridge. He looked over and grinned. It was the XO. Harry when they were in the wardroom or ashore, but the Executive Officer, the ship's First Lieutenant when they were at work. Lt Commander Harry Selby was dripping in sweat, his tropical whites limp and damp. He's been in the hangar, Marston thought. Pretty much open to the flight deck, it was the only large internal space without air conditioning and inside, away from the warm breeze that dried sweat at the pores, it was a bitch of a place to work. The helicopter maintenance crew worked stripped to the waist, and standing orders required them to drink eight litres of water a day. No one had to enforce the rule. The lads knew. At the start of the six-month patrol period they had taken on six water dispensers with built-in coolers and the first one aboard *Winchester* was placed in the hangar. The bridge and the officer's wardroom were the last to get them. That was the Captain's decision. For Commander Channing the lads always came first.

Marston pointed out at a supertanker and looked at Selby who had taken his cap off and was wiping the sweat from his face with a hanky. 'I'll bet she has a small swimming pool and her mate is sitting in it right now, a cold drink in his hand.'

Selby grinned. 'Not that one. She's Korean. No such

comforts. They are cooking just like us.' He looked down at his watch. It was 11.50.

'Lt Wallace. Who relieves you?'

Selby knew. He did the roster. He also knew that Lt Wallace knew he knew. But protocol said that watch-keeping officers always relieved each other just before the end of the previous watch, not after. The fact he had asked would get back to the lieutenant concerned and that would be enough. Marston, in front of Wallace and looking straight out at the sea, grinned.

'Lt Allbeury, sir. He won't be long, I shouldn't think.'

'I hope not,' Selby said and just as he finished speaking a figure entered the bridge from the internal stairs.

'Permission to enter the bridge,' he called.

'Yes, please,' from Wallace, still looking to seaward. The Royal Navy has singular traditions – warships are individual things, each fostering its own customs. The *please* thing was a quirk exclusive to HMS *Winchester* and her batch 1 flotilla mate, HMS *Birmingham*.

'Hello, all!' Lt Allbeury called cheerfully, taking in Lt Wallace, the duty QM on the wheel and a rating on lookout. 'Here to relieve you, Sally.' He hadn't seen the XO and the Navigator. 'You and me, Sally. Like Bogart and Hepburn' – he swung an arm expansively – 'on the African Queen.'

'I'm sure Lt Wallace is pleased to see you,' Lt Commander Selby said dryly, as the young lieutenant turned to face him. 'As it takes time to hand over the watch and it's now eight minutes to noon, and as on *Winchester* the relief takes place before the watch ends, if I were the off-going OOW I would be pissed off. Get my drift?'

'Aah – Yes, sir,' Allbeury uttered sheepishly.

'Hand over is at least fifteen minutes before the end of the watch, Mr Allbeury.'

'Yes, sir.'

'And you are too bloody young to have seen that movie.'

'BBC One practically every other winter Sunday afternoon,' Allbeury replied.

'Seen it there often,' another voice said. 'My wife loves

11

it.' It was the Captain, and both the duty QM, newly at the wheel for his watch, and Lt Wallace straightened their backs involuntarily as he slipped into his pedestal-mounted seat, looking out at the approaching tanker.

Commander Channing had appeared like he usually did, without warning, like a ghost.

Unlike most destroyer captains who held the rank of commander, he was a real four-ring captain, or about to be. His promotion had come through and this was to be his last few days in command of a warship for some time, maybe ever. His replacement was due in a week and he would fly home. Once back in Portsmouth he would take over a desk at Nelson. This would probably be his last sea command. After this to go back to sea he would have to get either a squadron or command of an aircraft carrier, and there weren't many of those.

Channing was a small-ships man through and through. Other than a tour as XO in HMS *Invincible*, his entire seagoing career had been aboard small ships, and with the exception of a year in a frigate, all in destroyers.

The year on the frigate had been interesting. In the last years of the cold war, as a watch-keeping lieutenant, he had served on a brand spanking new Type 22, and the boss in that ship knew his craft. Not for him the noisy, public departures Portsmouth usually witnessed. He would gather his crew aboard with no shore leave for maybe a couple of days, and then, always assuming they were being watched, he would slip silently out of Portsmouth in the pre-dawn darkness, the ship's passive systems already working as she entered the Solent. By the time it was light and people noticed she was gone, her patrol had begun and she would spend the next two weeks seeking out Russian submarines in the North Sea.

Happily back in destroyers, Channing had taken the lesson on board and he was now a master at disguised intent. Tall, lean, his dark hair prematurely flecked with grey, he had piercing grey eyes and a disarming habit of saying something funny, usually an observation hooked into a very human piece of behaviour, when you least expected it.

'For years my wife said she thought that everyone who knew how to thump an engine with a mallet should look like Bogey. Quite disappointed when she began meeting real seafarers. Especially me,' he finished dryly.

Lt Wallace looked over and smiled. Commander Channing was a very good-looking man, better than Humphrey Bogart any day.

A few minutes later, the watch handed over, Lt Wallace and Lt Marston went down to the ward room for some lunch, the second sitting. With twenty-three officers on the wardroom strength, and a table that would only seat eighteen at a push, they had to eat in two shifts, which worked well because there were always officers who needed to eat earlier for one reason or another. Lt Wallace had forgotten what she had pre-ordered for lunch, so she checked the list on the clipboard, and then took a seat. She had ordered an omelette and was pleased because the ploughman's, selected from a buffet-type layout, looked colourless. It was pretty good when they left England, but that had been eaten, and many of the salad items that came aboard in Ghana had been condemned by the medical orderly. One look and he had pronounced them to be carrying more bacteria and unknown substances than he could imagine, and said they would all have to be boiled before eating. Boiled lettuces didn't appeal. There was now a lot of squash, corn on the cob, pumpkin and beans. Such was life. The steward put her plate down on the non-slip mat on the table and she began to eat thinking about the afternoon. One of her division had cocked up on SOCs, the standard system operating checks, that morning, wasn't at his station when his systems were to be checked – not a career-enhancing move when the Captain was listening to the checks being run – and after she had seen him, she was down to run a class for three ratings who were going for extra GCSEs.

Lt Commander Selby dropped into the seat opposite, the one in the middle of the table that tradition said was always available to him as Chairman of the Wardroom. If he ate at the first sitting then it was free to anyone who needed somewhere to sit, but if he hadn't eaten, then it sat empty until he had.

'Harry, rumour has it that you have found a video we haven't seen,' Marston said.

'I have,' he said, beaming. 'Thought we might invite the Captain down this evening.' Several people looked up along the table. This was news. They had seen every tape in the ship's library at least twice.

'What is it?'

'It's a pirate copy but apparently it's not bad. Ladies and gentlemen' – he nodded deferentially towards Sally Wallace and Toni Banks, the Australian dentist – 'tonight for your viewing pleasure we proudly present *Saving Private Ryan*.' There were whoops and a few cheers, and a muttered 'Believe it when I see it', and a 'Probably porno'. The film had just gone on general release in England as they left and it certainly wasn't out on video in England yet, let alone in Ghana, their last port of call. No one had seen it.

'You may all thank PO Steward Pincher,' Selby said, pointing to the steward who stood by the galley door.

Just aft the wardroom in the Chief's mess they were also settling down for some food. Upgraded Type 42s with the new weapon and engine fits are technologically advanced ships; but, in the old hulls, with some of the old equipment, they are still manpower intensive and the chief's mess was large. Nineteen men – there were no women chief petty officers on *Winchester* – were seated eating when the last two entered the space together. Chops M (missiles) was the older of the two. Although his battle station was down in the ops room manning the missile and main-gun firing systems, he was also responsible for the ship's defence in close quarters. In particular while tied up in port, or in restricted waters where she might come under low-tech attack by terrorists or insurgents.

Pragmatic, traditional, hands-on, when not on a defence watch or at action stations he worked in the warfare office down aft. CPO Davies, in charge of the Phalanx close quarters Gatling guns was younger, more ambitious, and currently considering applying for Dartmouth and a commission, relatively easy in the modern Navy, the ultimate meritocracy.

There were four men in the wardroom who had come up the hard way, one now a Lt Commander, and Davies knew technically he was as good as anyone on the ship. He could make his Phalanx guns do things no one else could, with a speed and simplicity that Captain Channing liked very much. For CPO Davies the operating manual was a guide only, a standard to be bettered.

Chops M Roberts sat down first and Davies followed him into a chair opposite.

'When's the raffle draw then?' Roberts asked.

Davies was currently mess chairman. 'When some bastards buy the last three tickets?' he replied with a grin, looking up hopefully. 'Come on, Bob. Dig deep.'

'Fuck off. I've got four already.'

'So what's another couple then?'

'Ten fucking quid that's what,' Chops M replied indignantly. 'Pass us the salt. Anyway. There's only fifty-six petty officers on this ship. What silly arse suggested a book of two hundred tickets?'

'Head of the charity committee. Master at Arms,' Davies replied, passing the salt. 'Watch the top. It comes off,' he finished.

'He fucking would, wouldn't he? What about the Tree? Has he bought any?'

The Tree, called that because he wore a camouflage DPM rig, was Sergeant Conners, Royal Marines. Sgt Conners headed up the ten-man Royal Marine detachment that were embarked for this last phase of the deployment. The only marine in the PO's mess he took a constant ribbing, but he was thick-skinned and rose above it with great aplomb.

'Yes, he has.'

'Fuck it.' Chops M muttered. 'OK. Gimme 'em. I'll shift 'em.'

One level down on the main deck, sandwiched between the two long passageways that ran the length of the ship, was the seaman's mess. The crew lined up in the port-side passageway and got their food through a servery hatch from the galley, moved a few paces aft, and stepped over a watertight door coaming into the mess hall. Considering the number of people to be seated it was small, with just eight fold-down tables that each seated four. People had to eat and move on to allow the next person in.

Leading Seaman Tusker looked around for somewhere to sit. With a surname like Tusker, his nickname of Nellie was predictable. He was a killick, the Navy's version of a corporal, and for most who knew him, a fine shipmate. He was generous, forgiving of others, in constant good humour and gently took the piss out of anyone senior without ever really allowing anyone to take offence. He was mildly overweight with a sloppy, ready smile and cheeky eyes. As he slid into an empty seat, he looked round his dining companions. Two he knew well enough, but the third had only come aboard a few months ago, and like most of the twenty-two women on the crew she kept herself to herself and mixed mainly with the other girls. Her name badge on her overalls said Teller. She was of medium height, chunky without losing any femininity, and her strawberry blonde hair needed cutting. Her eyes were blue, the palest blue, offset rather fetchingly he thought by a smudge of grease along her right cheek.

Without being asked, one of the others took some things from the little closing locker above the table and pushed salt, pepper and brown sauce down to him.

'You'll need that, Nellie. Fuckin' pie's tasteless.'

Nellie grinned and looked at Teller and jerked a thumb at the lad leaving the table. It was an unfair slight on the galley. Food on the *Winchester* was bloody good, even by modern naval standards. 'If he hasn't had curry he hasn't eaten. It's Jenny isn't it? I'm Nick Tusker. Lads call me—'

'Nellie,' she said. Her accent was northernish. Liverpool maybe, he thought.

'Aye that's it.' He grinned.

'Just don't offer to show me your trunk,' she said acidly, without looking up from her meal. She was on her pudding, a blob of steamed treacle pud smothered in custard, and Tusker watched her lift a spoonful to her mouth.

'I wasn't going to,' he said honestly, a little taken aback at her brittleness.

'Good,' she said, standing. She collected her tray and walked away.

'What's got into her then? She always like that?'

'Dunno, like,' the other bloke said. 'They were up on starboard sponson this morning, taking the piss a bit. Wasn't that bad though, no worse than the lads give each other.'

'Well, it wasn't me,' Tusker said, but as he said it, he knew it didn't need to be him. The first women ratings had arrived on *Winchester* together, enough to fill a mess deck, and had met some resistance. It was natural enough. Some people didn't like change. They were usually the older ones, and that was true in this case. There were mutters about the *Winchester* not being a real warship any more. Not wif wimmin aboard. Tusker hadn't seen any ribbing or discriminatory behaviour – the old man wouldn't have it, not on his ship – but he was sure it was there in some form, and it would take a few months to settle down.

'She ain't had no mail,' the bloke added. 'From home, like,' he said with a shrug, like women expected it. ''Eard 'er telling her oppo.'

Mail. They had taken mail on board in Ghana. News from loved ones. Reassurance. At times it was all that kept you going at sea. Shame, he thought. Better get over it girl, he thought. It's not good on a ship.

When she left the mess, Operator/Maintainer Teller cut through to the starboard side and down aft to the stairs up to the weather deck. She had twenty minutes of her lunch break left and she found a quiet spot in the shade where the breeze would keep her cool and looked out at the sea, dark green – sometimes blue – the swirling foamy surface left by the ship's

17

bow wave almost mesmeric. She liked her job – liked the ship – and for a moment she regretted her prickliness with the fellow in the mess. Wasn't his fault. He was probably just trying to be nice, but she had known enough men in her short life to find most of them after one thing only, and so she was defensive until she had reason to be otherwise. She was frustrated too. She was in, in the mob, but she knew she was capable of more than they were demanding of her. She was bright, very bright and it irritated her to be reporting to people with less intellect and ability simply because they were older or male.

There was a sound to her right, running feet on the deckplates, and in silence – just the sound of their breathing and their footfalls – ten men wearing shorts and training shoes – but in webbing and packs and carrying rifles – ran up towards her. She pulled herself against the guard rail and they moved past in single file at a clipped jog. The ship's PT man – called 'Clubs' by all – ran exercise sessions, and some of the ship's company ran round the ship's weather deck in the early evening: seven laps from the helicopter deck round the forward end by the gun was a mile. Only one bunch did it in the heat of the day, though, and only one bunch did it with webbing, packs and weapons. The detachment of Royal Marines. As the last man passed her, he gave her a fleeting smile and then barked at the front runner to lift the pace. Their sergeant. Connors. He was lean, wiry, dark-haired, in his early thirties. The rumour was that when they embarked the XO had asked if it was wise running round with their rifles? What if someone slipped, dropped one over the side? The word was that Connors had replied, 'If a rifle goes over the side then someone will shout "Man overboard", because someone else will be holding it. My men don't drop their weapons. Ever. Sir.'

'And if they do?'

'Then it's still man overboard, sir,' the Sergeant had replied. ''Cos the bastard that dropped it will be going in after it!'

The detachment was from the fleet standby rifle company, currently Zulu Company of 45 Commando. She knew that. She had been gently corrected the day before by one of them when she had said 'Forty-Five'.

'Not Forty-Five,' he had responded. 'Four Five.'

'So,' she replied, thinking that she should know about the Navy's own, 'it's Four Five, Four Two, and Four O.'

'No. Four O is said as forty.'

She looked at him, her expression saying, Men! Make your bloody minds up!

She smiled and turned and watched them running up the ship away from her, up the long curve of the weather deck, everything steel, everything grey. A warship. She was serving on a warship. At sea. What she had always wanted to do. She smiled fleetingly, her features softening. After two months she still sometimes found it hard to believe. She really was on a Royal Navy warship.

HMS *Winchester* was a Type 42 destroyer. Four hundred and twelve feet long from her sharp stem to the edge of her helicopter deck over the transom, she was crammed with the technology and weapons of an area defence platform. With small Tyne cruise turbines and twin 25,000 horsepower Olympus gas turbine engines – the same used to power Concorde – she could move at a maximum speed well exceeding thirty knots, throwing up a rooster tail behind her higher than her quarter-deck.

Designed to protect 'high value assets' on the high seas – be they aircraft carriers, refuellers or troop ships – from air attack, Type 42 destroyers were the long-reach eyes and strike arm of the fleet. *Winchester* was old, due to be decommissioned at the end of this deployment. But she was still a formidable fighting ship. Her radars could see out 200 miles, assess threats and deliver that information to her crew, who could then choose the optimal weapon solution from an array that included everything from helicopter-launched Sea Skua anti-ship missiles and Sea Dart anti-air systems to the optical, radar, or laser-controlled 4.5-inch naval gun on the foredeck.

Winchester had a Lynx embarked for the deployment, cur-rently down in the hangar aft. The twin-engined attack helicop-ter was crewed by two Fleet Air Arm officers, but served and serviced by *Winchester's* crew. In the Navy the inter-discipline rivalry was strong, and helicopters – even those as robust as a Lynx – were, for the average sailor, notoriously complicated and unreliable. This was, of course, all the fault of the Fleet Air Arm chaps, who everyone said came aboard for three weeks a year and were either doing dramatic approaches to the stern, or standing mournfully around because their helo was broken. But either way they got all the glory and they were universally nicknamed WAFUs. Wet and Fucking Useless.

Type 42s were primarily anti-air area defence platforms, but if they needed to engage a ship at range, then it was the two men in their Lynx that became the ship's long-reach striking arm. Armed with Sea Skua missiles, they could go out, find and engage a ship. Sea Skuas are small, not big enough to sink a big ship, but they could certainly disable her, knocking out systems. If it came to that, then the Lynx crew were vulnerable, very vulnerable, because their radar targeting system was not fire-and-forget. They had to hover, or fly at the ship high enough for her targeting radars to see her and guide the missile the entire time it was in flight. That meant that, as the helo launched her weapons, the enemy ship would have seen her and fired anti-aircraft missiles at them, and as their Sea Skuas were in flight, the enemy missiles would be coming the other way, and they couldn't drop and hide, duck and run. Not if they wanted a hit. For those that knew, it was a case of, Call them WAFUs you might, but there was every chance they would never make it back from an engagement like that, so say it with some respect.

A Type 42, even an old one, was a formidable war-ship. An American admiral had once said they were as good as a US Navy Aegis-class cruiser, but this was only any good if you had the right commander – a commander who would make the best tactical use of the equipment, outthink and outguess the enemy, predict his next move, and then outfight him. By stealth, by guile, by being smart and, when the time came, by being absolutely committed, ruthless even, in the completion of the mission. And *he* needed the right crew. The correct people, with the right skills and training, the right initiative and the right spirit to fight the ship the way she was designed to be fought, in her optimal tactical environment, out in deep water, mid-ocean, her radars seeking out threats, her systems engaging over the horizon.

If deep sea was a destroyer's optimal tactical environment, then there were places they were never meant to be. In pack ice, inland waterways, dams and lakes – and they were never designed to go up rivers.

But this destroyer was about to do just that.

Democratic Republic of Congo
Tenta Mission

The car, an old Peugot 504, pulled over on the side of the road, and the three men got out and stretched their legs. Just ahead of them were the mission buildings, one of the places they had come to see. Makuma and Ndube wanted reports of these places. Numbers of people, police or army units, traffic on the roads, the usual stuff. Ndube was particularly interested in this place, because of the women, no doubt. He liked using white women, liked their struggles and screams. One of them felt his penis stiffen at the thought and he rubbed his crotch through his trousers and made a joke to the other two.

Their weapons were in the boot, except for two sidearms in the front with them, but they didn't come expecting trouble. There weren't another three men within twenty miles of them as armed, as aggressive or as dangerous as they were, so they were confident and joked for a while about how good it would be to get down in among them, see the nuns with their heavy, white thighs spread wide to take real men.

And there were men. Plenty of them. They laughed and got back into the cart. The mine now. See what was happening down there.

Congo

Way to the north-east, in Brazzaville, 40 Commando Royal Marines had their men scattered about the city in two hotels and at the airport. In a bedroom on the second floor of the Sofitel, Major Douglas McLean looked up at the maps that covered the wall for the thousandth time. It was his bedroom, but it was also the ops room. When he had arrived in Brazzaville two months before as the lead Royal Marine in their contingent, he had travelled with three much more senior officers, and on arrival they had found two French and three Americans all there to consider how to get their people out of Kinshasa when it all went 'tits up', as it was going to do sooner or later.

Across the river in Kinshasa – the other Congo, the old Zaire, now called the Democratic Republic of Congo – there were British nationals, French, Belgians, Americans, and a handful of other European Community types – some three hundred of them within reach of the embassy. The threat was rolling in from the east and the south, a rebel movement trying to overthrow Lauren Kabila's regime, the way he had overthrown Mobutu only two years before.

This was as close as they could get for a staging post, but it was, the Major had to agree, pretty fucking close. Kinshasa was only one mile away. Trouble was, the mile was water. Fast-flowing, brown, swirling with logs and trees and debris, and a class 4 rapid just a mile downstream. The Congo River. Mighty wasn't the word for it. The single way out to the sea for probably the biggest catchment area in the world aside from the Amazon. McLean had been a hundred miles up the Amazon, and even that wasn't a mile wide and flowing at ten knots.

At the first combined ops meeting, actually in the Brazzaville Fire Station due to the fact it had the only functioning air conditioning in the entire city, the senior officers had all looked at him, the most junior by about four ranks, the American saying, 'That's water. Needs boats and shit. Now, I know doodly squat about that, but you're a marine. General,' he said looking at the British Brigadier, 'I think your major should be ops.' He looked at McLean. 'We're working for you, son.'

And that was that. He was ops officer. The planner, the tactician. Which was just as well, because none of these officers had been this close to the nuts and bolts of a small operation in fifteen years. It was odd, because as ops officer and with only them there, they were his only resource and had to roll up their sleeves and get stuck in and do what he asked them to do.

McLean had moved fast. He got the comms going, used the combined muscle of the senior officers, got an advance team in, and three days later he had four rigid raiders and two hovercraft coming in on a transporter.

With a beefed-up troop from his company on the way, and with lads from 539 Assault Squadron, the first task would be getting the boats and the hovercraft the three-quarters of a mile from the airport to the river bank. There were no trailers, not for the hovercraft. One of his lads, a coxswain, was – like most of the marines – a resourceful fellow, and the night before he had done a silent recce up the riverbank with McLean, slipping into any decent-sized boat they came across, checking the engine and giving a thumbs up if he could hot-wire it. This was part of McLean's plan. He hadn't told any of the senior officers – they didn't need to know – but if the shit went down before the rigid raiders came in, then they would be able to 'borrow' the boats to cross the river and evacuate the embassy.

He sent Horrocks out with an oppo, in uniform, in daylight, to see if they could locate a trailer that could be borrowed, hired, bought, or – if the worst came to the worst – temporarily 'twocked', as the coxswain called it. The first hours were a let-down. There was nothing. Brazzaville, corrupt beyond belief, was a city that had been ground into submission. With armed gangs roaming the streets at night, looting whatever they fancied, there wasn't much left to take. There was nothing they could see. If there was a light trailer out there it was under lock and key and out of sight.

That afternoon things started looking up, though. They found a mobile crane, the only one in Brazzaville. The driver stayed with the machine twenty-four hours a day to prevent it being stolen, and said that, for a fee, he would drive out to the airport and lift the boats off the pallets on to a trailer for them. The crane looked like it might not work. It looked pretty tatty. In the cab were the driver's clothing and a sleeping mat, and he paid street children to go and buy food for him, but he started the engine to prove it worked. Then he said that he knew a man with a trailer, and some money – US dollars – secured the deal. When the C130 arrived, he was there at the airport with his crane and his friend with the trailer. They hooked the trailer behind one of the two Land Cruisers they had hired from the Avis office and they were in business.

The troop began training, covertly crossing the river every night as far as the middle of the river – the border – making sure they could landfall at the embassy every time without being seen by the guards on either side – irrespective of how dark it was, the weather or state of the river.

During daylight it was dodgy, with the bored DRC troops training their ZSU anti-aircraft guns on the boats as they passed, but at night they were asleep or drunk or not paying attention.

During the day the boats were laid up on an island in the massive Stanley pool, where the river shallowed and spread out round what was now a series of low-lying islands. Bank to bank across the pool was some six miles in places, with Kinshasa and Brazzaville facing each other across the lower narrows.

With marines guarding the boats, and the Congolese Navy chugging up and down their side in odd river boats with a machine-gun pintle on the cabin roof, they were safe enough from looters.

The Commando followed. With the Commando had arrived its HQ operation, including the 2i/c, Major Nick Webber, who moved in with McLean and, as SO2, took over the duties of ops.

The door opened and Webber strode in.

'Wotcha,' McLean called cheerily.

'Fucking shithole, this place,' Webber muttered. 'You taking your lads out again tonight?'

'I am,' McLean answered. They had been there six weeks and boredom was now a real issue. Bored marines got pissed, chased women, got into fights. Not good. The river training was now more than that. It was something to do, something to keep them interested, and, with potential problems every night, there was enough to keep things exciting.

'What's pissed you off?'

'There's no rule of law here. Fucking anarchy out there.' He had just been taken for $100 to get one of his vehicles past a police checkpoint. 'Fucking corrupt bastards. We should do what the French do. Take a few of them out. That's the only thing they respect.'

'Now, now. We can't do that,' McLean replied dryly. 'We have to respect their national right to run their country any way they like.'

'Can't believe these cunts have got a vote in the UN. They don't deserve it any more than . . .' He faded off, bending over to unlace his boots. 'Anyway. Be warned. The beast is ugly today.' He picked up a towel. 'I'm going for a swim.'

McLean smiled. He liked Nick Webber. They were from the same part of the country – Devon – and, although he had been to Sherbourne and Don had been a grammar-school boy, they had both sailed, both run competitively, and were both into canoeing, competing against each other.

McLean's parents now lived in Poole, but he had bought a house near Falmouth, his first step on the property ladder. His then girlfriend Penny – whom he had expected to make his wife – helped him choose it, but the relationship ended soon after. It had all but destroyed him. All he had ever asked for was honesty. Whatever it was, the truth was best. He was an honourable man and expected it in others. He caught her out. It wasn't the fact she had done it – maybe she couldn't 'cuff' the time apart, maybe it was just for the sex, he would never know – but it was the deception.

She had denied she was getting in over her head in a relationship – supposedly business – but on the third 'meeting' the man had stayed the night. She called him, told him the man was gone, but McLean knew better. He had driven over and found the man's car there, knew what was going in inside. He waited outside most of the night, his heart breaking, a knife in his guts. He had adored her, loved her to distraction, would have understood and forgiven her almost anything but the deceit. The lie. There were more lies to follow and immense pain. Emotional pain he had never imagined existed, and it was tearing him in half. She wanted to keep seeing the other bloke, wanted her freedom, told him that it was over.

Most men heal themselves by shagging everything that walks for a few months, but he didn't, he just threw himself into his work, and one day when she pitched up, tearful, wanting him back – the other relationship hadn't worked out, he had been a bastard, conned her, she was sorry, please would he have her back? – he thought, how could I ever love someone I couldn't trust? They have done it once, they will do it again. He shut the door in her face. He hadn't been in a relationship since.

He stood up and walked to the window and looked out. To the left was the Brazzaville waterfront. It was an odd place. The Congo was a huge country, the Republic even bigger, but their populations were rural. This was the capital but it was no bigger than an English market town, and into it was crammed every human unpleasantness that Africa could produce. Violence, theft, murder, nightly firefights between armed gangs, everyone corrupt to the extent that you could do nothing without paying *matabiches*, bribes. He looked out across the river. The only thing visible through the haze that was Kinshasa was the red-painted roof of the British Embassy.

What a place, he thought. On arrival they had been briefed by the number two at the embassy, his forte African history.

He had come across the river to meet them and, asked to give the marines a potted background, he shook his head slowly and began.

'If the Congo had a heyday it was arguably about the time that Ghengis Khan began his conquest of Asia. It's been going downhill ever since.'

There was some muffled laughter but the message was sound and McLean sat back and absorbed it, remembering most of it.

'From the founding of the Kongo Kingdom in the fourteenth century on the lands either side of the river by the coast, to the arrival of Christianity in 1484, finalised by the gleeful rush into trading slaves to the Portuguese on São Tomé, it was the place to be on the Atlantic coast of West Africa. From then on it went downhill. The Portuguese by now had established a settlement south of the river at Luanda to trade slaves, and supported the kingdom until 1571, when it was made a Portuguese vassal.

'Three hundred years later, in 1885, as another kingdom in the Congo basin – the Lunda – broke up, the Belgian King, Leopold, capitalised on Portugal's problems with her colonies and declared his own personal colony, the Congo Free State. That was a debacle. He extorted taxes and ivory and was cruel beyond belief. Eventually the stories began to trickle out and in the face of mounting embarrassment the Belgian government took it away from him.'

He looked at the five officers. 'Recent history in real terms? In colonial times neither the French administration up this side of the river, nor their European neighbours in what was to become Zaire and now the Democratic Republic of Congo, ever really penetrated much past the surface.

'As you know, both countries bordered the Congo River, one to the north of it, the other to the south. Imagine two countries bordering either side of the Amazon? The geography, the climate, the vegetation and the simple sheer vastness of land and the forests made the task almost impossible without massive investment, something neither country was there to do. French and Belgian policy was that you don't invest in colonial possessions any more than you have to, and this place they now had was huge, populated by many tribes, and dominated by the huge river with its brooding, dark rainforest either side. In those forests were undiscovered peoples, species unknown to man – some dramatic and obvious like pygmy people and pygmy elephants, others hidden, like viruses.

'Ebola. That little number you have heard of,' he said, taking an offered bottle from a tray. 'Last big outbreak was in Kikwit. It arrives from somewhere as yet unknown, hits a population, liquefies internal organs in its victims and then disappears again. That sums up the Congo best. The place is a fucking enigma. I think the flora and fauna here are less understood than in the Amazon. Things just happen here.' He shrugged. 'The Belgians? In truth the colonial task of opening up, civilising and then systematically reaping the colonies' wealth, be it minerals or agriculture, was, when viewing the sheer size of the central Congo basin, beyond any eighteenth or nineteenth-century colonial power's ability or interest. The Belgians never even scratched the surface. And in the light of the way they found themselves colonial rulers, you could argue they never even wanted it. They built a few roads, a few towns where they had found diamonds, some cash crops was the total of it. And when colonial Africa rushed into independence they left in almost indecent haste, the country already fracturing with a secessionist movement in what's now Shaba.' He jerked a thumb roughly south-east and sipped from the beer bottle. 'From the 1960s to the 1990s – as Zaire – it was systematically looted and driven into debt by Mobutu Sese Seko. The archetypal African dictator. Nepotistic, corrupt, brutal, strong, canny, a real survivor. But for the Congo it was an ignominious end to an ignominious story, and when Kabila finally ousted Mobutu two years ago, the few roads the Belgians had built were just potholed tracks, the infrastructure had collapsed, and much of the country's modern assets like mining equipment, hospitals, schools and clinics were rusted, abused, unpainted, derelict. Kabila took power, changed the country's name to the Democratic Republic of Congo and, according to his detractors, proceeded to do exactly what Mobutu had done.

'The only good news is that the Republic has a high literacy rate, courtesy of the mission schools, but that's about it. Kinshasa is now just a bigger, nastier version of Brazzaville, which makes Lagos look like a peaceful town.' He pointed out of the window. 'Each problem magnified tenfold. The rest of the country – about the size of Western Europe – with less spent on infrastructure, health and education than an English county. A population of poor people, disenfranchised, angry, hungry, ripe for the politicos to whip up into whatever new offer of wealth and freedom they could dream up, the gendarmerie and the magistrature corrupt, the national army unpaid and feeding itself at the point of a gun if necessary. And the cycle continues because now another bunch of rebels advance. Kabila has got support from Zimbabwe and Angola. Troops. Aircraft.' He faded away and then grinned. 'Puts thing into perceptive. See this and you'll never complain about a delay with your train leaving Waterloo again.'

The last couple of months had proven him right. McLean turned back and began stripping off to take a shower, one of the few benefits of living in the hotel rather than in a camp somewhere. That and hot food. It made an incredible difference to morale, and they rotated who lived in the hotel and who was either at the airport or on the island with the boats.

McLean was of middle height, five-ten and a half, with curly blonde hair and a fair complexion. He was fit, very fit, his upper-body strength the result of years of canoeing, and honed by the rigorous daily 'phys' they all did every morning. Green-eyed and with rosy cheeks that never tanned, he looked younger than his thirty-four years. He was confident – sometimes, senior officers thought, overconfident, particularly in his rather casual attitude to dealings with them. They would rather he was more deferential, but for McLean everyone had a job to do, and the modern Royal Marines were egalitarian. By all means respect the command structure, but they were too small an organisation for stuffiness.

McLean was fast-track. It came off him in waves to anyone who knew what the military looked for. Second-best marks ever on his course – when he made captain and got his own company he was the youngest Royal Marine company commander ever in peacetime. Afterwards he was promoted major when the Royal Marines aligned their ranks with the Army. He was lucky too. And no military officer can ever have too much luck. The CO of 40 Commando, acknowledging his youth at the time of the appointment, gave him A Company for one reason, the calibre of the Company Sergeant Major, who would be his eyes and ears on the ground. The CSM ran the company's support and admin functions, enforced discipline and very subtly kept the new commander on the right track.

It had been an excellent pairing, and when the CSM had moved on to a brigade job, McLean had been smart enough to benefit from his experience enough so that the new CSM was coming into a well-run unit. The new man was also young, but his style was similar to McLean's. Both were easy-going as long as everyone did their jobs. But neither would brook laziness or anything unprofessional. They were pragmatic, solid, practical. Marines.

The Royal Marines, only three commandos in size, was too small an organisation to have enough jobs for fast promotion for everyone, but it had its dividends. They were steadier, more experienced, more stable, more mature. It was just as well, because the Royal Marines' ethos was all for one and one for all. Shit or bust individualism, selfishness or 'lonerism' were counterproductive to that ethos. We know each other's strengths and weaknesses. We go in together, we fight together, and we come out together. We never give in.

Intercontinental Hotel, Kinshasa

Philip da Silva slung his bag on to the bed and tried to bump up the air conditioning. It was circulating air but not chilling it too well. He shook his head and walked over and opened the window. Friday night. He never spent the weekend down on the site. His manager, foreman and crew were there, with security. That was enough. Up here in Kinshasa he could at least get some variety of food, get out, see probably the best local bands in Africa, relax a little. He was an engineer running a short contract to build a series of new culverts under the railway line that ran up from Matadi. They weren't funded by the government – no one would take those contracts because you never got paid. This job was funded by the UN aid programme, and with luck, another two months and he would be out and back in Lisbon, waiting for the next job. He was a professional expat, travelling widely, mostly in Africa, building bridges, culverts, supported roads. He had spent a lot of time in Angola and Mozambique, the old Portuguese colonies. Luanda and Maputo were bad enough, but Kinshasa? The only saving grace was the club scene and two friends he had made, local men, who were into the clubs and music like he was. They knew their way around, kept him from being mugged simply because he had a white skin, got him into clubs that he would never have found in a million years, smoky dives that no European had ever seen inside, let alone heard the music. That made Kinshasa bearable. But tonight that would have to wait. On hearing his news, his friend the manager had made a phone call and arranged for him to go over and meet the British Ambassador.

He didn't mind. The clubs would be going all night, and this was possibly important.

His foreman had been to see him the day before. A bright, sparky, ambitious young Congolese chap, he had heard something and was uneasy. He had their mechanic with him and would translate. Rebels were in the area, increasing in number, from the south. 'We have security,' he'd said, pointing out at the gendarmes and army posts that surrounded his site.

The mechanic shook his head and spoke quickly in his native tongue. 'Not us,' the foreman explained. 'They are going to move north. He is worried about his village and the mission at Tenta. His children are there, at the school. He wants to take leave to go and move them.'

'The fighting is to the east,' da Silva answered. 'Not here.'
'It will be here,' the man answered simply. 'People from
the south.'

There was only one place south of them.

'Angolans?' da Silva asked.

The mechanic nodded. Da Silva said nothing for a moment
or two. The Angolans had been crossing into this country for
many years. In the seventies – much further to the east –
Angolan guerrillas had crossed into Zaire and attacked the
mining town of Kolwesi. They killed every European they
found, mostly French and Belgians. Butchered them along with
their wives and children. The Foreign Legion had recaptured
the town, and exacted their own peculiar revenge. They took
no prisoners. Their message simple. Don't mess with French
nationals. This time the Angolan Army were in the country
by invitation, but they were to the east, maybe a thousand
kilometres away at the closest.

But only two or three days ago another mine had been
attacked, not in the Republic this time, but at Yetwene, just
over the border in Angola. He had heard it on the BBC World
Service. They had kidnapped the Europeans. The Angolans
were blaming Unita forces, but that was crap he was sure.
Unita were still very pro-Western, and the last thing they would
normally do was kidnap Westerners. Bad publicity. He looked
back at his men.

'If they want the road,' he said, 'then why Tenta? That is
sixty miles the other side of the road.'

The men shrugged.

'All right. You can go. Move your family, but then come
back.'

There was some animated discussion between the foreman
and the mechanic, the foreman shaking his head, and then
finally the mechanic walked away.

'What was all that about?' da Silva asked.

The foreman smiled. 'Nothing. He wanted me to tell you
to warn the people at the mission. The' – he looked for the
Western term for it – 'witchdoctor said there will be much

death. I told him that you don't believe in that, so I wasn't going to tell you.'

Da Silva had been around Africa long enough to know that something didn't look right. Normally if a witchdoctor – be he a traditional healer or a shaman – made a prediction like that the people took it very seriously indeed.

'Much death?' da Silva said. 'You don't look too worried.'

'Oh,' the foreman replied, smiling. 'No. Not here. Tenta. There will be much death at Tenta.'

Da Silva blanched for a moment. There was the mission up there, and the mining camp. He knew the nuns and he knew several of the miners, one of them a young Swiss fellow he had become quite fond of.

Brazzaville

The door was open and CSM Harvey put his head round the door. 'Major Mac?'

'Yeah?' he called from the shower.

'Comms in from the embassy, boss.'

The Clansman was set up in the next room, plonked on the dressing table, the KL43 encryption device beside it.

'What does it say?' McLean called from the shower.

'Ambassador wants to know if someone can slip ashore tonight. Lend some advice. There's some int coming in. Some place called Tent.'

Slip ashore? In the Republic? That raised the ante a bit. So far they hadn't encroached more than ten feet on to the other bank. He walked out, thinking what it might be, dripping water, his towel round his waist.

McLean's new CSM was good. He had to be. Within each of the three commandos, each equivalent to an army battalion, there were only three 'fighting' companies, rifle companies. Although the Support and HQ companies had CSMs, their skills were different. The three commandos mustered nine rifle companies. That meant nine fighting CSMs jobs in the entire Royal Marines, and that was the job every young career marine aspired to.

McLean's was Don Harvey. A thirty-six-year-old climber and runner who had completed the London Marathon four times, excelled on the mountain leaders' course and the year before had had a crack at K2. But he was first and foremost a marine.

'If you go, boss, I'll come with,' he offered. 'Give us a chance to have a recce.'

McLean grinned. There were two special forces guys over there, 22 SAS, the Ambassador's personal minders. In Kinshasa, where the muggers got mugged, where cars were carjacked in broad daylight, he went nowhere alone.

They had drawn out the entire area, fields of fire, entry and egress routes, everything measured down to the last millimetre, thicknesses of walls, the lot. If they called for help they wanted it coming properly briefed and the intelligence was superb. There were even the builders' drawings for the embassy and residence, and overhead photographs of the street. There was no recce required. The CSM was bored. Champing at the bit.

He took the message and read it. 'Get someone to run it down to Major Webber. He's at the pool. Where's the CO? Do you know?'

'Airport, I think, sir. He'll be back for some scran soon.'

'OK, let me know if you see him. He may want to go over himself.' The CSM nodded and left, and McLean walked closer to the big maps on the wall. Tent? Where the fuck is that?

Two floors down and lounging around the pool were almost all of the assault squadron marines, and about half of A Company. The company was three troops, which each used to consist of three sections, each of eight marines. Now they had a new ORBAT – order of battle. The troop was bigger, and instead of just rifles and light section weapons, they now had a pair of GMPGs and two snipers in each troop. The troop commander – a lieutenant – had his sergeant, a radio operator and a runner-mortarman. A Rifle Company at full strength

34

was about 120 men. Many of those were sleeping, or at other things, but nevertheless the small pool area was full of people, all Royal Marines.

This was the routine. Up at 0530, an hour's hard 'phys', then – after breakfast – routine training and other tasks. At 1200 hours, lunch, then the afternoon off. Back into things at 1800 hours, till maybe 0300.

The 2-Troop marines at the river end of the pool were in good spirits. They had a couple of beers each, the ubiquitous Primus, but the lads next to them had ballsed something up, what their corporal called 'a shitfight', and he had imposed his own retribution. No beer today.

'Sad cunts,' one marine said, waving his cold beer at them. 'Look at 'em!' The speaker – in a pair of outrageous Bermuda shorts and Ray-Ban sunglasses – was Jock Roberts. Jock was just twenty, from Inverness, and had that skin type that never tans. He had slapped on 'factor fucking 682' and lay on his lounger like a well-muscled ice cream. Jock was fearsomely strong, but moderated the potential threat of his sheer bulk with very social behaviour. Like very many big men, he never had to prove anything. People just left him alone, and he was a congenial mate, a happy drunk, and a hopeless romantic who fell in love at least three times a year, and each time was for ever. He humped one of the troop's heavy automatic weapons, the cumbersome GPMG. He was strong enough to make it look lightweight. Jock was into butterflies, and could name any he saw and tell you all the breeding habitats and characteristics. Jock was also a dreamer. He would often be seen staring happily off into the middle distance, a little smile on his face. Sergeant Willis didn't like it. Didn't like the mind wandering, told him so several times. 'Do what you like when you're off watch Jock, but on my time you fucking concentrate and look like you are!' Jock grinned and nodded, amiable as ever.

Dave Hobson was the face in the troop. Clean-cut, clear-eyed, very good-looking. He was a New Zealander, and very laid back unless someone was playing rugby. He played for the Corps and it was on the rugby field that his real aggression showed. In his kit and beret he looked like a recruiting-poster Royal Marine, and women fell at his feet, much to the dismay of the man beside him.

Kevin Dawson, at only five feet nine, was the runt in the troop. He was the shortest and the smallest of them and so, jaw thrust out, he set out to prove he was better every chance he got. With three tattoos on each arm, and having occasionally affected smoking a pipe, he looked, someone remarked, like Popeye. He lay by the pool in a pair of Spice-Girl boxer shorts, Ginger Spice's flaming hair split and showing a coarser brown effect. Cocky, chatty, always with a wisecrack on his lips, he was a jaded cynical fellow who saw the flip side of everything. Kevin, his hair cut to almost nothing with a number one, was from Newbury in Berkshire, a town famous, he told everyone, for 'fuck all'. He also told everyone he was thinking of jacking in the job, heading for civvy street. Trouble was, he had no skills they wanted, and he was secretly pleased. The Marines offered him what he wanted: mates, order, fun.

Paul 'Furby' Davies was a couple of years older, craggy-faced, pockmarked by a childhood disease, and – much to Jock's dismay – burned the colour of mahogany by the sun, all in about two minutes. Furby was hard. From the wrong end of the Leigh Park housing estate in Portsmouth, he had earned money after school enforcing for a money-lender until his own brother took a beating from someone working for the same bloke, all over a spilled diet Coke in a club. Furby didn't like that. Kicked seven kinds of shit out of him and then dropped the bouncer. After that he was a marked man, and joined the Marines on his eighteenth birthday. Now twenty-two, he was steady as a rock. The Marines had channelled the energy, the aggression, given him a reason to be. Aside from the snipers and Sloth – who had trained as one – he was the best shot in the company and, in spite of his pockmarked face, he pulled more birds than any of them. They said he looked craggy and haunted and slightly wild, and they wanted to mother him, be ravished by him and run from him all at once.

He was called Furby because he was the complete antithesis of the cuddly little children's character. He was lean, committed and – unleashed on a task – he was focused to achieve. One of the lads once said to his girlfriend – who thought all he needed was a good cuddle – 'Cuddle? Jesus! Furby? I tell ya. Fucking glad he's on our side!' He was sitting with his face in a book, a big Wilbur Smith that he had borrowed.

Furby and Kevin's mate was Sloth. James 'Sloth' Holroyd was a sleepy, easy-going village boy from Milland in West Sussex. Tall and fair-haired, he was the son of a gamekeeper and tractor driver. He was as fit as any of them, but in spite of always getting there in the first two or three, he just seemed to move slowly. He was the best scout they had and a pretty fair tracker and – as point on a yomp – he was better than any of them. Although not one of the troop's snipers, he had done the snipers' course and was now entitled to carry a L96 7.62 sniper rifle if he wished.

He had befriended a stray dog. It was a skinny yellow cross-bred mut with a big head, which – much to everyone's amusement – had tried a dry run against Furby's leg within an hour of Sloth finding it. It was immediately christened 'Shagger'. Sloth was lying on a lounger, his eyes covered in a camouflage face veil. Shagger, putting on condition by the day, his stomach full of leftovers from lunch, lay asleep at Sloth's side.

Biscuit was the last of them. Edward 'Biscuit' Barton was their corporal. The fastest and the fittest, a quarter of his genes were from the shores of Antigua, and he was the colour of coffee with milk. When he arrived in the commando someone was trying to describe him. 'Well, he's not black. Not Asian either. He's a sort of – well – a biscuit colour, really.' Seeing he had gone right through school being called 'Horse' due to the size of his penis, this was – as nicknames went – not bad. Which was just as well because it stuck. At twenty-seven he was the oldest man in the section.

'Well,' Biscuit said, looking at the beerless section. 'Maybe

they will try harder tomorrow. Don't you cunts think I wouldn't
do that. I'm all-powerful. Remember, Hitler was a corporal.'
  'Fucking pongo corporal what's more,' Sloth muttered dryly.
Shagger looked up at his master, yawned and stretched, before
farting audibly. 'Jesus!' Jock said. 'He gets more like a marine
very day.'
  'Modelled on me, I might add,' Kevin said. 'The perfect
fighting machine.'
  'Na,' Sloth said. 'They would model something on a full-
sized action man, not a sawn-off little runt like you.'
  'I may be the compact version, but I'm all quality. Unlike
you small-cocked bastards. When I get out of the corps and
take my todger back to Newbury, the women of Taunton
will weep.'
  'Yeah, with joy,' Furby muttered.
  'What about you, Furby? Back to Pompey?'
  Furby shook his head. He knew he wouldn't go back. In his
heart he knew. He watched the Padre walk across towards the
doors, and felt the disgust rise like it always did.
  'There's no going back,' he said. 'It's never the same.'

British Embassy, Kinshasa

  'There,' one of the two SAS men said to the Ambassador. 'That
must be the place, sir.' He jabbed a thick, callused finger at a
point on the map.
  'Tenta. Could be, I s'pose,' the Ambassador replied. 'Be
here this evening, so we'll know then.' He ran his finger down
a brown line on the map. The line represented the trunk road
between Matadi and Kinshasa, the single-track railway line
running roughly alongside.
  'That's got to be one-thirty or one-forty miles to the turnoff
and another what, sixty into the river? The main road will
be OK, but up to the river? Christ knows. What was the
information he had?'
  'Didn't elaborate,' the Ambassador replied. 'Just that one
of their nationals has come in and there's something we may

want to know about. If it's likely to require or need a military assessment, then I'd like Cheyne's people to sit in.'

The call had come from the Portuguese consul, the manager of one of the hotels in Kinshasa, a man the Ambassador knew. He looked at the SAS soldier. They had come to know each other well, and without any military attaché at the embassy, his two diplomatic protection people were as close as he was going to get to having a resident military expert. The Ambassador had been in Africa quite a while. Before Kinshasa he had been in Nairobi as chargé d'affaires and then as HMA in Sierra Leone. He had learned to trust his instincts and there was something uncomfortable about this one. There was a sense of foreboding.

'There's a mission there, apparently. With Westerners.'

Two

M cLean walked into the hotel's restaurant and looked around. Cheyne was at the table he favoured several tables down from the door, next to the long eight-seater that had become the unofficial officers' mess table. He walked down. There were other marines eating – many of them – and the only civilians were a few local, wealthy Congolese, and what looked to be a pair of European businessmen down the far end.

'Excuse the interruption, sir.'

'Grab a plate,' Cheyne nodded. 'Sit.'

McLean got some food from the colourless buffet. It looked like it should have been beef stew, but could have been anything.

'Got comms in from the embassy this morning, sir,' he said softly, aware that others were around them. 'They would like someone to cross over tonight. Into the embassy. Got some int coming in. I got back on to HMA and he has someone coming over to the embassy tonight with the sitrep. He wants us to hear it, get our view. I'll be out with the assault-squadron lads anyway, but I wondered if you wanted Nick to go over or—'

'HMA's request?' There was no way any of them should be entering by way of the river bank and certainly not as MoD staff. There wasn't time to go by any other route either, or to get visas. It was the river or nothing, but if the Ambassador thought it necessary then so be it.

'Yes, sir.'

Cheyne thought quickly and looked at his watch. 'Grab Nick and let's get together at 1400?'

The meeting, up in McLean's bedroom, quickly became a planning session, an 'O Group'. Other officers were called in and eventually there were five of them there. The 539 Assault Squadron marines would be running four rigid raiders on exercise that evening. The raiders could carry eight marines with their kit, sitting on four motorbike-like saddles either side, with some limited room to stow their gear down the centre. The boats had inboard engines, but only had one engine each and so, in case of engine failure, and with a class four rapid just a mile downstream, they never went anywhere alone. There were always two boats moving together. The most likely problem was overheating due to blocked water intakes. The boats were designed for maritime rather than inland conditions, and the river carried that much debris and flotsam that the coxswains and mechanics stripped the intakes and cleaned them every day as they lay up on the island.

All four raiders would move off together, then two would go in closer. Colonel Cheyne and Major McLean would slip over their boat's flat, square bows and move quickly ashore where one of the two SAS men from the embassy would meet them. McLean would carry a short-range, hand-held VHF to communicate with the boats. The special-forces fellow had been developing a relationship with the two Republic guards on the riverbank, and he would 'facilitate' their arrival.

'Is anyone armed?' the 539 lieutenant asked. 'I know we're not supposed to be, but what if you step ashore and someone wants your wallet or something?'

'We'll be with one of HMA's SF blokes,' Cheyne said. 'But good point. Doug, we'll take a sidearm each, but somewhere discreet.'

That evening at exactly 2100 hours Colonel Cheyne slipped into a raider and nodded at McLean and the young Lieutenant. The Lieutenant tapped the coxswain on the shoulder and in moments the shallow cathedral hull was skimming across the water. The boats were capable of 40 knots, but in the dark they moved much slower because hitting a log at that speed would be very risky indeed. The coxswain ran down the river until he reached a point, lining up the lights on the Brazzaville side and then did a sharp left turn on to a compass bearing. They had done this drill many many times, but without actually crossing into DRC water. The engine in its padded casing was muffled down and incredibly quiet, and as they got closer to the shoreline, two marines in the fore section of the boat dropped down in the bows, their weapons pointed out. The coxswain cut the power, the boat stooging into the landing point, his line perfect considering the ten knots of current.

A torch flashed on the shore and as the boat ground gently to a halt a man stepped down, softly calling the Colonel's name. 'This way,' he said.

Cheyne and McLean followed him up the bank. A road ran along the shore, and the embassy's wall was on the other side of the road. A soldier, the river guard, was watching, looking down every now and then at the Swiss army knife he had just been given by the British special forces man. As they passed, the Congolese soldier stamped to attention and did an impressive salute.

'Told him you were a very senior officer,' the SF man chuckled. 'Good eh? That salute cost the FCO a Swiss army knife, ten US dollars and twenty Benson and Hedges.'

Three minutes later they were inside the embassy with the Ambassador. Tall, he was thin and almost stooped, with an academic air strengthened by the tortoiseshell spectacles he wore. He was pouring beer into glasses. 'I have let the staff go home,' he said. There was a knock at the door and it swung open. 'Ah. My wife, Pat.'

She came forward, offering her hand – a tall, slender woman in a summer dress and slip-on sandals. 'Nice to have you here, gentlemen. You have no idea what a relief it is to know you are just over the river.' Cheyne looked round the room. This was the dining room in the residence, the standard Foreign and Commonwealth Office watercolour prints on the walls. On the long dining table maps were spread out.

'I'll get something for you to nibble on.'

'We are fine, Mrs Hewitt.'

'Nonsense,' she said. 'Won't take a moment.'

'Introductions, gentlemen,' Hewitt said. There were two other men there. One was the number two at the embassy, a younger man, and there was a Mr da Silva.

McLean looked at the Portuguese engineer they had come to meet. He was lean – sinewy even – with short-cropped black hair. He was nut-brown from the sun, his nose was long and straight, and in spite of the untipped cigarettes he smoked, his teeth were pure white. All he needed was an earring and a red handkerchief on his head and he would have been the popular image of a pirate.

'Mr da Silva is running a project down the other side of Kimpese on the main road west. Yesterday two of his people came to him with some news.' Ambassador Hewitt indicated that da Silva should take up the story.

When he had finished, Colonel Cheyne nodded, looking at the map spread on the table. 'You know the place?'

'Tenta? Yeah. I know it.' He shrugged. 'Short time only. Maybe a month ago, the nuns, they have a puncture. No spare. My peoples fix it. They invite me for lunch. Long drive, but nuns . . .' He trailed off with a shrug that said, I'm Catholic – what could I do? 'It's shithole.' He shrugged. 'The village and the store is back from the river. The mine a bit nearer. The mission is at the river. Dominicans. The old one, Sister Mary, is Greek. We talked. She wants to go home one day. She's from a place called Heraklion.' He smiled.

Colonel Cheyne looked at the map again. 'The road stops at the river?'

'There was a ferry, but it broke, my boys tell me. River barges pull in there. People unload. You can get a boat across to Tadi sometimes.' He pointed upstream maybe two or three miles on the other bank.

Cheyne nodded. It was a long way in. If there was a rebel advance, it was a long way to go – into potentially hostile country – and if anyone going in to help the mission staff got caught up in trouble there was no means of support, egress or uplift. This was a job for helicopters, but at this

43

distance most would need forward refuelling, and that would mean a fuel dump somewhere. That in turn would have to be supported, guarded. All this on the basis of some very dubious intelligence that they couldn't corroborate in any way.

Da Silva saw the look on his face. 'Look, don't think I crazy eh? I don't know. I tell you he heard the rumours and went to the witchdoctor, he say same.'

'On the strength of this, one man's hearsay, a witchdoctor, a—'

'I know nothing about you job,' da Silva interrupted. 'I an engineer. I build things.' As he got more passionate he spoke faster, losing grammatical correctness, but his meaning was clear. 'The mine at Yetwene last week. I fuckin' know that place, eh? Built a road there. Five whites takens. A dozen of their boys killed. No warning. But I tell you this, eh? If it happens here and we knew, we been warned, and not notice the warning, then I don't know about you, but I didn't look myself in the mirror. What the fuck you here for anyway? Look good? Smart uniforms?'

The barb hit home, but Cheyne swallowed his compulsion to respond. The complex rules of engagement were his problem, as was the overall mission that had the commando here. It wasn't his task to explain all that to a civilian. Over in Brazzaville their movements were restricted. They weren't even allowed over this side of the river and if anyone was going to get down into the mission they would need to go from the south side of the river. Without the express permission of Lauren Kabila's government that would be seen as an armed incursion. Get a party of his people deep into the Republic, with all the logistics that would require, do an EO, and then back out again. Tactically it was a nightmare.

He looked at the Portuguese engineer. 'Do they even *want* to be evacuated?'

'They may have heard something,' da Silva responded with a shrug, 'but dunno. There's no phone lines in there. A radio. They must do because they can order supplies for the clinic and I saw a di-pole.' He looked at Cheyne, then McLean, then

44

the Ambassador. 'They won't want to go. They think God will take care of them.'

'And you?' McLean asked.

'This is Africa,' da Silva answered. 'Sometimes these peoples have more faith than brains, you know.'

McLean nodded. He had done his homework. In every conflict in Africa, missions were a soft target.

'Ambassador?' Colonel Cheyne asked. 'What chance of a temporary permission to enter the Republic? A small group, discreet, go down, secure the place, move the nuns out, whatever, and then return to Brazzaville?'

'From Kabila himself, not much.' Hewitt shook his head. 'But we don't have to go to Kabila. I am seeing the Foreign Minister first thing tomorrow. His brother is the interior minister,' he said obliquely.

Cheyne nodded. If – and only if – they got a permit, and if Northwood agreed, they would need a hell of a lot more information. He looked at da Silva. 'What more do you know about the area? Let's start with the road in?'

At that point things slowed as Mrs Hewitt came in with a tray. To McLean's amazement there were hot sausage rolls – not little cocktail varieties, but real sausages in pastry, mini samosas, and devils on horseback. He hadn't seen food like this in almost two months. 'And,' she said, 'my last bottle of HP sauce, so eat it reverently!' She smiled and disappeared again.

Two hours later they had exhausted the engineer's knowledge, and McLean had a sheaf of papers, notes, hand-drawn maps that he slipped into a rubberised waterproof map bag that slung round his neck inside his shirt.

The Ambassador thanked da Silva and showed him out to where a driver waited to take him back into town, and then came back into the dining room. Cheyne asked him the direct question.

'What's your take on this, sir?'

'I'm not sure. I'm uncomfortable about doing nothing, but from here there's not much I can do. Half the country is rebel-held, and even if I requested that the authorities provide some sort of security presence there, they would either ignore me or laugh. Quite simply, a few foreign nuns aren't high on their priority list. They have bigger problems.'

'Da Silva thought there were about fourteen foreign nuns and about four or five locals. Is he correct, sir?' McLean asked.

'Yes. Near enough. Spoke to the people at Médecins sans Frontières this evening. They have a doctor at the clinic there. They said it sounded about right.'

'Transport,' McLean said, looking back at the map. 'Sir? Do you know anyone who could lay their hands on some transport. A truck of some sort?'

Hewitt looked at his man, who nodded. 'I'll see what I can do. How many?'

McLean was a bit taken aback at the question. 'Not sure, sir. We haven't made any decision yet, but two would be good, in case we get a breakdown. And something smaller.'

'We have a Toyota 4x4 and a Land Rover here.'

'What chance of getting the permit, sir?' the Colonel asked.

Hewitt looked at Cheyne and scratched his long, bony face. 'I happen to know that there are several things' – he paused and smiled – 'he needs. He needs friends right now and, for a minute of his time and his signature, I think it very possible. This is, after all, a humanitarian act.'

'If Northwood agree – and that's a big if – what will be required at this end?' Cheyne asked.

'A permit the interior minister signs, and probably an escort. Two gendarmes or something. Its about nine hours down to Matadi on the train and the road's not bad. You could be down there into Tenta, have at least offered the people at the mission a ride out for the time being, and be back here in what? Twenty-four hours?'

When da Silva got back to the Intercon he decided against going out to one of the music clubs and ambled into the bar for a drink. There was another Westerner on his own further down, and two men immediately to his left, but the rest were locals by the look of them. He ordered a cold beer, drank it down in several swallows, the glass never leaving his lips, and then ordered another.

'Now there's a thirsty man,' a voice said. He turned. It was one of the two Westerners on his left. 'I'll get that one for you.'

Introductions made, they began to talk and about half an hour later one of the two men, a journalist – thin-faced, lean, jaded, but with bright, quick eyes – caught da Silva's eye.

'Do you play cards? Penny poker?' Da Silva wasn't a big gambler, and if it had been anything other than penny poker, a minimum-stakes, almost-for-fun game he would have said no, but the journalist pulled out some cards and indicated a small, round table that was free. They played for an hour or so, the small pot of US dollars, maybe twenty in total, moving back and forth. The journalist's name was Perrin Dalton, and he worked for the *Daily Telegraph*. He took his own photos and had been the paper's staff man in Central Africa for three years, based in Nairobi. He was waiting for a new press pass to go back into Shaba, a tedious bloody problem that raised its head every twenty-one days. Each three weeks he would have to come back up to Kinshasa and wait for two or three days, pay some bribes, cool his heels before he could go back to where the news was happening.

He was medium in height, wiry and wore jeans, desert boots and a khaki shirt with big patch pockets. He looked older than his thirty-six years, the result of too much sun, too much whisky and too many late nights. Thinning, sandy-coloured hair and lean, tanned cheeks framed quick, green eyes, and his humour was fast and dry, much of what he said laced with sarcasm.

He was English, born in Sussex, and schooled at a better public school. He flew each holiday to join his parents in Kenya, where his father worked for Inchcape. Other than a few spells 'at home' and on other assignments, he had been in Africa most of his adult life. He loved it, hated it, feared it, respected it, was in awe of it, addicted to it. As he had once said to a girlfriend – a pretty blonde he had met at Malindi, who wanted him to come back with her and live in her Bayswater flat – he just couldn't, and quoted Frederick Forsyth: ' "Africa bites like the tsetse fly. Once it's in your blood and its dust has been between your toes, you will forever want to return." '

His notebook, tape recorder and one camera were where they always were, in the bag beside him on the floor. The security – even in the best hotel in Kinshasa – wasn't great, and so usually he left nothing of value or interest up in his room, but rather kept everything locked in the manager's safe. Tonight was the same and he had two other camera bodies, three other lenses and his film stock in there. All were irreplaceable in the Democratic Republic of Congo. One of the cameras was a digital and he could download the pictures on to his PC and then send the stories and pictures back on the Internet.

The other man was an aid worker having a few days in the bright lights of Kinshasa and the conversation between the three was rambling and open. It was into the second hour when da Silva asked them if they had heard about trouble brewing in the south-west. Both said no, and it was only when da Silva said he was working down there and his people were getting nervy that Dalton looked up from his pair of nines. 'So I told people at the British Embassy. They had their soldier there to listen. Maybe they go down there. Move the nuns,' da Silva finished.

'What soldier? The attaché?' Dalton asked. He knew there were no British troops in the Democratic Republic. Nearest ones were over the river, the Royal Marine detachment in Brazzaville.

'No. From Brazzaville.'

'They came across. The marines?' Dalton checked. Da Silva nodded, looking at his cards. Three of a kind. He smiled.

'Where exactly are you working?' Dalton asked. This was getting interesting. Not only was this a new rumour about trouble in an unexpected place – and, for a journalist, rumour chased to ground formed much of the breaking news – but if the marines in Brazzaville were part of it, then this was something that his paper would throw straight on to the front page. He hadn't had a front-page story in weeks, just small bits on the international pages and two weekend features. The great British public, even *Telegraph* readers, were only so interested in political and tribal violence in some African sinkhole. But if there was a chance that British forces would be involved in something then it had an angle. It was worth following up.

His mind was racing. Shit, he thought, the whole of 40 Commando are over there. What's that in size terms? About five or six hundred, he remembered hearing. French, Americans, everyone was over there, waiting for it to go off, to pull their people out. He ran a hand back through his hair while he waited for the Portuguese engineer to answer his question.

'This site? On the main road, twenty kilometres west of Kimpese.'

They were all on whisky and Dalton decided it was now on expenses and time to get a bottle in.

2100 hrs Monday
Tenta Mission

The mission had been built by the Dominican order in 1958. All clapboard buildings, the main mission was a hollow square with interior and exterior verandas, the interior ones almost like cloisters around a central courtyard where a raised rock garden stood round the base of an old mature jacaranda tree that shaded the entire open area.

The northern aspect facing the river held the office, the clinic, two small wards and some of the nuns' cells. On the northern veranda there were wicker chairs and some benches, the wood old and polished shiny by many years of posteriors that had sat and waited for their turn in the clinic.

A large bougainvillea crawled the length of the roof and several flamboyant flame trees were dotted around the yard, where, over the years, thousands of children had played. The eastern end was all schoolrooms, three of them for children of different ages. The nuns had long ago given up trying to grow grass that side, and now it was just hard-packed red earth. The southern end, facing the road in, held the kitchen, storerooms and pantries. There was even an old concrete dairy, where the original nuns had persisted with trying to keep cows for years, though eventually they had succumbed to sleeping sickness. The tsetse fly had never been controlled along the river, and these days conservationists considered it a blessing because it meant no domestic livestock. Even so, here at the mission they had goats and made fine cheeses.

For the nuns it also meant no milk, but in recent years they had supplies of UHT long-life milk delivered with everything else. Even so, UHT milk was rationed. There was of course any amount of powdered milk, and the children drank gallons of it every day.

The western side held the chapel and the rest of the nuns' cells, and outside was the chapel garden. This was grassed and lush, and during chapel services, when they opened the shuttered windows, the vibrant colours of the flowers were uplifting.

In the noon of the day the heat seemed to shimmer up from the red-painted corrugated-iron roof, but inside, the polished concrete floors, high ceilings and open, mosquito-screened windows made it bearable.

Outside there was a big generator in a shed. The machine gave enough power for electric lights and electric power points in the clinic, the refectory and kitchen, and for the refrigeration system. The classrooms had never been wired for lights, as all lessons were in daylight, and the nuns took pressure lamps to their cells after vespers. They had a pickup truck, an ageing Peugeot that was driven by an American nun from South Dakota, a woman in her mid-fifties. She had taught the fellow who maintained it both to read and write and then to strip an engine, and between them they could fix the pickup, the generator and the old Perkins engine that pumped water up from the well into the header tank that stood over the utility shed.

As nuns went, they were progressive, pragmatic, and committed. They wore their brown habits if it was appropriate, but got into shorts and a T-shirt if it was required. They were chosen by the order for service in Africa dependent on their commitment, their energy and their skills. They were self-supporting and could do everything from growing food to baking bread, perform minor surgery, fix their equipment, teach and minister to all the Lord's children. Once a month a priest – Father Pascal – came through, performing baptisms and confirmations, but most of the time they were on their own, unordained but doing the Lord's work nevertheless. Two months before, there had been some excitement when they had had a visitor from England – a woman priest! An ordained woman! In spite of their order's conservative stance, they were all rather chuffed with that, and the Reverend had stayed three days with them.

They were an eclectic international bunch. The oldest nun was Sister Mary, at fifty-five she was tough as old leather, but in her youth had been a stunningly beautiful woman. Greek, she spoke four European languages and three Congolese dialects. The youngest was only twenty-four. Sister Sarah was Irish and a year younger than Sister Jo – an English girl – and the pair of them, who had arrived together the year before, were like a breath of fresh air. There were three Belgians, two French, two other English, another Irish, another American other than Sister Ruth, an Italian and a Dutch woman. There were three Congolese girls ready to take up the habit, all about to leave for the order's training seminary in France.

It was dark along the riverbank. Low cloud had shut out the moonlight, and the single bulb in the office was the only light out on to the veranda. Sister Marie-Claire was in charge at the mission and this was her after-vespers routine to finish the day. A short break, the only one she took. A Belgian, at forty-two years old she had been at the mission twelve years. Some of them only came for two years – that was the standard commitment – but some chose to stay, as she had done, as Sister Mary had done. Sister Mary had been there nearly twenty-five years, and before that she'd been down in Katanga. She had spent almost her entire adult life in the country.

Sister Marie-Claire was sitting in one of the wicker chairs, thinking about the day they had had and the one that would come with the dawn, talking to her Lord as she did every evening. Night time was never silent, but for some reason at night sound seemed to carry further – crickets, insects, the odd sound of an animal, and she could hear the comforting thump of the generator running. She had caught movement in her peripheral vision and turned and looked. An old man was settled politely and quietly under one of the trees about thirty yards away. He looked to have been there for some time. And what do you want? she thought to herself. I suppose you will come and tell us when you are ready.

The clinic was down the veranda to the right, and as a door opened she turned and looked, a smile crossing her face.

'Ah. Doctor. You have finished your rounds. Come and sit with me,' she said in almost unaccented English, patting the chair beside her.

Dr Penny Carter was English. Slim, slender even, her dark hair was piled up on top of her head. Beneath the light smock top she wore her figure was good, but she was a professional and looked the part, and the long sleeves helped beat off the mosquitoes. Her hair was glorious. Rich tones of shiny, dark chocolate that shimmered in the sun, glossy and full. Many of the Médecins sans Frontières people had a serious haircut before coming into 'the bush', but she couldn't bring herself to do that, and getting it up and out of the way was the next best thing. There was something else in it too, she would have to admit if pressed. Living with the order here at the mission, all of whom had their hair very short, she rather liked the fact it marked her as different. She wore cotton trousers and a loose, lightweight top, and as she walked down the veranda she rolled the sleeves down to try and keep the mosquitoes at bay. It was a warm evening, but the breeze blowing from the east, having crossed Africa, was heated by the land itself and all it served to do was dry the sweat on the skin and keep the humidity down. She walked down to where the nun, in her full brown habit, sat in her chair.

'It's Sister Jo's turn so we might have some of her delicious coffee soon,' Sister Marie-Claire said. 'Come. Sit.'

She took the seat beside the older woman and they talked of the day until finally, after a decent interval on small talk, the older woman looked across at the young doctor, who by now had seen the old man squatting on his haunches in the dark under one of the flame trees.

'There's someone over there,' she said.

'I know. Whatever his troubles, he will approach us when he is ready, or he may just go. It is their way,' Sister Marie-Claire responded. She turned and looked at the young doctor. 'And you? It troubles you still?' she said, softly enquiring.

'What's that, Sister?'

'Whatever brought you to us.'

Penny looked across at her. She had never said a word, not to anyone, but the older woman had seen something. 'I came here to work.'

'I'm sure you did,' Sister Marie-Claire replied gently. 'But something drove you out in the first place.' She smiled. 'I am not a worldly woman, but I did come to the order later than most, so I have seen. I loved a man once, two in fact. I have fallen. I have hurt and cried with the best of them. And I know it when I see it.' She paused and looked out into the dark at the river that glimmered as the moonlight broke through the cloud cover for a second or two. 'Whatever it is, make your peace with yourself.'

Penny said nothing. Just looked out into the night. She was from the south of England. Her father was a doctor with a practice in Chichester. Her mother had been a doctor. The family was steeped in it, the dinner-table conversation often medical in nature. She had wanted to be one too. Always. So she had. Some hard slog, top marks at school, into med school in London, an interest in cellular diseases, but that was for later. First came the years of eighteen and twenty-hour working days in the hospitals, in Accident and Emergency, in the other departments – failed relationships, personal time, time for friends all suffering as she followed her vocation.

Professionally admired, seen as the role model, tipped as the future consultant with a very bright future, it all seemed to be worth it. She would be, some said, the eminent cancer surgeon of her generation. She was bright, successful, the golden one, but it was beginning to tell. At the hospital in Bristol she was working ever-longer hours, feeling unloved, unappreciated. Her boyfriend was solid, kind, reliable – maybe too much so, because when the chance came for some fun, something new, something exciting, she took it. She started an affair and he found out. She challenged him, said she could live without him, wanted something new, knowing as she said it she was wrong – but having started the affair, made her choice, she now felt she had to justify it to herself, him, everyone who knew.

She had watched the pain he was in, seen herself as the cause, watched the opportunities they had smashed on the rocks of her own deceit and foolishness. And at that point her world began to go downhill. By the time she realised the mistake she had made and gone back to him he had strengthened, moved on. Didn't want her or need her. Couldn't trust her. That had been some months ago and her life had a huge hole in it. Looking back now, she wasn't even sure why she had done it. A moment of madness, compounded by her own stubbornness, and she had caused great pain to someone she now knew she loved – and to herself.

Later, Teddy, wonderful one-time partner, lover and now just old friend, had been the catalyst. Teddy – one-time city broker who had found religion, born-again Christian and now teacher in one of the toughest comprehensives in Bristol. He had used his summer holiday to join an aid team in Africa. She had told him – confided in him. And he had been wonderfully supportive for a few weeks, but then, worried by the slide in her he was seeing, he challenged her.

'Stop wallowing. OK, so you made a mistake. We all do that.'

'I've lost him. I am responsible,' she said.

'And you have another responsibility. To God. For the gift he gave you. You ignore that, you turn your back on the talent and the skill and the training. The gift. Then you're not the girl I know. Use it. Go somewhere they really need you.'

She turned on him. 'Fuck off, Teddy! Just fuck off and take your fucking useless preaching somewhere else!'

Two weeks later she knocked on his door. Contrite, she bore flowers, a small gift and an apology.

It took no time at all. She had decided to take his advice, and having contacted the French outfit she had seen on TV, she expected to be on a plane somewhere within a week, and was right. Here she was. Basic medicine. Fundamental stuff. There was some trauma, but most of her daily work was treating the results of poor diet, bad hygiene and unclean water. She saw every manner of tropical disease from malaria to bilharzia, from amoebic dysentery to hookworm. That day alone she had seen septicaemia, tetanus, and for the first time, beriberi. There was also the first wave of the scheduled river blindness prevention effort. River worm was endemic throughout West Africa. The worm spread by the black simillum fly burrows under the skin, causing itching that almost drives people mad. The end result was egg-sized swellings and blindness, but one tablet a year could make the difference. She had been doling out Mectizan all day.

It wasn't just the kind of work that was different. The people were also different. Unlike London, there was no fighting, no insults, no complaining about waiting or the lack of expensive drugs for free. The people who came to this, the only clinic in hundreds of square miles, queued for hours in the sun, bore their sickness and pain with great stoic strength, were grateful for any help they received. Routinely she had one of the local nurses – girls trained by the nuns over the years – wander down the line and do a triage, because – so dignified were they, and so patient were they – they would await their turn to see the doctor even if they were a genuine emergency case.

'Ah,' Sister Marie-Claire uttered. 'I can hear coffee cups.'

Sister Jo brought coffee out and left them to it. They were joined by Sister Mary, who settled in beside Penny. The Greek nun looked older than she was, the effect of years in the African sun, but she seemed as tough as any of them. Penny, who knew that wasn't the case, or wouldn't be for long, looked at her fondly. She had given each of the long-standing nuns a medical when she arrived. Neither Sister Marie-Claire nor Sister Mary had been away from the mission for more than a week in years, and neither had gone home on leave in the last two.

When she had given Sister Mary her check-up she had found something. A carcinoma on the back of her neck, another on the front. That was two months ago. The nun had refused to go home, and swore Penny to secrecy. No one must know. Penny had removed both the cancerous tumours. Had they been melanoma she would have given the woman six months at the most, but they weren't. Carcinomas were less virulent, but they had been there some time. Sister Mary was not a vain woman. She had no mirror in her cell. She had no idea how long the little dark lumps had been there. When Penny removed them, under local anaesthetic, she saw the cancer had spread inside the tissue below the skin. Without chemotherapy to hold the disease in check, Sister Mary might only have a year, maybe less.

'And how are you, child?' she asked.

'I'm very well, thank you,' Penny responded. 'And you?'

'I am as good as the good Lord wants me to be,' the nun answered cryptically, lifting her coffee to her lips.

Out in the dark, the man who had been sitting under the tree stirred and got to his feet, slowly, and looking a bit creaky, as old people do. He wore shorts and an old, much-patched shirt, and had a carved wooden walking stick. An old, straw, fedora-shaped hat sat on top of his head, and as he came closer into the light, he paused and raised the stick in salute.

'I know him,' Sister Mary said softy. 'His village is two days walk from here. I knew him in the old days at Isangi.' She put down her coffee cup and stood up. 'We were both young then.'

'*M'boh tay*,' she called, and then took the three steps down from the veranda to the hard-packed red earth and they shook hands. The greeting over, they were now speaking in a local dialect that Penny didn't understand and even Sister Marie-Claire, who spoke fair Kongo, couldn't manage this one much past a few words. The pair moved off at a slow walk round to the side where there were benches outside the schoolrooms.

'He was obviously waiting for her, then,' Sister Marie-Claire said. Ten minutes later Sister Mary was back, this time striding with purpose round the veranda. 'Excuse me, Doctor. Sister Marie-Claire. You should come and hear this.'

'He has agreed to speak with you,' she said softly. 'I will interpret, but he has always been very old-fashioned, and not good with strangers, so . . .'

Sister Marie-Claire nodded.

The old man wasn't old in Western terms – maybe seventy – but in a land where you were only as good as your own ability to survive, a place rife with malaria, blackwater fever, dysentery, dengue fever, sleeping sickness, and a myriad other tropical diseases, it was a venerable old age. In his youth he had been south – into the old Northern Rhodesia – and worked in the copper mines. He had travelled, mostly on foot, and on old buses, and he had seen and met whites down that way. But in 1963 he had come home – with some money for the bride price – and taken a wife. Other than two years over in the east of the country he hadn't been away again.

He remembered the mission being built. It was and remained the only exposure that the local people had ever had to Europeans until the mine opened, and there were only ever three or four whites there. He had thought about his children's schooling. He had never learned to read or write and had got by, and although he wanted them to learn the ways of books and numbers, their village was a full day's walk away from the mission, so none of his children – there were nine of them – had ever been schooled.

Then came the time of the sickness, and one day the God woman had arrived from the mission. She came with medicine, with water tablets. She was there for five days, sleeping like they did on the ground, eating with them, helping them with their sick. He remembered her, remembered her from his time during the killing in the east, when he was younger and foolish and had supported Lumumba, and rampaged with the others. But she didn't recognise him. Or he thought she didn't.

She had asked for nothing in return, but laughed and clapped hands with the children, who had been fearful at first, for they had never seen one with skin this colour. She was unmarried, yet travelled unchaperoned. She had no man, and yet said she was married to God, but would only stand beside him after she died. None of this made any sense to them, and clearly she was confused, but she had come to them when they needed help, and she wanted no money, no favour. At other times she was wise and clever, could read and write, and spoke of places far away where she had influence with the elders, and clearly her God protected her in his way, but maybe not this time and this was why he had come.

He looked round and stood respectfully as she arrived back with her elder, who seemed younger.

'Maneru, this is Sister Marie-Claire. She is our leader.'

He nodded and put his hand out and took hers and held it for a few seconds, the African development on the European handshake.

'Please sit down. We thank you for your visit, Maneru. Sister Mary says you have – news for us. Please speak.'

'You must leave this place,' he said, lifting his head as if looking them in the eye might convey the message more strongly. 'Soon. The fighting will come. Many guns. You are unprotected here. You have no men, no gendarmes. They will prey on you.'

'They will come here? Soldiers?' Sister Marie-Claire asked. She was sceptical and maybe it was in her voice. There was no fighting in the west of the Democratic Republic. That was all way over to the east on the borders with Burundi and Rwanda, and although she had heard it had spilled south, down towards Shaba, there was nothing over this way.

'Maybe yes. There is talk.'

'Who will come, old one? The Tutsi?'

'No. Not Tutsi.' He turned and pointed to the south. 'Congo men.'

Sister Marie-Claire nodded, showing she understood. The Congo people were widespread, speaking over fifty dialects, from well north of the river in the French Congo – she still though of it as that – down as far as Luanda in central Angola in the south, and several hundred miles east.

'When will they come, old one?'

Maneru shrugged and the nun nodded. Two days, a week, two weeks. It was all the same to him. She had seen a man wait a week for a bus. Africa gives its sons nothing if not incredible patience. She smiled at him. He was old and had walked all day to speak to them about this. 'I thank you for coming to see us. Will you rest here tonight?'

He shook his head.

'Then let us give you food for your journey.'

Sister Jo was called and she was back a few minutes later with two loaves of bread and two cans of corned beef, chosen because they did not require can-openers. There was also a bottle of water, and a mug of strong, very sweet tea.

Twenty minutes later he had melted into the darkness, but they knew he wouldn't be going far that night, to the nearest village perhaps, where they had a hut for travellers.

'Well,' Sister Marie-Claire asked Sister Mary. 'What do you make of that?'

2350 hrs Monday
Brazzaville

McLean pulled the pistol from his belt under his shirt, removed the magazine, made safe and put the weapon away in its webbing holster. With no safes in the rooms, side-arms could be handed back to the armourer corporal for safe keeping, but he invariably chose to wear it. Cheyne would be down in a minute, they had only been back two or three minutes at the most and he needed to round up the team for an 'O' group meeting.

He phoned downstairs and asked the night porter to bring up cold beer and bottled water, and as he finished, the CO and Nick Webber walked in.

'Right, let's get started. Where's—'

'Here, sir,' the assault squadron lieutenant called, coming in the door. His boots and the bottom of his trousers were sodden, and he squelched his way in. 'Can I have a minute to change, please?'

'Yeah, go,' Webber replied, then looked back at the others. 'Right. I'm going to talk to Northwood. Assume for the time being they say do it and we get the permits. You blokes get the beginnings of a plan together.'

Webber called to the duty corporal manning the Clansman next door and asked for OC Support to come over and join them.

'I'll be half an hour,' Cheyne said, lifting the heavy satellite telephone and its encryptor unit from the dressing table.

The Royal Marines' planning ethos is simple. A defined process that looks at all the headline issues and ends its first stage – mission analysis – with an initial warning order to a formation. Stage two is evaluating factors – the ground, the enemy, other friendly forces – and is worked through a relative strengths analysis – difficult with this mission, because they knew so little about any possible enemy. They then looked at surprise, security, time and other relevant factors before getting into COA. The courses of action. Stage four was 'commands decision' and selecting the courses of action.

By the time marines are deployed everyone has been briefed, knows the mission objectives, and the scope they have to achieve them. Everyone has been briefed and involved, right down to individuals in fire teams.

This was A Commando 'O' group. Next level was company, then troop, then section, then fire team. McLean knew that even if they came up with a course of action in the next two hours, then by 0200 they would have small groups of marines around the hotel in looking at the plan, challenging it, asking questions. They were looking to finish up where they knew all there was to know about the mission and the environmental factors. With this cascade effect, by the kick-off there would be corporals briefing sections, answering what they could, going back up to Troop for answers to things they didn't know. They were looking for decisions, options, for every possible scenario, from a boat engine failing, to a driver getting lost, to a truck breaking down, through to their meat and drink, the tactical issues. Troop commanders in turn would go back up to Company and so on. It was complicated but it worked.

In the commando 'O' group, Major Webber chaired the meeting. As ops officer this was his territory and he was, McLean knew, bloody good at it.

'Right. Items. One – Mission is clear. Let's agree courses of action is clear. Let's look back at re one dash a – permits. Two – resources. Three – logistics. Four – entry. Five – egress. Six – return Brazzaville – a) with EOs and b) without EOs.

Presumably they all have passports. Where was the old nun from? The one who wants to go home one day? Iraklion was it?'

'Heraklion.'

'Right, gentlemen. Operation Heraklion. The Mission. Let's define it.'

They began.

Upstairs in his room Colonel Cheyne sat on his bed, the satellite telephone beside him. It was late in the UK and he now had people at PJHQ Northwood trying to track down the correct decision-makers in that loop. He knew the problem. Northwood had authorised him to make certain decisions based on known facts, and they at Northwood were also set up to respond on other decisions but still based on those same facts. This issue had raised new sensitivities and there would be senior people on their way back to Northwood, maybe even ACOS J3 and people at the MoD. They would have already contacted RMHQ, Royal Marines Headquarters in Portsmouth, to bring them into the loop.

He was totally engrossed. He was the commander on the

ground. Much of what came back from Northwood would rely on his assessment. In this instance it was most likely that MoD and Northwood would authorise the attempt, if HMA could get the necessary entry permits, but would be unlikely to present orders without much stronger intelligence suggesting the mission was imperative. It would be down to him, his judgement on the unfolding local situation. Tactically, it was not a good scenario. It looked like a straight round trip, but if they hit any problems, they were a hell of a long way from help and support. Out of range of their standard comms gear, the PRC320 Clansman, which with its standard transmitter and aerial had about thirty miles range on an excellent day. In theory you could boost the transmitter and extend an aerial on a pole to communicate round the world, but it was notoriously unreliable.

It should go off without a hitch, but this was West Africa. The what-ifs outnumbered the givens. The ground situation was so unstable in most places that anything could spark it off. With luck, down in the area they had been asked to go into, it would be sleepy bush country, away from the pressure-cooker atmosphere of Kinshasa or the open fighting in the east. But the intelligence, sparse and unconfirmed as it was, suggested otherwise.

Down one floor an hour later, while Colonel Cheyne was still on and off the phone, they were talking about items three and four.

'Right, entry and logistics. Let's cover them together for a start and then split them out,' Webber said. 'One troop. It's too far for boats, we have no air, so we are limited to the road. Options?'

'Gotta be a heavy with a light vehicle in convoy,' the assault-squadron fellow offered.

Webber looked at the HQ Company Commander. 'The number two at the embassy is trying to find us something, but what are our chances of his finding something decent?'

On deployment it fell to HQ Company to manage supplies

and logistics, transport, communications, and the maintenance skills for all their equipment.

'Your guess is as good as mine, but I'd say not good, and when and if he does, I'd want to know what he has found so we can try and rustle up some spares. Fan belts, water hoses, filters, the usual stuff. That means one of my VMs going as driver. Need to know we can refuel too. Preferably somewhere out of the way, where we aren't going to have a million locals popping out to have a look and getting stirred up.'

'Round trip,' McLean said. 'Three hundred and forty miles or thereabouts. Couldn't we carry drums? Refuel ourselves?'

'We could, but we would need to find it first. Is fuel readily available over there?'

'Seems to be. I'll check.'

Forty-five minutes later they were on to the way out for the group. 'Egress, four options. Green, back out in the trucks the way you came. Red, back out to the road but then west to Matadi. Yellow, the river, downstream, cross, get some transport and pick up the road that loops back towards Matadi. Worst case is cut off from the road and no way across the river. That's Blue.'

'They'll be stuck there with those nuns. They will make the lads go to church,' someone chimed in and everyone laughed except Webber.

'Two of those options are going the other way, away from us. What do they do when they get to Matadi? They will need uplift,' McLean challenged.

'Uplift? Air, land. That's the port, so sea. Anyone?' Webber opened it up.

'The port? Shit,' someone muttered looking up at the map. 'That must be sixty, seventy miles up. How big's the river there?'

'Big enough to be navigable for small ships!' Webber snapped. 'Come on, people! Focus!'

'We could get air down. Have it standing by somewhere?'

Colonel Cheyne entered the room. 'Carry on,' he said,

dropping into a seat left for him. At the next natural pause in the flow he looked across at Webber.

'Where are we up to?'

Webber briefed him on what they had covered so far.

'Right, we'll have a decision from Northwood within the hour. If it's on, I want more than one troop. Two full troops, with an LMA, a couple of engineers and a couple of VMs.' He looked at McLean. 'The marines from A Company, please, Doug.'

McLean nodded. Two troops were the bulk of his company. That meant he would be with them. There was a knock at the door, and a head popped round. It was the commando's padre, Rory Chisholm. 'Can I join you?' he asked.

Cheyne smiled. 'Of course, Padre.'

'So, let's start from the top and work up a plan for two troops.'

'Sorry, but before I forget,' McLean said. 'When we get back on to egress, isn't the WADS somewhere in the area? It's HMS *Winchester*, isn't it?'

0300 GMT
England

There were now, at this unsociable hour, some nineteen people up from their beds and heading into their places of work. Nine of them were going into the PJHQ at Northwood in Middlesex, including ACOS J3 (Sea) and ACOS J3 (Land), the two heads of operations of their sections. J3 (Sea), a senior naval officer, was expecting to meet up with a senior Royal Marines officer on arrival.

Six of them were going into Headquarters Royal Marines in Portsmouth. Whatever happened they would now be very closely in the loop, twenty-four hours a day. As with the Army special forces people at Hereford, Royal Marines on deployment routinely channelled communications back into their own command, simultaneously with Northwood, the MoD, and wherever else it was required for joint or tri-service command decision-making. HQRM would channel communications if necessary and then prepare to do everything they humanly could to support their comrades if the mission went ahead, or if anything went wrong. For the 3rd Commando Brigade's SO2 ops this was a concern. One of his commandos was on an active deployment a hell of a long way from home and had been asked on the basis of some very low-grade intelligence to intervene outside the scope of what they were set up to do. In the event of a problem the very nature of the intervention made the mission virtually unsupportable, either by the rest of the commando, or the brigade. The what-ifs were hairy. It could be something as simple as a vehicle breakdown. With the local situation as volatile and unstable as it was, the possibility of the detachment being cut off a hundred and seventy miles from any help, support or uplift was not ideal.

Back here in the UK they would be almost totally reliant on the objective, on-the-ground, smell-the-smoke-and-feel-the-wind views of CO 40 Commando in Brazzaville. It would be his call, his assessment of the situation.

The Democratic Republic of Congo

The men, in their loose formations, slept in the bush anywhere they could find that was half-comfortable. About thirty miles south-west of Kimpese and spread out across half a mile, their command was on high ground above them. From their overnight bivouac they could make their objective in another day or so, their trucks down in the bush by the road on which they had crossed into the Republic that afternoon. There were some eight hundred in this group, but there weren't trucks for all of them, so some moved on foot, and there were another three groups strung out behind them.

This was a sizable Unita force well inside another independent state, but for these men, and for their forefathers going back four hundred years, crossing into this country was nothing new. Once it had almost been theirs anyway, but none of them knew that. None of them were students of history. They were not so much soldiers as fighters, and not so much driven by political ideal as by custom and habit. This was what they did. They had no other skills, were unemployable in a modern environment to do anything but backbreaking labour for a pittance. They had always done this. In the unit as in the rest of the Unita ranks there were men in their forties who had known no other way of life.

Unita, União Nacional para a Independência Total de Angola, were an Angolan rebel movement. Originally funded by South Africa and the USA in the seventies to combat the Marxist-funded MPLA, they had lost the war. The MPLA was in power. With the demise of apartheid in South Africa, that funding dried up, and then the USA pulled out after Unita ceased to honour any treaties struck with the now-ruling MPLA. They had fought on, stayed in the bush, and increasingly, their once anti-Communist moral high ground was eroded by atrocities and brutality. They raided, looted, robbed – killing as they went – but their aim was still the overthrow of the MPLA government.

Their commander was awake and brooding, looking north out over the bush as the warm wind blew through the darkness. It was quiet, only the light murmuring of his men below him. There were no animal noises, no bird cries. Even the crickets were silent. When he had got his orders to move into this area it was like an answer to a prayer for him, not that he would pray. Even though mission-educated, he was atheist, believing in nothing but the power of the gun, that the strong shall vanquish the weak. For him this was the natural order of things. He took what he wanted, when he wanted. Any resistance was met with extreme violence. Makuma took pleasure, almost sexual, in brutality. He was a psychopath, although he wouldn't have known what the word meant.

He had lived here once, dragged here by his mother, who had come to live with a man from these parts after his father had left. He had never fitted in, people laughed at his accent, and the man in whose huts his mother slept cared nothing for him, and beat him when drunk on home-brewed beer. At the school he was behind the others in his learning and they laughed at him, so he hit out at them, and many days he didn't come at all, preferring to be outside.

His anger grew, feeding something inside him that had always been there, and people began to fear him. That felt good. By the time he was twelve he killed purely for the pleasure, starting by taking a puppy and breaking its tiny legs in his fingers so he could watch it squirm and yelp. When bored with that and with watching it shivering and trying to crawl away on four broken limbs he slowly pushed a six-inch nail through it into the ground and waited till it died.

He was caught doing it. One of the nuns at the mission, a big-boned Irish woman enraged at what she had witnessed, had taken a stick to him and he had never forgotten it.

At fourteen, tall for his age, he took his first woman and killed a human being for the first time. He forced himself on her on a path, and when she spread her legs and he produced his penis, she laughed and suggested he came back when he was a man and it had grown. He was not well-endowed and knew he never would be. Other boys his age had things that swung down, heavy and potent. Not him. His was like a finger. He beat her brains out with a mattock handle, the greyish-yellow, bloody gore all over the implement. Then he had her, wishing she was one of the whites at the mission, using the dead body quickly, finished in seconds.

At the school they knew nothing, but they still didn't like him and he wondered what they would be like, the white women, God's wives. He wanted to use them, kill them, show them who was who.

There had been other killings, and in time people guessed who was behind them, and anywhere he went there were men with weapons looking at him. His mother had thrown him out of her hut and no longer spoke to him, so finally he moved on and, heading south, he joined up with the Unita people. They had guns.

Now he was back. A commander with many men and

many weapons and a roving brief. He had taken command of his first cadre simply by killing its real commander. He didn't even manufacture a reason. Just cut his throat as he slept. The commander – the equivalent of a brigadier in Unita's command structure – had had men come to him and complain, but he was pragmatic. If they would follow this Captain Makuma, and if he fought well with them, then he had other things to worry about. And he did. He seemed almost fearless, his brutality channelled enough to leave him to get along with it. Makuma, now a man driven by his own agenda, had heard about men complaining and acted with his group of immediate followers. The complaints stopped. In Africa men will follow the one with most blood on his spear. And Makuma's was dripping with it daily.

Three years on they were here. His and other elements were to cut off the supply lines from the coast and hopefully force the Angolan Army – in the Republic to support Kabila – to break off their fighting in the east and move towards them. That would free up Hutus under siege to advance on Kinshasa and, that battle won, the Hutus would move south and help Unita.

That was the Unita high command plan, but he didn't care. He never thought that far ahead. He thought tactically, wanted immediate gratification. He thought about Idi Amin, Mobutu – the great African strongmen – and saw himself as one of them. All he needed was wealth. Money to pay soldiers. His men were now more aligned to him than to Unita. They too wanted booty, women, money. With him they would get it and all he demanded in return was absolute obedience and loyalty. At times he was congenial, charming and almost acquiescent with the Unita power players, but the change in his mood could come within a heartbeat. If he came across dissenters he dealt with them, and his troops feared him more than they feared the devil himself.

His immediate core knew what they were going to do. Let the other cadres cut the road east. They had another task. One for them as men. They had raided the diamond mine last week. Working on Ndube's intelligence, they had taken what valuables they could, no diamonds worth talking about, but they had got some trucks and some white hostages. They all knew they were always good for cash money. They were down there with them now – four whites, two young ones and two older, one grey-bearded and holding his Bible like it would protect him.

They knew Makuma would have quite happily killed them all. But they had suggested, with great respect, that they were worth more alive, no matter how much fun it would be to kill them. And there was another mine, this one much less defended. Makuma said that the stories years ago said that it was not a big mine. Not much diamonds, people said. But it was there and poorly defended, and besides, these people were all liars. Ndube, his right-hand man had come back from Luanda grinning, with evidence, and had spoken of it all the time since. Plenty of wealth there. A good haul would make all the difference. Put money in their pockets and have some fun with the women in the villages they moved through. Then they could move back to the road and fight with the others.

Above them Makuma – a huge, evil, brooding presence – sat on a rock looking out to the north. He wanted more men. To the east there was another Unita unit. It would be easy enough.

Three

Terry Harris was awake. The morning air smelt of dew, and his clothes were damp. They had stopped in the dark last night and he looked around for the first time in growing light. Dry savannah bush, some jesse, the grass sparse and brown, red, rocky soil, flat-topped acacia trees, a massive-trunked baobab tree away on the flat ground to the right. An emerald dove called, and away somewhere a baboon barked a warning, a troop moving from their night's rest towards water in the dawn light, no doubt coming across some of the many armed men that were all around them.

He looked nearer, his immediate area. His captors were stirring. When they slept they just scraped out a hole for their hip bone and lay down, head to toe in a line. He knew why. This habit dated from the time they had spent doing incursions in smaller groups. If someone approached at night then the man awake, the sentry, simply touched the feet or head of the next man and they were up and moving. No words. No noise.

One of them stood, scratched his crotch and then blew his nose on to the ground, flicking the snot off his fingers, a yellow tendril arcing away like a mucus bolas, caught on a thorn and swinging in the morning light.

Terry tested his bonds as he always did, but the electrical wire held as it had done from day one. Three-phase heavy wiring around their hands and then all four of them tied to a tree. He wasn't even sure why he tried. Certainly to ease the circulation in his hands, but would he try and escape? He thought not. He knew little about surviving in the bush and they would soon find him out here. Also, an escape would just antagonise them and there were the other three to consider. They had seen the leader of this bunch. His men feared him. There was no other word for it. From the look of it they gave him complete and total obedience. Big – like an old silverback gorilla male – when he moved among them they fell silent, only his immediate cronies talking. They had been paraded before him, Francisco, their guard, pulling the wire that joined them hard enough to be painful, something he now knew to be out of character. He had clearly done it because that was what was expected of him. The leader – someone called him Colonel – had looked at them with a dark, blank, expressionless eye, assessing them. It had been uncomfortable, rather like being viewed by a large snake, a one-eyed snake, because this man's left eye was opaque, a contrast to the ebony blackness of his skin. There was no empathy. No emotion. Nothing. They might as well have been flies on a turd.

The Lord God would protect them. The two youngsters were bearing up well. Fit and healthy, they were strong. But he worried about James – feisty, sometimes truculent, always loyal James – who had struggled through yesterday. He was pale and seemed off-colour, but he said he was just dehydrated. They needed water.

Would there be a ransom demand? Who would they make it to? The company? They could pay. The authorities must know we have been taken, he thought. They would have done a count of the dead and wounded at the mine, known that the expatriates were missing. But would they care, he wondered? Care enough to mount a search, some sort of follow-up?

The sun was rising. Where are we? He knew they had been moving west. Others were up and moving now and he looked at the nearest of his colleagues. Tony next to him, one of the youngsters and a geologist, was awake.

'You OK?' he asked softly.

Tony nodded. Terry turned his head. He couldn't see James or Phil. Both were sort of behind him, their backs also against the tree trunk. 'The others awake?' he asked.

71

One of their captors was approaching. He was youngish. Spoke quite good English. Small, quick-eyed and intelligent. He was amiable enough considering everything, tried to talk to them at times, reassure them, but most of the time he remained aloof, as if he feared something. With some rudimentary awareness gleaned from a magazine on the psychology of captivity, he had tried to engage the process, asking the man's name, trying to establish a relationship of some sort that would benefit them. This was Francisco.

Terry looked up at him as he approached. The young Angolan was moving towards them fast, moving round stirring men, one of whom was urinating noisily into a bush.

'Can we have some water?' Terry asked as he got closer.

Francisco shook his head quickly. He flicked a look over his shoulder. 'No. No water.' He was worried about something. 'Quiet,' he said softly, quickly. 'Quiet.' His expression changing, saying be quiet, be grey, don't be noticed.

'Why not?' James asked loudly. He couldn't see Francisco from where he was, just heard the question and the first response. He hadn't seen the other figure loom up out of the soft, dawn light, but Terry had. It was their commander, the Colonel, and Francisco had come to a sort of sloppy attention. 'Christ, man,' James continued. 'You can't expect us to—' Tony, who could see who it was, nudged him with an elbow to shut him up. 'Piss off!' he snapped. 'I'm not fucking kowtowing to these cunts. All we want is water. Shit, man—'

Suddenly Makuma was looming over him, looking down. Every man within fifty yards had fallen silent, even the three or four who were always with him.

James looked up. 'Well, well, well,' he started, but whatever he was going to say just died in his throat. There were no witty, brave remarks. The menace came off this man like a smell. It was palpable, you could taste it. He was unpredictable and extremely dangerous, and they knew it.

Fight or flee instincts were academic. Tied like they were, they could do neither.

Makuma looked at Francisco and asked something, the

younger man responding quickly. Makuma grunted and stepped
forward. Oh no, Terry thought. Please, not like this. He could
see nothing from his side. James was on the other side of
the tree.

He heard the kick land, heard James's grunt of pain. Then
the next. Then the next. After the fifth, James stopped making
noises. There was just the meaty thump of each new kick
landing, and on the seventh, blood and teeth splattered out,
some of it catching Tony across the neck and face. Makuma
seemed to take his time, stopping every now and then, then
swinging a big leg back to go in at another angle. He was
smiling now, that turning to a grin as a kick shattered the
unconscious man's jawbone, that quarter of his bloodied,
broken face lolling downward. He kept kicking at the helpless
figure tied to the tree until it seemed the victim was dead.

Finally he pulled from a long scabbard a *panga* – a machete
– and in the peripheral vision of both Phil and Tony, sawed
through James's neck. Obviously the hostage's heart was still
beating, because blood fountained upward from the severed
carotid artery as the big blade cut through his throat, some of it
spraying on to Terry's boots. Then a few chops and it was done.
He held the severed head aloft, waved it in front of the two who
had seen him do it and then walked round to where Terry was
sitting, his eyes scrunched closed, praying and sobbing.

He pulled Terry's head upward by his hair, and dropped
James's head to the ground and then kicked it away between
two of his men, who laughed as it rolled between them, leaves
and dirt sticking to the bloodied, severed open area that had
been his neck.

'G-O-A-L,' Makuma roared, laughing.

He was pleased. He knew what he was going to do.

0630 local
Brazzaville

At the hotel the main 'O' group meeting had wound up and
now troop commanders were walking round smaller groups of

their people run by the section leaders, the corporals and lance corporals. This was to brief, discuss and understand everything they could about the mission, its various component tasks, and get every detailed thought or question out on the table. A hundred what-ifs, and a thousand details, but some of them were losing interest.

The chances of this job getting the green light and enough of the elements coming together to make it feasible were remote, but as one said, maybe get a ride across the river, really see a bit of the country rather than just a smudgy riverbank. A bit of a crack, innit? The 2-Troop lads were sitting round a coffee table they had pulled out on to the veranda overlooking the pool.

'Be OK,' Jock Roberts said. He lifted a huge, muscled, white arm and sipped from a water bottle. 'Must get some film for ma camera. Might be some animals, you know. Loads of butterflies when the flowers are out.'

Furby and Sloth looked up. 'You dickhead. There's no fucking game left,' Sloth said. 'These cunts have eaten everything that walks. They even eat monkeys.'

Sloth, son of a gamekeeper, was a conservationist, a rabid conservationist.

'If you have finished with the Attenborough shit, can we get back on the job?' Biscuit asked.

Furby looked back at the table and the papers and notes. 'What about some torch and radio batteries? If we get into the shit and end up staying a few days, we might want some.'

'We got a few. Not enough. Heavy as fuck they are,' Jock muttered. 'Who's gonna fucking carry them? Not me.'

'You'll carry what you're fucking told to carry, you pongo bastard,' Sloth muttered, leaning back in his chair.

'What about the frogs?' Furby asked. 'They might have some.'

The French contingent were also in Brazzaville. Their 3rd Regiment Parachutiste Infantrie Marine were just down the road, and they had been joint exercising. The swapping of kit and equipment and trying each other's gear had been going on for three weeks. Furby now had a natty French DPM T-shirt and Dave Hobson was sporting a pair of their issue jungle boots. Biscuit added it to his list.

'That it?' he asked. They all nodded.

'Right, it's light order, so day packs only.' He waved papers at them. 'Remember, nothing but seventy-two hours' food, water and survival kits. You'll need the rest of the space.'

Next to them the troop's other big section was sitting round on the floor with their own briefing. They were young, their average age just nineteen, with one who was even too young to legally drink. Their corporal balanced it out nicely. At thirty-five he was the oldest man in the company, and the lads called him Grandad. They dragged him into nightclubs he hated, marvelled at his capacity to drink copious pints of beer and still be able to think and walk, took the piss out of him, but as one of theirs. That just tempered the respect. He was the only man, other than the CSM, who had seen action. He had yomped in the Falklands war, seen his friends and comrades die and been wounded himself. With seventeen years in the corps he was salty. He had seen things they had only heard of, and when trouble brewed, it was to him they turned. It was he that had tagged them with their nickname after watching them trail back into the camp one night after hours of chasing girls without success, and pissed as rats the lot of them. Trouble was, in uniform they looked the business. Green commando berets squared away, super-fit, ramrod straight. But in civvies in a nightclub they were just spotty callow youths, and with girls or women they were collectively shy, awkward and stumbling. They occupied the same table in the same club every Friday and Saturday night, always with the same sense of hope and optimism, and always trailed in pissed, dejected and depressed, the girls inevitably having gone home with someone else, or giggling back to their mums.

One night Grandad had waited for them at the gate in case they had any trouble with the guard detail. 'Fucking 'ell,' he had uttered to the man beside him. 'Look at 'em. The love machine.' The name had stuck.

*   *   *

Up on the second floor in the comms room a corporal was on encryption next to the Clansman. Nick Webber was running over plan details with McLean.

McLean was functioning at one hundred per cent and Webber was pleased. He seemed to have put his personal trouble behind him, dealt with it. In the week after he had discovered his fiancée's deceit, he had told no one, and then one evening it had come out. Webber had gone into the A-company office late one night and found him. He was huddled in a corner, holding himself like a child, his face wracked in pain, sobbing. He was like a wounded animal, the pain so deep, so powerful, he could no longer hold it in, and it welled up and flowed from him like blood. Blood from his soul.

Webber knew not to say anything. Just went off, got a case of beers, and came back. He wasn't sure what to do, so he cracked the caps of a couple and sat down alongside him in the corner and waited. Four beers in, Webber looked at him.

'Come on,' he finished, getting to his feet.

'Where?'

'Never you mind.'

Webber took him to the best place he knew. His home, where his wife, Jenny, would know what to do.

Late that night, she sat up with McLean in the sitting room, and eventually he told her what had happened. It was rambling, painful, a catharsis.

'I understand why, you know, Jen. I know why people do these things. But it doesn't help.'

'You trust too much,' she responded. 'You want to believe people, even those you love, have your own values, your own honour. Your trustworthiness. They don't. Karma,' she said. 'What goes around comes around. You'll go on, intact, wiser, stronger even than before. She has her pain to come.'

'How come?' McLean asked softly.

'Because of what she did. She will have to live with that, and she will realise that her own actions cost her you. I know you. There would be no better, no more loyal man, no one

76

who would love more, honour more. There's the right one for you out there somewhere. This one wasn't. She would have destroyed you. I know, Doug, it hurts like hell. I've been there. But this I know. I know men. This is her loss, not yours. In the meantime, talk about it – to me, or anyone else you feel comfortable with. That will help.'

Jen had never told him exactly what had happened. She was a psychologist, and although this wasn't work, it was between her and Doug.To his credit, whatever had happened between him and his fiancée didn't affect his work, even in the immediate days that followed.

Webber looked over at him.

'Maps,' McLean said. 'I want fucking decent maps. Look at this shit!' He held up a 1:500 000. 'There could be some serious country in there – rivers, swamps – and you'd never know it.'

They were expecting the second in command of the French contingent, who was on his way over with all his maps, and an American major. The French still had the best maps of both sides of the Congo River.

And they were still awaiting a decision from PJHQ Northwood.

Northwood, Middlesex

It had been a frantic few hours. ACOS J3 had pulled in his people, and then advised the Chief of Staff. Three people had been rounded up and were coming in from RMHQ and there was now a small team in at the Foreign and Commonwealth Office trying to make contact with the Democratic Republic of Congo's ambassador, and trying for direct contact in Kinshasa. The phones had been working all night, the Ambassador in Kinshasa trying his best to get the communication lines open.

The planners and tacticians who had seen the outline plan had given it the thumbs-up. A simple enough task. If the permits were granted, they were happy to suggest that Colonel Cheyne be authorised to get his people down there to evacuate the staff at the mission. It was the Chief of Staff's call now.

He made it.

> With the necessary permission from DRC and in light of
> local intelligence, conditions, assessments and in-theatre
> dynamics, and remaining cognizant of your prime role;
> to take whatever action you deem prudent to ensure the
> evacuation and subsequent safe transit of non-combatant
> evacuees, specifically the foreign personnel at Tenta
> mission. Rules of engagement as normal for humanitarian
> mission. Do not fire unless life of non-combatant evacuee
> or own personnel in imminent danger.

In Brazzaville, Colonel Cheyne was standing beside the Clansman radio talking to the Ambassador over the river in Kinshasa,
when the satellite phone rang. He began by writing down the
formal message verbatim then reading it back. He then spoke
for ten minutes and replaced the handset on the briefcase-
sized unit.

'Corporal, find Majors Webber and McLean if you would,
please.' He walked to the window and looked out across the
river at the haze that was the Democratic Republic of Congo.

A minute later they walked in together. 'We have the
go from Northwood,' Cheyne said. He passed Webber the
message he had written down. 'As I expected, it's our call,'
he said softly.

'Then it all hinges on permits and transport,' Webber said,
handing the note to McLean. 'I have been thinking about this.
Coming from the south, right? Angola? Why? How about this?
Unita vs Angolan Army. Angolan Army is now here, which –
as far as Unita is concerned – makes it open season on raids.'
Webber was talking with his hands as he usually did. 'Kinshasa
is entirely dependent on the route up from Matadi. Christ, so
is Brazzaville for that matter. If they can take and destroy
the railway line, then prevent traffic using the road up from
Matadi, then surely Kabila and his Angolan allies will have to
move troops west to protect the supply lines. They have already
taken out the power supply for Kinshasa – what? Twice?'

'Maybe that's the bigger picture,' Cheyne responded. He had thought it through as well. 'But to go this far north of the railway line and the road? Maybe they have to cut the river off as well.' He pointed to the map on the wall. 'You could use the river indefinitely around that point. Stop traffic being routed round their area. There'd be no one to stop them. There's not much in there but a mine, and the mission.' He paused. 'I have just spoken to HMA,' he continued. 'He is meeting the Foreign Minister at 0930. Warning orders. Assume he gets the permit. Assume he can line up some vehicles. Plan on going tonight. If you are across and under way by 2100, you can be at the mission by first light. Turn around, head back and be back in Kinshasa at the embassy for the boats to bring you back over after dark tomorrow night. Review plans now and I'll look at them with you' – he looked at his watch – 'at 1000.'

Both men left the room. There was much to do, and as they departed, Cheyne turned back and looked out of the window. His decision now. Fourteen or fifteen European civilians in the middle of nowhere. To extract them – that is, even if they would heed the warning and leave – meant putting his people beyond support, beyond radio contact, one hundred and sixty miles into what could be a bloody mess. Looking across the river his spine tingled and for some reason the hairs on the back of his neck came up. He felt a foreboding.

Three hundred miles away and twenty minutes later, in HMS *Winchester*'s main communications room, down on the main deck alongside the ops room, the sophisticated communications gear whispered into life. A message, decrypted by the electronics into 'plainspeak', was pulled off the printer, and the rating, seeing the priority code, waved it at his PO boss, and left for the bridge.

Commander Channing was on the bridge wing. Early was the best time for this. Before the heat of the day, before breakfast and the daily standing checks. The water was blue, deep cobalt blue, the white froth from the ship's bow wave fluffy like whipped egg whites. The sun was up, bright in the sky, and already it was getting hot. They were running an exercise. Type 42 destroyers are manpower-intensive, and unlike the much newer Type 23 frigates, with their ultra-lean manning, the older 42s usually had a complement of midshipmen and young officers under training. One of them was now trying to con the ship round in a lazy circle to bisect the drift of a dan buoy thrown over the side for this purpose. The objective was to bring the ship alongside the drifting buoy, and at that point halt her in the water without them touching.

'That it?' he asked.

'Aah – yes, sir,' the young sub-lieutenant answered, looking out at the buoy, which floated along merrily sixty feet from the ship. He thought he had done a great job, since he had been given command half a mile away.

'How the fuck are we supposed to recover that?' Channing asked. 'Swim over to it?' – his voice a very good impression of John Cleese. 'Reach out with the buffer's telescopic arm? I know. We could launch 33!'

33 was the call sign of the ship's Lynx. The young man squirmed nervously.

'Right, move away and try again. This time, calculate the drift, see the line you want, get it as a bearing and call it. Use the engines. That's what they are for. Trust your instincts. OK?'

Channing looked across at the comms rating who had stepped out of the bridge wing door and took the proffered signal. He read it quickly, then reread it.

To: HMS *Winchester*
From: CINC Fleet
cc: FOSF
Priority: Immediate
Situation in DRC worsens. Int suggest armed incursion
from south into area west of Kinshasa imminent.

1. RM Brazzaville may be required to execute EO of +/-15 foreign nationals at mission, Tenta, situated 5° 31′ north 13° 38′ east. Circa 80nm upriver from Matadi.

2. RM entry and egress prime options are overland from Kinshasa and return but Options Yellow/ Blue are for uplift by RN vicinity of Matadi.

3. Proceed at best speed to make mouth of Congo River.

4. Plan to proceed upriver as far as operational limitations and conditions will allow.

5. Advise ETA.

6. Advise fuel state for Helo ops.

7. Advise at river mouth for confirmation of mission. Do not proceed upriver into DRC/Angolan national territory without final approval ACOS.

8. Given int on incursion assume area east of Matadi extremely unstable. ROE to follow. ACOS (Sea) available for voicelink.

'Officer of the Watch?'

'Sir?' He was standing behind Channing, listening with some amusement to the Captain's training style. Channing was in fact very good at bringing on young officers, but his manner sometimes had the professional trainers suggesting what they called 'developmental areas' to his style. He didn't change it. It was the way he was, and more importantly, it worked.

'The Sub will finish this exercise under your supervision, please. I am in the MCO. XO to join me there immediately.'

'Sir.'

'Then Ops, Nav, MEO, WEO, and aviators to join us in my day cabin in thirty minutes. And ask the nav to pull the charts for the Congo River. The approach into Matadi. He is to bring them with him.'

The OOW nodded.

'And try not to lose the bloody dan buoy.'

'Yes, sir.'

Two minutes later he was in the MCO at the satellite communications console, which allowed him to talk to virtually anywhere in the world. His voice was encrypted at the console, bounced off the satellite, and down in this case to PJHQ Northwood, where it came out slightly metallic, but otherwise all the vocal intonations were there. He had a fifteen-minute conversation with ACOS (Sea), a commodore, who had been at Northwood for several hours.

The XO, Lt Commander Selby, was beside him, and every now and then as Channing made notes on a pad he pointed to one and Selby looked over his shoulder.

Tenta Mission

Sister Jo had noticed it first, when the children – normally running round playing before school – were called into lines by the old bell that hung under a branch in the flame tree.

She had walked out, her habit swishing round her legs as she moved, smiling as she did every day at the thought of all the bright young expectant faces. There was no need to encourage an African child in school. They were diligent and worked hard way beyond what their Western counterparts would, even at a young age. They understood the value of education, the opportunities that being able to read and write and count offered. It seemed quieter than usual. Not only were there fewer children than usual, but there wasn't the usual volume of noise.

Odd, she thought. She walked over towards the bell, where three little girls sat under the tree. They were sisters and their bottoms were not on the red earth, but on plastic fertiliser bags to keep their clothes clean, the littlest one with a toy car made of wire. Its steering wheel was on a long wire extension, so the child could walk along pushing the car and steering the little wheels.

'*Sagebonhe*,' she said, noticing they were sitting together. Didn't usually do that. On arrival the older one usually went off with friends her own age.

'*Sa-ge-bon-he*, Sista Jo,' they chorused back in whispers. There were no smiles, none of the usual joyousness.

'You three don't look very happy,' she said, prompting a response. There was none.

Just two of the younger faces looking up at her, while the oldest of the three, Emily, looked down at the ground. Sister Jo squatted down so she was at their height.

'Do you want to tell me what's wrong? Come on now. Can't be that bad. It's a lovely day, the sun is shining down on us like the good Lord's love.'

There was no response, just huge, liquid, dark eyes looking back at her.

'Well if you want to talk to me, you know where I am.'

In the clinic, Dr Penny Carter was almost ready to open up. Her two local nurses were not in yet, but she quickly moved about her tasks, opening the shutters to let the light stream in. Today was the last day of this year's river blindness prevention programme, so she began opening boxes of the Mectizan. There was another problem.

The morning duty nurse for the wards hadn't come in yet and the girl who had done the night shift wanted to go home. She was agitated, and unusually uncommunicative.

'You go home,' she said eventually. 'Sister Sarah and I can manage.'

As she watched the woman go down the steps she noticed that the line of people that would normally have formed by now was a mere handful – and one of them, bleeding from the head, was clearly not here for Mectizan.

She walked over to him and looked at the wound, forgetting about the small turnout. He smelled strongly of beer and sweat and looked hungover. He had not covered the wound, so there was no bandage to lift, but the blood had congealed into crusty lumps and flies buzzed around it. It would have to be cleaned and sutured, and he would need antibiotics and an anti-tetanus injection. She knew what had happened. He had come second to someone in a drunken fight and been caught with a hoe, or a club, or had taken a glancing blow from a blunt machete or maybe an axe. Left, it would be flyblown and maggoty within days, but at least the maggots would eat the rotting flesh of a wound that had gone septic, as this surely would. He didn't seem to be in pain, but she had long since stopped marvelling at their stoic stance to pain. They seemed to be able to switch it off at will. She had seen people with the most horrendous injuries walk in – trauma that would have left most people she had ever treated incapacitated. Once, she had run out of anaesthetic and stitched a man's arm. He had thirty-six ripped puncture wounds in his left arm, the result of an attack by a juvenile crocodile. An adult he would never have been able to beat off with his right arm. She had cleaned and sutured the wounds, and bound the man's arm, and he had never murmured, not once. The pain must have been intense, she knew, but he never made a sound, just seemed to be in his own world, cut off from all around him.

'Come in,' she said.

A few moments later, Sister Marie-Claire appeared on the school veranda with two of the other nuns. She was a teacher too, all four of them were, and all four were looking out at the children already lining up, anticipating Sister Jo's ringing of the bell.

She took it in, in an instant. There were maybe only half the children who would be expected to attend. The old man's warning came flooding back. If he had travelled all the way from his village to warn them, then he believed it. Maybe others had also heard, and maybe this was why.

She looked at Sister Jo and nodded. Ring it, girl, she thought. Let's not dwell on this. We have a school to run. The bell rang out three times, and as Sister Jo walked back under the shade of the red-painted, corrugated-iron roof of the veranda, the children fell silent. Sister Marie-Claire watched them stop shuffling before she spoke, as she did most days, but something made her look out beyond them, to the edge of the cleared ground. There, at the tree line, was the old man. He looked back at her for a moment, and then without gesture, but with great dignity, almost sadness, he turned and walked into the trees along the path.

Makuma had sent a runner across to find the unit to the east and deliver a message, and the man returned inside an hour, sweat running freely down his face. He changed hands with his AK47 and did a sloppy salute. Breathing hard he said they were six miles to the east and were moving away when he reached them, but he had delivered the message.

Their Colonel, he was angry at the request, his advance would have to wait, and he and his cadre would meet them at the place described mid-morning. Makuma nodded and dismissed him with a wave. They moved off an hour later, the main column moving slowly northwards, Makuma and ten of his most loyal men in two four-wheel drives they had taken some months before, heading west for the meeting. They were waiting at the rendezvous point when the other unit commander arrived with what seemed most of his HQ element.

He was a minimalist. His second-in-command was there, as was his political officer, and just two others, runners.

He was slightly built, wiry, in direct contrast to the heavy, imposing bulk of Makuma, and at about forty years of age he was older than Makuma, and a solid Unita veteran. Trained in the early days by the South African Army, he had made his way up the ranks the old-fashioned way, with experience, hard work and commitment to the cause. He was fair but a stern disciplinarian, who punished men for looting and lax behaviour. He didn't like Paul Makuma, didn't like his methods or his command style. The stories of his sadism and brutality were commonplace and he certainly didn't like the way he had taken command of his first unit, the rumour well known among the older veterans.

He walked up towards them, his only weapon a Russian Tokarov pistol he had taken from a dead MPLA officer a decade before. His number two, a stocky major Makuma had seen once or twice, trailed him by a few feet to his left and he had a folding-stock weapon over his shoulder. The other three were all armed but their weapons were slung. Makuma took this in through his one eye like a snake viewing its prey. They suspected nothing – and why should they? he mused with a smile at the approaching Colonel, they were comrades, soldiers in the same liberation army.

'This better be good,' the Colonel said. 'My men are sitting like women around a cooking pot, when we should be on the move.'

Makuma knew that. He knew where they were, how many there were. 'My friend,' he said with a beaming smile. 'Comrades.' He included all of them. 'Please? Rest.' He indicated that they should sit.

'Get on with it, Makuma.'

Makuma's smile died. He did. He pulled his rifle up and, levelling it in one fluid move, he let go a burst of fire at close range into the Colonel and his four men. Makuma was strong, and the burst that began at chest height stayed there, all four of the victims dropping, jerking, to the ground, one of the runners staggering a few feet before he was cut down by one of Makuma's men opening up with his own weapon. It was over in seconds. None of them was dead, but all had multiple gunshot wounds in the abdomen and chest. Even the finest trauma teams in a Western hospital would have struggled to save any of them, but out here they were as good as dead.

The sound echoed off the nearby hills, and as the echo died away, Makuma threw the rifle back to the man he had borrowed it from. He walked a few steps forward to where the Colonel was lying on his back, trying to breathe, his chest making sucking, bubbly noises, his body going into deep traumatic shock. His mouth was wide open, his eyes staring upward. In an act that even his own men found distasteful, Makuma stood over him, undid his fly buttons and – careful that his men could not see his tiny penis – he pulled it out and urinated into the dying man's mouth. When the man's mouth was full and he was coughing it back in a reflex action, Makuma pissed into his eyes, and then back again into his mouth, laughing as he did so.

He shook it, did his buttons up and began to walk away, toward where his new unit was waiting for orders. The men he had shot would be left to die, or be ripped apart while still living by the big black vultures that were already appearing in the sky.

Forty minutes later – inching over the rough ground in their vehicles, his scouts out ahead on foot – he found the first of the elements of the now leaderless battalion, the left flank. Makuma called their officer over and told him to send runners for all the other officers and have them return to this spot.

While he waited his men spread a small tarpaulin from the branches of an acacia tree back to the Land Cruiser and set up two folding chairs and a table. This was equipment that had been in the vehicle when they had stolen it. There had also been an artist's easel, but that had been burned on a fire. Fifteen minutes later, with the two vehicles parked up and the awning out, it looked like a place a commander might sit planning his battles, but Makuma didn't sit down. He indicated that his two senior men should sit. They did so. They sat, but they didn't relax. No one did around Makuma. He grunted and walked away.

The senior man, Makuma's second-in-command, was Marco Ndube. Just twenty-eight years old, he was made from Makuma's mould and early on Makuma had seen this, a kindred spirit, someone as nasty and evil as he was. But Makuma thought he lacked strength, he was weak, needed leading, needed someone with vision to make the decisions. For Paul Makuma he was perfect. Small, wiry, quick-witted, he was also vicious, cruel, power-hungry. He would execute Makuma's orders without compunction, modelling himself on his leader.

In fact Marco Ndube was highly intelligent. He was also manipulative, cunning, ambitious, and absolutely without morals. He would do anything to get what he wanted and, unlike many, he knew his own limitations and therefore had learned how to use other people.

As they moved off, he thought about it. Diamonds. Enough

to be a very rich man for the rest of his life. It would be simple enough as long as he could keep Makuma focused, and he had become good at that over time, manipulating the thinking of the great, brooding hulk, like advisors and acolytes had done for powerful, ambitious men right through time.

The various unit commanders were gathering. Within half an hour there were fourteen of them – seven captains, each with his number two. They were standing around, confused, impatient, throwing questions at Marco Nbude, who sat back leisurely in his folding chair. Some who knew him, or had heard his reputation, were quieter, waiting to see what they had been gathered for.

Finally Makuma arrived, moving slowly, but like an elephant, seemingly light on his feet. All the talk stopped, and behind him Marco Nbube and the other man rose slowly and moved quietly round the group of men as if to hear their leader's address.

'Is everyone here?'

'All but Dennis,' someone responded. Makuma looked at him. 'His cadre are on the right. Maybe he didn't know,' he finished lamely under Makuma's stare.

'My friends,' Makuma began. 'In war things happen, men break. Men disobey. This morning your colonel was unwise enough to do that. Our units are to join for a major push, and he said he wasn't going to cooperate. He was fearful' – Makuma paused – 'and this is not for fearful people. I will not have cowardice!' He bellowed, moving forward, nearer them, his sheer bulk imposing. 'I will have obedience!' He swept his eye over them, awaiting challenge, and then in a second he was amenable, friendly, a big smile showing even white teeth. 'But in return you will find that with me you will have some fun, enjoy yourselves a little. Women? A man takes what he wants. My men do. On this march you will be able to put money in your pockets, because now I command you.'

Some of them were smiling. This was sounding better. Better than the previous rules. But not all of them. Two men near the back of the small group were silent, and then one spoke.

'Where is our commander?' he asked. He was tall, well-spoken, wore glasses and had pens in his pocket.

'Relieved,' Makuma answered. Ndube was moving round now, like a cat stalking.

'You command us now?'

'Is there any doubt of that?' Makuma asked.

'I'd like to hear it from our colonel.'

'He was shot for cowardice,' Makuma answered. 'But you can ask him all the same.' As he said it, Ndube stepped up behind the man and then moved. It was lightning fast, like the attack of a mongoose. The knife in his hand went straight into the side of the victim's throat, through the carotid artery. He pushed and it went clear through, and he cut forward through cartilage, muscle and the trachea, and out the front. Blood gushed out and Ndube let him fall to the ground twitching his death throes, his glasses falling off, the pens in his pocket covered in blood and gore. The gathered men were stunned, and Makuma stepped nearer.

'Anyone else want to hear it from someone other than me? I will not have disobedience! I will not have disloyalty! Victory for the cause is all that matters!'

Ndube smiled, looking down at the dead man, now lying still. He didn't like educated people.

'You?' Makuma stepped up near the man who had been standing next to the dead man.

'Will you follow me?'

'Yes,' he said with a nod, his eyes wide, stunned by what had just happened.

Makuma looked at Ndube. 'Find this Dennis. The rest of you' – he turned and pushed his way through them to where a map was laid out on the vehicle bonnet – 'swing your march to the west. Form up with the others and be here' – he pointed – 'by dark. I want the road cut at this point.' He began to issue orders.

Ambassador Hewitt was waiting in the Foreign Minister's ante-room. His private secretary and two other men kept coming and going and every now and then the typist sitting at the desk smiled wanly at him, the red of her lipstick like blood against her pitch-black skin. She had brought him tea and he sat and drank it without pleasure. It was served the African way, with lots of sugar.

The Foreign Ministry was – like most of the government – located outside downtown Kinshasa. The whole district had been moved out here to the west by Mobutu, not that he ever spent much time here towards the end. He had sat on his huge yacht in the middle of the river, where he felt safest, and ruled Zaire's slide into chaos from there.

Kabila had maintained the location when he took power, and at least he was here every day, although at the moment he was in Egypt courting Hosni Mubarak, who was trying – as a senior African statesman – for some sort of peace agreement. Mubarak had told the world's media he was hopeful of an outcome. Ambassador Hewitt knew otherwise. As long as Kabila had Angolan, Zimbabwean and Namibian support and troops, then he wouldn't concede an inch to the Hutu-sponsored rebels. It had taken him too long to wrestle power from Mobutu and he wanted his snout in the trough for as long as he could.

At last the door opened and the private secretary walked across to him.

'Ambassador, the Minister's apologies for the delay. He will see you now. Please follow me,' he said abruptly. He had obviously learned the words by rote but whoever had taught him had not bothered with the soft skills. The sentiment wasn't there. It was all attitude. This was no career civil servant. No youthful potential diplomat. A tribal appointment, Hewitt realised. Maybe even one of the Minister's extended family. Jobs for the boys. Good old nepotism.

Hewitt stood and followed.

The Minister was behind his desk. It was large, polished and shone like glass. The only things on it were a leather desk set, clearly a gift from someone, and a small, stuffed crocodile with his name on it, in case anyone was in doubt as to who they were in front of. Three telephones sat on a side bureau, and to Ambassador Hewitt's mild amusement, one of them was a Garfield telephone, the dial set into the cat's face. The phone was new. Obviously, the Minister liked it. Along one wall a long cabinet held books that looked as if they had never been read, and on the top sat a model of a big sleek motor yatch in a glass case. The name plate said 'Predator 80', its makers English, a company Hewitt had heard of based in Poole. Above the cabinet was a cheap print of an Alpine scene standing in stark contrast to the heavy wood panels of the wall. Hewitt wondered if the Minister's aspirations were clearly on view or if he had inherited the bits and pieces.

They began with small talk as a secretary – this one a young woman in a tight skirt – poured tea into garish little red glass cups. The handles were a sort of baroque gilt effect and the irony was accentuated by her pouring Nestlé condensed milk into the cups direct from the tin and stirring the tea with a spoon. She sniffed loudly, swallowed whatever mucus she had sniffed back, and passed Hewitt a cup. He smiled politely.

'Minister, let me come to the point of my visit.'

The Minister nodded and waved a hand. 'Of course.'

The haggling started.

Across the river at the Sofitel, the marine manning the comms was sitting at the chair at the dressing table, the Clansman, the KL43 and the satellite phone all arrayed in front of him. He jotted down a message, this one from a mile away at the embassy. He stood up, ripped off the page from the pad and popped his head round the door into the ops room.

McLean took it and read it. 'Comms in, Nick. The manager from the Intercon has found us some transport.'

There was a knock at the door. 'Major McLean?'

McLean nodded. He knew the fellow. The marine was a support-company communications man, trained to provide the up and down links and do basic repairs and maintenance to the Clansmans. He had McLean's radio operator with him.

'Comms, sir. We've tried the others. There are only two

sat phones in Brazzaville. The French have lent us theirs, happily, but it's taken a thumping, and they reckon it's intermittent. They have been using diptel.' McLean nodded. Diptel was the diplomatic telephone system, available to the French contingent, because they had an embassy on this side of the river.

'To be honest, sir, I wouldn't rely on it. We have the only other sat comms in Brazzaville, so that unit will have to stay, but we have another idea. There's every chance your Clansman is not going to work back up to here, you'll be out of range for only about eight hours, and if this phone' – he pointed to it – 'doesn't work, then we have something else. This is natty. It's an emergency transponder off a life jacket. This will work. Anywhere. It's satellite bounced. If you break down – or get in the shit – set it off. We'll know.'

'What can you do?' Mclean asked.

'Not much, sir, but we'll know,' the marine answered. 'He turned to the Captain's radio operator, a signals sergeant. 'It's currently unscrewed. To send a signal, just tighten it a full turn. Unscrew the battery and break the power supply to get your silence. Here's a code we worked out. One to four short bursts is egress intention. The other set messages are preceded by a long. As you start your transmission give it three minutes of continuous, then a ten-second break, then two, another ten-second break, then a minute. By then someone will have picked up the beacon. HQRM have borrowed some gear and will be listening out. They will let us know.'

The signals sergeant nodded and looked at the French satellite phone in its steel carrying case. 'What's wrong with this? Can't we ask the tels tech sergeant to have a look?' knowing as he said it that even the technical skills of the Signals Troop's best man weren't aimed at this sort of kit. 'Maybe not . . .' he trailed off.

In the UK, although permission had been given for the Royal Marines in Brazzaville to conduct what they had tagged 'Operation Heraklion', the decision at PJHQ Northwood had been that there would be no publicity, no press statements. The mission would be low-key, routine stuff, and the only release of information to the media would be after they were back in Brazzaville, and then only if they actually brought the civilians out with them. If the civvies refused to leave – still a possibility – then there was little newsworthy about the short mission and nothing would be said.

At the Sofitel marines were preparing their kit. As ordered, everything except food, water and survival kits was emptied out of their day packs. They wouldn't be carrying their big bergens. Sleeping bags, ponchos, mosquito nets, extra clothing, personal effects – everything would stay behind. They were paring down for what should be a twenty-four-hour mission, travelling light, and whatever they took would have to be absolutely essential.

Furby was working through his belt kit and vest. On the belt were two water bottles, shell dressings, a folding knife – his an American Buck knife – and a recent addition to most marine's kit – but bought and paid for personally – a Leatherman tool. For most of them it was the best sixty quid they ever spent, the multi-purpose tool kit built into a pair of pliers could do just about anything.

Hitched on the right alongside the water bottle was a gollock, a machete. Some of the lads had heavy ghurka kukris, but he had bought his here in the Congo, a heavy-bladed machete with a fifteen-inch blade and he had sharpened it to a razor edge.

His vest was state-of-the-art 'load-carrying equipment'. Based on the fisherman's vest with its many pockets, this was stitched around a kevlar fabric frame so it was load-bearing in the true sense. The wearer could hang any amount of ordnance and gear off its various loops and clips, and it would retain shape and be comfortable on a long march. The magazine pouches were ergonomically designed to be at exactly the right angle for a soldier with his weapon to his shoulder to change magazines as fast as possible without fumbling, and the front cloth panels and netting back panels were breathable gortex. He had customised the vest, and the left shoulder panel was reinforced so that when he carried link 'bandoleer' ammunition for an LSW or the GPMG it wouldn't chafe and wear through the vest.

The vest contained four magazines for his rifle, each loaded with thirty rounds, rifle grenades and hand grenades. It also held a maglight torch, a compass, his survival kit and a big, heavy-bladed knife, also sharpened, which was in a sheath that ran upward along his chest so the point was at his shoulder. To pull the knife out he just grabbed the handle and pulled downward. He was one of the old school and believed in the 'carry a knife and save a life' thinking.

Furby, like any fighting man who moved on foot, was very conscious of his feet, and in his combat-trouser pockets he carried a spare pair of socks, dry and clean – and kept that way in plastic sandwich bags – and foot powder. He also carried spare shell dressings and his own first aid kit, complete with butterfly plasters and antiseptic. He checked those and then looked into his almost-empty day pack. He knew there would be other gear to carry, and into his pack he stuffed a clean olive-green T-shirt. With his foil-packed meals in the side pockets, the rest of the space could take whatever the troop needed. He slipped his beret into one side pocket and his floppy hat into the other.

Beside him the others worked, quietly, professional in every way, Jock bent over cleaning his GPMG lovingly, talking to it like it was a woman. The Royal Marines, unlike the Army who got rid of their heavy GPMG section weapons and opted for the lighter LSW that fired 5.56, held on to theirs. Every RM troop still had general-purpose machine guns. They were big, heavy, required different ammunition from the basic marine's SA80, but they were devastating in action. With a heavy barrel, they could – in theory, in a cyclic rate of fire – pour out a thousand rounds a minute. They didn't need to. A long 7.62 round will shoot through walls and tree trunks, and the machine gun was the undisputed queen of the infantry battle.

Two marines arrived pushing the hotel gardener's wheelbarrow. 'Eh up, lads,' one said cheerfully. 'Got your toys here. The frogs have come through.'

Furby looked into the wheelbarrow. In it were boxes of 7.62 long-link ammunition for the troop's GPMGs and extra preloaded magazines of 5.56 for their SA80s. There were rifle grenades and hand-delivered types of white phosphorous, the green smoke grenades, frags, an exotic-looking portable grenade launcher with a rotary magazine, a sort of lightweight M19, and a couple of Claymore mines. There were also LAW rockets.

'If you ever wondered how the French enforce their foreign policy in Africa, this is the clear indicator,' the support company man, an armourer, said. Big Jock was looking through the material, oohing and aahing. Soldiers the same the world over. They love things that go bang.

Sloth wandered over and looked at the pile of ordnance in the barrow. 'Fuckin' 'ell,' he muttered. 'Where's the boss think we are? Fucking Bosnia?'

Four

W hile the two troops, the handful of attached men, Don Harvey, the CSM, and Major McLean made their preparations, the assault squadron team were making theirs. Their base was in the islands in the river, the largest so big as to suggest it was a piece of high ground that split the course of the river. Their island was small, and in the first days they had real trouble with the crocs, but they seemed to have made enough of a presence there that the big surians had moved on, across to the next island. They still had an armed marine at all times, and most of them – if they were working near the water – had their weapons close to hand.

The big island out behind them was a shithole. About ten nautical miles long and seven wide, and all Congolese territory, it was locally called Il Mbamou and the northern side was low-lying and swampy, but there were still fishing villages of hardy local people, trying to pull a living from the brown waters.

On their island there was just them, and as they worked they slapped at flying or crawling things that bit, and they sweated and swore and cursed fucking Kabila and fucking Africa, and fucking heat and fucking mosquitoes, and fucking snakes, and fucking crocodiles.

Their task was to transport across the river, silently and effectively, the two troops of marines, who would then drive down to Tenta, bring out willing non-combatant foreign nationals and then return to Kinshasa where the squadron

96

would get them back across the river in their boats to Brazzaville. With only four boats it meant several trips, so they were hoping that Colonel Cheyne would authorise use of the hovercraft.

Their prime mission in the region was the evacuation of foreign nationals and staff from the British Embassy in Kinshasa should the capital fall. In the worst case, the approach, loading and departure of each boat back towards Brazzaville would be under fire from unknown attackers. The hovercraft so far had been used in the exercises as a stable gun platform, there to protect the rigid raiders. Moving at speed up and down the shoreline, it could pour out suppression fire with a fifty-calibre and twin GPMGs, supported if necessary by marines with LAW rockets. This was a deterrent. You wouldn't want to open fire on the boats, not with the armed hovercraft – capable of turning on a sixpence at fifty knots – there like a big brother, prepared to make sure you didn't have a nice day.

On the raiders the engines were stripped and cleaned, new filters put on the cooling intakes, all excess weight removed, the two raised saddle-like seats pulled out. Props were changed, the chipped older ones – perfectly good for training – replaced with brand new ones, and tactical spares kits put on board.

The jobs done, the piquet was changed and coxswains and mechanics retired to the makeshift camp to get some rest. They lay under awnings and mosquito nets and sweated and scratched at heat rashes and bites and tried to sleep, the mighty Congo River, brown and broad, around them.

HMS Winchester

Commander Channing and his XO, Lt Commander Selby, had had three round-table meetings already. His prime group – the senior officers, the heads of departments – were first. These were the heads of operations, weapons engineering, mechanical engineering, and several of the ops team, including the navigator who would need to plot his course up the river, and the aviators, who would have a critical role if their mission went ahead.

The navigator was now in his hutch at the bottom of the bridge stairs. He would spend the next eight hours plotting the exact course, sightlines, bearings, and duration of each leg up the hundred-odd miles of river. It was a major task. Although navigable, the river had sandbars, banks, rocks and shallows. In places it flowed slowly, in others – where it narrowed – it punched along at ten knots. Engine failure up here would be calamitous, and running aground was unthinkable. There was no tide to lift you off, just the force of water flow pushing you ever harder on to whatever it was you were stuck on.

Once on the river, he would not leave the bridge. He would check every calculation two or three times, check every course change the officer of the watch called for, check every sight-line and beacon.

The weapons team followed. HMS *Winchester* was going right out of her optimal environment – deep sea – and its two-hundred-mile clear view for her targeting radars, and room beneath her keel to allow her massive Olympus turbines to earn their pay.

On a river, everything was close, threat and risk profiles were different. Along with the weapons engineering team were a clutch of chief petty officers, each with responsibility for a system. What Commander Channing wanted was thinking out of the box. Their task, in conjunction with the mechanical engineering people, was the protection of vital areas of the ship.

The MEO's team would take care of critical junction boxes, wiring points and conduits that ran along the inner wall of the hull. The WEO's people would look at how to protect the bridge and the men manning the 20-mills. from shorefire. The WEO had an idea.

'Well,' he said. 'We are going to be decommissioned anyway. Let's cut out some of the non-essential internal bulkheads and use the material to reinforce the critical areas, the passages, the area outside the ops room and the MCO, the bridge. It will all help.' He sent them away to think it through and report back. The next two were Chops (M) Roberts and the Royal Marine, Sergeant Connors.

'Chops, you and Sergeant Connor will work up how you will defend my ship with small arms. You will both report direct to the XO.' Selby was sitting at the table taking fast notes and he nodded without looking up. 'Think it through, agree your plan. The area we are going into is extremely unstable and we may come under fire. Consider attack from the shore, as close as fifty metres, maybe even from river craft. Mechanical engineering are in next. They and the WEO's team will do what they can to give us some protection on the main deck. We won't be stopping to fill sandbags and if we come under attack from the shore, our hull plates won't stop bullets, certainly not armour piercing. Am I right, Sergeant?

'You are, sir. Most of these countries use the old Sov Bloc kit. AKs. They fire a 7.62 intermediate. They generally lack the punch, but up close they'll put rounds through light steel plate no problem.'

Channing nodded. 'So, anyone not essential will be down below the waterline, and everyone else will be behind something solid. Master at Arms is looking at those safe places now. Work out which you want for your armed deck parties as reaction teams. Sergeant Connors, it's likely that once we have gone as far as we can go above Matadi, we will have to wait, either with a hook down, or under power. You may be required to provide an armed shore party. Your second task is to plan for that. XO will want you back here with him in two hours. Any problem?'

'No, sir.'

'Right. Make it happen.'

The MEO popped his head through the curtain. He wasn't a happy man. With him was his deputy and they had also brought along two senior ratings whose job was the coolant systems. This was their prime issue. Their machinery, their cooling systems, generators, fire water, all were designed for and dependent on water coming into the ship from intakes along the hull. Water in a marine environment. Salt water. Not only was sea water at the depth they sucked it into the intakes clean and debris free, but in a river the deeper you went below the surface the worse it got, with debris, leaves, mulch. Everything from tin cans and plastic bags to leaf debris, all being sucked up against the coarse filters on the hull, jamming them, or getting past them and getting caught in the next layer of finer mesh. The filters clogged, the flow of cooling water stopped. Machinery overheated, air-conditioning systems broke down. Someone had to go over the side and clear the intakes. Also fresh water had all its own problems once in the system, and most Navy engineering officers dreaded even going up the Thames as far as London. There was loads of preparation before going into a freshwater environment, and on this task they didn't have time for any of that.

One third of the way down the ship on the narrow deck above the weather deck, aft of the bridge, were the ship's close-in air-defence systems, their twin Phalanx six-barrel, computer-controlled Gatling guns. Down in his little world in the control room opposite the port Phalanx, Chief Petty Officer Davies opened the operating manual and began to sort through the troubleshooter section. He had an idea. The new software for Phalanx, which *Winchester* would never see, included a capability to fire along a bearing. With this existing software suite they could only fire Phalanx along a bearing for calibration testing, but converting that to a target couldn't be so hard. If the weapon system's computer – working on overpriced, piece-of-shit MoD software – could do it, then he fucking could. He began to work through the problem.

Tenta Mission

Penny Carter was busy. The day-shift nurses hadn't turned up, but she had completed the river blindness drug distribution herself. It hadn't been that difficult with so few, and now she was doing the ward work with Sister Sarah. This ward – the women's – had eight beds, eight old wooden beds made from local timber. They were high and, with ancient, kapok-filled mattresses, they weren't the most comfortable things, she knew that – she slept on one in her cell – but they were still better than sleeping on the floor.

'Never seen it so quiet,' Sister Sarah said. 'Is it a local holiday, do you think?'

Penny looked up. 'I don't think so. Sister Mary had a visitor last night. An old man from some village. He said there was trouble coming.' She spoke softly, although none of the patients spoke much English at all. Several of them had gone. Just walked out, hobbled out, people who should have been confined to bed.

It was lunch time. While the children ate their food – supplied by the mission and cooked in a pair of huge pots in the kitchens – most of the nuns and Penny Carter sat down at the long table for their meal. The windows, always without glass, had shutters and mosquito screens, but they were swung back to let whatever breeze was blowing shift the air.

The talk began around the non-arrival of so many children and the shortness of the line at the clinic.

Penny was listening, but only partially. She was thinking about some home leave, now just six weeks away. Shopping, visiting friends and family, wonderful food. She wanted to go to the River Café and the restaurant in the OXO building, see ten movies in a week, have her hair done, have a long, cold lager shandy and a Big Mac, and a chicken korma; maybe – maybe try and see him, call him, try again. The talk dragged her away from her fantasies and back into life at the mission and the talk round the lunch table.

'Well,' Penny said. 'We are foreigners and non-combatant medical people. All sides need us, so if fighting starts in this province, then I suppose we become very busy.'

'But why should it start here?' one nun asked.

Sister Marie-Claire – silent thus far – looked up. In spite of the warning, they were many hundreds of miles away from

Shaba, and there was no way she was going to let the issue dominate conversation at the lunch table until it got very bad and the authorities or the church instructed them to take precautions.

'Rather than indulging in speculation,' she said softly but firmly, 'we would be better thinking about our work.'

Sister Mary, the Greek nun and the oldest person at the mission, looked up from her plate at her old friend. She had a differing view from Penny Carter's, and from Sister Marie-Claire's, but one no less pragmatic. She had been in the Congo a long time. First the Belgian Congo, then Zaire, now the Democractic Republic of Congo, and in that time she had seen dreadful things. In Katanga in the sixties, missionaries were killed. She was there. A young woman. In that same province, now called Shaba, it happened again in the seventies, and she was there then, and now in the late nineties they were fighting there again. She suspected that missionaries and aid workers were no safer now than in the sixties, and knew that in Shaba most of them had been withdrawn by their agencies and orders, moved to safety.

She knew the reality of night attack, of flames and screams and machete blows, and spurting blood – the mass rape, ritual torture, beatings, and death and the horror of it. She had been there. Stayed to help identify the bodies. Some she couldn't, so badly were they mutilated. It was a butcher's yard. They had been gang raped, killed, tortured. That night at the mission, evil came calling. There was no other way to describe it. But help arrived. Belgian paratroopers later jumped into Stanleyville. Out where they were, young soldiers, Western mercenaries had arrived with the dawn, and rescued those still alive. And she had met Henri. He had fought his way through the smoke and the dead, kicked the door open and stood there, an angel. A smile of white teeth and clear eyes, an angel, pulling his own clothing over her, and standing over them, protecting them as the fighting finished.

When it was over he wiped her face, wiped the tears from her eyes with his handkerchief, pulled a red-spotted kerchief from round his neck and bound her hand, talking to her. And his young officer, who saluted her, and introduced himself like he was at a diplomatic reception.

Later, as Henri and the others, mercenaries she now knew, helped the others, he kept coming back to her, drawn by something. It was there. Chemistry, something mutual, love at first sight, even. When they left later that day, she never saw him again, but not a day had gone by when she hadn't thought about him, wondered if he was safe, where he was, who with – was he married, even?

She had kept the red kerchief, kept it all these years. It was wrapped in tissue paper and in plastic, and when she was feeling depressed or low, she took it out and touched it and sometimes even slept holding it. He never came back.

They had come again in the seventies, this time bandits from Angola, attacking the people at the Arian tracking station, killing sixty French civilians – men, women and children. And maybe there was divine retribution and perhaps even instant retribution, because it came again – like the first time – in the form of young men. But these were from Corsica, like her Henri. Foreign Legionnaires, who parachuted in the next day and stayed a week. The rumour at the time was that they hunted them down, followed the people who did it back to where they came from. An eye for an eye. A tooth for a tooth.

At the time when she heard she felt nothing – not pity, not sadness – and she prayed to God for forgiveness; for what she should have done was forgive them their sins, she should have prayed for their souls, but she didn't – couldn't. She wanted them roasting in the fires of hell for what they did, and that wasn't very Christian.

She looked back down the table at the faces. Some older, wiser – faces lined by a decade or more of service in Africa, service to their Lord God – others young, bright, hopeful – the future of the Church and of their holy order.

With her long years in Africa, and perhaps some deep instinct, she was fearful. But it was not her place to say so. Jesus put up with trials and tribulations and so shall his followers – this she knew and this she believed – but she felt a sudden unease, like someone had walked over her grave. She excused herself, stood up and walked straight to the chapel, her long brown robes swishing along just above the level of the red-polished, concrete floors. She entered, crossed herself, went to her place and began to pray, and for the first time in twenty years her hand began to throb, the old wound.

During the lunch hour the generator and pumps were normally shut down and from the silence of the chapel one could normally hear crickets and cicadas, or the call of an emerald dove through the heat shimmer, but today there was nothing. It was ominously silent.

6°36'N 14°2'E
South-east of Lufu

The advance was steady but slow. They didn't want to be at the road and railway line until later that night, so they were better off moving slowly up through the bush until that time. The Unita troops were experienced bush fighters, and needed little in the way of pushing or command while on the march. There were now over nineteen hundred of them, in columns, moving across nine miles of bush, some in vehicles, some on foot. Makuma had issued his orders, swung his men in trucks out with the farthest objectives. He would join them later, but for now he wanted to consolidate his command of the new battalion.

The bush was dry. Scrub, thorn, calf-high brown grass, long tracts of jesse bush, flat-topped acacia trees, rock outcrops and red soil. The ground shimmered with the heat and every now and then they could hear the cry of a dove carried through the bush on the hot still air. Ahead, nearer the river, they knew there would be patches of thicker vegetation – greener, lusher, with palms and bananas, the forest and savannah a mosaic of ever greener hue.

They moved in relaxed formation, in singe-file columns, a ragtag army – most wearing some form of uniform, possibly only a shirt or a pair of trousers, the rest of their clothing made up of their own or looted civilian clothing. Their weapons were slung, some carrying bandoleers of link ammunition, others heavier weapons or RPG7 rocket-propelled grenade launchers. Each man carried his own food and water. Some had hard-wearing, military-issue water bottles, but for most it was something more accessible, and although there were one or two big plastic Coke bottles, the most popular container was a plastic detergent bottle. They were strong and had a handle so they could be slung on a piece of rope. They were also in garish colours, and as the men moved through the sparse rocky bush, there were flashes of bright orange, sky blue and lime green.

Makuma sat in his Land Cruiser and watched his men file past. It had been a fruitful hour or two for him. They had found Dennis, the company commander who never showed up to the commanders' meeting, and Makuma had killed him in front of his men. He then promoted one of the junior company officers, making sure that the man understood that all that was expected of him was outright obedience or he would go the same way. Makuma then gave him money, a lot of money for a bush fighter and, with an evil grin, told him there was more where that came from. He had removed three other officers – men who might threaten his position – and now any sedition was leaderless. In the next days he would weld the unit on to his own and they would soon forget they were ever someone else's.

Most of his forward elements had been out there for three days now, but some as long as a week. He had four good men in an old Renault and they had been as far as the ferry crossing at Kinganga and Tenta, looking at the roads, and the old gendarmerie post at Lufu. They had sent back word. All was as expected.

The advance would soon break into three distinct elements. One would halt a mile short in the bush to hold the road, facing Kinshasa. The second element would swing west, and they, a few miles down the road, would prevent anything coming

through from Matadi. The third element, his own hard-core
followers – some four hundred men mounted in trucks –
would go north, take out the railway line and – further up
the road near Tenta – take down the power lines that took
electricity from the power station at Inga to Kinshasa. That
power station supplied forty per cent of the capital's power,
and no one would be in any doubt over who was in control.
That third element would then push on for the river and close
it to traffic.

That was the strategy Makuma had agreed with his high
command and that was what he would do, but not because
they were his orders, but because it suited him temporarily.
He was beyond that. He was now working to entirely his
own agenda. Because there was booty to be had, fun for his
men. And for him, there was the mine at Tenta, with plenty
of diamonds. He needed the diamonds. Keeping his men in
the field cost money. There was also his old village, and old
scores to settle. There were also the whites at the mission.
There was revenge. He sat in his vehicle, brooding silently, a
great, black, bear-like colossus, his one eye glazed and hard,
the hatred and the rage in him growing daily, fed by whatever
dark demons he carried.

HMS Winchester

Chops Roberts knew what he wanted and, what's more, the
Royal Marines' Sergeant had agreed. They had thirty rifles and
four portable machine guns down in *Winchester's* armoury.
Ten sailors, now riflemen, would man personal weapons from
the handful of 'hard' areas. Four of them would be on the
gun director's platform, where material from the buffer's store
could be built up to offer them some protection. The ropes
and netting stuffed into thick canvas storage bags would stop
a bullet, even armour-piercing. Another four men would be
down aft on the quarterdeck, where mooring lines would be
cleared and cases of stores brought up. Their field of fire
could cover the whole stern of the ship and out each side

about seventy degrees. With the last two men floating aft but high up, concealed by the sea-boat davits, they would have an instant if light reaction capability.

The heavier twenty-man reaction team would wait in the main mess. From there they could be deployed up the aft gangways to come out on to the weather deck behind the sponsons and engage, return fire, or repel boarders.

Connors' marines – ten of them – would man the ship's general-purpose machine guns, one on each bridge wing, and one aft each side. They also had one GPMG of their own, and an LSW, a light section weapon.

As weapons went the GPMGs were very very effective, but only in the right hands, and Chops Roberts had to admit that he just didn't have anyone on the whole ship's list who could consistently hit anything over one hundred yards away with a gimmpy. They simply never got enough practice time. The marines on the other hand were rather good at it. Much to the watching sailors' chagrin, even with a rolling ship they had consistently hit targets between four hundred and a thousand yards away, reloading and getting the weapon back firing incredibly quickly.

On the gun platform the mechanical engineering team were cobbling together some extra protection for the operator maintainers who would be manning the 20-mills. either side.

The single-barrelled 20-millimetre Oerlikon was a multi-role weapon. Primarily an anti-aircraft gun, it could, though, be depressed to train down at the water, and could therefore engage surface craft or indeed targets on a shoreline. One or two rounds would take out an aircraft – if the gunner could hit it – or a small boat's bridge – or indeed an armoured vehicle on shore – with armour-piercing, explosive-headed munitions.

Trouble was, it was bloody difficult to hit a moving target with the 20-mill. It was generally accepted that if there was a jet coming in to attack the ship, then Seadart had already failed and the best you could hope for with a manually operated, optically sighted, single-barrelled 20-mill., was to unnerve the pilot a little and hope he dropped short or cocked it up and let the Phalanx do its thing.

The extra protection was needed because, although there were armour plates either side of the gun that gave the operator some protection from straight ahead, they were not designed to protect him from fire from several directions at once, and certainly not designed to protect his loader.

For all its inherent weaknesses at a fast jet, when it was man on man, they all knew that if the 20-mill. opened up, whoever it was shooting at would be digging in with sheer terror, or running like hell. They all also knew that everyone else, however, would see it and be unable to resist shooting at it.

While the engineering people were doing that, Chops Roberts and Sergeant Connors were down aft with their men. Targets were dropped off the stern – condoms blown up and filled with some water to weigh them down. The sailors who would be using the ship's small arms and the 20-mills. were practising, getting their eyes attuned to firing at stationary targets from a moving vessel. But the training was limited. They simply didn't have the ammunition to waste, either 20-millimetre, or the small ball fired by the GPMGs or the SA80s.

Down the port side they were rigging the boarding gangway. When in use it had one end lowered down to the dock, or indeed near the waterline. Now it was being prepared to be lowered outboard and suspended along the ship's side, flat-on and parallel to the waterline directly outside the ops room and the MCO, places that would be manned and vulnerable, and places where one bullet coming through the hull could do major damage to electronic or electrical systems. It wouldn't do much, but it was another layer and it might deflect something.

The helo was going to be the problem. They were short of fuel. The Tenta mission, now plotted on a map someone had found – the Admiralty charts only went up as far as Matadi – was about a hundred-mile round trip from the rapids where

Winchester would have to stop. But they had enough for several sorties.

Commander Channing was in his quarters with the XO when the MCO rating knocked on the side bulkhead and put his head through the curtain.

'Comms in, sir!' He held out the message. Channing crossed and took it. He read quickly, then again more slowly. 'Northwood. It's on. HMA in Kinshasa has managed to convince the necessary people and RM Brazzaville have the go. They have transport lined up and will move tonight, ETA Tenta first light tomorrow. Give 'em, what? Two hours there?' he walked over and looked at someone's bright idea. They only had one chart showing topography of the area and that was the aviators' chart, which they needed. A photocopy of the relevant bit didn't work, not enough contrast, so someone had nicked some greaseproof paper from the galley and traced it – the river, the roads, the railway line, major high ground and features – and it did the job. He looked at the traced image and then back at the Admiralty charts that were stuck to the bulkhead with Blu-tack.

'Then back out. Even going slow they will be back out on the main road east by midday. If they have a problem, or they are heading our way, we'll know by then.'

'That junction to Matadi?' Selby, now standing and looking over the tracing of the air aviation chart, said softly, 'Got to be something between two and three hours. If they come our way they could be in Matadi by mid-afternoon.'

'That will work,' Channing said. 'We'll be off the river mouth by 0530 local. Get the go. Then nice and cautious, about ten hours up the river. We'll arrive about the same time. And if they go east and everything's hunky-dory, then we'll know by about midday at latest. We'll kedge or warp her round and slip out again.'

There was a knock at the door and Channing waved the man in. It was the Lynx pilot. 'Sir, just looking at the charts,' he said, laying a real pilot's navigation chart out on the table. 'You need to know, sir, this area around Matadi is restricted-use airspace.'

'Any indication of why?' Channing asked.

'No, sir. But whatever the reason, we will attract attention.'

'What do we know about their air force?'

'They have an air force,' the pilot replied. 'But if it's like their northern neighbour's then it's four old jets with flat tyres gathering dust somewhere. Their pilots aren't much chop. There's a story, documented in the Western press, about two of them flying from somewhere in the east back towards Kinshasa, which was locked in by weather, so instead of going for an alternative airfield, they just banged out. Ejected. Scratch two MiGs.'

Channing shook his head in depressed wonder. 'What about the Angolans, or Zimbabweans?'

'My guess is they would be operating much further east, but that's a guess only, sir. The good point is that there won't be anything flying in that area. If there is, then it's worth watching.' Channing nodded. No one in their right mind would tangle with an area defence platform like a Type 42 with anything short of six or seven fast-attack, anti-maritime jets – more than they could muster in this entire part of Africa – and no one down here had Exocet or other anti-shipping missiles. But that assumed they knew her capability. Someone who didn't might just be ignorant enough to think they could get away with it.

'The down side,' the aviator continued, 'is that if we fly, then we are going to have all sorts of people asking questions. I think we assume their radar is working and stay low, and just hope no one notices. This smaller restricted zone is more of a concern.' He pointed to a smaller circular area. 'Inga. That's a power station in there. See the high-tension lines coming away here? That will be defended in some form, so I think we should skirt that, come round to the south. Not much of a detour from the shortest route, but prudent. Bit of luck we'll be in and out and no one will ever know we were there.'

'OK. Otherwise happy?'

'Yes, sir. The seat and the weapons gear are out. Even with a winchman, if we have to uplift then we can cram in six or seven people.'

Channing nodded. There was another problem. Although they had charts for the river approach to Matadi, due to shifting sandbars and seasonal shifts in currents the Admiralty advice to mariners was not to attempt the passage without a local pilot, in particular the last leg from Boma to Matadi. The embassy in Kinshasa had a fellow who served as an honorary consul in Boma, and they were now trying to track him down to see if he could discreetly find them a pilot. Discreet had been the embassy's word. Nothing bloody discreet about a destroyer, Channing thought. They even turned heads in naval ports used to seeing them, their flared bows, their sleek grey menace. Moving up an African river in broad daylight, HMS *Winchester* would be about as discreet and as welcome as a turd in a bathtub.

He turned and looked at Selby. 'Harry? We still have some of those UN flags and bunting?'

Winchester had been part of the UN force in the Adriatic nine months before and had been equipped with UN flags of various sizes and light-blue bunting for identification of her sea boats. In typical services style, they had three hundred feet of the bunting when in fact sixty feet would have been ample.

Selby nodded. 'Yes, we do. Buffer's stores.'

'All right. That might make anyone think twice about challenging us – and this *is* a humanitarian mission. Get a message away to Northwood. See if they can get us permission to fly the UN flag.'

'If the UN say no?'

'We'll use them anyway,' Channing said. His mind was made up.

If the DROC authorities anywhere along the river suddenly took notice, then the UN flags would at least have them checking their paperwork and getting on the phone to someone. With a bit of luck they would be long gone before

111

anyone got an intelligent response from someone high enough up the ladder to issue a heave-to order. Disguised intent. He smiled. Pity he didn't have a band on board. They could rig an awning and play music, have the officers in dress whites, like arriving for a well-planned state visit.

Three decks down Operator Maintainer Jenny Teller was stripping down a pump. This was routine maintenance, but she wanted to check the filters before they went into what the Chief had described as 'fuckin' crappy, dirty river water full of foam 'n scum 'n sticks 'n leaves 'n shite.' The pump was for fire water and took its load direct from the big coarse filters at the under-hull intakes. Her next job was to do the same on the air-conditioning pumps in her sector.

Up on the gun controller's platform 'Nellie' Tusker – flash-hooded and helmeted and wearing the comms headset – was nominally controlling the operator maintainer crews' training on the 20-mills. He was one of the better shots on the ship, but his job was directing the communications with the ratings on the guns. If they got into trouble then he would be busy, stepping over the four ratings with SA80s, to observe the 20s and the main deck gun's local area sight each side. Like most of them he was quite excited. The possibility of going upriver into an area of 'increased tension' broke into the tedium of the deployment. They were all working at a pace and there was a buzz around the ship.

Kinshasa

Ambassador Hewitt rocked back on his chair and lit one of his wife's cigarettes. He had given up, at last count, five times, and always went back to it because he enjoyed it. He looked at the smoke curl up, and felt the smoke thump into the back of his throat and into his lungs and smiled. He then rocked forward again and looked at the ever-growing pile of papers in his in-tray.

The embassy functions were still running routinely. The consular section was busy, with two staff in the office collating and updating lists of nationals as people came and went. Luckily for them there were more leaving than arriving, but the queue for visas to 'visit' Britain was out of the door, and everyone knew that very few would be granted, just those for students attending bona fide courses, and one or two for genuine business reasons.

The military radio with its encryptor unit was in the ante-room, and the duty special forces man was in there with it. Colonel Cheyne, over on the other side of the river, was out at the airport, and the Ambassador was waiting for his return to advise him that they had the special entry permit for foreign nationals and the road permit for his people. The vehicles would be outside the embassy on the road by four that afternoon, so he and his small team had now done all they could.

There was a knock at the door. It was his secretary, the wife of a Brit who was in Kinshasa with the UN food programme, a Londoner with almost crew-cut spikey hair – dyed white – and seven rings in her right earlobe. She was incredibly efficient and he knew he would miss her when her husband's contract was over in December.

'Ambassador. A Mr da Silva is at reception. Said you'll see him?'

'Oh!' He looked up. 'What have I got on?'

'You're clear till three. Then the staff appraisals begin through till five.'

Bloody appraisals, he thought. The FCO Human Resources people insisted on them at this time of year but he found them unnecessary. He constantly appraised his people, agreed objectives – all the things that were now trendy – and had done so for years. He found being forced into a box a bore.

'OK. Ask him to come through, will you?'

'Tea?'

He nodded, then changed his mind. 'No. Something cold, I think. Could you rustle up a couple of rock shandies?'

She was back in a minute or so – a tray with two glasses in her hands – and ushered the Portuguese engineer into the

Ambassador's office. Hewitt stood up and offered his hand. 'Mr da Silva. Please sit down. You will be pleased to hear that we have managed to get permission for our people in Brazzaville to go down to the mission at Tenta. Let's hope they don't get told thanks but no thanks. It hasn't been easy.'

'Good. The trucks? Good?'

'Yes. Your friend at the Intercon was very helpful there.'

'It was not difficult. The contractor who owns them does work for me. If he wishes to continue to do so . . .' He shrugged. 'A small favour. And now I have one to ask of you?'

'Please,' Hewitt said, indicating that he should speak.

'My pickup is in shop here. Bushes gone. I need to get back down to the site. With a friend. Do you think your peoples can give us a lift that far? They are going down tonight, yes?'

'I should think that's OK. If you are here by about eight?'

Da Silva thanked him and then drank the cold drink. He was pleased. In the early hours he had made the journalist a promise – and he always kept his promises – to get him back down to the site, and if possible up to the mission. Da Silva could get him as far as the site, but to go on with the British he would have to work that himself. He looked at the drink. After all the alcohol last night it was just what he needed. He was pleased that the marines were going. Not only for the sake of the nuns, but also for the young Swiss fellow at the mine. They had met several times, shared a bottle of Scotch, and found much in common – two kindred spirits in the middle of nowhere.

Over the river in Brazzaville, Major McLean was with his troop commanders. He was light one officer, the Captain who commanded 2 Troop. He was away on a course, but he had opted to take that troop anyway because they had an excellent troop sergeant, and with him and the CSM along on the mission – in the unlikely event that something happened that Sergeant

Willis was unable to deal with – they were there. There would be two troops, each of about thirty-two men. In addition, the two vehicle maintainers from HQ Company, the LMA medic, two engineers, and his own command team of CSM, Signals Sergeant and his mortar fire controller trained marine, would form McLean's TAC, making up an additional section of two fire teams.

Just because this was a light, short mission, Colonel Cheyne had insisted they hump their standard deployment weaponry, heavy as it may be. They had individual and troop weapons, two light 51-mill. mortar tubes, six LAW rockets with each troop, and some kit the French had lent them. The rationale was simple. It looked a lot, but if nothing happened then it would never leave the truck. If something did happen, then they would be glad of it.

The lads packed and repacked their gear a dozen times. Only essentials, but you had to know where everything was in the dark, put your hand right on it. The rations were stored in belt kit and side pockets, boil-in-the-bag pusser's rations that most of the lads enhanced with something. Tabasco sauce was popular. A small bottle was light, lasted weeks, and could pep up the most boring meal. Some of them sought culinary excellence in another way and mixed the rations with Batchelor's dried instant noodles, fresh onions, garlic, curry powder or tomato puree. Although most of them just heated their food and ate it, one of the lads – Dave Hobson – prepared his rations, cooking with a devotion that was as serious as a Japanese tea ceremony. That morning he had slipped out into the town with Furby and stocked up on provisions from an Indian trader. They had curry powder, onions, garlic, Peri-peri oil – a Portuguese variant of Tabasco, if anything even spicier – and, wonder of wonders, Pot Noodles. They were well past their sell-by date, but no one gave a shit. He had also made friends with the cooks in the hotel kitchen, and they had given him some fresh oregano and basil that they grew on a roof garden. As Sergeant Willis moved among them he stopped at the section.

'Right. At 1630, main galley's open. Get some scran in

ya, and a wet. There's ice and cold water from the fridge if
you want to fill flasks. Back here by 1730, ready to move.'

In addition to load-bearing vests and old belt kit, all the
'Gucci' kit was out and used. Anything that wasn't issued by
the Pusser, standard issue, was considered 'Gucci'. This was
everything from the Leatherman tools they all used, to gaiters,
boots, clothing, camping gaz, and lightweight hi-tech stuff like
civilian sleeping bags, the favourites always 'softies'. There
was Gucci and there was Gucci, and then there was what Kevin
called 'mega-fucking-mega-Gucci' – anything designer, like
his Calvin Klein jeans that he always wore when out and
trying to 'trap'.

The lads were hard on Gucci kit. If you had paid for it
out of your own wallet then it better fucking perform, and
long debates followed any field test, or new development.
Whole fire teams could spend an entire evening arguing the
merits of their particular model of Leatherman or its clone,
hexy blocks versus camping gaz, and the new pusser's boots
with goretex inners were also a popular debate. There were
two or three lads who had bought 'Gucci' boots only to find
the new pusser's boots were better, and they were royally
pissed-off. Biscuit looked over at Kevin. 'You wearing those
frog boots?'

Kevin nodded. 'Fookin aye,' he said with a big grin.

'Have you yomped in them yet? What if they fall apart?'

'They won't fall apart,' he replied. 'Anyway, we are in
transport. No yomping.' 'Yeah,' someone muttered sarcastically. 'You wouldn't want to walk in them. Might get
them dirty.'

Sergeant Willis arrived. 'One hour. Galley's open. Get
some scran and back here by 1730.'

One of the Love Machine had a ghetto blaster and it was
playing while they packed their kit. When on the move
they split up the main CD player and the two speakers, so
each was carried by someone different. Anywhere they went
they had music. Someone changed the CD and the Verve's
'Bitter Sweet Symphony' came on. The Love Machine, as

one, stopped what they were doing and began to dance, a carefully choreographed routine, as precise as parade-ground drill. It was impressive – the cohesion, the timing – but that only fuelled the laughter round the pool.

'Fookin' 'ell,' someone yelled. 'If you cunts dance like that in clubs, no wonder you can't trap!' The speaker got a selection of extended double fingers but the dance continued.

Up in his room the Padre was also packing his kit. His brief was roving, and having only been with the commando four months, he took every opportunity to meet the lads, get to know them. The best place for that was in the field and he had just been authorised by the CO to join the two troops of Alpha Company for their twenty-four-hour operation. Rory Chisholm, as a naval chaplain, had no rank. Given the courtesy of an officer's equivalent meant he could move wherever he liked, with whoever he liked as long as he was doing his work.

He looked down at his day sack and smiled. A year ago he had been the Presbyterian minister on the Isle of Skye, and one day he just knew there was a different call for him. He had applied for a military chaplaincy, not just military, but the Royal Marines. They had a vacancy and he did the all-arms course with the rest of them, sur- prised himself and everyone he knew by passing, and a year later, here he was, a padre to 40 Commando, in the Congo.

The men loved him – well, all except Furby. He was everything they weren't – everything each of them knew in his heart he should aspire to be. He was kind, decent, gentle, compassionate, caring, tireless and totally egalitarian. His love and caring for them were unconditional. Look for the worst-off marine – the tiredest, the coldest, the hungriest, the sad, the hurt, the one in pain, the one whose wife had run off, or girlfriend had left him – and there you would find the Padre, arse-deep in mud, cold, wet, and suffering alongside them like a common bootie, a marine. But he was more. He didn't have to be there. He could be sitting at HQ, warm and dry, like the others. He was there because he chose to be, chose to be there with the lads, and that made him special and they loved him for it.

He wasn't just a marine. He was a warrior priest. He carried no rifle. But he had a Bible, his faith, his kindness, his compassion and he would walk beside them into hell itself if that's what it took. He carried no rank, and although everyone could call him Rory, from the CO to the newest junior marine out of training, the lads still called him 'sir' out of respect. And from the CO to the newest entrant to the commando he had equal time for each.

When the commando went into action or on exercise, the Padre carried little things that boosted morale. He looked down at his belt kit and stuffed the pockets with sweets. His wife had done a big shop at Sainsbury's only a week ago, and his last parcel, in only yesterday, had loads of things – eclairs, Liquorice Allsorts, fruit bon-bons, mini Mars Bars, Wine Gums and other bits and pieces. He also had a hip flask that was usually filled with good malt whisky, but he had run out of that, and that called for ingenuity. He found some cheap brandy and bought some fruit in the market. Three weeks later it was ready. The sliced fruit and sugar had taken the roughness off the brandy and now it was a silky-smooth apricot brandy

He filled the flask and moved to the door.

Down the hall Colonel Cheyne took a call from the officer commanding the French contingent. He had requested authority to offer the use of his one long-range Puma helicopter, and had been told that unless there was undeniable and immediate risk to the Westerners at the mission, then he wasn't to deploy the only helicopter with long-range tanks still operative in the DRC. Cheyne understood. They had had two hit by gunfire since they had been there – costly and embarrassing. If there was a change to the status he could act. He made his personal apologies. He knew and liked Cheyne.

It gets dark quickly in the tropics. One minute it's daylight, the next it's black as pitch.

The assault squadron were waiting for dark, and the moment the sun fell over the river, they knew their night's work had begun. The four rigid raiders stooged out from their island base and ran downriver for the first pickup.

The Company were trying to be discreet. Because people on the Brazzaville waterfront were used to seeing the rigid raiders running back up towards their island base, instead of a straight crossing of the river, in full view of everyone, they were going to move back upstream to the island and then run down the other side. This would add some time to the total crossing but it was deemed worth it.

The boats began running at 1812. With eight marines per boat on each trip, each of the four boats operating in pairs would need to run two trips.

There were four gendarmes waiting on the Kinshasa side. They had closed that section of the road so the marines could walk straight to the back gate of the embassy. Outside that gate the transport was waiting. There were not four, but three, trucks. Two of them were twenty-foot flatbeds, heavyweight vehicles with high, iron sides designed for moving earth. They both had canvas tarpaulin covers. The third truck was bigger. Articulated, with a forty-foot trailer, it had what looked like a new Renault tractor unit on the front. The trailer was set up for side loading with canvas sides that could be raised from various points so a forklift could unload pallets. There were three local men, the drivers, standing and talking beside the middle truck.

Major McLean, the CSM and the vehicle maintainers were in the first load of marines ashore and McLean stood back and watched as his men scrambled up the bank and crossed over into the embassy compound. The CSM was concerned with logistics, and now he had seen the transport he would be able to determine who would travel where. The VMs split up, each moving to a vehicle. The local drivers did the same, and in a dreadful pidgin Franglais, they began communicating with big beaming smiles while lifting bonnets, and producing torches. By the time the second load of men was in they had seen enough.

'Both the flatbeds are held together with years of botched jobs. Wire and welds. Incorrect spares. Its a fucking wonder they go at all. Brakes are dodgy. But you know what it's like here. They have been like that for years and will probably outlast the new one. But they wouldn't get an MoT in a thousand years.'

'They get us there and back?'

'Christ knows, Sar' Major! We have some spares that should fit the two old Hinos, but no guarantees. The Renault looks alright.'

Marines were filing across the road now, into the back gate of the embassy. Three Troop was all present, their Captain, Richard Lowry, counting them through the gates.

Harvey called one of the local drivers over. 'Matadi? *Pas de* problem?' he asked with a shrug, pointing at the trucks. The man grinned back and pointed to his battered old truck. '*Très bien! très bien! Camion beaucoup* good. *Camion* number one!'

I fucking bet, he thought. Number one for the scrap heap maybe.

Over on the Brazzaville side the last 2-Troop section was loading into raiders. Dave Hobson, Furby, Sloth and the others, with the two assault engineers. Shagger had tagged along for the ride down from the hotel.

'Don't even ask,' Jock muttered. He looked round his fire team. They were loading, concentrating on the task.

'Oi!' Biscuit said, looking at Sloth. 'What the fuck's the dog doing here?'

'Where, Corp?' Sloth looked up wide-eyed and innocent, like butter wouldn't melt in his mouth.

'Don't fuck about.'

'Jesus! Lighten up, Biscuit,' Dave Hobson said. 'We are going for a ride in a frigging truck. He won't be any problem, and if he has to go back now, then this boat is delayed. You didn't see it, right?'

At the embassy, the compound was crowded. There were now sixty-six marines, all with their day packs and extra boxes of stores scattered round the exterior wall. Da Silva was waiting inside with Perrin Dalton, the journalist he had met the night before. Dalton had met Hewitt twice before, but had deliberately not reintroduced himself. He didn't want his profession known till they were down the road, or he would suddenly find himself watching them leave without him. He wouldn't lie. He just wouldn't tell them without being directly asked. That seemed fair.

Hewitt had already asked McLean if he could drop the engineer and his friend back at his site, and with plenty of space in the trucks he thought no more of it, instead opting to spend his time with the Sergeant Major and his troop commanders sorting out the logistics. They were walking over to the gate when the CSM – a man who saw everything and missed nothing – spotted something. He turned and moved over to where Sloth was bending over his day sack against a wall.

'What,' he asked, 'is that?'

'Aah . . . that's Shagger, Sergeant Major,' Sloth answered.

'I know that. What the fuck's he doing here?'

Jock grinned. The CSM certainly did know the dog. To much raucous approval, Shagger had nicked his lunch that very day. The CSM had made a sandwich – chicken and chips – carried it out to the pool and put it by a lounger. Mistake. Shagger had it away in seconds, and Harvey – swearing and cursing all thieving cunts with four legs and two – had to go back into the dining room and make another, while the lads cheered and whistled and applauded. Sloth's silent yellow mongrel was now top of their hit parade.

'Mr Harvey, he can't stay here,' Sloth replied. 'The Ambassador's wife has got a moggy, and Shagger will have it, or vice versa. Come on, Sar' Major . . . Company mascot! Pongos have got goats, long-horned sheep. We have this proud, upstanding, hard-core bastard.' The CSM and McLean looked down at it. It was lying, snoozing, its belly still distended after a huge meal, snoring softly.

'Come on, Mr Harvey. Look at it. It eats, farts, sleeps and tries to shag everything that moves. He's just like us. In a few days we'll have it super-fit, highly trained, professional. If he was a human he would be a marine. Marine Shagger. Two Troop, A company, 40 Commando.' He paused, let the banter drop, became genuine. 'Please, Sar' Major? I'll take care of him. He's one of us now.'

Shagger opened one eye, looked up, yawned, and with a lazy wag of his tail closed his eyes again and went back to sleep. McLean walked off. This wasn't his problem. This was Don Harvey's call. Although he was responsible for discipline, part of his job was morale. He would get the balance right.

'Fuckin' 'ell,' the CSM said, weakening. 'I don't want to see it, right? One squeak, one incident, and it goes – and if it ever nicks my fucking scran again I'll clock you one.'

'This gets better and better,' Kevin muttered.

The CSM overheard that and snapped, 'And you can shut up too!'

'Yes, Mr Harvey.' Kevin grinned, but the grin faded when he saw Sergeant Willis standing and watching.

'Sergeant Willis,' the CSM said dryly. 'Well done. All your troop now needs is Rolf Harris.' Now they were in the shit.

Half an hour later the men began loading and McLean popped his head round the Ambassador's door. 'Right, sir. We're away.'

'Jolly good,' Hewitt said, standing up. 'I hope it's not too uncomfortable in those lorries.'

'We'll be fine, sir.'

'And we're to expect you back about this time tomorrow night?'

'All things going well. We'll try for radio communications on our way back, your SF chap will have a listening watch from about lunch time, and let you know what to expect in the way of people looking for accommodation and what have you. From the look of the transport it's seen better days. Otherwise it should be quiet enough.'

'Good,' Hewitt replied with a bleak smile. 'I assured the Minister no one will even know you are there.'

Ten minutes later, McLean, his radio operator, da Silva and a driver led the column out of Kinshasa in a borrowed Toyota Land Cruiser. Behind them was the big Renault truck, followed by the two older trucks, and up the rear in the second 4x4 was the CSM, his radio operator, a driver and Perrin Dalton.

In the first Hino were fifteen men, one dog and the Padre. There was animated chat for the first hour, lads sometimes looking out under the tarp cover, but it was dark and there was nothing to see and eventually the talk subsided into murmurs. The Padre stretched out his legs and within a short time followed the lads' example and dozed off.

Tenta Mission
0003 hrs

Sister Mary, unable to sleep, rose quietly and lit the lamp in her cell. The furnishings were spartan. A single bed with a kapok-filled mattress, a bedside locker and a small table and chair under the window. There was a little chest of drawers and space for hanging garments on a rail behind a curtain in the corner below the bed. She had four books on the shelf above the bed. There was a small Bible in Greek – very old and given to her by her parents – a much newer King James edition in English – also leather-covered and worn by time. Although she loved reading and had read thousands of books – novels and non-fiction – there was only one on her shelf – a copy of Terry Waite's story, his time as a hostage in Beirut. The last book was hardback, bigger than the others, a leather-bound journal of some quality. It was part journal, part personal diary, part photograph album – a collection of memories, of her life. There were news clippings, old photos, postcards, several dried flowers, a theatre ticket – momentos of various kinds – all around scores of handwritten entries that dated back almost forty years. Once, she had thought it vain and selfish to keep it up, but had done so anyway, and Sister Marie-Claire encouraged her to continue it, suggesting she leave it for the order's training school when she retired. It was more than just a diary now, it was a unique collection, a vivid memoir, a tangible summary of a lifetime's work in Africa, intensely personal and all the more powerful for that.

She took it down and sat at the little table, moved the lamp over so she could see, and opened the book at the back. She took a tissue-wrapped item out, carefully unfolded the paper, smoothing it out, and extracted the red-spotted neckerchief that Henri had given her and held it briefly to her cheek, her eyes closing for a moment. Finally she put the garment away, carefully rewrapping it in the tissue paper, and turned back to the next fresh page in the journal and began to write. The style was conversational, and although no one but Sister Marie-Claire had ever read excerpts, each entry was in letter form, all to the same second party.

She began this entry as she had done all the others, with the date, and then began with the French word, '*Vous*'.

In the soft light of the gas lamp the years fell away, and had anyone observed her, they would have seen fine bones, lips that were still full, something of the beautiful girl who many said looked like Sophia Loren, who had come to the Belgian Congo almost four decades before.

Outside, and unknown to her, a man approached and stood at the edge of the veranda and rang the little surgery bell. Sister Jo heard the bell go, and lifting the kerosene lantern, she walked out on to the veranda and held it up.

The man raised a hand in greeting and said he was from Tufu village, barely a mile away. She recognised him then. His children came to the school. '*Vous papa de Simone?*' she asked in her appalling French.

He nodded, smiling, and then said, '*Voir le docteur.*'

'*Pour vous?*' she asked. The man shook his head and pointed back to his village.

It didn't happen often – the local people were incredibly respectful of the medical staff off-duty time. Penny was woken barely once a month and often said she wished they would wake her earlier if it meant she could treat someone earlier, so Sister Jo took that to heart, nodded at the man, indicated he should wait, and went to wake Dr Carter. Five minutes later, in jeans, trainers and a denim shirt, she was following him across the compound towards the path that ran west through the trees, her bag in her hand, and a big yellow waterproof torch to light the way.

Twenty minutes later she was in the village, a small collection of huts and tilled beds of maize and pumpkins and sorghum claimed back from the forest. There was a young man waiting for her – a boy really – there to interpret for the old man who stood beside him. It was the same old man who had been to visit the mission the night before, the man whose own village was many hours walk further west.

He pointed to a stool beside the embers of a fire and indicated she should sit down.

She looked at him. '*Docteur*,' she said, tapping her chest. 'Who is sick? Take me to them.' The old man spoke to the boy. The boy looked back at her and smiled.

'My uncle' – the term was generic for any older male relative – 'says thank you for coming. Now you must stay here with us.'

'Why?'

The old man spoke again, the boy interpreting – somewhat unnecessarily – as he went. 'You are not of them. They stay for God. They were warned yesterday. You are not nun. You can go. You are doctor. You help us,' the boy said shyly. 'Bad men coming. They kill everyone. You stay here and if they come this far we will all hide in the bush.'

'When will they come?'

'Tomorrow. They will come tomorrow.'

'I can't stay here. I must go back,' Penny said. 'I must tell them to leave.'

'My grandfather told them. They not go. If you go back, you die.'

The three women had taken her, past other silent, empty dwellings, into their hut. The smell was that of wood smoke, sweat, cheap soap, ash and kerosene. She looked around. Sleeping mats were not rolled out, but rolled up, and belongings had been packed into portable sizes. She looked at her watch. It was now past one in the morning and everyone seemed awake and alert. These people, she realised, were ready to desert this village. They were taking the threat very seriously, and what's more, they were determined to protect her. The point was made. She was staying and it was for her own good.

Five

R ight about then and seventy-odd miles away, the three trucks carrying the marines pulled off the highway on to a temporary slip road that ran into the construction site where da Silva and his crew were building culverts under the highway.

As they pulled in, the vehicle headlights swept trees, shrubs and bush, the earth red and rutted after the blacktop highway. Da Silva looked out. The place was deserted. The hairs on his neck rose. Ordinarily there would be sixty or sixty-five men on the site – labourers, team bosses, plant operators, a cook, and the number two, the local engineer. The lines of big old army-surplus tents they slept in were still there, but there were no security guards, and the excavator was gone, as was the little dump truck.

'Something's wrong,' he said.

'What?' Mclean asked.

'Something's wrong. No people.'

'Keep going!' he said to the driver. He touched his throat mic. 'Charlie Charlie one' – Charlie Charlie was for everyone – 'Zero Alpha. Keep moving. I say again, keep moving. Follow my callsign out on to the road. Two, three, acknowledge.' Mclean snapped a look at his driver. 'Pull over a couple of hundred yards along.'

He spoke again into the radio. 'Zero Alpha. Two, three, acknowleged,' the CSM, Mr Harvey, came back immediately. The troop commanders followed him in seconds.

'Charlie Charlie, load. I repeat, load. As we halt, everyone debus, go ready and form a defensive perimeter. Alpha two, Alpha three, you copying this?'

'Zero, this is two. Roger that.'

'Zero, three, copied.'

'Once the perimeter is secure, troop commanders to the CP.'

The Land Cruiser in front slewed to a halt in the red dirt. McLean, the driver and the one marine in the back piled out into cover, cocking weapons to the 'ready' state as they hit the ground, deploying weapons at the high port. The second light vehicle tucked in behind it to leave room for the heavies, and forty seconds later the two troops were out in firing positions, McLean moving round them, checking that he had interlocking defensive arcs of fire. Suddenly it was quiet. Very quiet. Just two of the drivers, fearful, whispering to each other and debating whether to run for it. The third was hiding in his cab.

'Right.' McLean dropped down beside da Silva, his RO – his radio operator – there with him like a shadow. 'What should we have expected?' Captain Lowry, OC of 3 Troop, and Sergeant Willis both dropped down beside him within seconds of each other.

'Security guards, three of them,' da Silva replied. 'Lights. The machinery has gone, too. Two vehicles. There should be sixty peoples sleep there.'

McLean nodded. 'Draw me a layout of the site.' He flicked on his torch, its red-filtered lens designed to reduce loss of nightsight. 'This is the road we just came up.' He drew in the red dust. Da Silva reached down and finished a rough plan of the site.

'Were they expecting you back tonight?'

'No.'

'Would anyone be coming in here at this hour? Suppliers? Trucks?'

'No.'

No one was due here, so an ambush was unlikely. The place had been quiet, but there was no apparent damage, nor the usual detritus and mess that results after a place has been ransacked or looted. McLean looked at Captain Lowry.

'A section patrol, please, Mr Lowry. I want a recce. See if there's anyone still in there, or anyone hanging around.'

The Captain nodded.

'Be very careful, right!'

Three minutes later Lowry moved out, two fire teams moving slowly forward, covering each other in a slow, steady, absolutely silent advance. Half an hour later he was on the radio. The place was deserted. No one was there or in the bush behind the site camp.

'Sergeant Willis, secure here. Vehicles stay here and make sure the drivers don't scarper. Rest of 3 Troop will come with me. Mr da Silva, you better join us.'

They walked the two hundred yards to the site, and then da Silva wandered around looking at various things. Some personal possessions had gone, the men having snatched what they wanted to take, but other stuff had been left, and the cook's fire was still burning and there was food still in the pots, and not just food, but meat. No working-class black African ever left meat. It was too valuable, too expensive, too protein-rich. A marine shone his torch into the big pot and then looked at his oppo.

'This is like the fucking twilight zone. Weird. What was that ship? The *Mary Rose*? Where everyone had disappeared, leaving food on the table?'

'No. The *Marie Celeste*.'

Da Silva's own tent, always pitched a few metres way from the others, with his few bits and pieces, had been ignored. They had left in a hurry.

Lowry appeared by McLean's side. 'Sir, This is all a bit X Files for me. Feels v. spooky.'

McLean nodded, thinking me too, and then looked at the Portuguese engineer, who walked over to him. 'Well,' he said to him, 'everyone's gone in whatever of your transport they could find, Mr da Silva. No signs of violence. What would make them go? They ever done this before?'

'No. Anyone just piss off, no ask, and dey get fired. I got their pay.' He patted his trouser pocket. 'Two weeks' money.

Pay day tomorrow. But they gone.' Da Silva looked at the Marines officer. He lit a cigarette, closed the lighter with a flick of his thumb and looked back up at McLean. 'So, they frightened of something. Maybe this not a wasted trip for you, eh?'

'We better get moving. You could wait till daylight and hitch a lift back up, or wait for us and come back to Kinshasa, or do you want to come with us?'

Da Silva looked round the camp, and over Captain Lowry's shoulder he could see Perrin Dalton wandering around. 'No much choice, eh? We come with you. I get some stuff. Give me two minutes, eh?'

He went back to his tent and had a look around – carefully, as if looking for something – then shrugged, grabbed a pair of socks, a couple of clean shirts, and went out to rejoin the others. A few minutes later, as they walked back, he looked at the journalist, who was a few paces ahead of him. Got you this far. You on your own now. Come clean, he thought. He walked up beside him.

Three or four minutes later the trucks were loaded and Dalton, instead of climbing into the CSM's vehicle with da Silva, walked over to where McLean's command element were climbing into the other 4x4.

'Major McLean?' He walked closer to the officer. 'Might I ride with you on this leg? Truth is, I have a confession to make and it's a bit of a long story.'

McLean looked at him, his eyes narrowing. 'Well, shorten it, please, Mr Dalton.'

'I did want to come down here. See what was going on. I am a journalist. I write for the *Daily Telegraph*.' He looked for an expression on the officer's face, but McLean was giving nothing away. 'I was going to ask if I could journey on with you when you dropped Mr da Silva here, but it seems we are now stuck together. Irrespective of that, I'd like to be able to do my job. I won't get in the way, I promise, and this will be a nice little human-interest story. Royal Marines going in to bring nuns to safety. Bloody good PR, actually.'

Fucking marvellous, McLean thought. Colonel Cheyne had told him Northwood and HQRM's view of press on this story. Got to manage this – I don't want him riding with the lads. He jerked a thumb at the Land Cruiser door. 'There's not much you can compromise from out here, but if you've got a question, it's to me, Captain Lowry or the CSM. Leave the lads alone. Understood?'

Dalton nodded. 'What do you think has happened here?'

He wanted the Marines officer's view but he suspected he knew. In Africa news travels fast, and wherever armed men advanced, be they in armies or bands, the local population usually knew they were coming and fled, more refugees for a continent sinking in them.

'I have no more ideas than you,' McLean replied, but Dalton could feel the mood change and there were other very obvious signs that McLean was taking this seriously. While they were down in the camp someone had taken the back door of the vehicle and there were now two marines in the back, a machine gun between them. They were wearing what he knew was called CBA – combat body armour – and there was a belt of link ammunition in the gun's workings.

Ten minutes later they turned right off the main road and began the haul in towards the river. The road was appalling, rutted, potholed, no more than a dirt track in places, and once they had turned off the highway, their speed fell in places to a walk. Although it was only seventy miles through to the river and the mission, McLean knew that – averaging only twenty miles an hour – it would take them most, if not the rest, of the night to get there. He wondered if it was worth halting and trying to get the big aerial up and give the 320 a go. The Clansman could – if you got the right atmospherics, and the aerial just right – communciate round the world, but there were limitations.

Having said that, he once saw a comms bloke hook one on to a chicken-wire fence, and using that as his aerial, he was able to talk to almost anywhere. He decided against it. It would waste time, and although it was only a supposition, he felt there was something going on down here. His only evidence was a deserted camp, and the same spooky feeling that Lowry, and no doubt others had felt. But better to keep going.

They were in a tactical convoy mode now. What was the CSM's vehicle was now out in front, with a fire team and their coporal in charge. They were two hundred yards ahead of the others, who were following with big gaps between each vehicle. No bunching up, each able to support the others, but far enough away so that any attack or problem with an anti-vehicle landmine and the immediate damage and injury would be limited to one vehicle. The CSM was in the last truck, in the cab with his radio operator between him and the driver.

Tactical mode it may have been but they had been seen. The first group of Unita fighters had actually seen them turn off the main road from their vantage point a mile further down towards Matadi.

But they did nothing. These men had been ordered to cut the road at dawn, and it was not yet dawn. Besides, these vehicles were going off the main road, not coming on to it. Had they known that this was the same road that their commander and his mobile element had taken, they might have had a different reaction, but as it was they just settled back and tried to sleep. After all, they had said daylight. We close it at daylight.

Actually, three miles up the Tenta road from the turn-off there were two other bands of Unita fighters, one each side of the road. They were there to take out the Matadi–Kinshasa railway line that bisected the Tenta road, and their orders were to do that and then close the dirt road just before dawn to prevent repair crews being able to access the site.

The two lookouts looked at each other and one shrugged. Like the men at the main road their orders were clear and were to be followed. Makuma just wanted obedience. Not initiative. Not independent decision-making. Obedience. And that's what he got.

*   *   *

An hour later the trucks were crawling along, and according to McLean's GPS, had covered twenty-two miles.

Further back, in the back of the middle truck with the lads, the Padre found it odd. They had gone from the remote possibility of something going wrong to this increased state of readiness in moments. This wasn't an exercise. This wasn't training. They had found the deserted road-building camp and it had unnerved some of them. For him this was a new experience, seeing them mentally prepare for the prospect of something that an hour ago had been a very remote possibility. There was a machine gun set up on the roof of the truck's cab, and men who earlier had put their weapons down with their day packs now had them in their hands. Some had redefined their belt order or vests. Where they might have had chocolate, biscuits or other personal things within reach, they were now buried in daysacks and the only things within instant reach were magazines and grenades.

There was nothing to inhibit access to whatever they might need, and if someone wanted some of his chocolate, then he was happy digging for it. Some of the lads were eating now. One enterprising bootneck had his camping-gaz stove out, and was holding the base between his feet. Atop the flame was a piece of Gucci camping gear, a tiny, sealed, lightweight, two-cup kettle that actually clipped down on to the burner. Others had flasks out, some sipping cold drinks made with ice back in Brazzaville, and others – more traditional – had hot drinks in their flasks.

Everyone was awake now. They were quiet. Not silent, just quiet. There was some talking, some banter, but many of them were caught up in their own thoughts as they jarred along the road, the gears grinding up into third and then back into second over and over and over. The night was warm, the wind movement drying sweat on them. It was too bloody hot under the tarp cover and, with it being night, no one was going to see them anyway, so they had removed the tarp and it was now rolled up and those along the front were sitting on it. Many of the others, seeking to relieve their bruised bottoms were up and standing now, and from a standing positon they could see over the steel sides. Every now and then they passed small villages or pocket-handkerchief-sized cultivated fields illuminated by moonlight, but mostly it was bush either side of the road, and above them they could see the stars, bright and seemingly close enough to reach out and touch.

The Padre stood up beside one of the men and looked out at the night. The fellow the Padre stood beside looked at him as he took his pace at the sidewall. Just then the truck hit a pothole and the Padre, without a good handhold, lurched back. A hand reach out and grabbed his shirt and pulled him back to the side. 'Bet you wish you were in one of those 4x4s, Padre, in the comfy seats.'

'No, no,' he replied. 'I'm fine. Just stretching the legs a little.' He paused. 'The lads call you Sloth, don't they?'

'That's right. And that's Furby.' Sloth pointed to the Padre's right.

'We bought one each for our daughters last Christmas,' the Padre said, thinking, I fail to see the simliarity, ergo, the name is born of sarcasm. Sloth knew what he was thinking, because he said, 'If a girl tickles his tummy, Padre, he starts saying things to them. Things like, "Of course I love you," and "I promise I won't—"'

'Yes. I see,' the Padre said dryly. Beside him Furby had ignored the exchange, just looking out at the night. It wasn't the first occasion the Padre had noticed this, but he ignored the snub and looked back at Sloth.

'The lads have quietened down.' The comment was double-edged and Sloth knew it.

'Most of them have got sore arses and want some decent kip. Another – what – three hours or so, then an hour on the ground, then another nine or ten back in here?' He paused. 'Fancy a wet, Padre?'

'Yes. Thank you. I have a flask,' he offered. He bent down to his day sack, as did Sloth, and when the Padre carefully slopped hot tea from his flask into the two mugs, Sloth looked at him and said softly, 'Don't mind Furby, sir. He's . . . he's like that with your lot. Tell you why one day.'

The Padre nodded and, reaching into his belt order, pulled a plastic bag out. 'Lucky dip?' Sloth reached in and took a piece of something and the Padre stood up and began to offer the bag to everyone else. He looked down. It was half a biscuit. He put it to his mouth with a smile The Padre had broken his own ration biscuits into peices to offer to everyone else. The rations were determined by the MoD after consulting nutritionists. In a twenty-four-hour pack there was enough to keep a man in the field for that length of time. No more, no less. And there he was offering his own food to everyone else. Even Shagger – up till now asleep with the Love-Machine lads who were sprawled down beside Sloth – got a bit of biscuit, his yellow tail wagging in appreciation.

0400

The motorised elements of the rogue Unita force were now just seventeen miles from the mission and ten from Tenta village. Makuma had pushed the advance hard, with almost five hundred men crammed into nine trucks of various sizes. They were going to be even more crammed in now, as one of the vehicles had broken down. The driver, a man who actually had a real driver's licence issued in Botswana, said he would try to fix it, but in his heart he knew he couldn't. They had been pushing the trucks hard, very overloaded, and the grinding over rocky bush was running them hot. Short of oil, they had in fact drained some out of one truck's engine for another only the day before. He suspected this engine had seized, but he wasn't going to tell Ndube that and certainly not Colonel Makuma. Just that he would try and fix it. Let it cool. Try it again.

He watched as the column moved off with crashing gears and revving engines, men crowded on to the back of the trucks, hanging on for grim life, one actually falling and having to run after the departing vehicle, his friends laughing at his attempts to reach the high rear end.

Ndube said they would try and find some oil and bring it back with them, and then had left three men with him. Experienced men, Makuma's own, to ensure that nothing happened to the vehicle. It was too valuable and important to Makuma's plans to be left on the roadside unguarded.

0440

Penny Carter was awake. In the hut the three women, each sitting beside the possessions they had packed, had all nodded off. It seemed quiet enough and she peered at her watch. The watch, a present from her parents, had a luminous face, and it was glowing softly in the darkness. Twenty to five, she thought. She looked round the hut's interior again and carefully, her decision made almost without being aware of it, she stretched her legs out and then gathered them back and silently stood up, stepping over the legs of the woman asleep by the doorway.

Outside, she took a moment to orient herself and then walked quietly down the dry, packed-earth path through the collection of huts and found the path she had come down earlier that evening. Flicking on the torch she began to walk back to the mission. Normally she would have had to convince herself it was safe, that there were no man-eating animals lying in wait for her, but it never occurred to her to worry. Her need to get back and warn the others was stronger.

Makuma's trucks drove down the road into the mission grounds like they owned it, no thought given to a reconnaissance, or that there might be any danger for them. They were all-powerful in these parts, and Makuma knew his arrival would be unchallenged.

Sister Jo, awake and on the hospital ward, heard them approaching – the grinding gears and revving engines. There weren't many people in the beds. Those who could leave had done so over the last two days, so she wasn't that busy. She wondered who it might be, realised there was more than one lorry, and taking the lantern from the window sill behind the nurse's station, she walked out on to the veranda and round to see who it was. Someone from the mine maybe? Had there been an accident perhaps? She knew that Dr Carter wasn't back yet, but thought she might be waiting for daylight to begin the walk back, so she worried for a moment in case there had been an accident – could she cope alone?

Others were rising in the mission. Routinely, they gathered for morning prayers before the sun rose, at 0530, so when the lead truck halted and armed men jumped down and began to run through the mission buildings, none of the nuns was actually still in bed. All were in various stages of dressing after washing.

Sister Jo, standing to welcome whoever it was, was still holding up the lantern as the first man reached her, his rifle butt taking her in the stomach. As she fell retching, she dropped the lantern and the glass broke and it rolled across the veranda and dropped to the ground. She heard men shouting, orders being yelled, other excited calls. As she rose – holding her stomach, stunned and shocked, disbelieving – someone else running past her swung a kick and she went down again.

There were screams now, coming from the inside, as the attackers moved through the hospital ward hacking at every-thing and everyone with huge-bladed pangas.

Makuma had said he wanted no witnesses and there was to be no mercy. A man at the end of the ward sat up in bed, his eyes filled with terror as five men in a frenzy of bloodlust moved down toward him, killing as they went. One wearing a mutant ninja turtle T-shirt, his eyes red on *dagga*, swung his panga and chopped his feet off before starting up his body.

The patient opposite him tried to stand but was too weak and the attackers fired several shots into him. Within a few minutes the rebel Unita men had been through the mission, emptying rooms of occupants, rounding everyone up, beating them and herding them outside to where Makuma waited.

While this was going on he had walked through the class-rooms. Slowly at first, he had smelled the chalk dust, touched old, tired books, and at one point stopped and ran his hand down an old, scarred desk. But there were no fond memories. This was no nostalgic moment. The rage was building in him, and as his one good eye misted over, he snapped. With a roar he swung his foot and kicked the desk over, swinging round and round in an ever-increasing circle, pushing and kicking out at desks and chairs, ripping children's paintings and pictures from the walls until the room was a shambles.

Ndube watched him from the door, dispassionate, with half a smile on his lips, like he was observing an animal in a cage.

Only three hundred yards away Dr Penny Carter, within a minute of leaving the forest and entering the compound had heard the gunshots. She wasn't alone. The boy, the one who had interpreted for her the night before, had found her gone and caught her up about halfway from the village. She had stared him out, refused to go back with him, and then, tired and grubby, she pulled rank.

'I am a grown up. You are a child. You don't tell me what to do. Now I am going back to tell them. You can come or you can go back.' Clearly having lost his fight to convince her, he did the next best thing, and that was to stay with her. She moved slowly closer, the boy following, and could now hear the yelling, the shouts. She moved a bit closer till she could see through the foliage, and watched, horrified, as the scene unfolded.

'Please, Doctor? We go,' he urged in a whisper. 'This very denge-rus.'

0508

'I know you,' Sister Mary said, her heart sinking, trying to keep the fear and revulsion from her voice. In nearly forty years of teaching, twenty-five of them here, she had rarely met children who were bad. Born bad. Evil. One or two in all that time. One, by then a teenager, had died in a fire in his village – a kerosene-burner accident – and when she heard the news she felt nothing but relief, thinking, now you can face

God and account for yourself. The other, worse by far, now stood before her. Paul Makuma. He had filled out since she had seen him last. He was a big man now, hulking even, his small ferrety eyes above a horribly scarred left cheek. His right eye had gone milky – river blindness – and, standing before her, he exuded rage, evil. She crossed herself.

He had arrived at the mission as a child – a sullen, brooding seven-year-old – and just got worse. People didn't want to be in the same room with him. He gave off something almost palpable, a blackness, a consuming hatred that would flash out in a second. By his teens he was suspected by local people of several killings in the bush, travellers who were attacked. But not ordinary attacks. Savaged, slashed. He had last been heard of maybe ten or fifteen years ago, when he had gone south, back to Angola.

He was wearing trousers of the DPM – disruptive pattern material – favoured by Unita, a pair of what were once good-quality boots, the yellow leather now discoloured with dried blood. A filthy, red T-shirt covered his torso, and over that he wore a sleeveless fisherman's utility jacket, the type favoured by journalists and photographers. That too was stained with blood, and from the tears in the fabric, the original owner had been shot or stabbed and this was his blood. On his head he wore a baseball cap, with a pair of women's sunglasses resting on the peak.

'You are the spawn of the devil,' she said in Greek, 'and may God's retribution upon you be swift and terrible for what you do here today.'

Makuma looked at her. He didn't understand a word of it, but he knew her, too. Remembered her. He punched her, a big, powerful, straight punch that left his massive shoulder and took her full in the face. She collapsed, and three of the nuns dropped to help her, the American nun looking up at him, beseeching him for mercy. 'In the name of God,' she began. He kicked out at her and then looked at Ndube. 'The radio?'

Ndube nodded.

Makuma looked at the nuns. He pointed at Sister Mary, the

American nun, and one other – Sister Sarah, the Irish girl. 'Let them have these three. Save the others for when I am back.'

Ndube grinned. He would slow the men down, let them have one of the white women at a time, so he could watch all the action. As Makuma climbed back into his vehicle, many of the men piled back into the trucks. It occurred to Ndube to have some men do a sweep of the perimeter, and get others to see what food there was in the kitchens. If there was food it would be good. He was looking forward to that, and to watching the men have some fun with the whites. He hated whites. It would be a good start to what should be a good day. As Makuma drove off, he looked round their captives. Three old ones, the rest younger.

Seventeen miles from the mission, the marines' leading vehicle came round a bend. Ahead, pulled over on the left, was a truck. In the headlights they could see two men on the road, both armed with automatic weapons, one holding his hand up. There was another one to the side, on the right maybe ten feet back from the two in the road. 'Oh, shit,' the driver muttered.

'Quiet!' the Corporal snapped, thinking fast. Corporal McEwan didn't recognise the exotic DMP trousers one was wearing. These aren't police and they aren't DRC troops. How many more? he thought. Shit! The bush could be thick with them. He knew about roadblocks. The actual block point was invariably supported by a stop group further up in case any vehicle broke through. What size force? What size stop group? There was no time to call it in for orders, no time to stop the vehicle and turn it round.

'Slow down, slow down, crawl forward. Wait till he walks over. If he raises that weapon and looks like he's going to use it I'll cap the cunt,' the Corporal said, drawing and cocking his 9-mill. 'Taff, get the one on the other side OK? Wait for my command!'

Taff was in the middle of the three seats, far enough from the door to be able to lie his SA80 across his lap, and that of the driver, the barrel pointing outwards.

The two marines in the back with all the packs, ammunition boxes and the radio hastily shoved gear aside. Each slid back the window on his side for the marine opposite to lean forward and shoot through.

'If it goes off, Mick, take the one on the right. Aim dead centre. Three rounds. Make sure they don't get up! Right! All of you! Then max suppression fire. Taff, get a smoke grenade out on the road behind us. Eddie,' he said to the driver. 'Then you get us out of here and don't fucking stall it!'

There was no time for a full sitrep for the boss, but he could alert them. He touched the button on his throat mic and spoke quickly.

'Zero Alpha, Zero Alpha, three seven two. We have a problem. We are on to an armed roadblock, repeat armed roadblock. Slowing down, got my flag card ready.'

He pulled out the Union flag – A4-size and pasted on to cardboard – and held it up in the window. The vehicle ground to a halt and the two men armed with AK47s walked forward confidently, cockily, in the headlights.

Two hundred and thirty yards behind them McLean ordered his vehicle to stop and jumped out, signalling the vehicles behind to halt, jerking his thumb at them, indicating that they should get out quickly and quietly. Lt Lowry, the CSM and Sergeant Willis had all been listening on the net, and urging silence, they pointed off both sides of the track as the marines began to bale out and take up defensive positions.

Up at the roadblock Corporal McEwan was focused, watching the man walk towards the vehicle door. 'Wait for it, wait for it. On the command,' he snarled softly, spooling them up but containing the aggression. 'Fucking wait for it. When it goes off, fucking do it! But on my command.' He put his head to the window and looked out.

'British. We are British. *Anglais. Britainnie*,' he called holding up the small Union flag to illustrate the point, smiling widely. In his other hand, out of sight, he had his 9-mill., the hammer back on full cock.

The approaching man walked closer, looking at the flag

card. It meant nothing to him, and inside the vehicle it was dark, so he could see no detail. But the voice was a foreigner's. In a millisecond – a millisecond where fear outran reason, or where the opportunity for another good vehicle seemed easy, or he had seen the DPM material of the marines' smocks in the dashboard light – the Unita fighter made his mistake. He swung his gun upwards, eyes wide, going for the trigger.

Corporal McEwan, from the wrong end of Leith, was ahead of him. He shot him twice, the first round going into his chest dead centre, the second into his head. 'Hit 'em!' he yelled. 'Go, Eddie!'

Taff, with his rifle lying across Eddie's lap, fired as he saw his Corporal's weapon snap up, a short burst going through the door into the man who was now standing at the driver's side door. In the rear, Mick – who was already sighted on the third man – let rip as the vehicle lurched forward, the other three pouring out suppression fire as they left the scene.

They never saw the fourth fellow who was under the bonnet of the truck still trying to see what was wrong. He, knowing in a heartbeat that he was in deep shit, was into the bush at a run, fleet-footed as a deer, the vehicle racing away one way, he at forty-five degrees the other.

Corporal McEwan, in the bouncing Land Cruiser, the adrenalin racing through his blood, called, 'Stop! Stop! Zero Alpha. Three seven two. Contact! Contact! Contact! Firefight at the roadblock. Three enemy down. Saw no others. Repeat, three enemy down. Saw no others. Their broken-down vehicle at the roadside. We are clear the immediate scene, over.' No stop group yet. He switched the mic back to press-to-talk, to allow the net to function. 'Fuck fuck fuck, stand to. There may be a stop group. Change magazines! Everyone alright? Anyone hit?' There was a babble of talk, yells. 'Shaddup! Anyone hurt? Mick, Eddie, Taff, Bloater?'

'Three seven, three seven, Zero Alpha.'

'Zero Alpha, three seven, send.'

'Three seven, confirm figures. Three, repeat three, only, over.'

'Roger on the three Zero Alpha.'

'Three seven, Zero Alpha, pull over when you can, and get clear of your vehicle. Go into a defensive position and wait for the company. Did you receive that, over?'

'Copied, Zero Alpha.'

'Three seven, we will approach the scene, sweep through, and RV with you, over. Do you have any casualties, over?'

Shit, McEwan thought. I forgot that, the Land Cruiser haring away up the road. They were now some distance from the scene. 'Zero Alpha, three seven. No casualties, over.' He suddenly thought – no stop group. That wasn't a roadblock. An armed carjacking, maybe? 'Zero Alpha, three seven. There was no stop group. I repeat, no stop group. Maybe this was a carjacking over?'

'Aah, roger. Thanks, three seven. Zero Alpha out.'

McLean moved fast. He put a ten-man section – two of the new fire teams – each side of the road in the bush, and with them advancing through the rocky savannah in the moonlight either side, he put a third up the road thirty seconds behind them. If the section on the road came under fire then he had a flank attack and a second axis on which to engage.

Fifteen minutes later they were at the scene, and four minutes after that he was calling the transport forward, eager to link up with Corporal McEwan. The Corporal's assessment would seem to be right, he thought. This seemed to be more of a carjacking than a roadblock, but he was getting increasingly concerned. There seemed to be no tactical reason to stop road traffic here but the the dead carjackers were heavily armed and some in bits of uniform.

'Part of a bigger force up ahead somewhere?' Lowry asked.

'Could be. I don't like this. Too many unknowns,' McLean said. 'Let's go. I want to get in there, lift these people out and get the hell out of here.' He looked at his signals sergeant. 'See if you can raise Commando.'

A few minutes later, the big aerial out – two marines having walked it round various compass headings – the signals sergeant shook his head. 'Nothing, sir.'

143

McLean elected to leave McEwan and his team in the lead vehicle. After their contact they were charged up and incredibly alert, and that was what he wanted. He had a few quiet words with each – praise, encouragement, making sure they were alright. They were. Morale was high.

Half an hour later it was different, and McEwan felt it. They had gone quiet, and it wasn't the enforced silence driven by tactical issues and environment. The adrenalin had worn off, there had been time to think. Absorb it all. Taff was the quietest. He had been looking into the man's face as his rounds hit, the memories of the man jerking as the rounds hammered into him vivid.

Makuma and his trucks rolled into the mine at 0530, splitting up, some stopping at the senior accommodation, a rough, prefabricated, wooden building like a stable block, others at the office. One truck came to a halt at the labourers' lines, men piling out, rounding up workers, shooting at those who were already fleeing into the bush.

There were three senior people present at the time. Two local men – both middle-aged, and both experienced miners – and a young Swiss expatriate, an engineer. One of the local men was still in his room and the other was walking down to the shower – a drum suspended seven feet high in a frame surrounded by a canvas privacy screen – as the Unita fighters rolled into the camp. His towel round his waist, rubbing the sleep from his eyes, he was confused for a moment or two. They were expecting no one. Supplies were due in from Matadi, but not today and certainly not at this hour of the day.

The Swiss engineer had been there only three weeks. The mine had been losing money and he had been sent down to close the operation and bring out the equipment for the owners, as they had another site in mind. The new upsurge in diamond mining had been covered by the papers a few months before. *The Times* had done a colourful article on the new imperialists, the new breed of late-twentieth-century buccaneers and their high-risk, high-return investment strategies. But these people weren't the new breed. De Waal Webley – his employers – were now part of a much bigger concern – Empire Mining Holdings – but had been involved with mining in Africa since the golden days at Kimberley.

Tenta mine had been mentioned in the article much to the amusement of those who knew the place. There were diamonds in the river beds there, but they were small and poor quality and in their view no one was going to get rich.

They had proved to be right, and the Swiss engineer – twenty-six years old, fresh from Europe – was looking forward to getting the equipment out and on to the new site that would be his to manage. In true irony, the river bed had at last begun to offer good quality stones, but it was too late, he was there to get it all wound up and the equipment moved. In the way of these things he was in for a share and excited about the great adventure he was on. He was still under the sheet on his camp bed – a big American job with tubular aluminium legs – trying to work out what the yelling was, when the armed men burst through his flimsy door.

On the other side of the compound the Unita men had broken into the mine store and shop. It was there to sell everything the mine workers and their families might want. From soap to cigarettes, from Cokes to food, from buttons to cheap clothing. There was beer, cases of Primus, plastic tubs and brightly coloured blankets imported from the Indian subcontinent. The looting began, everything loaded on to the trucks, the men stuffing their own pockets with small, high-value items like cigarettes and sweets.

There was still some sporadic gunfire as his men took potshots at mine workers they found, but Makuma ignored that and followed others of his men into the mine office. Two battered old metal desks stood against a wall decorated with cheap calendars and working rosters and shift schedules. In the corner was the safe. It wasn't old like the desks. It was new. Shiny and heavy. He smiled. This was what he was looking for. Diamonds.

He looked at the combination lock and told someone to bring

him the office workers and the bosses. Of the latter only two were still alive. The man who had been walking to the shower had run for the bush in his flip-flops, nothing but a towel round his waist, and had been shot in the back.

The other was tied up, and he and the young Swiss fellow, both terrified, were dragged across the compound by their bound hands.

At the mission the first pink skies of dawn were laced with rising smoke. The generator shed and garage workshop had been looted of anything of value and were torched, the old Renault pickup, so lovingly maintained by the American nun, loaded with tools and bits and pieces and ready to be driven away.

Round the front of the mission the frenzied bloodlust of their arrival had tempered into something equally appalling, the gang rape, abuse and torture of the mission staff.

Ndube had enforced his colonel's command so the men were only allowed three of the women for the time being, the three he had pointed out. The men had spread them out on the ground, pulled up their brown habits, and had formed lines – the longer line at the younger woman. The men were laughing, shouting, pushing and jostling each other – enjoying this – and the women were crying, weeping, one screaming every now and then when someone did something to her. The best bit for Ndube was that he had lined the other nuns up and made them watch. He had one down on her knees in the front and every time one of them dropped their heads or closed their eyes, he had the kneeling one hit with a rifle butt.

Sister Marie-Claire stood upright, her back straight, her eyes open but staring into the middle distance, praying to God, praying for the three women on the ground, for courage, for fortitude, praying that he might deliver them from evil. Next to her, Sister Jo was sobbing, her eyes wide, unable to take in what was happening to them. The men were laughing and jeering. One came over and felt her breast and another walked down the line waving his penis at them, leering, showing them what they would get when their turn came. There were about two hundred men present, and another fifteen were still out sweeping the perimeter.

They were hurrying lest they miss out on the fun. They were too well disciplined or too fearful to stop, but moved fast round the treeline, and it was the speed of their move that allowed them their capture.

Dr Carter was watching from the trees and didn't hear them. Her eyes were fixed on the scene across the compound, on the flames and smoke, on the gunshots and what sounded like drunken laughter, on the awful screams and moans, on the men fighting amongst themselves.

They heard them at the same moment. The boy, smarter, more aware, said something – a whispered warning – and was away, fast like a gazelle through the trees. As Penny stood, her heart pounding, liquid terror in her guts, there were shouts and someone was upon her, someone big, unwashed – his odour pungent, heavy.

A few minutes later she was dragged, terrified, across the compound by her hair, towards the systematic gang rape that was in progress. Ndube smiled and looked at her like a snake looking at a mouse.

McEwan pulled over and let the convoy catch him. As McLean walked forward he pointed at the rising smoke.

'I reckon that's it, sir.'

McLean nodded, thinking quickly, and touched his throat mic.

'Charlie Charlie, Zero Alpha. We could be too late. All stop. Troop commanders forward.'

I've got to see the ground myself before we leap in feet first, he thought. Time on recce is never wasted, but I want some protection and another good pair of eyes for the ground. As they arrived McLean knew what he wanted done.

'OC three, send me Corporal Gillespie's fire team and make sure he and Lance Corporal Dallaglio bring their L96s. Put another fire team on the high ground to our left and make sure we aren't surprised. Rest of the troop hold here. OC Two, hold your lads here. Get the sides of the vehicles up and remind everyone of their vehicle debussing drills. We won't have time to dawdle if we need to go down at the rush.'

Lowry's sergeant had appeared with his OC as Gillespie's fire team came forward. Concurrent activity and anticipation at all levels, he thought, delighted that he had such a professional team.

Gillespie looked at his team, making sure they were watching him. He unslung his rifle, looked at his lads and said in low, clear voice loaded with menace, 'Keeping your weapons pointed in a safe direction—' He worked the action on his rife, the mechanism sliding forward and putting a round into the breech. He slipped the safety on. 'Ready and make safe.'

The fire team did that and piled into the Land Cruiser.

'Ted,' McLean said to Captain Lowry, 'while I'm away, get da Silva. I want him to draw us a map of what he remembers the compound layout looking like.'

They drove the last two miles and then stopped the vehicle and moved forward through the bush, moving fast, a skirmish line. This was dangerous. Incredibly dangerous. A recce patrol moves slowly, does not get compromised, does not get seen – but McLean pushed that to one side. He knew that with four marines with him they were effectively a fire team, could deliver some focused firepower, and fight their way out of any trouble with a piquet group or small patrol in the bush. He needed to get forward, see what the fuck was going on, and do it fast.

They dropped back in pace and moved slowly up the last sixty yards through the bush to the edge of the compound clearing. They were maybe one hundred yards from the road off to the left, the compound out to their right. He settled down, deployed his team and pulled his binoculars up. Smoke was rising from fires, armed men scattered everywhere, but a big group were in front of what must have been the mission buildings. He could hear the screams of the women and laughter from the men gathered round them. Bastards. You fucking bastards. He swung the glasses right, taking everything in. Many weren't even carrying their rifles, but shambling around, eating, sitting, watching. Men jostled each other in the lines for what he knew must be women. Nuns. Fucking cunts. You filthy fucking heathen cunts. He felt the anger building. Contain it, he told himself. He crawled back.

Back with the company he lifted his beret and wiped the sweat from his face, the cam cream smudging. This was against every instinct, every tenet of his training. This was almost a knee-jerk reaction, but there wasn't time for lots of recce, lots of planning, lots of think through. People were in real trouble down there, and every minute counted.He spread the drawing that da Silva had done out on the bonnet of the Land Cruiser.

'Charlie Charlie, troop commanders and Mr Harvey to the CP.' He quickly told them what he had seen. 'We go in.'

'Two troop leads on this axis here,' he began. The problem was space. What he wanted was a fire support troop perpendicular to the main 3-Troop axis of attack, and his snipers and TAC with that support troop, but there was no room for something so defined. 'A 3-Troop fire team as cut-off here. Swing round us to put yourselves nearest the river. Again. First we are going to engage the group at the northern edge, the river side, where the nuns are. Stop vehicles, debus and engage. Sweep through. Fire teams stay together! Secure the front and civilians. Captain Lowry's troop then takes over. Round the back of the mission, supporting the cut-off section and engaging whoever is out on the right. Snipers take them as they cross the open ground.

The moment the exterior is secure, one section from 2 Troop will clear the mission buildings. The other is in reserve. While that is going on, Captain Lowry, your troop then to sweep inland. Set up and secure a perimeter. Got it?' The five men nodded. 'Snipers, where are they?'

'Here, sir.' The men pushed forward, and from the corner of his eye, McLean could also see Perrin Dalton, inching forward, his eyes alive.

'We engage the group at the northern end. Our vehicles will stop here. There are civilians in there. I'll call. Tell 'em to drop,' he said. 'The enemy is in mixed kit, some DPM, fawn and brown-coloured. They are all black and all male. Take 'em fast, anyone threatening the civilians.' He pointed at the drawing, looking at the snipers. 'Your angle of fire is in here between 2 Troop and the fire support teams. You'll have maybe fifteen seconds before 2 Troop are skirmishing into there. Make it count and then cease fire when you can't shoot, but stay put and turn your rifle this way. The company will sweep through and live ones will be crossing this ground. After my command, fire at will. Got it?'

They nodded.

'All of you, listen carefully. I don't want this becoming a hostage situation. We have to hit them fast and so hard that anyone not going down or running away is unable to think or issue orders. Right, let's move. Brief your teams as we go in. There's people dying down there.'

They had taken Penny Carter into the hospital – or rather Ndube had, with three of the men. Bodies of the sick, hacked to death earlier in the attack, were strewn around.

She was thrown on to a bloodstained bed, bodies either side on the floor, and held there while Ndube undid his trouser buttons. He wanted this one first. He knew he could, because she had not been there when Makuma had left, therefore in his logic she wasn't one of the ones he wanted left until his return.

Outside, the line of nuns were still standing, just. One of them, overcome with shock, her mind unable to deal with what she was seeing, had fallen over, and been kicked to her feet. The line of men was concentrating on just two of the women now. Sister Sarah, the young Irish girl, had fought back just a little too much and one of them had punched her senseless. The next, angry, not wanting to vent himself into someone comatose, slapped her a few times and, wanting a reaction and getting none, he went beserk and stabbed her with his bayonet between her legs. Others, angry that he had ruined one of the women for fun, pulled him away and a fight ensued.

Sister Marie-Claire was still standing ramrod straight, staring into the middle distance, and when she heard the trucks it barely registered. Just their leader coming back. Now it was their turn. '*Lord God above, we beseech you,*' she began.

The surprise was complete. There was no doubt that many of the Unita fighters thought the trucks and vehicles were their Colonel returning. When the leading vehicles drove up – among them a Toyota Land Cruiser very like Makuma's – few paid any attention.

'*We ask that you receive us into your kingdom . . .*'

In front of her was a man walking past. As he passed her – without warning and seemingly without reason – his head snapped back as if he were punched, and blood spumed outwards as he fell. Another – one of the men pointing his rifle at them – went down to his right, and the report of a gunshot followed by another rolled over them.

The vehicles were there. As they rolled to a halt, suddenly a voice was shouting and men were jumping to the ground, men in green uniforms with black – no, green – faces, and the shooting started.

'British forces! Royal Marines! Drop down! Lie down! British forces!'

Sister Jo, the Londoner, the youngest and newest of them, and most exposed to the media, who as kid saw the Iranian Embassy thing on TV, who also saw the movie *Raid on Entebbe*, on video, and the most fluent in the dialect – was the first to react. She came out of her trance, shrieked at the others in French, and pulled Sister Marie-Claire backwards on to the ground by her habit, telling them to lie down, lie still.

McLean's driver entered the compound, the two trucks in front of him. McLean was totally focused. Behind him his radio operator was ready to talk to the snipers, but McLean was watching for reaction from the people they were approaching, watching the last few yards roll under the bonnet. Every foot closer was a bonus. Still no reaction. This was unbelievable. Little or no reaction, almost like, shit, no vehicles here. Closer now. One of the enemy even waving at them, the two trucks now rolling into position in front of them, facing away so the troop would engage left to right across their front.

'They think we're theirs,' a marine muttered out of the side of his mouth. His cam cream at a distance made his skin look black. McLean could hear the section leader in the back spooling his men up – low commands, charged with aggression.

'Keep going, Mufti,' McLean said to Sergeant Willis, surprised his voice was so steady. 'Try and get to within thirty feet of that mob, side-on.'

Closer, closer. The GPMG was set up, all that was needed was the canvas side hauled up.

'On the command,' McLean said into his throat mic. 'Stand-by, stand-by. Snipers, open fire! British forces!' he yelled out of the window, the door opening. 'Hit 'em! Open fire!' – into the mic. Then yelling again, 'Royal Marines! Drop down! Lie down! British forces!'

All hell broke loose. The machine guns opened up, two heavy-barrelled gimmpies and two section automatic weapons, ripping, tearing into the crowd of men queuing for their turn at the women. Marines were piling out, debussing like they had practised hundreds of times, section leaders calling orders, fire teams going to ground and opening fire. McLean dropped to the ground with his radio operator to command the battle and by the time he was in his position, the carnage was at its height, and whatever Unita men weren't down, dead, wounded, or jerking as rounds ploughed into them, were running for the trees or for cover. Two Troop were up and rolling forward, furious fire ripping out, marines peeling round prone fire teams to engage, the ones they had moved in front of up and moving around them in turn.

A few of the Unita men were fighting back, but they were no match.

In the small ward the three men holding Dr Carter down for

Ndube scattered, one running for the door out into the daylight and being shot down, the other two going the other way into the mission building.

Ndube, a natural survivor, made no attempt to lead his men, or to rally them into some sort of counterattack or defence, and he made no attempt to do what he had come to do. Fast as a weasel, he was down the length of the ward, through the nurses' station and clinic in the middle, into the next ward and out of the window at the end, running for the cover of the trees at the eastern end of the compound, leaving them to their fate.

On the bed, Dr Carter was trying to assimilate what had happened, what was going on. Suddenly her attackers were gone. They would be back, she reasoned. She shrank back, trying to be small, unnoticeable, trying to be inconspicuous, trying to disappear into the sheets – and then she remembered the blood. The sheets were wet with blood and there were bodies at her feet, severed limbs, pools of blood. She sat up. There was noise, incredible noise, screams of rage and pain, confusion.

Oustside, the action was furious but one-sided. The marines were a much smaller group, but they were professional soldiers, disciplined, highly trained and highly motivated. Some of the rogue Unita men close to their weapons tried to return fire and died in a fusillade of bullets. Biscuit shot a look at Sergeant Willis and he nodded and pointed.

'On me!' Biscuit yelled. His fire team rose as one and, as they ran forward past the other section, he shouted, 'Coming through!' Sloth, Kevin Furby, Jock and Dave Hobson moved past the team they were peeling round, and set themselves up with an axis that could see both the group of nuns and down the eastern side of the mission.

In amongst the many dead and dying men by the nuns, one wounded fighter rose. Sloth swung his rifle and fired two shots into him and then scuttled forward, putting himself into the six-foot gap between the women and the bloody pile of wounded and dead Unita fighters.

There at his feet was a woman, one of the nuns. She had been treated brutally, but behind the terror in her eyes he could see the real person, and he flicked a smile – a smile that said, don't worry, we're here now, you're safe. Somewhere in there, in the smoke and gunfire, there was recognition – she knew she would be saved. He dropped beside her and re-entered the fight.

Biscuit didn't like the exposed layout of his new position and could see that if anyone was inside the mission, up on the veranda a good two feet above them, they would have a clear field of fire on to his position.

He looked at Sgt Willis, twenty feet away, and pointed into the building and then at his own chest. Willis nodded and held up a hand, and twenty seconds later, a fire team from the other section were sprawling round them, taking up the position so they could cover the east side of the mission and the carnage surrounding the nuns, while Biscuit's fire team cleared the position in the building.

'Zero Alpha, Three Alpha. We are exposed to fire from the building. I have a fire team entering the front to secure and hold there, over.'

'Roger, Three,' McLean responded. Willis was good, using his experience.

Biscuit called to his team and they raced forward, three of them down the verandah to the end while he and Dave Hobson went into the door and began to sweep the rooms along the front.

It was Hobson who found Dr Carter. She was sitting up on the bed, clutching her shirt together at the front where they had ripped the buttons away, eyes wide. All she saw was a uniform and Hobson's face, dark with cam cream, behind the levelled weapon and SUSAT sight. Hobson took it in. Bodies on the floor. Blood everywhere. His senses reeled for a second, but there was a figure. Someone up. He swung the weapon on to her. A woman. A white woman.

'You alright?' he called.

She looked at him. Staring. Eyes wide, not trusting herself to believe the voice she had heard. He could see no one else in the room, not alive anyway, but he took no chances and waited till Sgt Willis was there before he moved forward.

'You alright?' he asked again. '*Très bien?*' he tried in been-across-on-the-ferry-for-smokes-and-booze-a-few-times French. She just looked at him then nodded, once.

'Get down on the floor.' He looked down. Blood every-where. 'Come on. Right now, please. Over there in the corner,' he said, like he was speaking to a child, and took her hand. 'You're safe now.'

'Who are you?' she asked. He heard her speak for the first time. English. She was English.

'We're Royal Marines. Forty Commando.'

She put her arms around his neck and began to cry.

Ten minutes after 2 Troop had joined up with 3 Troop, Lowry had led his troop into the bush to set up a perimeter, while 2 Troop secured the mission buildings. McLean's radio operator was setting up the aerial for the 320 and hoping like hell he could get a signal out.

Dalton was moving around the scene now, taking pictures, recording what he was seeing, and da Silva was sitting hunched over, in with the nuns, talking to them. McLean noticed, with bleak approval, that he had already taken an AK47 from the ground and armed himself. This wasn't over yet. Not by a long shot.

The road out was now suspect. The bush was crawling with the men who had escaped, and who knew how many others, and it was high-risk. It was then that someone noticed the smoke rising to the south-west and pointed it out to the Captain.

That's where they are, he thought. The rest of them, with their transport.

For the other marines, the first job was clearing weapons from any enemy who were still alive and capable of using them. There were dead and wounded everywhere, mostly Unita fighters caught by the machine guns in the first furious attack. Three marines moved among them removing weapons. There had been two marine casualties. One man had taken a round through the upper chest above the lungs, which exited four inches further up out of the top of his shoulder. The other, a 3-Troop marine, was fatally wounded when he took three rounds from an automatic weapon. He was lying prone at the time and two of the bullets hit him in the head. Out the front of the mission the leading medical assistant had his work cut out. The wounded marine was stable and he was working through the nuns – incredibly, only one of whom had been hit in the exchange – running his own triage.

'Any chance of a casevac, sir? There's one of ours and at least three of the civvies that need a hospital.'

'We are having trouble raising comms,' McLean answered. 'The moment we can get word out we will get a helo in. This,' he said rather bleakly, 'is inside the French ROE.'

'What about them?' the LMA asked, nodding at the Unita wounded. There were three marines standing over a handful of able-bodied prisoners, and they had put them to work tending to their own wounded. 'At this rate,' he told Captain McLean, 'I'll get on to the worst of them in about an hour. That's if you want me to,' he finished. McLean looked at him. 'What I am saying is, sir, we are a long way from home, and that' – he pointed at his black, rolled-out medic's pack – 'is all the kit we have. If a helo is coming in, can I put an order in?'

'Sure. Tell the CSM what you need. In the meantime there is stuff inside,' McLean responded. 'Treat who you can while we are here. That's all anyone can ask.'

The LMA nodded, and as he went back to work on one of his patients, a nun in her fifties, he looked across at the Padre, Rory Chisholm.

The Padre was on his knees, wearing his purple vestments, covered in blood, holding one of the nuns. The LMA knew the woman he was with was dying, he had seen her already. She was bleeding out, going into massive traumatic shock. By the look of it she had been repeatedly raped and then bayoneted several times – the last few between her legs – because she was bleeding heavily down there. The Padre had closed her legs and pulled down her habit to try and give her back some dignity, and was holding her now.

It was Sister Sarah, the Irish girl. She looked at him and saw the cross at his throat, the vestment. A priest. An ordained priest.

'Father?'

He nodded. 'Don't talk now.'

'Are they OK? The others?'

He nodded. 'Aye, child. They're OK.' God forgive my lie, please?

'Pray for me, Father.' She whispered it so softly he had to lean forward to hear her. 'Bless me, for I have sinned.'

He smiled at her. The goodness, the decency, the caring, the compassion came up off her like a bright light. Sinned, he thought. You've never really sinned. You don't have it in you.

'I have thought bad things of others,' she said, weakening. 'But I forgive them.'

Dr Carter had been sitting for the last ten minutes just staring into space. Sister Marie-Claire, who had been moving among her people comforting them, saw her and walked over to her. 'Penny? Penny?' she said softly. 'Put this aside for now. We need you. We need the doctor in you.' Penny looked round at her and her eyes focused.

'Yes. Yes, of course. Sorry,' she replied, realising something, appalled she had been doing nothing. She stood up and walked into the mission building. A minute later she dropped down beside the LMA, a cardboard box in her hand. In it were some instruments, bandages, drugs. She looked down at the marine's patient. Sister Madelaine. 'I'm Penny Carter . . .' She struggled, trying to do what Sister Marie-Claire had asked, put it aside, 'I'm a surgeon You're . . .'

'Gubby. I'm the leading medical assistant.'

'Navy?'

'Aye aye, marm,' he said through his gap teeth.

Good, she was thinking. The Navy trained its medical assistants well. Often they were the only medics on a ship and were good enough to temporarily set bones, deal with trauma, and be talked through minor surgical procedures. A colleague of hers had done it once, talked a Naval LMA through an appendectomy.

'OK, Gubby. What have we got here?'

Six

McLean's signals sergeant had collared da Silva and had him walking around with the end of a wire aerial as he tried, without success, to get a response on the big PRC320 Clansman radio. The 320 was a skywave set, an HF radio, and on a good day with the right conditions it allowed communications at very long range. But not today.

'Zero Zero Zero . . . Zero Zero Zero, this is Golf One Zero.'

'Zero Zero Zero . . . Zero Zero Zero this is Golf One Zero.'

They were doing it gingerly, the marine snipers were still active, and da Silva ducked involuntarily every now and then as a gun went off somewhere, moving round a few feet as the radio operator indicated.

A few yards away the nuns were on their feet and active. Incredibly, some of them were now in among the Unita wounded with the prisoners, staunching bleeding, helping and comforting them.

Furby, preparing to enter the mission as part of the sweep team saw this and shook his head to himself. 'Fucking hell!' he muttered to Sloth. 'Look at that. They are helping the cunts who ten minutes ago were gang raping them before killing them. I'd leave the fuckers to die.'

'That's why they're nuns and you're a bootie,' Sloth responded quickly. They were on a high, a post-firefight rush, with adrenalin still in their blood. He looked across at the nuns and as he did so the one he had dropped down beside earlier looked across at him. Her face was swollen from a blow, but her eyes were clear and when she smiled at him her whole face lit up. He smiled back.

McLean walked past. His signals sergeant, still struggling to get a response, was getting pissed off. 'Zero Zero Zero . . . Zero Zero Zero, this is Golf One Zero.' He looked up at McLean. 'This area is shite, sir. I've had a recce inside. The mission radio has been trashed. The pricks even pulled down the di-pole. That would have been useful. And this kit? Too hot and too humid. Can't even get the World Service.' He pointed to the Clansman. 'I'm not sure if we can get a signal out at all in daylight. What about the beacon jobby?' he asked.

Egress. McLean was thinking. Thinking fast. Quite simply, without communciations in warfare, you could lose. His company net was functioning, but they needed support and uplift and the radio link to Commando was critical. Without that no one knew their situation.

He had already walked enough of the mission to know it wasn't defensible. Light timber-frame walls on a concrete floor. Nothing to stop a bullet anywhere except the kitchen block, so there was no way it could be fortified into a defensive position, and the perimeter was too large. We have wounded. We have used up a hell of a lot of our ammunition, the lads have already dug into their rations. If we wait here for support, it may be days. We have to get out of here. Get out where we can determine events, get out where we have the initiative, where we can expect uplift and resupply by the French. Their big, long-legged, lovely Super Puma. Come on, boys.

He looked at the smoke to the south-west.

'I'll tell you in five minutes. Keep trying.' He looked at the Portuguese engineer. 'Mr da Silva, who is in charge here?' Da Silva pointed out Sister Marie-Claire, who was on the ground bent over Sister Sarah, the Padre the other side.

He crossed the few feet to where Sister Marie-Claire was. McLean stopped beside her. 'Sister, I believe you are in charge here.'

She looked up at him as he knelt beside her, and nodded.

'I'm Doug McLean. I'm with Alpha Company, 40 Commando of the Royal Marines.'

'You are the commander?' she asked.

'I am. Can you spare me a minute?'

'Of course.' She rose. 'I must thank you, on behalf of my people. You were quite literally the answer to a prayer.'

He smiled. 'No,' he said sadly. 'We were too late. Sister, can you tell me what might be burning over there?' He pointed to the smoke rising.

'Could be a village but it's more likely the mine. Tenta mine.'

He nodded. 'Were there more of these people than we found when we arrived? There was no transport here.'

'*Oui*. There were many more. They drove off.' She grimaced. 'Their *colonel*' – she said the word with distaste – 'is a brute of a man. He was at school here in his childhood. Sister Mary remembered him. She said he was pure evil. An evil person.'

'How many more?' he asked.

'Many hundreds. They had many trucks. All full of them.'

'Think, please,' he asked. 'How many?'

'Maybe three or four hundred others. I don't know. Maybe they will be back,' she said. 'This Paul Makuma was saving us for when he got back.'

They have the road out, he thought. Seventy-odd miles of places perfect for ambush. They have us bottled up here. He could see the jetty on to the river. There was no boat, so crossing was out. It was on foot from here.

'Thank you. I'll see you a little later.'

He flipped open his notebook and looked something up, walking back to where his radio operator was still trying to raise the commando.

'The beacon. Use it,' he said. 'Egress option blue.'

'Blue?'

'Blue,' McLean repeated.

Inside the mission a section of 2-Troop marines were clearing and securing the building room by room. Shagger, who had disappeared during the firefight, had reappeared and followed them in, right on Sloth's heels, then moved ahead.

They were all looking at him now. He was hunched down, his hackles up in a ridge the length of his back, his teeth bared, growling, his eyes on the storeroom door. Biscuit and Kevin dropped to one side, Sloth and Furby the other. Hobson and his oppo were further up, but all looked at Shagger, whose eyes never wavered from the door.

Furby held up a grenade and raised an eyebrow at Biscuit. Use this? Biscuit held up a hand. Not yet. He pointed at Furby, who moved across to him. 'Get round the back. See if there's a window. Make sure there are no civvies in there. If it's OK, fire a signal shot, one round, and use it – we'll come in this side immediately after it goes off.'

The big marine nodded and skittered off on the shiny red concrete floor. Shagger hadn't taken his eyes of the door, and Sloth pulled him gently back out of the line of fire. Biscuit tapped his magazine and nodded towards Sloth's rifle. Sloth nodded back. They were ready.

Furby moved quickly through the kitchen and to the back door. Smoke rose from somewhere out the front and the wind blew it over the rooftop making the sky a leaden pink. He looked out of the door.

The section's other fire team were there, two in a defensive posture, the other two stripping weapons away from four dead enemy. One looked to be only sixteen or seventeen, his face peaceful, untouched. The one beside him had taken a round in the side of his head and the exit wound was large, a gaping hole where his forehead had been, brain matter and blood everywhere. Sniper, he thought. Hit by one of the snipers.

Furby looked at the section's corporal. 'There's someone in the storeroom. Biscuit and Sloth are waiting to go in.' He pointed round the corner. 'I'm going round to see if there's a window. Have a look.'

The section leader nodded, his eyes leaving the edge of the compound and the treeline for barely a second or two. The area was far from secure. Firefights were still breaking out. 'Go with him, Boff. Don, you and I cover them from the corner.'

Boff – who seemed to be thoroughly enjoying himself – grinned widely and moved, crouched over, to the end of the kitchen wall. Furby moved past him, his weapon, butt to the shoulder, ready to fire in an insant. Northern Ireland all over.

A few seconds later they were at the point along the outside wall adjacent to the storeroom and there were windows all along. Furby peeked into the first one. Kitchen. He moved along. Had to be this one. As with the rest of the mission windows there was no glass, but in addition to the fly screen, this window had bars. He signalled to Boff, and holding his breath, he snuck a look into the room. Couldn't see shit. It was dark in there, and trying to look through the fly screen into a dark room wasn't easy. He tried again and heard something move and two shots rang out, one bullet blasting chips off the edge of the wall, the other going out through the fly screen.

Fuck this, he thought. He pulled the grenade out of a vest pocket, pulled the pin, let the spoon fly clear, counted to two, banged off a single shot and punched his closed fist through the old fly screen and let the grenade drop. Two seconds later came the nasty flat crack and maize dust blew out of the window, the fly screen blown out by the concussion wave.

From the other side, Biscuit and Sloth came through the door firing, each taking a side, frightened and not knowing how many were in there, so pouring rounds into every hiding place for five or six seconds. There was one man down at Biscuit's feet, and another pair of legs, wearing cheap, brown tennis shoes, were sticking out from behind the maize-meal sacks. He changed the angle on his weapon and fired a burst down into the hole behind the sacks. 'Stop!' he called. The man on the floor moved and Sloth fired another two rounds into him to make sure.

'Furby, you OK?'

'Yeah.'

'Stay that side. Get ready to move down to the next room when we do.'

Shagger was in by then, sniffing the action, his nose smelling the blood and the death and the cordite. Biscuit looked at him, his heart pounding, the adrenalin still coursing through his blood. 'That,' he said, 'is a fucking ace dog. Real Gucci. Will he do that again?'

'Let him go ahead,' Sloth said. 'We'll see.'

'Grab their weapons and let's move.'

Outside, the two assault engineers attached to the company were moving through the enemy dead stripping them of heavy stores. They had quite a pile. Three Claymore mines, a pair of RPG7s and about fifteen rockets, four anti-vehicle landmines and one bit of kit that they were both poring over, a SAM7 launcher with two missiles.

McLean was moving through the civilans, talking to them, getting a feel for morale, and had squatted down beside Perrin Dalton, who was sitting beside Sister Mary, one of the rape victims. She had obviously just died and he ran his hands over her eyes closing the lids. One of her colleauges was kneeling on the other side, crying softly, when the firing began. It ended almost as quickly.

Dalton looked at him.

'Clearing the building,' McLean answered in response to the look.

'They obviously found someone,' the journalist muttered. He looked down at the old nun who had given all her adult life to the poor, the weak, the forgotten, and had now died in the process. 'She thought you were John Peters,' Dalton said.

'Sorry?' McLean took his beret off and wiped his brow with his face veil. 'Who?'

'John Peters. Hero to some, villain to others. She was obviously in the first category, and I think I know why.'

The name rang a bell for some reason but McLean couldn't remember why.

'Don't know him,' he said. Somewhere off to the right there was a burst of fire, followed by another series of shorter exchanges that died way, the sound muffled by the dense rainforest vegetation. He looked back at Dalton. Whoever that was would be calling in.

Dalton pulled a hip flask from his pocket. 'I am an Africanist. Means I know lots of fucking obscure little things about this huge, savage, wonderful bitch.' He swung an arm expansively and took a sip of the fiery brandy and offered it to McLean, who shook his head. 'John Peters, a mad northerner, ex-SAS or something, who was here, or rather down in what was then Katanga, with Mike Hoare's 5 Commando in the sixties. Remember them?'

'The mercenaries?'

Dalton nodded. 'She kept mentioning a place name – she's old enough to have been there – Yangambi. Peters had a small detachment of the commando. He was almost Hoare's second-in-command, but had this small group mounted in Land Rovers. Later on it was enlarged and called Force John John.' McLean grimaced. It was coming back. He had read a rather dry account of the action only six months before in a book on the region.

'They were going to a mission downriver from Stanleyville,' Dalton continued. 'They got there and the Simbas had moved the priests and nuns. They found out where, and kept after them. Rescued them. But Peters and a small detachment split off to go to a smaller mission where there were a handful of staff. They arrived at dawn. The rebels had spent the night raping and killing and torturing the priests and nuns. Peters never hesitated. Flat out in the vehicles, straight into the mission area, machine guns blazing. A few minutes later it was all over. His lads had done the business. Three priests dead already, but they saved two nuns. For them he was the answer to a prayer. I think this woman was there. She thought she was back there, and she thought you' – he indicated McLean and his marines – 'were Peters' boys. She was reliving a nightmare. What was it Churchill said? Study history or you are doomed to repeat it? She was.'

It was quiet for a second or two, just the sound of the doves calling in the trees until the sound of another short contact rolled over them.

'So, do you remember what they did then?' McLean asked.

'Yes,' Dalton said seriously. 'They reformed with the main commando and drove to Stanleyville with fifty other survivors from the main mission at Isangi.'

So, now the story differs, McLean thought. Because there is no main commando here. The enemy force is out there in undetermined strength, and we – sixty-one marines – are on foot. We are almost certainly outnumbered, with limited ammunition, in a very hostile environment, one hundred and sixty miles from our support elements and about seventy miles from any friendlies, with casualties and non-combatants.

'Be nice if that bit repeated itself,' he said, thinking, thank Christ for helicopters. Turning, he looked at his signals sergeant who was coming to his feet.

'Wouldn't it just,' Dalton agreed.

The signaller ran up to him and handed him the small Clansman, the 351 that he needed to speak on the company net, and just as he did so a furious contact broke out up the road. 'Zero alpha, two alpha. Contact, wait, out.' It was Sergeant Willis's radio operator. He had the left flank with the Love Machine, the other half of 2 Troop.

'Contact! Now. We have approx forty enemy crossing to our left. We are engaged at this time. Over.'

That was serious enemy activity. In Western terms a reinforced platoon on the move. Either they have rallied or the others are back. Here we go, he thought.

At the mine, smoke drifted upward from burning accommodation lines. The mine had single quarters only, so half a mile away a village had sprung up, where wives had built huts and had begun to till the soil. That was burning too.

Makuma had been sitting at a desk with his feet up, watching as his men questioned the two mine employees. The local man was terrified, jabbering that he didn't know the combination, he was a miner, not one of the adminstrators, and that all there was in the safe was petty cash. The young Swiss man was down on his knees, his hands bound behind his back. He was in shock, trying to take it in, trying to get his head round what was happening. He was Swiss, gay, a pacifist vegetarian in an enlightened age. He had never hurt anyone in his life. It was unbelievable, a nightmare, and he kept wanting to wake up.

Then they turned on him. There wasn't even a question in the first instance, just a kick between his legs. He grunted and dropped forward, the pain so deep, so intense, it winded him. Unable to breathe for a few seconds he finally gasped a breath and let out a moan, his face a mask of pain.

'What is the way in?' one of his captors asked.

'Dunno,' he groaned in French, and then vomited. 'Dunno. Not my job.'

The next kick took him in the kidneys, and then another man kicked him in the face.

'Show us!'

Makuma looked over. He was getting bored with this. Obviously the diamonds were in the safe. He got up and walked over.

'We can't get in. Don't know the combination. The safe has nothing but a few francs. I'll show you. Get me explosives. From the store. I'll blow it open for you,' the local engineer offered.

Makuma thought about that and nodded, and two of the men dragged the hapless miner away to get the explosives. Don't need this one any more, he thought, except as an example. When his men arrived back with the Congolese miner, they were carrying packets the size of cigar boxes wrapped in greaseproof paper, detonators, a roll of wire, a battery and an electrical initiator.

Makuma, whose knowledge of geology, physics and chemistry was clearly limited, looked down at the fellow. 'If you break the diamonds, this will happen to you.' He turned round, bent down and pushed his knife, filthy-bladed but honed sharp, into the young Swiss fellow's stomach from the side, and pulled the blade laterally across his abdomen, sawing through the heavy abdominal muscle tissue as he went. The man's eyes widened for a second, his brain unable to deal with what was happening, and then he screamed an animal bellow of pain as his intestines and viscera spilled on to the dirty floor.

The international search and rescue coordination centre took the transmission from the life-jacket transponder and plotted it.

Emergency transponders are tracked globally. When activated they can lead rescuers – everything from a Nimrod S&R aircraft for downed aircraft or ships in trouble, down to avalanche rescuers with small hand-held radio direction-finding equipment – right to the spot.

The people who watched the screen were experienced and had seen mistakes and hoaxes before. They had once talked Glasgow police on to an emergency transponder that was transmitting, but in fact was sitting in its life jacket on top of a wardrobe in that city. They had dealt with hoaxes, people who set them off just to watch the emergency services turn out, or attention-seekers, but they never ignored an emergency transponder. Once or twice a day there were genuine emergencies, and somewhere on the globe, someone with a transponder was in trouble.

In fact, they were keeping a watch out for this one, and the moment it came on air, they began to record the signal emission, while another of the two duty staff phoned the number they had been given. It was a Portsmouth number. It was answered immediately.

'Turn your receiver on,' the staffer said. 'Your transponder came on air, exactly where you said it might, thirty seconds ago. What? yes? The Democratic Republic of Congo. Map ref . . . OK. No problem. I hope they're OK. Cheers.'

At Royal Marines Headquarters, the Royal Marine warrant officer, one of two sitting in this early, switched on their receiver and the tape deck it was attached to, while the other pulled out the sheet that described the codes.

'Fucking 'ell,' he said. 'Heraklion's gone pearshaped. Its

option blue.' He made two phone calls, one to his boss, the 3rd Commando Brigade ops officer, who was at home and in the shower, and the second to PJHQ at Northwood, where a marines officer, a major reporting to ACOS till these lads were out safely, made three calls himself and then walked over to a whiteboard. The board title was Operation Heraklion. Against the egress column he wrote, in that colour, the word BLUE!

Tenta

The miner, who had used explosives on and off for years, had always used them in mining operations, where they drilled a hole and inserted the charge. The fact it was inserted in the hole meant the energy was contained, and that was its real power. He hadn't used it much on this site, because this was water mining, sifting the riverbed for diamonds, and he only occasionally used it to move a piece of the riverbank.

He had also never blown something where the charge would be attached to the outside, so he made sure he used plenty. Three charges. One on each hinge and the third on the lock itself. He was pretty sure that he would get the safe open, but he wasn't at all sure what would happen to the immediate area, so he told everyone to leave the office, and praying to God, he pressed the initiator switch. The blast was impressive. It blew the fly screens in the windows out, lifted the roof and blew off the office door, sending clouds of dust into the air.

Three Unita men ran forward. The safe was open, the door was hanging on one hinge, but the opening was wide enough to get a hand into. There was what the engineer had said there would be. Some Central African Francs, some papers, a petty cash tin and not much else.

Makuma, six feet four and eighteen stone of him, rounded on him, lashing out with his fists and boots, demanding to know where the diamonds were. If he had listened to the man he would have heard in among his dying words, his pleas, but he didn't hear it or didn't believe it.

His rage satiated, he looked down at the body, kicked it once more and stepped back. He reached into his pocket and pulled out a piece of folded newsprint and read it, his lips slowly forming the words. He read it twice and, satisfied, he folded it back up again and put it neatly in his pocket. Then he went back into the ruined office and looked down at the white man. The eviscerated young Swiss fellow was finally dead, killed by the massive blast only two feet from his head, and flies were now hovering over his intestines.

Makuma looked at him, thinking. There were diamonds here. Many diamonds. So where would he put them? Where would he hide them? He knew what he would do. Bury them somewhere. Where would a white man hide his diamonds? Where would he take them? The other whites! The mission! Ndube was right. They would be at the mission. He would give them to the dried-up old mothers of whores at the mission! He began to yell orders.

Brazzaville

Colonel Cheyne was called into his comms room by the corporal. It wasn't radio comms coming in, but the satellite phone. PJHQ at Northwood. He took the call, spoke for a few minutes, hung up and looked at his number two, the ops officer, Major Webber, who just walked in.

'That was Northwood. RMHQ have picked up transmissions. Doug has activated his transponder. They have gone option blue.'

'That means—' Webber began.

'They are cut off. Can't get back to the road for some reason,' Channing uttered. 'And Doug wouldn't have activated that bleeper unless that meant some risk attached for his people. They have asked *Winchester* to get a move on and once she is in range to get her helo up and try and get comms. They have also been on to the French. This has opened up their ROE, so right about now our colleagues down the road will hopefully be getting an authorisation to assist.'

Webber nodded. The French contingent had a pair of Super

Puma helicopters in Brazzaville at the airport, and they had previously offered to assist the British with non-combatant evacuations, and if necessary do it without the permissions of the authorities in either country. It was high risk, however.

The first time they had flown, within days of arriving, they had ignored local advice and ended up taking ground fire from somewhere, and they thought it was from DRC troops. The Puma had limped back trailing smoke with a very embarrassed and very pissed-off pilot.

'Get on to them. Let's see how soon they can get going,' Cheyne said.

Webber nodded again. He was already thinking it through. He knew what Doug McLean had taken and he was now imagining what he would be doing, going through his available resources in his mind: His CSM is very good. One troop officer – young but smart – and he has specialists. He has a sergeant signaller, good man. Troop sergeant in Two is a swimmer canoeist, an SBS bloke, on a broadening job away from the Boat Service, with excellent skills. Sergeant in Three is a PW1, a weapons man. He has got two assault engineers, four snipers – one of them has done the weapons instructor course – and another marine, sniper-trained but missed his last 1000-metre shot. He has a leading medical assistant and two vehicle maintainers. Good skills base for ops.

The good news was that HMS *Winchester* would have begun broadcasting already, trying to raise them. She could belt out 500 watts on her communications, and while McLean's HF320 could only manage 20 watts on the skywave, if they had their antenna up, they might be able to pick up *Winchester*'s comms, but they would be unlikely to be able to reply. So, they are stuck in there unable to move back to the road. He has troop and section weapons and some Claymores and kit from the French, enough to make themselves an unattractive target prospect. Not only could they shoot back if they came under fire, but after all, he reasoned, Britain wasn't a combatant nation in this conflict, and so no sane person would attack them directly.

But then again, he reasoned, this is Africa.

171

Mike Lunnon-Wood

Tenta

Makuma got his men loaded with the usual shouting and
yelling. They were carrying what booty they had found, mealie
meal, tinned food, sorghum, bread, cigarettes, beer, some cheap
Zimbabwean cane spirit, rolls of fabric, sweets, crates of Coke
bottled in Lusaka, odd bits of clothing. One man even had two
cases of Sunlight soap. Others were arguing over what to do
with other things. One fellow was attaching a small donkey
cart to the back of one of the trucks and another was still
passing cans of kerosene up to his freind as that truck pulled
away. Much to everyone's amusement – except the man who
had stolen it – the driver of the truck with the donkey cart
wired to its tailgate put it into reverse gear to move back to
get around the truck in front. With a crunch the cart tipped
over, ending up under the back axle, and everyone laughed
at the thief's misfortune. They were in a hurry now. There
were women at the mission, white women there for the taking.
That and some booty. For some of them life didn't get any
better. Crowded under the feet of the Unita men in one truck,
still trussed like chickens, the three surviving European men
abducted from Yetwene in Angola sweated and tried not to
get stood on, Terry whispering words of encouragement when
he could.

McLean, aware that the full enemy force might return, had
not redeployed his own people, but rather sent up some kit,
the LAW rockets, the team who covered the road in. They
couldn't advance too far up the road or they would be flanked
on both sides by the men they had chased out of the mission,
but the 3-Troop sergeant, a weapons instructor, had moved
with a GPMG-equipped fire team far enough up the road that
they could see half a mile along its rutted surface. Any vehicles
coming down that route would come under his fire. He also
had the troop's two snipers with him.

With the immediate area secure, and confident that they

172

would get as much warning as they could expect, McLean
had begun his second phase. He had prisoners digging graves
– three of them – beneath the trees along the riverbank. The
bodies of the two nuns and the marine who had died in the
firefight would be interned here at the mission. Other prisoners
had dragged the bodies of their dead comrades round the back
of the mission into the open ground between the chapel garden
and the trees, out of sight of the civilians.

Inside the building in the clinic Penny Carter and Gubby, the
LMA, were working on the wounded marine. He was stretched
out on the high, narrow operating table.

She had decided that she wanted to go into the wound at
the entry point and suture several blood vessels, and with
a hefty dose of local anaesthetic in the area, the marine
was quite happily chatting as she worked on him. She was
back in full doctor mode now after a momentary relapse a
few minutes before. She had been doing her basic prep and
had gone to take his pulse when she realised her watch was
gone. The lovely, big, chunky, black-faced, luminous watch
with the big, red sweep hand, which her parents had given
her, was gone. They had taken it. As they were preparing to
rape her, they had stolen the watch her parents had given her.
The violation hit her again. She walked away into the nursing
station and dropped her head and began to cry. Bastards, she
thought, you horrible evil fucking bastards.

'Doc, you OK?' Gubby asked.

She wiped her eyes, looking round at him. 'Yes. Of course.
They took my watch,' she said, a smile breaking through.
'Don't know why, but it got to me. My parents gave it to me.'

'Inanimate things,' Gubby said. 'You're fit. They didn't get
you. That's what matters. Get a grip, Doc, and let's get Dinger
here back to his mates so I can get a wet on,' he finished with
a cheeky grin.

McLean looked up from his position and saw two marines,
Dave Hobson and Big Jock, going through the pile of captured
weapons. His look got the response he wanted.

'We're low on ammo, sir,' Jock said. 'Sar' Major said to get the best ten of these, and plenty of mags for 'em.'

McLean nodded. The CSM – part of his job was supply – wanted everyone back to 120 rounds each, and that meant some of the lads would have to use enemy kit.

Da Silva was with him to interpret and he looked back at the man sat in front of him, one of the prisoners, one who others had looked to for leadership and who had asked one of the marines for a cigarette in English.

'What's your name?'

'Philimon, sah.' His eyes were wide. He was frightened.

'Rank?'

Nothing.

'Don't fuck us around!' da Silva snapped in bad Kongo. 'Rank!'

'Captain.'

'Where are you from, Philimon? Where is your home?' McLean asked.

'Near to Luanda, sah.'

'You are from Angola?'

'Yes, sah.'

'Unita?'

'Yes, sah.'

'How long have you been with Unita?'

'Sickeze years, sah.'

'Is this how you fight? You attack missions? Women? Violate them? Is this the Unita way?' The man said nothing. Just looked at McLean.

'Where is Makuma?' The eyes widened again, surprised that this white man knew his colonel's name.

'He went to the mine.' He pointed off to the south-east.

'How many men does he command?'

'Eh, one thousand, but there are two of us now.'

'Two units?'

'Yes, sah.'

'Two units each of one thousand men?'

'I think so, sah.'

'Are they all here?'

'No, sah. Some are at the road.'

'Which road?'

'The road, sah, from Matadi to Kinshasa, sah. And maybe some more at the railway line. I don't know, really.'

'Your English is very good.'

'Thank you, sah. I was waiter at Victoria Falls Hotel,' he said with a smile. 'In Zimbabwe.'

'Tell me about Makuma.'

The man's eyes widened. Fear. Pure fear, McLean realised.

'Why did he lead you here?'

'Money, sah?'

'Money?'

'Diamonds, sah. He said we officers would be wealthy men.'

'What will he do now? Did he have a plan?'

The man said nothing. They could come back to him, but now McLean needed to verify the rest of the intelligence, and he got up and walked away with da Silva. They found a second prisoner, one who spoke Portuguese, and da Silva interpreted.

Seventy feet away Perrin Dalton was at work. He had taken lots of photographs, some on 35-mill. film and some on a little digital camera. He had walked back to the transport, collected his overnight bag, and from it pulled out his laptop, knowing he would be fine for the next few hours anyway, the battery was fully charged. He had written the story quickly, made a few changes, and then downloaded the images from the digital camera on to the computer file. This was breaking news and not just another African tragedy. It had everything to appeal to his masters. It involved Westerners, and not just Westerners but civilians, nuns, from half a dozen countries, caught up in something barbaric, and then rescued by British troops. This story would be syndicated everywhere.

He looked at his watch. It was 0650 local. London was two hours behind. They had all day to follow up on this one, and the power of the pictures could domimate the front and then a centre spread of pages. He put the laptop down, reached into his pocket and looked up a remote dial-in number.

That done he reached back into his bag and took out what looked like a smallish, metal attaché case and flipped it open. Inside was a satellite telephone, part of the kit supplied by the newspaper. He flicked the power switch and watched the little 'battery charged' light glow with enough greens on to know he could get an uplink. He then plugged his modem out line into the port and began to dial, and then stopped as there was a massive blast followed by automatic weapon fire somewhere close by. He swore softly, an old familiar feeling he recognised as fear running through his gut, unplugged the laptop, closed both and stuffed them into his bag.

Three hundred metres away on the road in, just out of sight of the mission buildings, the 3-Troop sergeant had been settled in, waiting for the enemy to return to the mission. They had found no radio equipment on any of the captured or dead Unita fighters, so conceivably the returning force had no idea that the marines were there, or that there was any danger for them.

The lead truck, overloaded, was grinding its way over the potholed road, the engine revving high, followed by another heavy and a lightweight 4x4. Out behind them there were other trucks in a column going round the corner out of sight.

Men, heavily armed, were crowded on to the back of the trucks, and kit and equipment seemed to hang off every point. Some of them were singing, others raising bottles of beer, and from one of the trucks came the sound of a drum being beaten in a hypnotic rhythm.

The sergeant watched it get closer and then looked across at one of the men with him. They were twenty yards apart on a rise in the ground and were down the track from the gun team to give themselves the right firing angle for the LAWs, but he had another option and he went for it. He was the company's senior weapons man so the assault engineers had brought out to him one of the two RPG7s they had recovered. He pointed to the trucks, held up two fingers and pointed at the marine. The man nodded and swung his LAW slightly to the right. The sergeant lifted the heavy RPG launcher – it weighed almost twenty pounds with the rocket-propelled grenade loaded – round on to his shoulder, sighted on the lead truck and fired.

The grenade fired out of the barrel, dropped a foot or so, then as its own motor cut in, it streaked away over the sixty yards at the leading vehicle, hitting it in the engine compartment with a mighty blast. The LAW fired by his companion was away half a second later and struck its target as the first truck's nose rose into the air and it careered sideways off the road and rolled over. Off to their right the GPMG had opened up, the rounds tearing into the following vehicles as men were jumping off and running into the bush. Fire was being returned now, but it was everywhere, up in the air, back down the road, everywhere but at the marine positions, and ten seconds later, as the sergeant fired his second rocket-propelled grenade, the marines broke contact and melted back into the bush to get back to the mission before they were cut off.

Ten minutes later they were back in their lines, the sergeant peeling off to report what he had seen to McLean, furious gunfire still going off back at the ambush site.

'We saw four trucks and a 4x4, but the column went back round the bend. Couldn't estimate. Maybe another four? Maybe eight. Don't know, sir. The ones we saw were all heavily loaded. Maybe eighty or ninety blokes on each. Some of them were getting pissed, waving beer bottles, drinking, singing. We hit the two lead trucks and then the gun team raked what they could see. I got the 4x4 on the second volley but whoever was in it had baled out. Return fire.' He paused, and pointed with a bleak grin. 'Well, you can still hear it. They are firing at shadows, each other, Christ knows. A real clusterfuck. No discipline at all, but having said that, they weren't expecting trouble. Next time might be different.' He paused and wiped the sweat from his eyes. 'Oh, yes, sir. The road is now blocked, so if you wanted to go out that way, the wrecks would have to be towed clear.'

*   *   *

Makuma had lain in cover behind a rock listening to the gunfire all round him and finally realised that whoever had ambushed them were probably gone and his men were firing wildly at nothing. He stood up, yelling orders. 'Stop shooting! Stop shooting!' He kicked one wide-eyed man, who was firing rounds into the air. Gradually the order filtered down the line into the scattered groups wherever they had run to take cover.

'Leaders to me,' he called. He looked at one of his henchmen. 'Go and see what happened to the trucks and my car. You' – he looked at another – 'take some men. Go to the mission. See what has happened, get Ndube, and report back here.'

As his officers arrived he told them to move their men back, regroup, and then carry out his orders. Those orders were to spread out through the bush, and he showed them how he wanted them arrayed by drawing in the red dirt with a stick. What he had drawn was a tactical envelopment, three formations, each two companies strong, one at the centre, one on the left, and one on the right around the mission. Whoever had ambushed them was maybe still in the area and he needed a central point. He tried to figure it out. The ambush could have been done by as few as twenty men. There was certainly no sizeable force in the area. The biggest group, DRC troops, were guarding the power station at Inga many miles away. With his men at the mission he had a full battalion, and if these people were still in the area, he could track them down and make them pay. But first he needed to see what had happened at the mission, what his men had seen or heard, if anything. They were preoccupied, he realised, fucking the white women, so maybe they had seen and heard nothing until the ambush.

What he had drawn was one thing. What he got was another. Irregular troops are not trained to move in large formations. Their whole ethos is that of the small, highly mobile band operating almost independently. Moving through thick vegetation or forest in large formations requires discipline, training and planning, and is incredibly difficult. Within ten minutes, lines of march had lengthened, the main columns had become a series of groups, and some small bands of five or six found themselves on their own. Normally on a march this didn't matter. Like soldier ants, the conga line lengthened and shortened, but everyone found themselves where they should be eventually.

In a tactical environment this wasn't ideal. Groups moving faster than others overtook each other, and invariably overtook the group where their officer was moving slowly enough to make sure he didn't get lost. Most of these men weren't happy. Their natural fighting environment was the wide, open savannah country of Angola, much of it semi-arid, dry, brown, knee-high grass with visibility that stretched for ever. But they didn't complain. They were too frightened to. They had laid enough landmines in their lives to know where they would be put, and although the forest was thick, their leaders stayed clear of game trails and paths.

Francisco, the man who had been leading the white captives, herded them along with his unit and they moved out, pleased to stretch their legs and breathe fresh air.

On the move forward – on two sperarate occasions within minutes of each other – two groups of the rogue Unita fighters, very mindful that they had just been ambushed, and a bit too edgy, opened fire on each other. Then the inevitable happened. A group moving through the bush happened upon a group who had fled the mission. Surprising each other, keyed-up and ill-disciplined, they opened fire on each other, and this time there were four wounded.

One large band was moving parallel to the river, looking to link up with their command element, and inadvertently swung north, edging closer and closer to the defensive line of marines.

In the dark-green DPM, and with cam cream on their faces, they were invisible from four feet away, and when the Unita men walked into a once-cleared area that was now calf-height vegetation, they – in their fawn-coloured hotchpotch of uniforms – were very visible indeed.

In the shadow of the trees on the far side was Captain Lowry with two fire teams of his troop. He saw something and swung up his binoculars. White men.

Seven

There is a thing called the command loop. It is that decision-making process between something happening, a change in the tactical environment, that new information being moved to whoever must process it and make a decision, and then that decision being communicated back to the points where action is required.

The command loop that goes from troop to company can be from ten seconds to a full minute, from company to commando longer, and from there to brigade, and division, and on to corps, even longer, sometimes even hours or days. This is for good reason. Any intelligence or report that needs to go to brigade or up from there has, by that very fact, got major implications, maybe even at the strategic level, and the modern military attempt to get it right first time. That means think it through.

At section and troop level it is very different. This loop is seconds, and often an officer with considerably less experience than his troop sergeant will have to consider all the factors, the implications, the safety of his men and the overall objective, and make a decision instantly. Quite simply, there is not time to seek advice or call it in to his company commander.

Captain Lowry looked out, saw white men, bound and being pulled along by the enemy. Captives. These people could be assumed to be non-combatant European civilians, and therefore covered by their rules of engagement. After what he had seen at the mission he didn't hesitate. He touched his throat mic and told the section to let them pass directly in front of the position. Then, on the command when he called out to the captives, the team to his right would enage the front markers, the team to

181

his left the men at the rear. Then, while the gun team laid down covering fire, the team on the left would skirmish round on a new axis, with their LSW covering their left flank – the route the Unita men had come in on – in case there were others behind them. They would grab the hostages and make their way back to their positions, all the while under covering fire from the other fire team.

He touched his throat mic. 'On the command, after my second yell, hit 'em hard!'

He rose up four inches, filled his lungs and yelled, 'Get down! Drop down!' A second later there was a hail of gunfire as his men engaged. The Unita men were very alert. Those not hit in the first seconds were gone into the trees, the captives, bound together, pulled to the ground by the first to hear the call. As the gimmpy began its suppression fire he looked across at the left-hand team and touched his mic. 'Corporal Jacobs, go!'

The team were up and moving, the aggression levels high as they skirmished round the flank. Lowry watched them go, and as they swung round, he pointed them out to the gunner, who nodded. The gunner shifted his aim and put some fire into the trees to their right as three of them dropped into cover, the other two pulling the captives up and into a running huddle. A minute later they were back with three bewildered, frightened men.

'You're Brits!' one of them said, unable to believe that in seconds they were in safe hands. 'You're Brits.'

Five hundred yards away at the mission buildings, McLean swung his head to listen to the contact and contained himself. Wait for the sitrep he said to himself, wait for it. Thirty seconds later his earphones hissed. It was Captain Lowry.

'Hello, Alpha this is Three Zero Alpha. Sitrep. Got visual on a band of fourteen or fifteen armed men and saw figures three, again figures three white men, bound and obviously in custody. We inititated contact. We have figures two, I say again figures two confirmed enemy dead, four wounded and down. The rest broke contact. Captives now in our care. No casualties our side. Three men are British nationals. They were taken from

Yetwene mine in Angola. I say again, Yetwene mine in Angola last week. Area is secure at this time. Need a medic out here, over.' There was another burst of fire, the fast, tearing sound of an LSW, and then single shots, then a gimmpy opening up, its heavier beat thumping through the trees and then dying away. Silence again.

'Roger, Three Zero Alpha. Is that your gunfire, over?'

'Alpha, Three Zero Alpha. No. Fire is to the north, approx 200 metres, over.'

Brazzaville

The two French Air Force pilots leant over the map that was spread out on the oily work bench. Major Phillipe Pascale was in his flight suit, the top half dropped down and tied round his waist in the heat, a cheroot between his lips. He was feeling good about the world. That very morning he had spoken to his wife and daughters, the little one Danielle gushing about the new doll she had been given by her Uncle Jean, his brother.

Major Webber was briefing them as best he could, using their TPC M-3C tactical pilot's chart. At a scale of 1:500 000 it was crap as maps went for a soldier, but it was perfectly adequate for the pilots. He pointed out Tenta, and Pascale leaned closer and looked at what route they might take, tracing it with a finger. Over the Congo's territory, into the DRC, turn overhead Luozi, cross the river, then run in from the west along the river.

They had two Super Pumas, but only one with long range tanks. It had less load capacity but, with a range of about 700 miles, a much longer flying duration. The other, with standard fuel cell configurations, could take more load, but it didn't have the range to get down to the mission and back safely.

The Pumas were big helicopters. Almost seventeen feet high and over fifty feet long, with the standard twin Turbomeca Makila 1A1 engines, they could lift out four tonnes, and with fuel on board, that equated to twenty-four people in the cargo cabin.

As they were looking at the chart, the crew chief walked over with his clipboard to hand over the aircraft.

'Sir, Quebec Yankee has an intermittent radio fault on the VHF. We pulled it out yesterday but the radio is OK, so it's the antenna. A dry joint somewhere maybe. It is working now, but . . .' He trailed off.

Pascale remembered it. Reception was breaking up, just for a second at a time, but it was bloody irritating, particularly when the first objective of this mission was simply to raise the group on the ground. Everything had to be said twice. But he didn't have much choice. The other aircraft didn't have the legs for this mission. It was this one or nothing. He shrugged with a certain Gallic nonchalance, nodded, and the engineer passed him the clipboard to sign for the aircraft, the radio fault acknowledged in a remarks space at the bottom of the page. Other than a crack in the plexiglass windscreen on the right-hand side, everything else was fine. The weather was superb, with a good tail wind to get them down there on scene, the skies clear, with visibility that stretched for ever.

'OK, we raise them. Relay back. Then what? If they want to be lifted out?'

'They are cut off. We don't know why. But you'll be on scene. It's you or walk out to the west.'

'A long walk, *mon ami.*' Pascale grinned.

'It is. Eighty people, eh?'

'Eighty-four. Sixty-seven of ours, fourteen missionaries, three drivers.'

'That's four trips. Be ten hours before the last men are out.'

'Can you help if necessary?'

'Of course,' Pascale smiled. It was a glorious day, and it would be good to get some flying in.

McLean walked past his signals sergeant, who was now sitting scanning the frequencies, into the mission hospital where the doctor and his LMA were just finishing off their operation on the wounded marine.

He entered and saw her and stopped dead. She looked at him for a second or two in silence. 'Hello, Doug,' Penny said.

He was stunned. 'What are you . . .' He trailed off, not knowing what to say next, the pain returning, slashing into him like a knife.

'I'm the doctor here,' she said breezily.

He looked away from her at his LMA. 'Remember hearing about those four Brits kidnapped in Angola last week?'

Gubby nodded. 'Sir.'

'Believe it or not, Captain Lowry has just snatched three of them back and he wants a medic. Get out to him, please. CSM will show you where they are.'

'Can I leave him with you, Doctor?' Gubby asked, picking up his black medic's kit. She nodded and he darted out of the door.

McLean looked at her again and then turned to his marine, whose upper chest and shoulder was covered in a large dressing. 'How you doing?'

'Fine, sir.'

'Food alright. Boots fit? Mail getting through?' McLean asked, very tongue in cheek, trying to be normal, two feet from the woman who had almost destroyed him.

The man started to laugh. 'Everything's peachy, sir . . . aagh, that hurts.'

'That's enough, gentlemen,' Penny said, a half-smile on her face. She looked at McLean. 'I want my patient resting now, please.'

'Of course. Can you give me a minute?' She nodded and followed him out on to the veranda.

'First of all, thank you for your help,' he began. She gave a small, bitter laugh.

'No, Doug. Thank you. We would all be dead by now if it weren't for you and your men. You owe me no thanks. How are you? I couldn't believe it when one of your men told me his unit. Thought I had heard it wrong.'

He smiled fleetingly, bitterly. I'll fucking bet you couldn't, he thought. Of all the companies in the world to come in here it's mine, you deceitful, lying bitch.

'I need to know the medical state of the group.' He paused. 'We have to leave here sooner or later. Marine Clusson, the nun, Sister . . .'

'Sister Madelaine'

'Sister Madelaine, these three men coming in now. Can you look around? Give me an opinion on who can move. Walk. And who we will have to carry.'

'Walk?'

'I'm afraid it might come to that. Hopefully, we have got a helicopter lined up. We are trying to raise Brazzaville on our radios, but we are having trouble. All we think they know is that we can't get back out to the road. They have no idea that we are under attack, or that we have casualties. So we can't assume anything at this stage and need to know our options. One of those is to leave here and walk out.'

'How far?' she asked. She knew where they were. In the middle of nowhere.

'Matadi,' he replied. 'We might have to walk out to Matadi.'

'That's a hundred and seventy miles! That is impossible, Doug!' she said disbelievingly.

'On the roads, Doctor,' McLean corrected gently. 'As the crow flies it's only forty-something.'

'Only forty-something,' she repeated. 'You are going to walk to Matadi through the bush. Look,' she went on, 'I know what you do. God, I nearly married you. You guys do this stuff. Yump—'

'Yomp,' he said dryly.

'Yomp. But we have wounded, we have older people, weaker people. They can't do this.'

He let the bitterness fall away. 'Look, there's every chance we will go by helicopter. But there is a chance we might not. We will be moving slowly,' he said, trying to sound reassuring, but as if on cue, sounds of gunfire rolled past, and she looked at him, the realisation dawning.

'You are saying it will be slow because those people out there will probably try and stop us?'

'It appears that way.'

'Look. It's' – she was thinking fast – 'God, its nineteen ninety-nine. I can't believe that we have to walk out of here carrying people. Isn't someone going to come? Every time you turn on a television there's helicopters, ships, planes—'

'Until we can get communications I don't even know if they know we are in trouble here. But there are two helicopters in Brazzaville. French Air Force. The moment we get word out they can help. But we need to get word out. There's also a Royal Navy ship, a destroyer, which is going to get as far upstream as she can to help us, but that's only as far as Matadi, and that's it. She has a helicopter, but with very short range to carry loads. It would take two or three days to get resources here from the UK, and that's if they had somewhere to operate from and the authority to do it. For the time being we are on our own, Doctor. We have to accept that and work with that.'

'Can't we stay here?'

He had thought about that option. He had sixty fit men and of those ten were already preparing to use captured kit. The lads had been dipping in so they only had rations for another full day. There was food at the mission but not for this number. With a Western adversary, tonight would be crunch. You attack under the cover of darkness. But here. From what he had been told and experienced, African troops didn't like fighting in the dark, and how long would the Unita force keep attacking them? Why, was a better question. Diamonds, the prisoner said. But they could think better of it and break contact and move out today. They should have done. Their plans to rape and pillage the mission had partially failed. It was no longer a soft target. So what was keeping them here? Revenge? Unlikely. Diamonds? In a mission?

This was a Unita force. Part of a rebel army that was the military wing of a political group, and all political groups have to be aware of public opinion and the world's views. So, what was it? And whatever it was, whatever the reason, was it enough to have them hold on for another day, or another three or five days?

'No,' he replied. 'Our objective was to evacuate you people to safety. Defending a position is a tactical exercise that supports a larger strategy. You would have a very good reason to stand and fight. You would have food and ammunition in abundance and resupply and support. We don't have any of that. We will run out of ammunition, food, supplies.'

'But how long will they keep this up for?' she asked.

'This isn't a bunch of bandits. This is a very large force of Unita, a long way from their usual operating area, and they haven't come this far to give up.'

'Unita. No. The Unita I heard about see themselves as anti-Communist freedom fighters. These are just bandits. Animals,' she said venomously.

'I agree with you. Their commander is known to the mission staff. But they are out there, and as long as we are here, we are using up what we need to walk out. In a few days someone might come looking for us, but at this rate we will be unable to fight by this time tomorrow. We have to take the initiative and move while we can determine our own actions.'

'And that means what? Walking out and fighting?'

'It means using what resources I have to move you all to safety,' he responded formally.

She looked at him. 'Doug, How many men do you have?'

'Sixty-odd.'

'I thought your company was over a hundred?'

'Only two troops here.'

'And how many of them?'

He said nothing, so she asked again. 'How many? I think we are owed some honesty.'

'Between here and the main road?' he replied. 'Two thousand. Probably half of those in the immediate area.'

Her face said it all and the conversation dried up as Gubby appeared leading in the three British miners who had been kidnapped in Angola the week before.

*　　*　　*

HMS *Winchester* was now moving upriver. Her 280 crew had been working frantically and were still hard at it. She didn't look like she had two hours earlier. She was now festooned in pale blue. The UN bunting was strung from the yardarms aft, fluttering gaily in the breeze. A creative type in the PO's mess had looked up the recognition book and painted a large Democratic Republic of Congo flag on to a white sheet, and this courtesy flag was now suspended from her yardarm.

An awning, collapsible in case they needed it down in a hurry, was secured to the aft section of the hangar and spread outwards over half the flight deck, and a cassette player was hooked into the main broadcast system, so as they passed Boma – some hours away yet – they could reinforce the illusion of a foreign visiting warship on some goodwill type mission.

A shabby customs launch had chugged past at one point, its paint peeling, the confused officers on board returning the salutes of the British officers high above them, and looking at each other in confusion. Commander Channing, just inside the bridge, was grinning wolfishly as they chugged away without challenge.

She was doing twenty knots through the water, but only fifteen over the ground, the flow running at a steady five knots. Further upstream the river's pace picked up considerably, and twenty knots through the water would be only ten over the ground.

Marston, the navigator, was on the bridge, where other than for short breaks to eat or go to the heads, he would stay while the ship was moving. The river was too narrow, too shallow in places, with too many navigation hazards for him to be anywhere else. Channing had the same view. As Captain he would also be on the bridge with only the OOW, the officer of the watch changing with the watch-keepers.

Channing's round-table meetings were now all held on the bridge, and the latest had been to advise his department heads that Operation Heraklion had struck a problem, the nature of which was as yet unknown, and they were now on foot and had reported that their only way out was to head for Matadi.

This put a whole new series of issues on the agenda. Instead of arriving at the same time as the marines, lifting them out and heading back downstream, they now might have to wait somewhere.

The options were on the table now and Channing didn't like any of them. Below Matadi there was just too much traffic to be discreet. You couldn't park four hundred feet of warship round the back of a chip shop. The only other option was above Matadi to the base of the rapids. They were substantial and the first point at which the river became unnavigable. Three or four miles up from Matadi, they could stooge round there for a while and be out of sight to a degree.

The MEO, the mechanical engineering officer, still had most to do because the ship was now going to be in a freshwater environment for what could be a few days. Pumps, air conditioning, firewater inlets, main coolant intakes – all worked up for a short foray – would have to be watched closely. In addition, although the protection for the gun crews on the exposed upper works was finished, the engineering team was now split, some below doing what they could along the passages on the main deck to protect the MCO and ops room, and a handful of others up in the bridge doing the same thing. They had cut steel bulkheads out of accommodation areas and were using them as a second layer, and where they could, they were stuffing the area in between the outer hull or bulkhead and the inner layer with whatever they could find – rope, stores, anything that would slow down or catch an armour-piercing round.

Jenny Teller, the operator maintainer, was working in this group when one of the others looked over at her, another of the few women on board. 'Bet you didn't expect to be doing this, eh? Going up a river in deepest, darkest Africa?'

'Naa, you're right. Think anything will happen?'

'If the shit hits, we'll be well down below the waterline. It's them lads up on the director's platform that'll be in the thick of it. Nellie and that lot.'

'What's he like? Nellie?' she asked.

'Tusker? He's OK. Straight, ya know. I've been out wi' worse. Bloody nearly married worse.' She grinned back. 'Why? Fancy him, do ya?'

'No,' Jenny replied.

'Bollocks. Anyway. He's a good bloke. But don't do nowt out here, don't even encourage him, or one thing will lead to another and you'll both be for the high jump.'

Jenny looked at her. She didn't have much time for men. Most of the ones she had known were either unemployed, and therefore alternately angry and resentful, or insensitive, shallow bastards. Tusker seemed nice enough, and he had got the short edge of her usual reaction to approaches from men, however nice he was. Maybe, she thought. Maybe. Finished there, she crossed the four feet into the main communications office. An extra plate had been welded on to the outside wall, and just feet from her the comms ratings were trying everything to raise Operation Heraklion. Punching out 500 watts on their radio transmitters, they began and kept calling the marines.

'Golf Zero Alpha, Golf Zero Alpha, Golf Zero Alpha. This is *Winchester*. Do you receive, over? Golf Zero Alpha, we have your blue. I say, we have your blue. Bravo, lima, uniform, echo. We are proceeding to uplift at blue. We will be in range for helo ops at fifteen hundred hours. I repeat, helo airborne at fifteen hundred hours, using VHF, VHF. If you are hearing this, give three longs. I repeat, three longs on your transponder. Over'

The ops officer ducked his head round he door and passed the rating at the radio console a message. 'Include this in the call.'

At Tenta mission the signals sergeant caught something and looked across at da Silva who had been co-opted back into his aerial-holding duties. 'Hold it! Back a bit, come round. Hold it!' He wound up the volume, eased the squelch, pulled on the headphones, and closed his eyes to concentrate.

'. . . at fifteen hundred hours. I repeat, helo ops at fifteen hundred hours, using VHF, VHF. If you hear this give three longs on your transponder. I repeat, three longs on your transponder, over.' There was a fifteen-second pause.

'Golf Zero Alpha, Golf Zero Alpha, Golf Zero Alpha, this is *Winchester*. We have your blue. I repeat, we have your blue. We are proceeding to uplift at blue. Stand by. We will have helo ops from *Winchester* at fifteen hundred hours. Helo from Brazzaville, I repeat, helo from Brazzaville airborne at 0850, helo from Brazzaville airborne at 0850, echo tango alpha your location 1030 local. I repeat, echo tango alpha your loc at 1030 local. If you hear this give three longs on your transponder.'

'Yes! You fucker!' The signals sergeant pulled off the headphones and punched the air. He scrabbled around in his tunic pocket and pulled out the transponder, eased the battery back in and out to give it three longs, and then touched his throat mic to talk to Major McLean.

McLean was with the three British men as Doctor Carter gave them the once-over. All had lost body mass, and were thin and weak, but other than one with a cut that had gone septic, they were in good condition considering their ordeal.

One of them, Terry Harris, looked at McLean. 'I had thought that you came for us, but looking around . . .'

'No,' McLean responded. 'I'd like to say we had but we didn't. We had no idea you were even here. Your release is sheer good fortune. I think you can expect to be quite disoriented for some time. Doctor Carter will know better, but you must certainly be hungry. I'm sure someone can find you something to eat.'

'Tea,' Phil, one of the younger pair, said. 'I'd like about ten cups of tea.'

'I'm sure we can organise that,' McLean said with a smile, adding, 'There were five of you reported missing.' The atmosphere changed dramatically.

'They killed Don the day we were taken.There were four of us until a couple of days ago,' Terry said.

'James. James was the fourth,' Tony, the other youngster, said. 'Their colonel killed him. Kicked him and kept kicking him till—'

'You don't have to talk about this yet,' Penny Carter said softly. 'Not till you are ready.'

'I'm ready,' Tony said angrily. 'I am fucking ready! James was tied up, tied to a tree. We all were. He kicked him till he moved no more, and then he – he cut his head off with a knife. When he had done that, he used it as a football. Kicked James's head along the ground and shouted "Goal!"' he said angrily. There was a second of silence and then he looked at McLean. 'That's who's out there. That's who you're up against. He's a fucking nutter. Believe me, now. This man is certifiable.'

'I believe you,' McLean replied, and then he straightened up as the radio message came into his earphone. 'Zero Alpha, Zero Alpha.'

'Zero Alpha, send.'

'Sir, we have comms coming in from *Winchester.*'

'I'll be right there.'

HMS Winchester

Because, in the course of her duties, she might be required to perform search and rescue work, in among the impressive state-of-the-art electronic equipment aboard HMS *Winchester* were the same receivers as used by the international S&R centre in the UK and installed at RMHQ. The small box took the signal direct from the satellite, which had plotted the position of the transponder, and threw that position up on a small LED screen at the same time as sounding an audible alarm, a beeping sound rather like an alarm clock.

The alarm going off surprised the MCO communciations ratings, one of whom had been looking at it and wondering if it would ever go off. They had been transmitting for an hour now.

'Shit! There it is!' she shouted.

'Is it ours?' someone asked.

'Dunno. But it's three longs. That's a GPS fix. We need a map.'

'And some bastard who can read it,' the PO muttered. He scooped up the telephone handset.

'Officer of the Watch, MCO.'

'MCO, Officer of the Watch. Go.' Also on the bridge were the Navigator, the Captain and the XO.

'Bridge, we think we have a response from Heraklion. We have three longs coming in from a GPS position—'

'Get this down, please,' the OOW called to the yeoman, but the Navigator, Lt Marston, was already on it. 'I have it,' he replied, bent over his chart table. The coordinates came through, and in five seconds he looked over at the Captain and raised a thumb, a big grin on his face.

'That's them!' he said.

'Outstanding! I'm going down,' Channing said, and he slipped out of his seat and began to make his way down the three levels to the MCO.

When he got there, creative thinking was already underway, the PO and his two comms ratings were standing with a third, an operator maintainer from mechanical engineering who was bullet-proofing their bulkhead.

'What about morse?'

'No one uses morse any more, encrypted bursts more likely for them, and anyway,' he grinned, 'they're blokes who dress up as trees.'

As Commander Channing stepped through the hatch, the youngest rating, the operator maintainer, was about to speak, but at the sight of her captain, she closed her mouth. It was Jenny Teller.

'Carry on,' Channing said. This was the MCO. These were the experts. He hadn't seen the mechanical engineering patch on her arm.

'Speak,' the PO said.

'Well, sir. I thought that we could do a Q and A. Give them some questions in – each only requires a bleep answer. We can learn a lot—'

'Like?' he asked.

'Like, what prevents you returning? Transport, one bleep.

Road closed, two bleeps. Enemy activity' – she said that rather embarrassed, it sounded melodramatic – 'three bleeps, and so on. If it's three bleeps, is it finished – one bleep – or are you, you know . . . still shooting at each other – two bleeps . . .' They all looked at her, she thought, like admitting that there might be something seriously wrong was raising the ante, and bad form. 'Well, you said, sir, that it could be hostile.' She was quite wrong. Channing was chuffed. 'I did,' he replied. 'And that's good thinking! Well done.' He looked at the PO. 'Ask the XO to join us. Let's work out what we want to ask.'

'What about the RM sergeant, sir? Connors,' the PO suggested. 'He may have some input on the soldier stuff.'

'Good, get him, too.' Ten seconds later it was over the main broadcast system.

'Do you hear, there? XO and Sergeant Connors to the MCO. XO and Sergeant Connors to the MCO.'

Five minutes later they had worked up a bunch of generic questions, and then Connors spoke.

'If they are in contact, sir, then resupply. We need to know if they need resupply, and then that first helo out needs to take 5.56 and link for the GPMGs. Also, if they are in contact they may need casevac on the return.'

'Do you need ammunition? One long bleep.' The woman comms rating spoke as she wrote it out. 'And do you require – what was it?'

'Casevac. Casualty evacuation,' Connors explained. 'Move their wounded out.'

She went pale for a second, this was all getting too real, and looked down at the pad. 'That will be the fourth and fifth in the second batch of questions.'

'That's probably enough for now,' Channing said. 'Let's get it on air.'

'Sir,' Connors said. 'I'm happy to take my detachment out to support them till things are worked out.'

Channing looked at him. 'I'll think about that, Sergeant, but there are other issues to consider and I might need you here.'

For issues, read mission slippage, Connors thought. Jesus.

They are already talking slippage. He knew about slippage. When you commit more and more resources to a situation that should never have happened, or should have been contained. When the planners started quoting slippage, they were already admitting that they wanted no more resources expended on what might be a no-win situation. Vietnam was the classic. It began with a handful of advisors and US marines, and ended up with half a million men under arms. Clearly the Captain was already considering the possibility that to put him and his detachment in to support the 40 Commando lads might be a resource committed and possibly sacrificed on a no-win situation.

Channing looked at the young woman, who was back down on her knees on the deck, stuffing laundry tightly into the spaces between the two layers of steel, the one who had made the Q&A suggestion.

'Sorry. I should know everyone on this ship. It's Jane Teller, isn't it?'

She looked up, stunned that he even got her surname right. Her name patch was smeared, and he hadn't read it there.

'Jenny, sir.'

'Well, Jenny, lateral thinking. A rare thing. What else are you good at?'

'Numbers, sir,' she replied. 'I like numbers.'

'Well I have better uses for a brain like yours than that task you are on. Want to work with these people on this? Keep the ideas coming?'

Her face lit up. 'Yes, sir!'

Channing looked at Selby, his XO. 'Make it happen.'

0910 hrs

Makuma was glowering, pulsing with anger. Not only was whoever attacked him still in the area but they had attacked his cadre at the mission, killing and wounding many and frightening the rest into the bush. Now they held the place, and the people with the diamonds. Ndube had finally turned

196

up and reported his version of events. He had been honest enough to admit he didn't know how many there were, but he had seen three trucks from the forest. 'But,' he said, 'to have routed the men, there must have been several hundred of them.'

'What? In three trucks, two of them small ones?' Makuma challenged. 'Did you have sentries out? What were the men doing when they drove in?' Every question made it worse, and he soon established that almost every one of the two hundred-odd fighters had been with the women – many with their weapons put to one side – and that there had been no challenge from anyone when the trucks rolled in.

'We thought it was you returning, Colonel. Victorious from the mine,' Ndube responded. He was frightened, but knew Makuma could be pandered to, flattered. 'After all,' he finished, 'in this country only you go anywhere with such boldness. Others are more like women.'

'So, who are they?' Makuma growled. Some of the men had said they were green-coloured, some said evil demons, also green-coloured, but one or two of the more educated ones said they were whites. He had thought French, Legionnaires, but Kabila wouldn't let them into the country, and another man had said he heard shouted English. So maybe it wasn't the Legionnaires. He had felt a trickle of fear when that thought had crossed his mind. He had heard about the French Legion men. Gave no quarter. No mercy. So, who? And how many of them? English, maybe? Unlikely. This was West Africa. They had no place here, no interest, and they hadn't fought anyone here since, since – he tried to remember but couldn't. It was a long time ago.

'Whites,' Ndube said. 'They are whites. But not South Africans.' He knew South African troops. Knew their ways, their uniforms. Years ago as a kid he had fought alongside them, back when they were killing Communists.

'They are soldiers. I don't know the uniform,' he said. 'Not like this.' He touched his own DPM. 'All dark greens. And short rifles, all the same.' He had seen pictures of SA80s over

197

the years but couldn't remember what they were called.

That said a lot. In an informal military force where there was an odd hotchpotch of weapons and clothing, that became the norm. When you saw a unit where they were identical it was noticed.

Makuma looked at him. Soldiers. Whites. It registered as a problem for a moment or two and then his ego and his arrogance took over, the anger building again. He would get his diamonds, and if anyone stood in his way they would die. And besides, white, green or black, they had attacked him, killed his men, ruined his trucks, made him personally jump into the bush in fear of his life. He would get the diamonds and then they would pay for that. He would capture them, torture them, kill some of them and maybe keep some for ransom. The diamonds. He looked at Ndube. 'They better be there. At the mission. You better be right.'

Ndube nodded.

A man ran into his camp. He had been looking for Makuma for at least half an hour now, criss-crossing trails in the forest, and he wasn't looking forward to this.

'Colonel,' he panted, 'Fungabera sends word. His men guarding the whites were attacked without warning and some were killed. The whites were taken.'

The men with him, including Ndube, scattered as he came to his feet like a gorilla male, bellowed and began lashing out.

Where the two sides were in contact the fighting had subsided into desultory exchanged shots, both sides now tired by the emotional tension and stress, and both husbanding their ammunition. There were sections of the line where there was no movement and McLean's marines could detect no presence.

Sensibly, the old man came in on the water, in fact by canoe, paddled by his two sons to the jetty at the front of the mission. Clearly the two sons were not impressed with this venture and paddled from hunched-over positions, but the old boy sat bolt upright, his expression saying, it's my river, always has been, and I'm not skulking around on it for anyone.

McLean's signals sergeant saw them approaching, put the transponder down, pulled his rifle closer and touched his throat mic.

'Zero Alpha, Zero Alpha, Zero. I have movement on the water. A canoe coming in.'

Twenty seconds later, two marines skittered round the side of the mission and took up positions, weapons ready, but both Sister Marie-Claire and Penny Carter recognised the old man at the same time.

'Don't shoot!' Penny called. 'He's a friend. Don't shoot!' she ran down and intercepted Sister Marie-Claire a few feet from the bank as the old man climbed out of the canoe and pushed it off. In his hand he had a burlap bag and he carried a stick, chest-high, the top a smooth knob, once a gnarled old tree root but now shiny with handling.

'Maneru. Welcome,' Sister Marie-Claire greeted him. He nodded at her and looked at Penny. 'You live,' he said in English.

'Most of us were spared by the goodness of the Lord,' Sister Marie-Claire responded. The old man nodded and looked around the group of nuns, some with Unita wounded, two still with the injured nun, Sister Madelaine, who had been gang raped. He couldn't see who he was looking for. 'The old one? My friend?' he asked. Sister Mary, Penny thought.

'She was killed,' Sister Marie-Claire replied. 'So she is with our Lord now in his kingdom of heaven.'

The old man nodded and said in his Kongo dialect, 'So, her marriage is consummated at last. She will be pleased.'

Neither of the two women understood what he had said, and McLean, who had been out at the back end of the mission, arrived in time to hear her ask, 'So, Maneru, what brings you to this place at a time of such danger?'

He looked at McLean.

'This is the . . . the officer of the soldiers who saved us,' Sister Marie-Claire said in English. 'Major McLean, this is Maneru. He lives in a village two days' walk west of us.'

'He knew they were coming. Tried to warn us. We wouldn't

listen. Tried to save me last night,' Penny said. 'Sent word that a doctor was needed in a village just a mile or so away. He was waiting there to explain, and I ignored his warning.'

McLean looked at him. Tall, thin, with greying hair and beard, he was clear-eyed, straight-backed, and had great presence and dignity. Almost noble. He put his hand out and took McLean's. He pointed off to one side and indicated that they should talk. He didn't look at Sister Marie-Claire again. There was another man present, a leader, young but an equal, and he would now conduct his business with him.

Maneru squatted down in the red dust and from his pocket produced a tin of tobacco and an old meerschaum pipe and filled it in silence. He offered McLean some of the tobacco, and when the young Englishman refused, he lit his pipe, puffed to get it going and then looked at McLean.

'You come to care for the God women?' he asked.

'Yes,' McLean responded, and then remembered his manners. 'Would you like tea?'

The old man nodded and McLean called for someone to get a wet going.

'They were warned bad men come. They are women. They not listen.'

McLean nodded. He wasn't going to discuss who ignored what, or women for that matter. He wanted the old boy to come to the point.

'I live' – Maneru pointed with the walking stick to the west – 'that way. Tonight when these *tsotsi*' – he used a word he had learned in Southern Rhodesia many years ago, meaning young troublemakers – 'fear the darkness and hide like children, I will take you. It is safer than here.'

McLean nodded. 'I thank you, but there are many of them and I think they cover all sides. Leaving with such a number of people will be hard. Also, a helicopter' – he wondered if the old bloke knew what that word was – 'is coming from Kinshasa. The nuns, the God women, will go on the machine.'

'If they go, you stay?' Maneru asked. 'To fight?'

'The machine is not big enough for all, and it will have to

200

return. Once they are safe we have no fight with anyone. But, if they attack us, then . . .' He shrugged.

The old man nodded. 'I will stay till they have gone on the *n'degi.*'

A marine arrived then, with tea served in a cup from the mission kitchen and carrying some sugar in a bright blue enamel bowl. 'The stove inside is a wood burner, sir. CSM got it going, save our hexy. Didn't know if the gentleman wanted sugar.' The marine, one of the VMs, passed Maneru the cup and watched in amazement as he spooned in four or five sugars. Maneru stirred it and sipped audibly and appreciatively, and as McLean rose, one of the nuns passed him a hunk of bread from one of the few loaves not stolen and eaten during the attack. McLean looked at it and walked over to Sister Marie-Claire.

With fifty of his men in the defensive perimeter, McLean had just six others on various tasks who also formed a reaction element in the immediate mission area. These were his signaller, the two VMs, the two assault engineers and the Company Sergeant Major. He had one driver sorting enemy kit for later use and the other brewing up a huge urn of tea on the stove. One of the engineers was scrabbling around for things he found 'useful', the other standing guard over the thirty or so unwounded Unita men they now had as prisoners, and the CSM himself was going through the stores at the mission to see what he could find to keep sixty men fed in the field. That was also McLean's worry. A twenty-four-hour ration pack was just that, and his blokes had left Brazzaville with three each. He didn't know how long they would be here, so he wanted them eating fresh while they had it.

'We have had word that a helicopter is due in at 1030 to lift you and your people out. Can you ensure they are ready with one small bag each only. Just passports, clean underwear, valuables, that sort of thing. There will be room for all of your people and the other civilians on that first run out. It will come back for us.'

'Very well.'

'Having said that, I'd like to plan on the assumption that

we are going to have trouble getting everyone out of here today. One of my men tells me the stove is lit, but they are committed in the line and I have no one to pull back in. Are any of your people up to going into the kitchen? I'd like hot food for all, whatever you can muster, and tea for everyone. But if you can, cook lots, stuff that can be eaten cold, carried for a day or so without going off. Eaten on the move. My people will reimburse you for anything you give us. Can you help us with that?'

'We can. How many of you?'

'Sixty-one. It's a lot of food,' he said.

'Left here it will only rot, and it's the least we can do.'

The nuns were now all in the central courtyard, the safest place. With them were the three local drivers, all visibly frightened by the events and the continuing rifle fire around them. Da Silva was still outside with the signals sergeant who, having found a place where he could get a signal, 'wasn't bloody moving', and ducked every now and then as a round buzzed past them. This was what da Silva noticed, his memories of his own time as a soldier flooding back. The sound of bullets in the air. They buzzed, cracked, whirred. They were anything but silent.

He was jotting down the questions as they came through from *Winchester*. This was the second batch of five. That done, they called McLean over to get his answer to each and then sent the answers back with the transponder.

Perrin Dalton was moving round the nuns, talking to them, learning what he could about them and their pasts, filling in the human side of the story, in particular, learning what he could about the two dead women and the surviving American woman, Sister Madelaine. She was now sitting up, but in deep emotional shock, in an almost catatonic state.

HMS Winchester

They were now four hours up the river, moving at ten knots over the ground. They had passsed the big fork in the river where the wide, brown waters passed either side of a huge island called Grand Isle Mateba. As the island narrowed at its western end, Channing knew the town of Boma would heave into view. This was where the honorary British consul was trying to find them a pilot for the last stages up the river to Matadi, much narrower and faster flowing.

Outside the facade was complete with awnings, bright-blue bunting fluttering from the yardarms and masts and music playing. On the bridge all was reality, and Channing was looking at the latest set of answers back from the beleaguered marines and their non-combatant civilian charges at Tenta.

'Oh dear,' Channing said, almost under his breath. This was one of his idiosyncrasies. He was a man who used four-letter expletives in almost every conversation, but the worse things got, the less he used swear words, and the more he understated things, until his men knew, when things were getting really serious, he would be using words like an aging country vicar at a tea party.

'This is not good at all.'

'Captain, boat leaving Boma, heading our way.'

He was looking at the replies that had come in. They had put together thirty-five questions so far and the picture was becoming bleaker by the response. He reached for a signal pad.

The OOW was looking out through huge binoculars. 'Customs launch by the look of it.'

Northwood, Middlesex

People of various ranks and from various services were hastily gathering in the ACOS J3's office at PJHQ. They were all J3 SO1s, commanders, ops people. There was someone there from Met, from Navigation and Royal Marines, and they were waiting for people from J2 – Intelligence – and J4 – Logistics. The signal from HMS *Winchester* was being passed round while they waited for the others.

'It says here two thousand. This isn't a typo, is it?'

'Not from Channing,' the man who had passed it to him replied. 'If it says, "McLean reports prisoners interrogated say enemy force possibly two thousand," then that's what we work on.'

'What about McLean?'

'Shit-hot,' the marine answered in defence of his comrade-in-arms. 'CO 40 rates him very highly.'

ACOS entered then, followed by a rating, with a huge map board, a map of the western DRC, Congo and Angola under a clear plastic wipe-off surface. Another carried charts of the Congo River.

'Stick it up there against that wall,' he said. He drew a red circle round the word Tenta. 'Right, how do we support them and get them out? What are our options?'

'For now it's got to be *Winchester*,' someone responded.

The J4 team, two of them, arrived then, and ACOS (Sea) looked round. The place was getting crowded and the intelligence people were yet to arrive, and ACOS (Air) was on his way over.

'PO Fletcher.'

'Sir.' Fletcher, who was his writer, popped his head round the door. 'We are growing in number. Find us somewhere else to work, would you?'

'Done, sir. You have 3/4 and 3/5. They are sliding back the partition now. And the Chief of Staff has cancelled his 0900 at the MoD and is on his way down.'

'Very well. Let COS's sec know where we are, will you? Let's move, people.'

As they trooped into the hall – an RM major lugging the map boards – they were joined by another officer. He was a serving major and head of public relations at the PJHQ end of things at Northwood. His job was briefing the media and managing the interaction between Northwood's military people and the ever-hungry national press, and providing purely factual imformation. His rather cynical view was, if you give them the facts, they don't have to make them up.

'Sir, the media. I know the original decision was to keep

this under wraps till they were back in Brazzaville, but I think we should prepare a statement.' The Fleet PR man was not military, but a civil servant, a grade seven, and he had long made it his personal rule never to call anyone less than three-star rank 'sir'. But he was a mere major and spent a lot of time calling lots of people sir. 'That was also HQRM's view, but I think we must revisit this,' he finished.

'This soon?'

'Yes. I think so. British forces are under attack, and returning fire in the process of completing a humanitarian act. You might keep it quiet for a few hours, but the PM or Secretary of State for Defence will want the house advised. That will happen at 1400, or shortly afterwards. We need to get a statement prepared and agreed before then, and put together a media briefing team and a press conference for 1500 or thereabouts. I've got to liaise with Fleet PR too.'

'What do you want to do?'

'Grab a moment with COS before you start. If he's happy, then I can get that underway for you. I'll have something for you and COS to look at within the hour.'

'Very well.'

At that moment in central London, a senior official at the Foreign and Commonwealth Office was tracking down his counterpart in Lisbon, using a three-way phone call with people at the British Embassy in Lisbon. Unita, like many political organisations illegal in their home countries, had a representative office, an unofficial embassy, somewhere else. Unita's was in Lisbon, and the FCO official wanted to track down their senior representative in Lisbon and establish exactly why they were getting reports from their people that, while performing humanitarian work, they were under attack by Unita forces in a third independent state. On the basis of that conversation, its tone, tenor and content, the Secretary of State could then talk directly to the senior Unita person available anywhere and start wielding the big stick.

Boma

'He wants us to heave to for inspection,' the OOW called.

'Does he now?' Channing muttered. 'Who's got the best French?'

'Mine's not bad, sir.' This was from Marston.

'OK, let's get her stopped over the ground, holding position. Boarding ladder away.' The OOW started to call orders. 'Let's have them piped aboard. Mr Marston, you and I will meet them.' Channing grinned. 'Just interpret everything. Exactly. OK? No bloody laughing.'

Marston grinned back at him.

Fifteen minutes later, three DRC officials were coming up the boarding ladder to bosun's whistles and shouted pomp. This was all way over the top, but Channing was betting they had never seen a foreign warship up here. He stood resplendent at the side of the gangway, waiting to greet them. Two minutes later all of them were up in Channing's quarters, Marston translating. 'You see, there has been the most dreadful foul-up,' Channing said. 'You were supposed to know. Discreetly, of course. It's a surprise visit for your President Kabila, to present him with the freedom of the city of Winchester. An honour, sir, this ship is proud to bestow upon him.' The senior customs man swallowed visibly at Kabila's name. 'He will be in Matadi tomorrow to meet with us, and there is much to do. I don't suppose his people will be very happy with anyone holding us up, or indeed, not keeping this quiet? Eh?'

The customs men left, promising to keep it quiet, feeling very important, and loaded down with cigarettes from the ship's store.

Tenta Mission

Furby, Sloth, Kevin, Jock, and the rest of the section were settled in. They had used the terrain, scraped holes and dug in where they could, and their fire team and the other team on the section now held the eastern edge, down to the riverbank and across out to their left.

'We'll be in the trucks,' Furby mimicked, looking at Sloth, who grinned at him. 'Bastard! Road's fucked. We'll be yomping out of here, boys.'

'Helo is coming in,' Sloth replied. 'We'll be going out in style.'

'Bollocks,' Furby grunted. 'The civvies might, but not us. We're scumbag fucking grunts. We're fucking walking out. Feel it in me blood.'

'Yeah,' Kevin responded, 'but will these cunts follow us? They don't look like leaving. It's either us or the mission they want. Tell you what, though – if it is us and we piss off and they chase us, I will personally be setting records for distance covered in light order.'

Furby grinned and Sloth joined in. 'Aye, me too. These bastids will be following a trail that began in my arse, ran down my legs, and on to the ground. A wide brown trail all the way back to Norton Manor. Anyone want to carry my gun? When I am terrified I run better without it. The only man faster will be Kevin with his go-faster Gucci boots.'

Furby was sorting through some food from his pocket. He found some biscuits – the infamous garibaldi biscuits – pulled off the green foil wrapper and bit into one. 'Tell ya what,' he said through crumbs. 'We could all wear numbers, and make it a race.'

They started giggling then, like a bunch of kids, and Biscuit looked over and shook his head. This wasn't atypical. With Royal Marines, the worse it got, the more they joked about it. It was usually a sign of solid morale, but as a man who inevitably took the bleak view of everything, it always surprised him. It was when they went silent you had to worry.

About a minute later they heard the helicopter.

Phillipe Pascale looked out of the plexiglass viewing port at his feet. The rainforest stretched out ahead like a green carpet that went on for ever. To his right and behind them was the Congo, the green canopy stretching to the north as far as the eye could see, the odd patch of cleared ground with some cultivation the only thing to break the image. They had been in DRC airspace for a short time now and down to the left was the river, broad, almost a mile wide, brown, swiftly flowing, mighty. Even from two thousand feet it looked imposing. Across the other side the rainforest petered out and became fawn-coloured grasslands, savannah country, with ribbons of trees following watercourses and the smaller rivers and streams feeding the main river. Several attempts to raise the British troops had failed but he knew why. Until they heard his approach they would be on their own channels. Once they heard his engines they would switch over to aviation frequencies. The update from Brazzaville wasn't good. They would definitely be coming out. There had been an armed incident with some group or other and they had casualties. The approach they had agreed was in over the river, but the Puma was big – very big – and very easy to hit, and he wanted to reduce the chances of that. An approach over a mile of water was offering up a target if they were still in the area. Without better intelligence they were better coming in over the trees, reducing the time she was visible to anyone below.

His co-pilot pointed out of the windscreen to the left and up the river. There, ahead, a clearing, red corrugated-iron roofs. Time to cross the river. Pascale nodded, shifted slightly in his seat and brought the big machine into a tight turn, losing height, and bleeding off some airspeed. The mission was now just a couple of miles away.

Back at the mission buildings McLean could hear it too and looked out trying to work out which direction it was coming in from. That way, he thought. East. Sounds like they are coming in from the east.

'Raise 'em, Sergeant. Let them know we can hear them. Suggest they come in over the river from the north.' He was relieved. They could get the wounded and civilians out, hold until the helo came back. If necessary do a fast egress, a quick yomp somewhere a few miles away and await uplift on the helicopters return trip.

The signals sergeant was using the LZ Common frequency and picked up the handset in time to hear their first call coming in. 'Golf Zero Alpha, Golf Zero Alpha. This is Quebec Yankee Four.'

The signals sergeant could hear it now, it was definitely somewhere to the east of them and getting closer by the second. Dalton, his digital camera out ready to photograph the landing, was beside him and people were coming out of the mission building, the nuns with small bags, the three Englishmen, da Silva at the rear.

'Shit. He's going to come in right over them! Warn 'em!' McLean snapped.

'Quebec Yankee Four, Zero Alpha. Your approach to Lima Zulu is hostile. Repeat, your approach Lima Zulu is hostile,' the signals sergeant called. 'Suggest you approach from the north. Turn right, turn right, over.'

'Golf Zero, Quebec Yankee. Sorry, we missed that. Breaking up. Say again, say again, over.' They were closer now, the heavy beat of the rotors reaching them clearly.

'Quebec Yankee, be advised your approach route to Lima Zulu is hostile. Your approach to Lima Zulu is over enemy-held ground. Suggest you approach from the north. From the north, over. Turn right, turn right, over.'

'Golf Zero, roger. You say north is hostile? North is hostile?'

'No, Quebec, No, your flightpath is hostile. Abort, abort, abort . . .' and as he said it, there was a ripping sound, heavy ground fire was arcing up, and the signals sergeant looked up from the radio.

'Fucking thing!' Pascale snapped, going for the power settings, discs forward. There was no mistaking the word abort, and as the big rotors clawed at the air, he hit the right rudder pedal, looking out at the river to his right, and rounds began to hit, like hammer blows.

'We're taking ground fire!' the loader yelled from the back.

No kidding, he thought. 'Prepare RDP. Blow chaff and flares,' he called. The rearward defence pod had chaff and flare dispensers, and as the co-pilot leant forward to arm the system, he jabbed the left rudder, then the right, his hands on the collective and the column, throwing the big machine round the sky, altering height and direction every second.

The Puma, visible now, was taking evasive action, jinking left and right. From their position at the mission they could clearly see the tracer rounds and something flashing upward, leaving a thick, grey-white smoke trail.

The signaller grabbed the mic again. 'Quebec missile inbound! Blow flares, blow flares!'

He was too late. The missile was too close, the helicopter too low, the heat emissions too strong. The SAM7 hit the French Air Force Super Puma in the jet pipe of its starboard turbine engine and exploded. There was an immediate secondary explosion as fuel tanks errupted and the helicopter was a falling fireball, its tail boom broken clear, all but one of the main rotors snapped off, that last one slowly rotating as it hit the trees about half a mile from their position. Pascale was alive as it hit the trees, still trying to fly the falling, burning wreckage, the cockpit filled with flames and smoke, his flight suit on fire, thinking about his crew, the people on the ground he had just let down, his baby girls and a doll from Uncle Jean.

There was silence. Absolute silence from everyone who had gathered to see it land – this, their link with the world, their rescuers, their lifeboat.

It was the Padre who spoke first. Still wearing his purple vestment, its richness now stained with dried blood, he sank to his knees and dropped his head.

'Lord in heaven' – beside him several of the nuns went on bended knees and he continued – 'we bequeath you the souls of these brave men, who ventured in harm's way to save the lives of others' – If any of them are still alive, Lord, he thought to himself, hold the pain at bay, make their end merciful – 'Grant them peace and a place at your side and bring comfort to their

loved ones, their friends and family in this their time of need.'
He paused again. 'Lord, we ask that as our trial continues
you look favourably upon us. Grant us steadfastness of spirit,
courage and fortitude in the face of peril, and we remain in
your safekeeping, now and evermore.'

Dalton had caught the entire thing – five images of the
burning fireball falling to earth, but the last picture the most
poignant. It was of the Padre, a back view, flanked either
side by the nuns in their dark-brown habits, in prayer, as
a pall of thick black smoke rose from the crash site in
the forest.

Round at the front of the mission the mood had changed in
the small group. The three ex-hostages felt it the worst. For the
youngest it was all too much, to be so close to a way out and
to see it plucked from them. He lowered his head and began to
cry. Dr Carter sat beside him but left him to cry, knowing that
it would be as therapeutic as anything else, but when he looked
up and saw her, he quickly wiped his eyes, and muttered an
apology.

After the helo had gone in, the lads were silent. There was a
hushed twenty seconds or so while they took it in before Sloth
said it for all of them.

'Aaaah, no,' he uttered. 'Jesus, no.' He looked at Furby as
the pall of smoke rose from the top of the trees. 'They were
unarmed. Fucksakes. They were unarmed.' And the anger
began to build. No one even asked if they should go out and
look for survivors, the risk for anything less than a troop-sized
patrol was extreme and they all knew that it was unlikely that
anyone would have survived the crash. No one said a word,
each with his own thoughts.

If any of the marines felt despondent it didn't show. The
anger did, but they contained it, channelled it, and they didn't
have to wait long to use it. Flushed on their success at
shooting down a helicopter, a group of about twenty of the
Unita fighters did a fast flanking move around to the left,
the jungle off the eastern end of the compound. They moved

quickly, skirmishing through the undergrowth into an area that had yet to see any fighting, then into the clear ground under the trees, straight into arcs of fire set up by the last elements of 2 Troop to get into position.

Biscuit and his fire team, the heart of which was big Jock and his GPMG, had settled in there after clearing the mission and were hoping for a nice quiet time as they guarded the approach. This close to the water the ground was surprisingly clear of vegetation, just big tree trunks and a thick overhead canopy.

Less than two minutes later the Unita advance crossed their arcs. Jock eased the barrel of his gimmpy round and sighted on the leading bunch. He would initiate the contact, but he waited, traversing slowly until what looked to be fifteen or twenty men were visible, running through the trees towards them, all armed with AK47s and one with an RPG launcher.

He waited and waited and when they were only fifty yards away he opened fire, short bursts, keeping his barrel cool. Either side of him the section opened up, an LSW off to his right tearing rounds into the attackers, who were crumpling and falling and jerking in the withering hail of fire.

It only took fifteen seconds from start to finish. The attacking force had run into arcs of fire set by professional soldiers with automatic weapons and had been totally wiped out. There were wounded. Many of them.

One staggered to his feet, his face a mask of pain and confusion, holding his mid-section. Another scrabbled upwards, still holding his rifle, and tried to make it back into cover, but Sloth took him down. Furby looked through his SUSAT, sighted and shot the standing man in the head, and he collapsed backwards like a rag doll.

Biscuit looked at him.

'Don't fucking start, Biscuit! Like Sloth said, the French lads were unarmed. That's fucking not on!'

'Yeah,' Jock added. 'They just changed the rules. Well, fuck 'em!'

Aside from the emotional response, there was a brutal

tactical rationale that wasn't spoken of, but was understood by everyone.

In Western armies, where they cared about their people, it took seven people to take care of one wounded soldier. In tactical terms this meant that shooting someone in the leg consumed the opposition's resources and tied him down. That was preferable to actually killing the enemy. But here the thinking was different. This was an irregular force and there would be scant support for wounded. After the dreadful mass rape at the mission and the attack on the unarmed helicopter they knew there would be no quarter, no mercy shown by the enemy for any of them captured, and that hardened their resolve. The reality was that for the marines defending Tenta mission one less of these attackers simply meant one less to deal with later.

Furby bit into another biscuit but already the anger had cooled. The next wounded man who began to crawl away, leaving his rifle on the ground where he had fallen, was left to fate. Shagger, who had disappeared when the firefight started, slunk back in alongside Sloth and lay down panting in the heat.

Dalton ran back to the truck, where he had stowed his bag. With the French helicopter shot down the story was gathering pace and now had even more of an international urgency. He opened his laptop, added five paragraphs to the main story and quickly wrote a smaller piece that would need building back at the office in London by another writer with access to files, research material, and the French authorities for comment. He uploaded the digital shots from the camera, compressed them and attached them to the story and then opened up the satellite phone again. He dialled in, logged on, and then hit the send button. That done he dialled again through to the main switchboard in London and asked them to track down the foreign editor, page him, whatever it took, but get him now.

It was at this point that – hearing the one-sided conversation – the signals sergeant looked over at where the journalist was sitting under the shade on the verandah. His eyes widened and he walked over. He was, like all of them, tired, grimy, dirty, dripping in sweat, his entire uniform damp – and now he was 'well pissed-off'.

'What's that?' he asked, knowing full well what it was.

'My uplink to the office,' Dalton replied dismissively, listening carefully with his other ear.

'You fucking tosser! You have had that all along! You've been watching me trying to get some comms and you had a fucking sat phone all that time? What sort of fucking idiot are you?'

Dalton put the handset down and looked up. 'I beg your pardon!' he snapped.

'This, you cunt!' the sergeant snapped, pointing at the metal case. 'This! Give it here! We need to use it. You can have it back later.'

'I won't!' Dalton reacted.

'Fuck you. It's commandeered. 'He pulled the handset out of Dalton's grasp and picked up the phone set, kicking the PC connector cables back towards the startled angry journalist.

Dalton suddenly realised. He had seen the sergeant's efforts, but had been so engrossed in the story, and so blasé about his own bit of kit, and so much the journalist – where you observed only, you never got involved – that it hadn't occurred to him to offer them its use. But he was also angry. He wasn't being spoken to like that by anyone.

'Who the fuck do you think you are?' He went to snatch the phone back. 'If you want that—' The words were cut as the sergeant's fist flashed out and took him full in the mouth and Dalton ended up flat on his back.

'I'll fucking tell you who I am!' the sergeant snapped, realising that his promotion prospects had just ended, but he was beyond caring. 'I am the bastard trying to get some communications running and get some support in here. If you had offered this before, then those French lads would still be alive and the sisters and those poor bastards would be out of here by now. Instead, you got some pictures of them dying. What sort of a cunt are you?'

'Stand easy!' the words were snapped, but pitched low. The CSM had appeared, like he did, from nowhere. He reached down and pulled Dalton, who had a hand to his bleeding lip, to his feet.

'He had comms, Sar' Major, had a sat phone all the time.'

'Go over there. Back to your radio,' the CSM said evenly. He looked down at the satellite phone in the sergeant's hand, and then at the journalist. 'Mr Dalton. You don't mind if we borrow your kit, do you?'

Dalton, eyes down, took his hand back from his lip, looked at the blood and then shook his head. 'You ask so nicely,' he responded sarcastically. 'How could I? And while we are asking each other things nicely, could you, when you have a minute, explain how one levels a complaint?'

'I will be back in a minute, sir,' the CSM said. 'And I will be pleased to hear it.'

Harvey walked the twenty yards over to where the signals sergeant was setting up the phone. He was aware that it had gone quiet again, out on the perimeter.

'On your feet!' The man rose and faced the CSM. 'Dave, you are a prize fuckwit!'

'Fuck him, Sar' Major. There's a downed helo and dead lads and that could have been prevented. So, fuck him.'

'Three stripes on your arm, seventeen years in the Corps and you behave like a fucking pongo! He makes a complaint and you're history. All that time up the shitter. Now listen to me. Get that phone up and running. Do your job and do it like a professional. I saw what happened, and because of that, irrespective of what that fucking civvy says, you are in the shit. Deep shit. Goddit?'

'Loud and clear, Sar' Major.'

CSM Harvey walked back over to where Dalton was picking up his laptop, camera and the connecting cables. There was a burst of fire and the hammering note of a gimmpy from over on the eastern side.

'Mr Dalton, isn't it? I'm Don Harvey. I'm the Company Sergeant Major and as such responsible for day-to-day discipline. When things quieten down again I'll come and find you and then you can tell me what happened.'

Dalton nodded, his indignation already cooling. Over the CSM's shoulder he could see Captain McLean already heading over to his signals sergeant, and the CSM intercepted him and spoke briefly.

Off to one side was Maneru, the old man. He had seen the helicopter go in, the anger and the punch, but had made no comment to anyone. McLean nodded to him as he passed.

For McLean, he had more than this incident to worry about for the moment, namely, who to call first. *Winchester*, Commando or Northwood? He opted for Commando because, in amongst everything else they would need to contact the French contingent and advise that their aircraft had been shot down and post the crew missing, believed killed.

It was now 1050 local and McLean spent the next hour on the telephone.

The Padre had done all he could, comforting people within the group of civilians, and he now wanted to get out with his own people. Everything he needed to do his job was in a little zip-up green bag that contained his vestment – not something he often wore, but it helped people identify him – a Celtic cross, a hip flask of something, currently apricot brandy, hard tack for communion and two or three orders of service. He didn't need any of that, just some sweets and his lucky-dip bag of biscuits, so he grabbed his belt order and went out of the door into the sunlight, pulling on his helmet, in doing so realising that he was the only one wearing one. The marines, particularly A Company, hated helmets, and either wore their berets, floppy jungle hats or, in this heat, nothing at all. So, he took his off, pulled on his beret and five minutes later he was in the scrubby low bush at the edge of the compound clearing, belly-crawling in what he thought was a very professional, stealthy manner towards the perimeter line, where he knew the lads were.

A couple of minutes later he was looking down a gun barrel.

'Get slotted creeping around like that, sir,' a voice said. It was Kevin.

'Gosh – aah, yes. Well, I didn't want to call out,' he said with a disarmingly pleasant grin, reaching into his belt kit for some sweeties. 'Care for a chocolate eclair? They're a bit melted, I'm afraid.'

Kevin grinned and took two, passing one to his oppo. 'Thanks, Padre.'

'Where are the others?'

'Biscuit and the lads off to my right, the Love Machine on the left. Sar' Willis is about forty yards that way.' He pointed. 'But when you go, I'll take you, or you will get shot. Alright?'

'Has there been any—'

'No, not here. Biscuit's lads a few minutes ago – plenty round to the right – but we ain't seen jack shit. And that's the way we like it. You know, Padre, some of them have got fucking machetes and spears – oops, sorry.' He finished, midly embarrassed at having sworn in front of the Padre. The Padre could see he was clearly appalled at the thought of being slashed or stabbed. Shot was obviously OK.

'I see. How are you chaps, then? Alright? Need anything? I can go and get some water, or—'

'Couple of cold cans of Stella would be good, Padre,' Kevin responded. There was the crackle of gunfire behind them, on the far side of the perimeter, and the two marines looked at each other for a second. 'Yeah, and a ploughman's lunch,' his oppo added. Neither man had looked at him as they spoke, both looking back out at their section of the line. The comment was laced with sarcasm.

'Would be nice, wouldn't it?' the Padre agreed. 'Well, you two seem chipper enough. Biscuit's lads this way you say?' he asked, pointing.

'Aye,' Kevin replied looking away from the line briefly, and pointing. 'Out the back of that bush, you can see Furby's legs. See 'em?'

'Yes. Thank you.'

Half an hour later he was still at the eastern end, settled in with Sloth behind the gnarled roots, a tree exposed by flood waters. He had made his way down the line talking to each man in turn, his lucky-dip bag out. Only one had ignored him, Furby. The big man shook his head at the offer of a sweet and just looked out to his front. He looked back at the Padre as he crawled past. He shook his head softly, like he was seeing something he didn't trust. He didn't like priests. Hated them, and twelve hours ago he wouldn't have pissed on the Padre if he was on fire, but he had done the business back at the mission, and he didn't have to come on this jolly. It had been his choice to be with the company, but deep down Furby was still unconvinced that this one was any different to the rest. The snub was witnessed by Sloth a few yards away, who felt for the likeable, gentle Scots chaplain, who was trying to do his work within sight of the dead and the dying.

Only one man was still moaning out there. It was unsettling and, truth be told, if they had known who it was they would probably have put him out of his misery.

Sloth ignored the moaning and watched the Padre come the last few feet his way, thinking he was due some explanation about Furby's attitude. They talked for a few minutes and then Sloth pointed down the line at Furby.

'He's funny, Padre. It's not you, it's not personal . . .' He looked at the Padre, then pulled his water bottle and mess tin from his belt kit. 'His parents are Catholics. The local priest was the usual type. Round for tea. Very friendly. Too friendly. He came home once, caught the bloke shagging his mum. Tearful scene later. My true love and all that from his mum. His old man had pissed off by then.' He poured some water into the mess tin and put it down in front of Shagger, who rose up and drank it quickly, lapping noisily.

'So, this goes on, this hypocrisy. A few months later he catches the bloke, the priest, the celibate, Catholic priest with the big cheesy you-can-trust-me grin, trying to feel up his little sister. He went ballistic. The bastard couldn't do his next service because he had a wired jaw, and knowing Furby, he would have kicked his bollocks to a pulp. Anyway, he thinks that all your lot are suspect.'

'With good reason,' the Padre responded. 'Thanks for telling me.'

Above them the sun was high and bright and they were thankful for the shade from the trees, but it was still hot, humid. Sloth looked up and wiped the sweat from his forehead and then put the mess tin and bottle away.

'Got the time, Padre?'

'It's half past eleven.'

'Jesus,' he muttered, looking at the dog. 'We've only been here six hours. Feels like for ever, doesn't it, boy, eh?'

Suddenly the dog's ears came forward and he rose up, his body tense.

Eight

'There's a boy,' Sloth whispered. 'What have you seen, eh?' He made a soft, clicking noise, and Furby immediately turned and looked at him. Sloth pointed at the dog and then out at the forest and looked quickly at the Padre. 'You should go back,' he whispered. The Padre shook his head.

Sloth's warning had gone right down the line, passed from position to position as far as the Love Machine, and they were all stood-to, silent and ready. It is movement the eye sees. Looking out through the trees, sunlight came through in dappled spots on the forest floor. An elephant standing still would have been almost invisible but there was movement and Furby saw it. A figure, then two, moving up silently. This was an enemy recce. Now three, now four.

They weren't going to try and rush forward again, they were trying to establish where the marines were positioned, and that meant they could have a rocket or something heavy waiting. Furby didn't try and point the four figures out to anyone. They were sixty or seventy yards away, and he knew that if he took his eyes from them for even a second he would lose them, so trusting his own camouflaged position deep within a bush, he peered through his 4x SUSAT sight and zeroed on the leading man's chest. A shift to the right and – he was right – the second man was carrying an RPG7. He could take him. He was a good shot. Not as good as Sloth, who had only failed the long, onerous sniper's course on his last 1000-metre bullet, but snipers didn't count. He rated as a marksman with the SA80, and other than them, he was the best shot in the company.

He sighted on the leading man, fired, swung right, fired two

more rounds, and both figures dropped, one – the leading man
– coming up again for a second. The other two jumped back
into cover and Furby turned back and fired again, and the
leading man went down and stayed there. He looked across
at Sloth, who raised an eyebrow in question, and in reply he
held up four fingers, then did a throat-slitting motion and held
up two fingers, and then tapped his chest to show where he had
hit. Sloth nodded, grinned and raised a thumb, but the Padre –
who saw the silent exchange – felt no elation. He closed his
eyes for a second and prayed for the souls of the men who had
just died.

McLean had spoken to Colonel Cheyne at length, then direct
to Northwood, and lastly to the captain of HMS *Winchester*.

Colonel Cheyne was angry. He was impotent, and unable
to help or support his people in any way, and the moment he
was finished talking to Major McLean he was on to RMHQ
in Portsmouth and Northwood to see what was happening at
their end.

The French had been advised and he wasn't going to ask
them to risk another crew in an unarmed transport helicopter
that would need a botch job on its fuel tanks to make the
distance. That in itself would need another twenty-four hours
at least to complete.

At Northwood they had quizzed McLean at length and had to
support his view that Option Blue was all he had. A helo extrac-
tion, if that could be managed, or air support – equally difficult
to put together – could both be delivered wherever the marines
were, and if McLean, as the senior officer on the ground,
wanted to move for tactical reasons, then that was his call.

For the time being they were looking at the possibility of
trying to get Angolan government permission to fly support
ops from Angolan territory. The FCO were going to play
the ally and guilt cards heavily. The first card was that
Britain was supporting her people against a common foe. The
second was that Angolans, whatever their political persuasion,
shouldn't be attacking British troops in the Congo anyway.

They wanted permission for six Harriers and support elements to use Cabinda airbase. Cabinda was on the coast in the small Angolan enclave north of the Congo River. That would put RAF ground-attack jets less than a hundred miles from Tenta mission.

The FCO gave the idea about one chance in five of getting approval, but were going to try.

Winchester had been warned about the ground fire that had downed the French helicopter and were advised that any approach must be low over the river and in behind the mission building. They agreed one initial run, to bring in ammunition and, if possible, take out those wounded who couldn't walk. Any further helo ops would be once they had put some distance between themselves and their attackers. This LZ was just too hot.

1200
Brazzaville

At the 40 Commando HQ in Brazzaville Colonel Cheyne and his ops officer, Major Webber, were ensconced in Cheyne's room with a handful of other officers from B, C and Support Company.

'What about an ammo drop?' Webber suggested. 'Maybe we can get a charter organised down to Matadi. There must be an airstrip there. Then *Winchester* can uplift it.'

'Or, if *Winchester* can supply them for today and tonight from her magazines, then we could drive stores down there. But getting to her. According to Doug's int the road is now closed anyway,' OC Support suggested.

'How about offering the Congolese help to get the road open? Against these wankers it would take about ten minutes flat,' the major commanding B Company muttered aggressively. Cheyne smiled. Fat chance. Even if the DRC authorities agreed, no one would countenance that, not even him. That really was mission slippage, dropping headlong into someone else's war.

'How about stopping above the roadblock and having the helo pick up stores from the back of a truck?'

The options and ideas kept coming until there was a knock on the door. It was the number two from the embassy over in Kinshasa. A boat had just been over to get him and he had news from the FCO.

'The Unita delegation in Lisbon has denied knowing anything about this. They say this commander, this' – he looked down – 'this Colonel Makuma, is no longer under orders. They say he is beyond their reach and operating to his own agenda.'

'Christ,' Webber responded 'So what have we got? A two-battalion-sized force with a rogue commander?'

'What chance his troops will rebel, sir?' the OB B Company asked. 'Resist? Just refuse orders?'

'This is Africa,' the chargé d'affaires answered. 'None. He will just make an example of anyone who disobeys him the old-fashioned way. They know it. You must remember the basic African mentality. Your average African will follow the man who is strongest. Who behaves that way, exhibits the power, uses it. Since organised society began on this continent, that's been the way. There are always tribal loyalties, but in essence they follow the one they fear. From before Chaka, to Idi Amin, to Obote, to Sergeant Doe, to Mugabe. They will follow the one they fear most. Only when it's an equal contest do they take sides, and it's unlikely in a force this small that anyone has risen up to challenge this man and survived.'

'Fucking marvellous,' someone muttered. 'Two thousand of them.'

On board *Winchester* Commander Channing was now working with the new intelligence. It was now patently clear that, whatever the FCO were trying to negotiate with the Angolans, for the time being his ship was the marines' only method of support and eventual uplift. But with the French helo being shot down the ante had been raised. The enemy were now confirmed as having shoulder-launched anti-aircraft missiles. They could

223

only be SAM7s in this part of the world and you didn't need to
be a rocket scientist to use one. Stinger and Blowpipe were both
modern Western systems, and both needed complex training to
use. Not the good old Soviet SAM7. Like the other old Soviet
weapons, it was simple, robust and anyone could fire one. It
had been in use in Africa, Asia and Afghanistan for the better
part of twenty-five years and still worked well.

Which was a bugger when it was your people they aimed
it at. The difference would be that *Winchester's* Lynx was not
an unarmed transport and did have defence systems, as well as
chaff, flares and some very basic ELINT suppression gear.

But all of that was heavy and cut down her load. The aviators
were now working out what they could haul in the way of
ammo and food, carry out in terms of wounded, while also
defending themselves and still getting home.

'They want three out, right? Maybe six but three definitely,'
the pilot said, looking at the Captain.

'Yes, three wounded. But there are twelve civvy women,
the three people from the mine and the other two that went in
with them. That's seventeen holding him back, slowing him
down,' Channing corrected. 'Without them his lads can move
very quickly. I want options to get all seventeen out.'

'Well, I'd like a door gun. We can do the first seven and
still have room for a door gunner. Without that, we're too
vulnerable. No way of suppressing fire as we come in, or
answering back. Then, let's see. I mean, when they break
out, and as long as we have fuel and an operative aircraft,
if they can move ahead of the scrotes, just a mile or so, then
we can get to them again and again.'

'Scrotes?' Channing muttered. The P1's brother was a
II-Para officer. It was one of their expressions that came out
of Northern Ireland. 'You've been mixing with your yobbo
brother, haven't you?'

'Rocket pods would be nice,' the observer said.

'A squadron of Apaches would be nice,' Channing responded.
'But we don't have them. What have you got for them?' He
looked at his supply officer.

'Right, first trip – 3000 rounds of 5.56 and 6000 rounds of link.' That isn't much, Channing thought, about fifty bullets each, and twenty minutes sustained fire on the gimmpies.

'Is that all?'

'All we've got to spare. I have to resupply our lads if it comes down to it,' the supply officer said. Channing nodded.

'Main galley is doing something for immediate consumption. Also there are bread rolls, canned beef, baked beans, creamed sweet corn, cup-a-soups, sweets, Kit-Kats and stuff from the shop – smokes, matches, paracetamol, bog roll, soap, all packed up as individual ration packs – some bottled water, and stuff from the sickbay stores. Trauma stuff, anti-malarial tablets, water-purification tablets, insect repellent. It's all in bin liners, can be kicked out of 33's door.'

'What's the weight?' the P1 asked, trying to keep his tone professional. He was frightened. They had already taken down a Puma. This was one hot landing site.

'The rations, just over a kilo each, times seventy-five. Medical stuff eight kilos total.' The P1 was listening, converting it all into pounds as he did so. No problem with weight. 'Batteries?' They needed batteries, Channing knew, for the Clansmans, torches, and for the sat phone.

'Engineering is rustling something up, sir.'

At the mission it was quiet again. This lull in the fighting had lasted half an hour now, and McLean had been right round the perimeter, speaking to his people, looking at dispositions, sensing the enemy out beyond them in the forest. Now he was back at the mission building and talking with the three men kidnapped in Angola the week before.

'He took something from me,' Trevor said. 'A page from the *Sunday Times*. It was an article about Angola and diamond miners, the new yuppie adventure,' he said distastefully. 'This article was also about the other side. The lost money, the gambles. It cited the mine here at Tenta as an example of one where big money had been raised to exploit it. Maybe. Maybe he thought it was worth going after. They were all pointing at it. Much talk. One of them read it to their leader, but badly. The thing is the whole inference was that it was a gamble and that the Tenta mine was an example of something yet to prove worth the investment. But thinking about it, the inference was just that. An inference. Anyone other than a native English-speaker might not have picked that up.'

'They think that somewhere there are diamonds,' McLean summarised.

'I believe so.'

'Not just you, I'm afraid. One of the men we questioned said the same. But why the mission?'

'We didn't have much. Maybe ten grand's worth at Yetwene. So they come here. All this way, days of travelling. If they didn't find them at the mine, they can't search a million square miles of bush. I guess this is the next logical place to look. I dunno . . .' He lowered his head and wiped his face with his hands, tired, exhausted by it all. 'Fuck it. Think about it. If you were at that mine and wanted to hide something, give it to someone, who would you trust within a hundred miles of here? The good sisters of the holy order. Nuns. And these bastards probably think a) they exist, and b) they are here.'

It was possible, McLean reasoned to himself, but from what Sister Marie-Claire had said they had made no attempt to search the place methodically. They had just killed the hospital patients and then almost immediately begun the rape and trashing of the place. But if Makuma had gone to the mine, not found anything, then assumed the diamonds were here, he would have headed back knowing his men already held the place. And he was stopped on route. Hence a sustained attack? This made some sense. It was possible. There was precedent.

In 1997 when the Royal Marines had been in Brazzaville the first time, on this occasion for Kabila's march on Kinshasa, a section of marines were unloading big, white document bags that had been transported across the river from the embassy in Kinshasa. They were almost killed by a mob that were turning nasty because they believed the bags contained diamonds, and this was in the presence of the local police. The mob was all along the riverbank, expecting to be able to take valuables from fleeing Kinshasans as they stepped ashore in Brazzaville but there had been no exodus. Just the one boat from the embassy. The mob converged on it, and even local police firing their guns in the air and the prospect of having to take the bags off seven armed marines barely deterred them.

McLean had met the marine corporal who commanded the section. He had been decorated for bravery, for standing facing his frightened men, with his back to the crowd that numbered several thousand, all with weapons of some sort – clubs, machetes, spears or sharpened implements. And that was a mob, he thought. No leadership and no modern weapons. These people have both.

London
1400 British Summer Time

In London it was a glorious autumn day, the best that September could provide. Bright warm sunlight bathed the streets, taxi drivers took their shirts off, people lay on the grass in Green Park and ice cream vendors were busy with the tourists. Pubs with beer gardens did a roaring trade and at the Palace of Westminster as Prime Minister's question time was about to start, the Speaker called the house to order to hear a statement from the Secretary of State for Defence. Across from the Millbank studios in Whitehall, in the lobby of the Ministry of Defence building, a press conference was about to start. A Royal Marines Brigadier flanked by two MoD press minders would take questions after a junior defence minister had read a statement, the exact duplicate of one being read in the House by his boss.

'Acting on intelligence received, that unarmed civilians, including British, EU and US nationals, were under threat in an area of the Democratic Republic of Congo hitherto uninvolved in any fighting, a detachment of the Royal Marines based in Brazzaville were tasked to travel down to the area and conduct a non-combatant evacuation operation. On arrival there early this morning, at 0603 local time, the marines found the mission had already been attacked and atrocities of the worst kind being committed. They regained control of the situation and rescued most of the non-combatants. I say most, because it is with regret that I must advise the House that two of the civilians, nuns of the Dominican order, one a Greek national and the other Irish, were raped and killed along with some local people in the hospital wing of the mission.

Further to this, in a follow-up contact with the attacking force, they observed other Western captives, who turned out to be three of the five British nationals kidnapped from Yetwene mine in Angola last week, and after an exchange of fire they in fact rescued the three men.' There was a smattering of 'hear hears' and noises of approval.

'I also have to advise this House that the fifth man died earlier, and that the fourth man kidnapped at Yetwene was killed, according to reports, personally, by the commander of the attacking forces. We are informed they are a rogue unit of Unita, an Angolan rebel faction, who crossed into the Democratic Republic of Congo to attack the mission and the mine at Tenta.' At this point there were noises of disapproval from the Members of the House, the overall effect a low growl. 'The current situation is grave. Our forces are still at the mission, protecting European and US civilian non-combatants, aid workers and nuns of the Dominican order,' he stressed. 'They are, as we speak, under fire, and they are cut off from their planned return route by these same Unita forces. But morale is high, and after consultation with my colleagues' – he indicated the people either side of him on the front benches – 'I have charged my ministry to work out how we best support them and get them all out, hopefully safely. Furthermore I strongly commend their courage, their decisiveness and their actions to this House.' The initial shock and intense interest became a chorus of approval.

The only senior cabinet minister not present was the Minister of State for the Foreign and Commonwealth Office, who had two meetings back to back inside forty-five minutes – with the ambassadors from Angola and the Democratic Republic of Congo.

In Paris and Brussels the legation heads from the DRC, followed by Angola, were at the same moment in front of the respective ministers for foreign affairs, having huge pressure applied. In Lisbon the Angolan Ambassador was in front of no less a person than the Portuguese Prime Minister. The French were incensed by the deaths of their aircrew and their stance was unequivocal. The DRC will cooperate, or else. The Angolan Ambassador, waiting for his meeting in the outer lobby, could hear the shouting.

In the lobby of the MoD the questioning had begun, the Royal Marines brigadier fielding them like the expert he was, but the real action was taking place further up Whitehall where the Minster for the FCO was being unusually blunt.

'Let me make it quite clear. This facsimile authorisation has your Interior Minister's signature on it. It is approval for some of our people to complete a humanitarian task, and in the process of completing that task they have come under attack by a force of two thousand soldiers who shouldn't even be in your country! Now, you were unable to prevent this happening. These things happen,' he said reasonably. 'But make no mistake. We wish to support our people, with whatever it takes to do it, to get them out of there. The best thing your government can now do is to allow us to do something positive. That something is laid out in our letter, and in every communication we have undertaken.'

'I have already tried that. The President is out of—'

The Minister stood up. 'Then try again. You get on the phone. You talk to Kinshasa. Now, if you will excuse me, you have some calls to make and I have a meeting with the Angolan Ambassador. I shall expect news from you within, what? Two hours?' As he left the room, the Minister picked up the telephone and asked his senior secretary, a professional civil servant, to contact MI5 at Vauxhall Gate. 'I might want to lean on this bastard. See what they have got on him.'

The media went at the story like a wolf, the *Daily Telegraph*, three steps ahead with their on-the-ground story and colour pictures from their correspondent, who everyone now wanted a phone link with. But for some reason his phone was switched off, and when it was on, it was engaged, or callers, all wanting on-the-spot interviews and follow-ups to his now widely syndicated reports, got a terse rebuttal from someone else.

HMS *Winchester* was now just seventeen nautical miles from Matadi, the small Isle Oscar off her port beam, steering 270 degrees in 17 fathoms of fast-flowing water. There was no pilot waiting at Boma, in fact no word from the honorary consul at all.

Lt Marston and Commander Channing were both on the bridge, Marston having been there since 0430 that morning. Marston was looking at sheet 637 of the Admiralty's African west coast chart series. The river's course charted at 1:50 000 came out at well over an inch to the mile, seemingly plenty. But when rivers change flow, sand banks move and shift, and the soundings can vary by ten feet according to the season, anyone bringing a ship up here required a local pilot. But needs must, and they were on their own, powering up the river, trying to get the Lynx in range, the colourful blue bunting fluttering in the breeze, music playing, members of the crew in going-ashore rig, looking very smart indeed, waving at boats and other river traffic.

Channing, the XO, Ops and his aviators had completed their briefing and down aft on the landing deck the Lynx had been rolled out and the rotors extended and locked into position. The awning on the landing deck had been taken down and the Lynx had been loaded, with a door gun fixed on the pintle, and was ready to go.

Tenta Mission
1520 hrs local

McLean had consulted Commando HQ, spoken at length with Colonel Cheyne and Major Webber, and made his decision.

At nightfall, they were going to slip out of the mission and move west, into the bush, out to where he could determine events rather than have them dictated. He had done a third sweep round the perimeter, briefed his two troop commanders and the CSM, and now sought out the old man, Maneru, who earlier that day had offered to guide them out to his village. McLean could navigate, but in unknown country, with rivers to cross, there was nothing like local knowledge.

Maneru sat in the shade of a tree and McLean squatted down beside him.

'You saw what happened to the helicopter?'

Maneru nodded.

'Another will come, a smaller one from the river.' McLean pointed out at the dark brown muddy waters. 'If it can approach it will, but it will only take out the wounded. The rest of us stay until dark. Then we go on foot. Will you stay till then and guide us west?'

'The women. They will travel under the protection of your rifles?'

McLean nodded. 'Yes. My men will guard them.'

'I will stay and show you.'

'Thank you. We will leave when it gets dark.'

Maneru shook his head. 'No. Wait till the moon is up.'

'Why?'

'On dark the . . .' He looked for the English word, couldn't find it, and them mimed an insect biting, and slapping his skin.

'Mosquito?' McLean offered.

'Yes. The mosquitoes come at dark. The *tsotsis* will be bitten and will be awake for maybe two hours. Then they will get tired.' He put both hands up to mime sleeping. 'Then we go.'

McLean smiled at him. 'Fair enough,' he said. 'How far to your village?'

'Two days' walk.'

'How long to walk to Matadi?'

Maneru thought about that, and swept a look round the

people he could see. He had never been there, but he knew where it was, and was judging their fitness for the journey. 'Three days, maybe four for the young ones. The old women?' He shrugged. 'Longer.'

Fair enough, McLean thought. But that's walking along at a normal pace. So, really push the civvies and let's halve that. Let's aim for two, and allowing an extra day for fuck-ups, tactical movement, and LUPs on the second night, settle for three. I want to cover twenty-five miles a day minimum.

Everyone would be going – seventy-nine people – except whoever went out on the helo, and he remembered then to talk to the three civilian drivers. They would need the choice. Go with his company, go on their own. They couldn't stay, that was for sure. They would be killed by Makuma's men.

His signals sergeant called across the twenty feet to him. 'Got *Winchester*'s helo, sir.'

McLean walked over and took the radio mic. He wanted resupply in, his wounded and some of the civvies out and no repeat of that morning's tragedy. He had thought this through to minimise the risk for everyone.

'Whisky 33, Whisky 33, . . . Golf Zero Alpha, go.'

'Zero Alpha, 33. We are now twenty minutes from your location. What's the sitrep on our lima sierra, over.'

'33, Zero Alpha. Suggest you approach from the north, come over the river as low as you can, and straight in. Your lima sierra is directly in front of the mission building, between the building and the water's edge. Trees either side, but you have figures one two zero feet, that is one twenty feet, between them for your landing. We have three to four knots of wind from the east. We will lay smoke to cover you from the treeline and I will have five men to unload and reload you over.'

'Roger, Zero Alpha. We can take seven out with us, over.'

He called the CSM.

'Mr Harvey, *Winchester*'s helo is inbound. Twenty minutes. The lads are ready with smoke. I want five men to unload stores and then get seven people back into it in record time.'

'Right. The three wounded and who, sir?'

'The civvy bloke with the infected leg better be one, then ask Sister Marie-Claire. Three of her people, the weakest. The ones most likely to slow us up. But you choose 'em and have them down here in ten minutes. No bloody heroics. None of this, I'm-staying-if-she's-staying shit. OK?'

Harvey grinned and moved off. As the two driver mechanics were carrying the two wounded nuns down to the edge of the LS, he worked his way through the mission. He told the young British fellow with the infected leg wound to make his way down to the front of the mission.

'I'll stay with the other two. I'm OK. I can walk.'

'Bollocks,' Harvey muttered. He could see the youngster was just playing the game. There was no way he would be able to keep up and he knew it, and what's more he knew they knew it. A bit like someone saying 'You shouldn't have' when they got given a birthday present, it was just good form. 'Get yourself down there, lad.' Terry, the oldest of the three nodded in agreement.

Most of the nuns were on one of two tasks, caring for the Unita wounded, or in the kitchens, and Harvey very quickly found the three he wanted out on the first uplift. Predictably, all three looked at Sister Marie-Claire for a lead and she saw the look in CSM Harvey's eye. One of them was the American, Sister Ruth, who had been limping from a strained knee ligament for days before the attack, and now it was swollen with fluid. There was no way she could walk even five miles slowly, let alone quickly.

'Go,' she said. 'We will see you back in Kinshasa.'

The three women, with nothing other than the clothes on their backs, made their way out to the front of the building.

The Lynx called in on long finals, and McLean gave the order for smoke. At four points round the perimeter smoke canisters were thrown, the light easterly breeze dragging the colourful purple and green smoke until the entire forest edge was wreathed in it. The helicopter came in fast over the trees to the north on the far side of the river, dropped very low and began bleeding off speed. As it approached the bank the pilot turned it side-on, and as it settled he came all the way round so he was facing out over the water again. Before the wheels touched the red earth the door was slid back and the gunner began throwing bags out on to the ground, three marines running in one side, and two on the other, to help.

The heavy stuff was the ammunition cases. A last man stood in front of the cockpit ready to signal to the pilot, and as the last bag was coming out, the first person was going in. The last two, who should have been on stretchers, were loaded carefully, and as the last one was in, and the men cleared the sides of the aircraft, the marine at the front raised both thumbs at the pilot. He darted to the side as the pilot coarsened the pitch and dropped the disc forward. The Lynx lifted a foot, moved forward, and once over the water gathering speed, it began to gain height, just enough to skim the trees on the far side.

The whole thing had taken under half a minute.

There was furious fire somewhere back in the forest, but if the helo was the target, it was through the smoke and unaimed. The helicopter didn't get hit until it was well out over the water, and that was from the east, upriver from the mission, beyond the smoke, a hundred yards upstream from where Sloth and Furby held the right flank. Three bullets hit the machine, the second hitting a wheel strut and the third harmlessly into the tail boom, but it was the first strike that did the damage. It came through the side of the plexiglas windscreen, penetrating into the cockpit instrument panel and tumbling a good fourteen inches before lodging against a side panel.

'Everyone alright? Anyone hit?' the observer yelled, looking back. 'Check 'em,' he said to the gunner through his headset.

The Lynx didn't have redundant instrument systems, and as the pilot gained height and turned west to find the *Winchester*, half of his instrument panel was dead. He was now flying on experience, and thanking Christ that it was clear weather. He flicked a look back over his shoulder. People, hurt, blood-stained bandages, a marine with a bandaged shoulder, up on his knees helping a woman who was in a shit state.

Better see if we still have comms, he thought. He opted for

234

the lads on the ground at the mission rather than *Winchester* because he would need more height to get VHF that far.

'Golf Zero Alpha, 33.'

'33, Golf Zero Alpha. Go.'

'Golf Zero Alpha, we are clear. Took three hits and got some damage but we should get back OK. Talk to you later, over.'

'Roger, 33, thanks for your help and safe journey.'

McLean looked across to where the CSM had his blokes dragging the ammunition cases and bin liners and sacks back into the mission. He walked across.

'Let me know our supply status when you can, please, Mr Harvey.'

The CSM was grinning. He had opened one of the bin liners and it was full of individual ration packs.

With the two engineers and the two VMs going out at various points with food and ammunition, that left the eastern end for the Padre, and he moved out carefully, dragging a case of 5.56 and a sack of food behind him.

When he arrived at the 2-Troop right-flank position, he pulled the bag up and began passing out foil-wrapped packages. The lads in the main galley on *Winchester* had done them proud. Big chunky bacon rolls, three per man, with a wedge of processed cheese and a sachet of tomato sauce.

'Where'd these come from?' Furby asked.

'HMS *Winchester*,' the Padre replied with a smile. 'They've made up ration packs as well.'

'Scran!' Sloth muttered, appreciatively unwrapping the foil.

'Aye. Fucking Gucci scran!' Jock called. 'Bacon sarnies! You see, God loves us grunts after all!' He tucked in. The Padre smiled and moved down the line.

The Lynx was back on *Winchester* and the wounded had been carried below. The wounded marine had agreed to be debriefed, to fill in the gaps to help everyone better understand what had happened and what the current scene was at the mission. To get the most out of him it was thought that this was best done by Sergeant Connors, the marines detachment commander, speaking the marine's language, but they would be observed by the XO.

While the aviation artificers swarmed over the Lynx to see if they could get her up again, Connors handed the marine a couple of powerful analgesics sent up by the LMA and sat him down, feet up and comfy on the padded sofa seat in the PO's mess.

He handed him a huge mug of tea and a doorstep-sized beef-and-pickle sandwich and a plate of chips. 'Right, scran and a wet. Get that down ya, and when you're ready, tell us what happened, from the start.' Selby was off to one side, but the marine didn't look at him, just at Sergeant Connors.

He described the deserted road construction camp and the journey into Tenta.

'Then we had the contact on the road. Three lads with a corporal in a Landy drove round a bend into what they thought was a roadblock. It wasn't. Their vehicle had broken down and they wanted ours. Presented weapons at the lads, things going pearshaped quicksmart. This cunt has his rifle pointed at Corp McEwan and is squeezing the trigger but McEwan gets his shot away first, slots the first one with his 9-mill., the others take the rest. Then we knew.'

'Knew what?'

'The cunts were ahead of us. Half an hour later we can see smoke over the mission. The boss does a recce. Fucking diabolical, it was. They wuz gang raping the nuns. Killing everyone.' Then he grinned. 'We go in like the cavalry. The boys all spooled up. Fuckin' 'ell. It was like a duck shoot. They are all there lining up for their shag, weapons all over the place, and we drive in, unchallenged. Not a fuckin' dicky bird. They thought we wuz their own blokes. Well, we had gimmpies on the vehicles, snipers out, the lads charged up. There was about two hundred of them, maybe more, but it was fucking carnage. It was all over in maybe a minute. Bodies everywhere, the cunts who could run long gone for the bush.

We got secured, the medic got to the women.' He looked at the sergeant. 'Know what?'

Connors shook his head.

'They stabbed one of the lasses between the legs with a bayonet. She were an Irish lass, oh, about my age, like. Stabbed her in the . . . with a bayonet, over and over again. Why would someone do that?'

'I don't know,' the sergeant replied honestly, steering the marine back to the issue.

'What about the surrounds? Can you describe the countryside as you approached the mission?'

The Master at Arms, the man who had provided the tape deck they had played the music on, was leafing through his collection of cassettes. His taste was eclectic, with everything from the BBC's recording of the 1998 last night of the proms, to Louis Armstrong, to Works Brass Bands. He found one cassette, looked at it, smiled, slipped it into his pocket and made for the bridge, where his cassette player was hooked into the ship's main broadcast system. It was a compilation of music from the band of the Royal Marines. They could play that as they moved past Matadi. The irony would be delicious.

By four p.m. the team in the kitchen had done it. In addition to what *Winchester* had provided, they had for each person, wrapped in greaseproof paper, a loaf of bread, cold potatoes in an oil dressing, a large chunk of rich fruit cake and a boiled egg. Containers of every size and description had been co-opted into service for carrying that lifeblood, water.

The engineers had also been busy. One of them had found his 'useful things', including bits and pieces from the ruined clinic and the unburned part of the vehicle shed, brake fluid and, for some reason – probably water purification – chlorine powder.

Now, an hour before sunset, McLean sat down for the first time, a wet in his hand and his bacon rolls unwrapped. He hadn't eaten since before leaving Brazzaville almost twenty-four hours before, and he was hungry. He was lifting the mug to his lips when a shadow loomed over him. He looked up.

'Only me,' Penny Carter said, brushing her hair back from her face and settling down beside him on the step. 'Can I join you?'

'Of course,' he replied stiffly. He held out his foil package, offering her one of his rolls.

'No thanks,' she replied. 'I had some. They were bliss. Hadn't had a bacon sarnie in God knows how long.' She looked at him. 'Thanks for getting the wounded away. It was – aah – impressive.'

He smiled. 'That's the way it should be. We practise that. Should have been like that this morning.' He bit into his roll.

'And what now?' she asked.

He held a hand to his mouth and then swallowed. 'We get out of here. We got ammunition in on that helo, but they don't carry much stock of small-arms stuff, so I suspect that's all they can give us. But we have that and we have food. It's time to slip out of here. After dark, Maneru, your friend, is going to show us the way out of here.'

'And then?'

'We move. Fast as we can within the circumstances. Hopefully they will lose us, or get bored and just let us go.'

'And if not?'

He looked at her. 'Then we fight as we move.'

'Aah,' she said. 'A fighting withdrawal.'

He looked at her, surprised.

'I remembered that much.' She paused and brushed the hair back behind her ear. Her uncle had been a marine. Older than her father, he had been in Korea.

'I wish I'd listened more to his stories now. Did you know he was at Inchon?' she asked. McLean nodded. 'You told me.'

In a corps where they had withdrawn under fire hundreds of times in hundreds of incidents, some big and some small, it was the Royal Marines' most famous fighting withdrawal. The Red Chinese pouring over the border, they hooked up with the US Marine Corps and did a fighting withdrawal from the

Inchon reservoir that lasted for weeks and covered hundreds of miles.

'You never met him,' she said with a smile, like he should have, would do.

'There's a lot of people I never met. Like the bloke I caught you with. What was he, a medical rep?'

'Look, I was wrong. I am sorry. Can't we—'

'You can be wrong once,' he cut in softly, remembering the night he drove down, the song on the radio, the disbelief, the pain, the hurt. 'I trusted you, but you did it again and again in spite of the pain you caused me. Can't we what? Start over? I can't trust you, so no, we can't.'

The smile faded. 'What can I expect? I'll need to know what equipment to bring?'

'Best be prepared. Whatever you can to deal with trauma,' he said casually. 'My blokes will carry it for you.'

'Can we do it? If they keep coming at us. Can we do it? Cross all that open country and get to Matadi?'

He nodded. 'HMS *Winchester* is there waiting for us. Yeah. We can do it. We are going to try and get the helo back to meet us. Lift people out.' They could do it. If he had managed to get all the civilians out then he would have yomped his company out in a day and a half. Cover the first five miles very fast, at a jog, then the next forty miles without stopping for anything more than water and scran. That would have them well clear, and there wasn't a unit in any developing country that were as fit as his men. There would be no catching them. But with the civvies?

'I would have liked you all out, but it just means we move slower. We can get there.'

'So, if the helicopter can't get back it's just a matter of moving fast and being alert?'

'Yeah,' he responded. 'That's about it.'

Bullshit, she thought. Slower means they can follow us, attack us. Two thousand of them scattered through the bush. In real terms, if they decide to keep after us the chances of us all getting to the ship are slim.

'Doug, why am I getting the feeling you are telling me what I want to hear?'

'I'm not. Granted, that's the optimistic view, but—'

'What's the pessimist's view, then?' she interrupted softly. 'Be honest, please.'

We break out, he thought, straight into a contact. Fight through it, move fast, so fast we have people going down, we may have wounded. They will need carrying. Ongoing contacts, attrition. Depending on what the vegetation is like we may move at night and lie up in the day or vice versa. With less ammunition and more casualties all the time, we will be getting weaker. We will run out of food in two days and it will be long journey even without hold-ups.

'In truth?' he replied. 'The pessimist's view is that, in a worst-case scenario, not everyone will make it to the ship, and those that do will be in a bad state. I have to accept that, plan for that, and then work to minimise the chances of that happening.'

'What's best case?'

'The helicopter can take all of you out and then begin lifting us out, but that means we have to be far enough ahead of them that the helo can land safely. Each time there are fewer men left, that affects your fighting strength, and the less you want to contact the enemy. The last fire teams would be almost jogging to stay out ahead.'

'What about help from the outside?'

'Possible, but it's a long way away. It would take days to get here, even if they were allowed to enter. In truth, I don't think the DRC authorities care about what's happening to a handful of people at some remote mission. They have bigger problems. They will need to reopen the road from Matadi to Kinshasa, but that could take a couple of weeks, and any positive effect that had on us would be a by-product of a larger offensive against Makuma's people.'

'Why's he doing this? All this effort against a mission station?'

'Diamonds. He thinks there are diamonds here,' McLean answered honestly.

240

'That is preposterous! Sister Mary remembered him,' Penny said. 'Said he is a psychopath.'

'Which means?' He knew the word, could have defined it, but wanted her medical view.

'That means he has absolutely no empathy, no social consciousness, no morality. He does not judge his actions by our measures. Extremely dangerous. I'm not a psychiatrist, but it could be very complex and, well, he won't be easy to understand or predict. She also said he was a sadist, one who took pleasure in killing. Said he was evil.'

It wasn't a word that had a medical definition. It was a theological word, an emotive word.

'I can't—'

'Penny,' she said. 'Jesus, Doug. Can't you even say my name?'

'OK. *Penny*. I can't guarantee you anything. All I can say is this. We are going to do everything we can to get you people to safety. I don't have sadists and I don't have people who take pleasure in killing. But I do have my lads.' The popular conception, a misconception, was that they were men of simple tastes, the old 'If you can't eat it, drink it or shag it', but for McLean it simply wasn't true. The company had one fellow who had cooked on *Masterchef*, one who designed high-performance parachute canopies on his computer, another who had walked from Land's End to John O'Groats to raise charity money.

'First and foremost they are professional soldiers and they have the ancient warriors' code. The first rule of the warrior is to protect the weak.' He smiled. 'There's only sixty of them but they are rather good at what they do.' His voice hardened up, it was utter conviction. 'We are Royal Marines and we *will* make for our ship. A fighting withdrawal. If Makuma comes at us like he has done today, then we will give him a fight he'll wish he never bloody started, and one he'll never bloody forget.' His tone changed again, softening. 'They're my lads, but that's all I can ask of them.'

241

'That's all you can ask of anyone,' Penny responded. 'That and forgiveness,' she muttered softly.

'Pardon?'

'Finish your lunch.'

McLean watched her walk away. Keep your mind on the job, son. Forget her. She did it once, she would do it again. You can't trust her. You love her but you can't trust her. Move on. This is the job. He forced his brain back on Makuma. He was thinking. This snake, as nasty and evil as it was, wouldn't function without its head. Unlike Wellington at Waterloo – saying that it wasn't the business of commanders to shoot at each other – in modern days it was sound tactical thinking to take out enemy officers and commanders. More so than ever with this one. Kill Makuma and his men would give up, evaporate into the bush and head back to Angola. He would get a description of this Makuma and issue it to the troops, with open rules of engagement, in particular to the snipers. If they could get a visual and take him out the whole situation would change.

London

'They can't allow us airfield access. Not being a good neighbour,' the policy advisor said.

'Good neighbourliness!' the PM snapped. 'That's bloody rich. It's their domestic situation that has spilled into the DRC in the first place!' He thought for a few moments. 'Consult with Kabila. I'd like to be able to do that. Does anyone know where he is?'

It was his senior policy advisor who spoke. 'I could get on to the IMF. See where Angola sits on their agenda and how much they are in hock for. Then find out how we leverage that. Get some pressure applied.'

'Claude, you are a prize shit,' the PM said, marvelling at the man's streetfighter thinking. 'Can you make that happen without my intervention?'

The advisor nodded.

'Then presumably we could also do the opposite, get some favourable treatment offered?

The advisor nodded again. 'Certainly. Whichever tack you want to take.'

'Carrot and stick is always best. Get it underway. Keep me advised.'

The advisor nodded and he and the FCO Minister stood together and left the room, the Minister going directly back to his office, where the Ambassador for the DRC was waiting for him.

There was no positive news from Kinshasa and he came straight to the point. 'You explain our position, and let me tell you this quite unambiguously so you can make sure the message gets through to them. If your government does not allow us free access into that area to support and remove our people, then we will take a very dim view of it. Aid will stop. By that I mean British, French and Belgian. All European aid will stop. Furthermore, I will use every endeavour of my office, and let me tell you' – he was up on his feet, stabbing with his finger – 'that as a permanent member of the Security Council, that is considerable, to ensure that any American and UN aid stops as well. Have I made myself clear, Ambassador?'

'Yes, Minister.'

'One last thing, and this is personal. If I don't receive word direct from your government, then you will suddenly find that you have a temporary problem with your diplomatic accreditation. That means that the one hundred and seventy-six parking tickets you personally are responsible for, and for which your are abusing your accreditation, will suddenly be actionable. That will be an arrest and a summons and I will also tell the bailiffs collecting the money you owe Harvey Nichols and Harrods, and furthermore, I will suggest to your government they enquire where you got the money to pay for the three flats you bought in Camden. The ones where you house, at a grand a month each, so many of your countrymen, while they wait for the Home Office to issue status, acting on your advice and ripping off the British taxpayers by abusing the welfare system while they do it. I'll also suggest they look into the bank accounts you have in Jersey.'

The Ambassador seemed shaken by that. He didn't think anyone in Kinshasa would give a damn about his rather cavalier view of debt repayment responsibilities, but he had no idea anyone was aware of his other business interests, and that would be a problem.

'Yes,' the Minster said. 'I know all about that, and don't think I won't do it!'

Nine

The men rotated back in turn to replace ammunition, each take a ration pack, then pack, repack and pack again their day sacks to cram everything in. McLean was now regretting their decision to bring only the smaller day sacks rather than their much bigger bergens.

They would now need to carry everything they had brought in the trucks – the Claymores, extra ammunition, the mortar tubes and bombs, and the food – much bulkier than their ration packs. There was also the extra weaponry they had captured. The captured kit they couldn't take they were going to burn. It didn't take long to warp barrels in a fire, and everything they burned could never be used again. That finished, each man would have time to get some scran, grab a wet and then return to the line. Most of them wouldn't be back into the mission building.

For a few, the next time they came in it would be to form up in fire teams and sections and begin the withdrawal, but for most they would move from their fighting positions in a carefully orchestrated manoeuvre, out on to the track through the enemy's cordon. From then on it was tactical movement. Everything would be in silence as far as possible, muted talk on radios, but otherwise it was all hand signals.

The most critical few minutes was actually clearing the mission grounds and moving through the scattered Unita groups that formed their line. The old man, Maneru, had disappeared half an hour ago and suddenly reappeared again, a chimera. He had found a way through, a hole in their line down by the water on the western end. He said that, moving quietly, everyone should be able to get through that point. McLean knew he could fight his way through without a problem, but that defeated the purpose of leaving quietly, and he had decided what he wanted to do.

Two Troop would slip out first, with the civilians in their centre, while 3 Troop held the mission for another two hours. A full-scale night attack was unlikely, but they might probe the line, and the 3-Troop men scattered round the perimeter could give the appearance of everyone sitting tight. They would slip out later, fight their way out if they had to, and rendezvous with 2 Troop, Company HQ and their civilian charges the next day.

By having the company mortars out with him he could support 3 Troop and be able to turn them back on the mission area if called in by the defenders. The 51-mills. could throw a bomb two thousand metres if needed. Other than that, 3 Troop would be on their own until they linked up with 2 Troop and HQ the following day, but that was preferable to the reverse, leaving 2 Troop. Without their regular troop commander it would have been an unfair burden to place on Sergeant Willis. Troop sergeants would pick up the troop if their commander went down, but McLean felt that deliberately putting one in that position when you had another alternative simply wasn't fair.

He looked at his watch. It was now four thirty. The CSM had the two VMs throwing what captured ammunition they didn't want into the river – it was too dangerous to burn it – and piling the weapons on to a wood pile. Some diesel left in the generator shed was poured on to accelerate the flames, and he touched a match to the twigs at the base, and the flames caught with a satisfying crackle. The CSM was also overseeing the marines who were coming in, in twos and threes to get fed and sorted.

Now it was time to get the civvies preparing. McLean gathered them in the central courtyard. He looked at them. The nuns, young and old – physically all very different – Penny Carter, the two remaining miners, da Silva, Perrin

Dalton, and the three local drivers. The drivers were very unhappy men. All Kinshasans, they weren't rural people, didn't like the bush, didn't like the thought of dying out in the middle of nowhere for no other reason than that they were driving to the wrong place.

'Thanks for gathering.' There was a dry chuckle from Perrin Dalton, whose lip had swollen nicely after the punch from the signals sergeant. 'That's alright,' he replied. 'My diary was clear anyway.' A few other people laughed or smiled and McLean appreciated the effort at humour. He looked round the group.

'What I'd like to do is brief you on the situation. I know you know much of it, but it will be useful if we all work off the same basic information.' He explained where *Winchester* was, the risks to the ship's helicopter, its crew. He explained that even if the Lynx had got into the mission safely once, they couldn't guarantee that again, and given their shortage of ammunition and stores, the only option was to move out. Make for the ship.

'A couple of hours after dark, at 2000 hours – eight o'clock,' he emphasised – 'we will leave here and begin the journey. As you have seen, my men are making preparations. Think about what you want to take. I suggest as little as possible. You will carry your own food parcels, water. Other than that, just your passports and a change of clothes. Please wear long sleeves, long trousers, colours that match the environment – green, khaki, whatever you have got. Bring several changes of socks, stout walking boots if you have them, foot powder. No smellies please. By that I mean anything perfumed. Smell it for miles in the bush. Those of you who don't have a lightweight day bag of some kind that will go over your shoulders, let me know. I'll get my chaps to re-rig what you have.

OK? Everyone with me?' There were nods from the group. 'When we go, we will leave in single file. The old man, Maneru, who many of you from the mission know, will be our guide. Now please listen carefully. We will travel in silence. At all times. Unless I tell you it's OK to talk, you

247

will keep quiet. That's critically important for the first mile or so. Watch where you are putting your feet. Watch the back of the person in front, just those two things, Eyes down, eyes up, eyes down, eyes up. I want no noise, no crashing around, no talking, no falling over. You will go in two groups. It's dark, so you will be holding on to a piece of rope. If we get into . . . bother, just do as you are told. Go to ground. Cover. There will always be a core team of my men with you, but much of the time you won't see the rest. Do as the men tell you to do, instantly, and in silence. OK?'

'Everyone with me?' Nods from the group, people listening intently now.

'We will leave with half my men. The other half will stay for a few hours and meet up with us tomorrow. Any questions?' There were plenty, most of which McLean couldn't answer, and when they petered out he finished by saying, 'Now, unless there is anything else anyone wants to add, a short session on non-verbal communication. CSM Harvey will show you all a few hand signals you will need to recognise and understand. After that I suggest you start thinking about what to wear, what to take. Please be back here ready to go by half past seven.'

CSM Harvey had joined the group and now stepped forward. McLean moved round to talk to the three drivers, something more than a smile for the first time since arriving that morning.

'You men will have to choose what to do. This is your country. I will be taking these people away from here. You can come with us for tonight, then make your own way out, or stay with us till we reach safety. I would not stay here if I were you.'

One, with some loyalty to his employers, looked at McLean. 'What about our trucks?' he asked in bad French. 'If you go, they will be taken.'

'That is true, but to stay to defend them would not be smart,' McLean replied, realising for the first time that they were probably uninsured, or if they were, they probably wouldn't be covered for acts of war. 'We must protect people first. Are you coming with us?'

'You go west. I will come as far as the Kinganga road,' one of them replied. The third, who had remained silent, nodded, and the man concerned with his employers' trucks shrugged and nodded too. 'I will come. To stay would be to die.' McLean nodded and pointed to the CSM and asked them to listen carefully.

Dalton had broken away from the group and McLean intercepted him.

'Know the stuff,' Dalton said. 'I was with your chaps in Brazzaville in '97. We played with the boats on the river.'

'How's the lip?' McLean asked. 'My CSM did tell me what happened. I apologise for not getting to you sooner. I believe you wish to lodge a complaint.'

'I do, but it will wait. You have other things to worry about.'

'I do, and I appreciate your forbearance. I might say, that although I don't in any way condone his action, his career has been exemplary this far—'

'I know that,' Dalton interrupted. 'All he had to do was ask.'

McLean's eyes narrowed briefly. 'Can I suggest, Mr Dalton, that all you had to do was offer it?'

'How was I to—'

'Mr Dalton' – it was McLean's turn to interrupt – 'my problem, and the one I will address, whether you officially complain or not, is Sergeant Phillips. Believe me, he will be dealt with. On behalf of my company, my commando and the RM, I apologise for what happened.' But he was thinking, you have just said you were with the Royal Marines in '97, long enough to know our hand signals. You must have seen us trying to get word out. It would have occurred to anyone caught here in this situation with a sat phone to offer it. Even after he approached, you still didn't offer it. 'Now, if you will excuse me?'

A few minutes later the CSM's quick course over, Penny

Carter came up to him. 'I'm afraid I don't have anything green or brown. Black is nearest, I'm afraid. I've got dark-green trousers. Combats actually,' she said, her voice heavy with irony.

'I'll give you something,' he said. 'What about a pack? Have you got anything?'

'Yeah, a day bag thingy. It's green khaki. From Gap.'

Twenty minutes later one of the VMs looked at her little green pack and handed her some burlap sacking and a needle and thread. 'Your bag isn't big enough. Stitch these on to it,' he said, adding, 'Marm.'

Forty-five miles away, *Winchester* had hove to, two miles west of Matadi in the massive Cauldron d'Enfer, a huge pool a mile across with 800-foot-high cliffs on the northern side. Channing had decided that he would rather ghost past Matadi in the dark than blatantly power past in daylight and invite reaction. Then they would creep the last three miles up to the pool at the base of the rapids, risking the perils of river navigation in darkness.

Marston wasn't happy. Although the watch-keeping officers were fresh, they were following his courses and his instructions, and he had now been on the bridge for twelve hours. He was tired and this was no time to be doing high-risk passages through narrow river waters where the charts were dodgy at best. There were no navigation markings, sightlines or bearings on the chart above Matadi for the last two miles, and although the water was deep enough, if the sky was overcast with no moon, then it would be dead reckoning and compass bearings and the GPS. Even with the bridge blacked out for the night watch-keepers, there was still ambient light enough to make seeing into pitch darkness bloody difficult. He looked across at Sally Wallace, who had the watch. The air conditioning in the old 42s wasn't great and her clothing was damp with sweat, and she had a sheen of perspiration across her brow. She swung her binoculars up and strained in the dying light to see a boat coming downriver towards them. Marston looked away back at the water, thinking about the last leg. The ship was the Captain's responsibility, but he didn't want to be the vasco who drove his ship on to a sandbank one hundred and seventy miles up the Congo River. A successful trip would look good on his record, a fuck-up with no chance of recovery vessels would look like shit.

Channing was reading his thoughts. 'XO, when she gets underway again I want a seaboat out for that last leg, running up ahead of us. They can zigzag ahead of us and we can follow a median line.'

There was traffic on the river, but as darkness approached there were fewer and fewer boats. On the boats that passed, people waved at them, studied them curiously, and moved on.

'Pilot, course, please?' Channing called.

Martson had been bending over the binnacle-mounted gyrocompass. '071 degrees, Captain.'

'Officer of the Watch?'

'Officer of the Watch,' Sally Wallace responded.

'Let's get under way. Your course is 071 degrees.'

'Aye aye!' She turned to look across at the QM at the little butterfly-shaped wheel. 'Forty-six per cent on Olympus. Steer zero seven one.' That would give them fifteen knots through the water but only five knots over the ground.

On the deck they were ready. The Lynx, still undergoing repairs to her cockpit and instrument panel, was back in her hangar, but elsewhere they were ready, or as ready as they were going to be.

Chief Petty Officer Davies, the Phalanx controller, had spent much of the last twelve hours in his little controller's hutch opposite the port Phalanx gun, working through the software troubleshooting manual. He was one of the new breed. Twenty-nine years old, the youngest Chief in the 42 Flotilla, he had made Chief on his technical brilliance and solid performance. He was creative, imaginative, innovative, and at the same time utterly reliable and dependable. A rare combination. He smiled. He thought he had cracked it. The

251

Phalanx would fire along a bearing for calibration testing, but the old method of changing the bearing and elevation was slow and meant manual entry. Without the new software he thought he had worked out a way to bypass bits of the old programme and pre-enter one degree left and right traverse, and elevation changes, while the gun was firing.

But would it work? The next calibration testing wasn't due for a week. He needed to try it, and for that he needed the XO to sign off, to be able to run the standard operating checks, then the standard procedures for the LCP, the local control panel.

In the main mess Nellie Tusker, the last of the special-duty men from the upper deck weapons and gun controller's platform to come down to eat, had collected food from the port-side galley hatch and went in to sit down. The place was quiet, just a handful of people scattered around. The Captain had the ship on defence watches, and it could come to full battle stations in under ten minutes, but for now the port watch was off-duty and most of them were asleep. At 1800 hours they would change over.

He put his tray – steak and kidney pie, and treacle pudding with custard – down on the table and pulled out a chair. He pulled out the two Cokes he had bought from the store, opened one and sat down and began to eat in silence. He had been aft when the Lynx had returned and had seen the people coming off. Women who had been battered, raped. The word had run through the ship like wildfire. They had killed nuns. Someone said five dead, three of them stabbed in their privates with sharpened stakes. Even allowing for the rumour machine to have got it partially wrong, it was an awful thought. Cunts, he thought. Fucking evil bastards. How could anyone do that?

A figure loomed past him. 'Hello, Nellie.'

He looked up. It was Jenny Teller, the girl from lunch the other day. The pissed-off one. Surprisingly, she put her tray down and dropped into the seat opposite him with a little smile.

'Oh. Hello,' he replied, dropping his head back to his food. He wasn't saying anything this time.

'I got a bollocking,' she said. 'From my mate.'

He looked up, his expression quizzical.

'For being horrible to you. She said you were one of the nice ones and – well, I'm sorry I shat on you. Forgive me, then?'

He looked up and smiled. 'Don't worry about it,' he said. He cut a piece of his pie and forked it into his mouth. 'I hear you been put into the MCO by the old man. Bloody 'eck,' he grinned, chewing. 'It'll be the PO's mess for you next!'

'Naa,' she replied dryly, pleased he had heard, pleased he was interested. 'I thought I'd go straight into the wardroom.'

'Fancy a Coke?' he pushed the second can towards her. She had an impish little smile, and her eyes creased up at the edges as she took the can. She had missed the shop opening and this was a godsend – and Nellie knew someone in the galley, because these were cold. 'Thanks. I'll—'

'Just drink it,' he said. They talked for a few minutes. Beneath them the ship trembled. 'We're moving again. Better finish this and get back up.' He picked up his can and drank deeply, before spooning several mouthfuls of treacle pudding into his mouth.

'Me too,' she said.

'I'll – aah . . .' He stumbled, unsure what to say next, just that he had enjoyed chatting with her, enjoyed her smile, her presence, being with her.

'Right then, I'll – aah – owe you a Coke,' she finished.

'See you later then.'

'Ya.' She grinned.

London

The *Evening Standard* had the story out first, with the only picture that the *Telegraph* would allow to be syndicated prior to their own multi-page spread planned for the morning editions. The papers were swept off the stands, not only by the people who regularly took the paper, but by everyone who saw the banner: 'Brit Troops Under Fire in Congo – Rescue Goes Wrong.'

There were four linked stories, the main piece from Perrin Dalton, the MoD and parliamentary statements, the downing of the French helicopter, with the photograph of it going in, and a background piece on the Congo situation.

Extra editions of the paper were published and couriered to Taunton, Poole, Arbroath, Portsmouth and other 'marine towns'. In Clapham, a woman with two sons in the Royal Marines, both in 45 Commando, bought it thinking, there by the grace of God go I.

At Waterloo station Henri Lefage, now a grey-haired man, his back ramrod straight, the grey hair clipped short and exposing – if one looked carefully – a scar that ran round his neck up into his hairline, bought one of the papers. He read the first paragraphs of the stories quickly, finishing by shaking his head. The memories came flooding back. The 'Wild Geese'. He knew it then, they all did. This problem was not going to go away. The violence, the savagery, the volatility, would haunt men for ever. The Belgian Congo, as he still thought of it, was a vast, sprawling, sweaty, violent, Godforsaken place that had always ground men to mincemeat and always would. His experience there had scarred him, physically, mentally, and emotionally. But it was like a drug and kept drawing him back. In the beginning he had been with 5 Commando, Mike Hoare's command. Joined them in Salisbury, fresh out of the Legion. They had roamed across Katanga, sometimes working alongside the UN but – with differing objectives and ideologically light years apart – more often clashing with them. The memories came flooding back, vivid in their clarity. After being with Hoare he had worked with 'Black' Jack Schramme and Charlie Watts, but his favorite time was with Hoare, or more correctly, with John Peters. He had been with him when they rolled into the little satellite mission at Yangambi.

When it was over, they had found a girl, a young Greek nun too beautiful to give her life to the cloth.

Mary was her name. Big dark eyes you could look into for ever, skin like caramel. He fell instantly and hopelessly in love, but he was just a young ex-Legionnaire and she was a nun. When they left Stanleyville she took the crucifix from round her neck and placed it round his and called him an angel of the Lord. He had never seen her again, but had thought of her every day since. Every day for forty years.

He found a pub and sat down to read it again. He got further down this time, and then put down his drink and his Gaulloise, and read it again slowly, the blood draining from his face. It mentioned a nun dying, a nun called Sister Mary, from Greece, who had been in Katanga in the sixties and had been rescued before, at a mission beside a lovely bend in the river near Isangi, but this time they had come too late, just minutes too late. There could not be two. Not with the same name, not both beside a lovely bend in the river at Isangi? That was Yangambi. There was only one rescue there. He slipped his hand inside his shirt and touched the cross round his neck, a great silent tear running down his cheek.

People in the pub who saw him – the young brokers and traders, commuters – didn't know who he was, or what he had seen. He was just an old bloke who had had one too many by the look if it, crying into his beer. Someone laughed, and Henri Lefage just stood up, folded his paper and walked out.

Da Silva had armed himself. From the stack of captured weapons that were not going to be destroyed he had found a solid-looking, Belgian-made FN-FAL 7.62 and some of the old-fashioned chest webbing. The wooden stock was scarred and marked – this rifle obviously dated back to the seventies and early eighties when the South Africans were supplying Unita. The FN-FAL was the Belgian version of what the British Army and Marines had used for a long time, their 7.62 SLR. He went to find someone who could check it out for him. Some of the lads who were repacking their packs and rations were envious, Sloth among them.

'Fucking hell,' he muttered. He looked at Sar' Willis, who

was checking it over for the Portuguese engineer. He stripped it quickly and expertly, looked at the mechanisms, the firing pin, and nodded. 'Looks all right. Grab a cleaning kit from somewhere and give the moving parts and barrel a good clean and a light film of oil.'

'Sarge?' Sloth asked. 'Any more of those 7.62s?'

Willis just looked at him. No one liked the SA80. For all its hype it just never cut it with the lads, and the fact was that in every unit in the British forces that could choose their weapons, they had opted for something else. Some went for M16s, some the H&K G3. The old 7.62 SLR needed to be kept clean or it sometimes jammed, but it was generally reliable, and with the long cartridge it could put bullets through six-inch tree trunks and take out the bastard on the other side. Soldiers like that kind of firepower. 'There's one other. Use your own rifle. Once you need a replacement, we'll see.'

None of them was entirely happy with the prospect of civilians carrying weapons, but given what had happened, they couldn't prevent them doing it. Both the Englishmen had also taken weapons. The CSM's concern was safety. In a contact or action, highly trained men do what they are trained to do, in a disciplined and professional manner. Having some terrified civilian with an automatic weapon caught up in that situation could present as much danger to his men as the enemy, and he wasn't happy.

Sloth, Furby and Kevin were repacking their day sacks. Sloth dug around trying to find somewhere to put the boiled potatoes and shrugged.

'Fuck it,' he muttered. He ripped open the bag and began to eat them, 'carbo loading'. He wasn't the first. Many of the marines had just eaten what they couldn't find space for. 'I've only got so much space, and you can't shoot potatoes,' one had said, when one of the nuns looked at him quizzically.

'Yeah,' his mate said. 'And fruitcake blocks up the barrel!' – stuffing some cake into his grinning mouth. He was one of the Love Machine, and what he didn't tell her was that part of his day pack was taken up with one of two little speakers.

256

Another had the second speaker and a third had the main element of the ghetto blaster. They were fucked if they were leaving that behind.

'How far we yomping?' Furby asked.

'It's forty miles as the crow flies, the Mufti reckons,' Sloth replied, round a mouthful of potato. Furby shrugged, thinking, Willis wouldn't get that wrong, and we can do that in a day if we have to on our own. He looked out at the sky. The sun was down now, night falling quickly, incredibly quickly. A night tactical march. He liked the night. Was good in it. Moved like a big cat. Kevin wasn't keen. Didn't like the thought of homicidal black men with machetes and spears creeping up on him, but like a big predator, Furby was better in the dark than in daylight.

Sloth pushed another potato into his mouth and licked the oily dressing from his fingers, and pointed at the ammo they had to find room for. One of the nuns came past, looked down at Shagger and smiled.

'We have some meat. It's left over and it's no good to us now. Will he want it?'

'He'll love you for ever,' Sloth answered with a grin. 'You're Irish,' he said.

'Sure I am,' she said. 'Do you know Ireland?' The lightness was forced. She was tense, edgy.

'No not really. Drunk my way through it on rugby tours.'

'Aah, God loves you anyway,' she replied with a forced smile. 'Well, I'll get the meat then.'

She was back a few minutes later with a big, old, battered, aluminium dish full of what looked like mutton. She had mixed in some maize meal or sorghum with some powdered milk. Shagger was up, his tail wagging. As she bent over to put the bowl down his expression became more earnest. Sloth knew the signs. Fucking hell, he's going to shag her leg, he thought, grabbing his bandanna collar quickly, before the dog could try it on.

'Thanks,' he said, grinning sheepishly.

'Pleasure,' she replied. Shagger dropped his head and

tucked in, and she looked at the dog eating for a minute and then back at the two marines. 'What do you fellas think? We gonna get there, then?' Kevin had seen the signs also and was grinning. Shagger was living up to his name.

'We'll get there. Don't worry. You do the prayin' we do the slaying,' Furby said flippantly repeating something Kevin had come up with earlier. Immediately he knew he had said the wrong thing. 'Course we are,' he said. 'Don't you worry, now.'

'Yeah,' Sloth added, giving Furby a withering look. 'We'll get there. Nice ship. Hot showers. Good scran.'

She nodded and smiled and moved away.

'She doesn't know what scran is,' Furby muttered.

'Aah, yeah. And you, you insensitive bastard, you don't say "we do the slaying" to a nun!'

'Well, we do.'

'I fucking know we do,' Sloth muttered. 'But they're fucking pacifists, aren't they?'

'Well, they ought to be fuckin' glad we do the slaying because they'd be dead pacifists by now otherwise,' Kevin chimed in.

'They know that.'

'Well, what's wrong with me saying we do the slayin'?' Furby asked.

'Aaah, shit! Never mind,' Sloth said with exasperation.

Outside, suddenly it was dark. Pitch dark.

It was time. The redeployment in the line had taken place as the men had returned, alternate fire teams of both troops around the perimeter. As 2 Troop withdrew to begin slipping through the Unita line with the civvies, the 3-Troop marines spread and moved back to form a smaller perimeter. Other than sporadic exchanges, there hadn't been a serious challenge on the perimeter since about four o'clock, and hopefully it would be quiet till dawn.

McLean looked across at where Sergeant Willis was with Maneru and spoke into his throat mic.

'Two Alpha, Zero Alpha.'

'Alpha, this is Two, go, boss.'

'Let's go.'

It would take twenty minutes for Willis to get his men into position. Sneak out and form a defensive corridor with two big machine guns and two section weapons. The corridor would move, the fire teams leapfrogging each others' positions, the civilians in the centre, all this along a jungle track, all this in virtual silence, Maneru in front.

Any time they had a contact in this first critical phase, McLean wanted firepower where it counted. The men were 'well tooled-up' and were openly carrying fragmentation grenades, white phosphorus, and LAWs. There wasn't any armour out here, but an LAW would make a hell of a mess of a dug-in position.

He waited with his TAC HQ element and the civvies, and when Willis called in and said he was in position McLean looked round the tense silent people.

'OK, folks. Time to go. Remember, no talking, no noise. Eyes down, eyes up, and if something happens, listen for instructions from the marines with you.'

Penny Carter was – like most of them – frightened. As they followed a marine out into the dark, and he just disappeared and then loomed up beside her, she really understood the use of camouflage and face cream. She was pleased she had taken McLean up on his offer, and she was now wearing his spare DPM shirt.

The mission was in darkness, the last lamps extinguished half an hour ago to let everyone's night sight settle. It was warm and the sound of crickets and cicadas filled the night air. A mosquito sang past her ear, and somewhere out over the river a bird called, all sounds so familiar, and yet tonight they were foreign, scary.

She told herself no noise and set about following the person in front toward the dark line of trees, her heart pounding so loud she thought they would hear it, and began to say a prayer.

A few feet short of the trees and a young marine motioned for them to lie down on the ground. 'Numbers one to seven will go first. The enemy is one hundred yards that way,' he whispered. 'You' – he pointed at the first half group – 'come with me. Very quietly. Two metres between you. Hold the rope at the knots. Rest of you wait here with Dave.'

They moved off down the track, huddled over, each holding the piece of rope, passing the first marines with a machine gun then going on. The forest under the canopy was dark, but there were cleared areas, and when the moon broke through, they could move faster. Penny's heart was pounding. She was convinced that every leaf she stepped on sounded like a branch breaking. When the cloud rolled over again they slowed. It was twenty minutes before they were told to go to ground. There they waited for what seemed an eternity, until the second group dropped down beside them, and as they watched, four- or five-man fire teams moved past them, leapfrogging their position, silent wraiths in the darkness. Soon all there was behind them was the last group of marines, the tail-end Charlies.

Then it was numbers one to seven up again, and this continued for the next two hours.

McLean then formed them into one group and, clear of the immediate danger area around the mission, he had them moving down the track in single file, slowly and cautiously. There was still no noise, no talking, no torches, no light. If something needed saying, then it was whispers into another's ear.

Three miles from the mission at two a.m. the following morning, the lead elements hit the banks of the Lunionzo River, a tributary of the Congo that crossed their path at right angles. McLean halted the party there, and moved up to have a look at what they had to cross.

The track stopped at a sandy slope that led down to the dark water, the vegetation heavy and overhanging. He lifted his night sight and looked at the green hazy images and could pick out the opposite bank. The water looked deep and was flowing steadily.

Maneru loomed up out of the darkness.

'How do you cross?' McLean asked him. 'Is there a crossing place?'

Maneru shook his head. 'Many crocodiles.' He pointed off to the south. 'There is a small village there. Just a few people. They have a boat. In daylight they will carry for a price.'

'It's better they don't know,' McLean replied, somewhat relieved. 'Where's the boat?'

'It is up at the village.'

'Will you show us?'

Maneru nodded. McLean nodded and spoke into his throat mic, and a few moments later Willis and the CSM dropped down beside him. Willis was a swimmer canoeist trained by the Special Boat Squadron.

'Sergeant Willis. Take someone with you. There's a small village upstream. Maneru will show you. There's a boat of some sort there. Borrow it. Quietly. Mr Harvey, the troop is yours till Sergeant Willis is back. I want a defensive perimeter and a recce party ready to go over first. Sergeant?'

'Sloth and Furby, sir,' he replied without hesitation.

'Good enough. The civvies down in the hollow here. Have a rifle keeping an eye on the water. Maneru says there are crocs.'

'Magic,' Willis muttered, shaking his head. 'Crocodiles.'

McLean grinned in the darkness, then looked at their guide. 'Maneru, should we leave payment?'

The old man smiled in the dark. 'Yes,' he replied. 'Tobacco is good.'

Willis, two marines and Maneru disappeared up the riverside path, and as they went, the Padre dropped down into the hollow with the civilians.

'Well,' he whispered cheerfully. 'We'll be here for a bit. Everyone alright?'

One of the nuns murmured something, but otherwise they were silent. They were, frightened, absolutely alien in this environment, so he sat with them and offered his goody bag of bits of broken garibaldi biscuit around in silence.

Thirty minutes later Maneru, Willis and two marines were back, this time coming downstream in a wide-bottomed canoe hewn from a single tree trunk. The bow was taken up with sacking, traps, and other odds and ends, but it was quite a big craft, and would hold at least ten people.

Willis dropped Furby and Sloth on the far bank first, an armed recce, then took across the rest of Biscuit's fire team. The far bank consolidated, they could begin moving the civvies. McLean watched, transferring his command with the second boat of civilians, pondering the chances of 3 Troop actually hitting the river at this point, and how they might get the boat back over to the eastern side.

'Wouldn't bother, sir,' Willis said softly. 'They have another two that we saw. We can leave it on the opposite bank where they can see it.'

McLean looked at his watch as the moon broke through. Captain Lowry would be on the move with his troop now, and hopefully they were clear of the mission already. They would be fast. Once clear of the Unita positions, they would move almost at a jog.

They pushed on till dawn, moving in single file, Maneru finally swinging them south away from the river towards the areas where the vegetation was a patchwork of thick forest and areas of wide-open savannah. The road up from the main highway to Kinganga was now only four miles distant and McLean wanted to be over that and well into the bush on the far side by first light, within striking distance of a patch of high ground. The spot was unnamed and unmarked on the map, but for its height at 1801 feet. That was RV Alpha where they would rendezvous with 3 Troop.

Beyond there the going would be easier, and there would be plenty of room for the ship's Lynx to land, but also enough thicker bush to remain hidden. There would be no daylight manoeuvring through open country if McLean could help it. He was pleased. They had put good distance between them and the mission, had evaded the enemy, and so far things were going well.

But too well.

Three miles behind them 3 Troop were about to have their first contact.

Ten

C aptain Lowry had swung his troop south almost immedi- ately, and moved them fast, parallel to the road into the mission, the road blocked and held by Unita. His plan was to cover the fifteen miles back to where the power lines heading up to Kinshasa bisected their route and the road, swing west and cross the Lunionzo River, and then follow the power lines west. The first stage of the execution was also to be obvious, so the Unita units would think that everyone had gone that route, and follow them, rather than look around for and discover the tracks of the first party to leave. This had been agreed with the McLean. Lowry was confident that once he was in front of the chasing enemy he could outdistance them and lose them, and then turn west, leaving the Unita people thinking they were going for the main Kinshasa highway.

They were moving in an arrowhead formation, a five-man fire team out in front, two ten-man sections on the flanks, with machine guns and snipers outside of them, and a tail-end-Charlie team. Lowry was in the centre with his radio operator, a prudent full tactical bound from any of his men. This tactical bound was intended to keep him out of the immediate contact area and able to see the bigger picture, command, divert resources and support the team engaged with the enemy. His troop sergeant was out on the right flank with the 51-mill. mortar.

They were moving directly away from the river and the terrain and vegetation was opening out, patches of quite dense forest interlinked with acacia thorn trees and knee-high grass.

264

The Unita unit was under orders from Makuma and advancing towards the mission. They had been ordered to stay off the road and so were walking through the bush parallel to it. Following the easy ground they had drifted more than a mile away from the road, but heading in the rough direction of the mission. The light was improving by the minute and there were eighty-five of them moving in small bands, relaxed, chatting among themselves, when they were heard and then seen by the 3-Troop marines on the left flank. The three-man team with their GPMG went silently to ground. Behind them and thirty yards further over was their sniper. He saw them go into cover in his peripheral vision, and as he settled in he knew that whatever they had seen was directly to his front and heading his way. The section leader, Corporal McEwan, the man who had had first blood two nights before, swung up a hand to the rest of the section, touched his throat mic, and called it in. He was making instant decisions. The gun team needed support and the sniper was on his own. He rolled over and signalled to Captain Lowry and redeployed his section – five rifles to support the gun from the right and two men across to cover the sniper's left. They moved fast, huddled over, before going to ground.

The seconds ticked past and McEwan, while not doubting his men for a second, was wondering what they had seen when he heard the voices. He swept his eyes over his section. Everyone was in position and ready. Would they walk past? Would they see them? How many of them were there? There. Movement. More movement, a gaggle, moving and talking with each other. More. He could now see about nine or ten through the bush and trees, and a second group behind them.

As the fighters walked, the marines' axis of attack was swinging to the left. In a minute or so it would be the sniper and the two men covering him who would be in the thick of it. For a soldier armed with a bolt-action rifle designed to engage at distances of a thousand yards, being within feet of the enemy was not good, not good at all.

He watched them approach and whispered to Captain Lowry,

his hand covering his mouth, the sensitive throat mic picking up his voice. Sixty yards behind him and to his right Lowry was redeploying the rest of the troop, bringing the second GPMG across, fire teams dropping into position, either ready to engage or to support. Ideally, Lowry wanted no more than one third of his troop engaged at once. That meant he could have another third in support and the last third manoeuvring themselves into position before they took over the fury from a new axis, which would then free up the first section to move up or back, under covering fire from the support section. That was the 'one foot on the ground, one in manoeuvre and one in reserve' doctrine. But he knew that was a luxury he might not have time for.

McEwan watched them approach. They would be within twenty feet of this team as they passed. If any of them was seen, if any of the Unita fighters looked to his left and saw one of the marines, even camouflaged as they were, then the shit would hit the fan.

He resisted the temptation to select automatic, and slowly, very slowly, raised the rifle. It was too close even for his SUSAT x4 telescopic sight, so he looked across the top of the sight down the ironsight.

A bead of sweat ran down his nose, a fly buzzed and settled at the droplet, and he could feel his heart rate increase. The leading man was past now, chattering happily with the others. McEwan could smell him, a mixture of body odour and wood smoke. Others passed, one young – seventeen maybe – wearing flip-flops and a Benetton T-shirt, humping an RPG7, picking his nose as he wandered along after his friends.

A shout, movement. McEwan fired, taking the head off the kid with the rocket launcher and then swinging right and putting two rounds into another man. The GPMG opened up and all hell broke loose as the five-man fire team with the LSW engaged.

'Contact! Wait, out.'

On both sides marines were pouring fire into whatever enemy they could see, then moving forward into better cover, grenades going off, a burst of white phos, screaming. It was the beast unleashed, a vicious rolling firefight up close, the marines using concentrated firepower with discipline. There was no quarter given. One of McEwan's section fired upwards as a Unita fighter, probably trying to escape the carnage, ran over him. The man took the rounds in his groin and fell to the ground, going straight into shock. A few seconds later he began to scream in pain. Someone shot him – you don't leave live enemy behind you, not unless they are truly incapable of any more fight – and then turned back to the fight in front, skirmishing forward. There were bodies and wounded in small pockets, who lay where they had fallen, one sitting up, looking through wide, staring eyes at the blood leaking from his stomach. A marine skirmished past him and fired at a prone figure who was aiming fire at them until the firing stopped. He turned back and levelled his rifle at the wounded man, but then lowered it, crawled back and made sure his weapon was out of reach.

'Contact. Three alpha, Three two. The left flank is in contact with forty-plus enemy moving right to left. We are engaged, over.'

The other section was coming up now on the left, their GPMG hammering out through the bush. Suddenly it was over. The Unita unit did what irregulars do when ambushed or in unplanned contact with a force of unknown size. They break and run. It was like most short-range contacts in nasty little African conflicts. Brief, bloody, terrifying. Men dead, others moaning or crying, the victors' hands shaking as adrenalin still coursed through their bloodstreams, stripping weapons from the dead and living.

'Roger, three two,' Lowry came back. 'Three one is moving around to your left and will engage. As you can, move forward and swing left to create an axis to their rear.'

Furby heard it first. They were crossing savannah – a rocky, dryish vlei covered in knee-high grass, dotted with acacia thorn trees – moving in troop formation. McLean and his company command element were in the centre, 2 Troop arrayed in order of battle around them. They were in an arrowhead formation, with the GPMGs on each flank, and a sniper further out still.

Biscuit's section was the arrow's head. Sloth was out on point, his fire team just fifteen paces behind. Moving slowly, his eyes swept the bush before them like a hunter, his rifle at high port, always looking for the next bit of contoured ground, the next place he could drop into if fired upon. Shagger was out ahead of him. The dog seemed to understand. Maybe he was a hunting dog once, and had done this with his master, but whatever his chequered past, he seemed to know what he was doing. Nose up, testing the wind, then down on the ground – eyes everywhere, he moved forward in a sweeping lope, back and forth ahead of his new master. Sloth kept his eyes on a line of ground maybe sixty metres ahead. The closer ground he had looked over and he now focused on another imaginary line out ahead, the 'green wall'.

Ideally, it should be a hundred metres or further out, but a marines 'green wall' was limited by thickness of the vegetation and the contours of the land. Every now and then he flicked a look at the dog. That's my boy, he thought. Sniff out an ambush and I promise you doggy heaven for the rest of your life.

This far ahead of the section there was no break contact drill that really worked. If they were ambushed he had three choices, all determined by how close he was to the troop: go to ground and stay put, fighting, allowing the troop to skirmish forward or waiting for the contact to end; retreat down the centre line of the section that would be returning fire, but that only worked if they were close, bloody close; or go for cover left or right and withdraw by swinging round the side of the section and rejoining them from the rear. That was dangerous because you could run into the enemy's flank, or get shot by your own blokes.

Then Sloth heard it, the dull whump of a grenade at distance, then the dull beating tattoo of a GPMG and the crackle of 5.56 some way off. Sloth went down on one knee and raised a hand. He listened and looked back at Furby, who nodded and pointed out behind them and to the south.

Seventy yards behind him, McLean was down already, his head cocked, the signals sergeant with the PRC320 beside him, listening to the radio. A marine waved the civvies to the ground, pointing and telling them to lie down. They were tired, had been walking all night, and although daylight made it easier to see where they were going, the risk had increased and the marines were silent, watchful, alert and wary, their eyes sweeping the bush, rifles up to the shoulder, using their SUSAT sights to magnify things.

McLean listened as Lowry reported in. They had had a contact but the enemy had disengaged and run. There were nineteen Unita dead and injured, and miraculously there were no RM casualties. This was a function of two things, the fact they were in cover and ready when the contact started, and better training. Most of a modern Western soldier's training was how to stay alive, and untrained or badly trained soldiers suffered casualties at ten times the rate of well-trained men. It was basic stuff – when to move, when not to, how to move, when to shoot, how to shoot, how to support and be supported – basic food and drink to a Royal Marine. It made all the difference, again and again – but as Lowry finished his report, McLean knew their luck couldn't hold. In twenty-four hours of almost constant fighting, they had only one dead and one wounded. It couldn't last.

The risks for 3 Troop of hitting a second group were high this close to the road and McLean agreed for Lowry's troop to do a dogleg and head for the river immediately.

A few minutes later he looked out at Willis and nodded, and the troop was up and moving, corporals with comms passing on the news that 3 Troop had had a contact and won, no good guys hurt.

Out ahead, Sloth could see the high ground they were making for, and had also seen Maneru through his sight, the old man walking back towards them, with long mile-eating strides, his stick in his hand.

*   *   *

Makuma rampaged through the mission buildings like a madman. His men had done an assault on two fronts at daylight, and met no resistance. He had spent the night alternately pacing back and forth, and sitting brooding, thinking the people at the mission were going nowhere, almost hoping they would take to the bush where he could hunt them down at leisure, but knowing they wouldn't. They would stay where it was familiar, where the diamonds were, and hope that someone would come along and rescue them.

At first he had been pleased, thinking that his surprise had worked, but then it became apparent that the mission was deserted. They had slipped out during the night. He had wanted to capture the nuns, interrogate them. One of them must have hidden the diamonds from the mine and he would have just worked through them till someone talked. There was no way he could search everywhere – it would take days or weeks, and they were getting further away every minute. He upturned beds, pulled open lockers, smashed his way into desk drawers, spittle on his lips, his one eye red and pulsing, bellowing in rage.

The prisoners who had been sprawled out on the ground, thinking they were still under the watchful eyes of the British soldiers when his men attacked, said they last heard noises some hours before first light, but most of them had been sleeping.

Makuma kicked his way through them, glaring at everyone, wondering for a second why the whites hadn't just killed them. He would have. He looked at Ndube.

'Well?' he bellowed.

Ndube said nothing, feeling the fear. He had ridden the back of the lion and it was looking back at him.

'Well? Where are the diamonds?'

'If they weren't at the mine, they must be here. With the nuns.' He moved forward pulling a news clipping from his pocket, one exactly the same as Makuma had. 'There are diamonds, Colonel. See?'

'I don't see any!' Makuma bellowed. He looked round,

controlling his madness, then back at Ndube. 'We better find them,' he said, his voice low and menacing.

He looked round his gathered captains. 'They are out there. In the bush. Find them! Get the others back up from the road, just leave one cadre there. Find them!' He issued orders, telling them where he wanted men, stop groups – then with some deep predator's instinct he swung his arm westwards. 'That way. Kill them, but leave the old women.'

Marston had conned the *Winchester* the last few miles himself. The OOW was Sally Wallace, but he wanted the feel himself, the control himself. He cleared the area between the quarter-master on the wheel and moved between him and the compass binnacle constantly, looking out at the sea boat that skimmed back and forth between the extremities of what seemed the main channel of the river. He had inched her upwards on the Olympus engines, twelve knots over the ground, but only two through the water, knowing that if he got into trouble and inched on to a sandbar, then he had fifty thousand horsepower of reverse thrust into two big screws and the power of the water's downstream flow to pull him off again.

It would be more dangerous coming out, because if they grounded going downriver, then the flow of the water would be pushing them on to whatever it was. For this reason he had Lt Sally Wallace behind him, and as he moved the ship upriver, he called out reciprocal courses to her to note down for the return passage.

Eventually they had made the pool, the mile-wide deep expanse of water that sat below the class 4 rapids. There were navigable stretches above this, some of them for hundreds of miles, but nothing crossed this point up or down. Finally, with the sea boat stooging in alongside, Marston looked across the bridge at Commander Channing.

'This is as far as we go, Captain.' The ship was now facing into the current, her engines running enough to keep her stationary in the fast-flowing water. Channing looked at him. Marston had been on the bridge for twenty-one hours

– twenty-one hours of extreme concentration and awesome responsibility, and his eyes were grainy and red-rimmed. He was exhausted.

'Anchor party, close up. Special duty seamen, close up.' He looked at Marston. 'Good job. Officer of the Watch?'

'Officer of the Watch, sir,' Sally Wallace called back.

'In the log.' He looked back at Marston and called out. 'Outstanding effort from the navigator. Best bit of pilotage I ever saw.'

'Aye, aye, sir,' she replied with a smile.

'Mr Marston, go below,' Channing finished with a grin. 'Get your head down.'

They had dropped the anchors just after two a.m., both anchors down and guarded by an anchor watch party headed up by the OOD. In case the anchors didn't hold, warping lines were laid out and ready, but for now they were holding hard on the bottom. The ship was blacked out. No lights showed and marines and armed ratings patrolled the weather decks. Channing came off action stations and let one watch get their heads down for some sleep. He was pleased. His ship had slipped past Matadi in the dark and was now in position.

Now, in the soft dawn light, Channing wanted to see if he could get her turned round so she was facing downriver. The early light had shown him something unnerving. The main channel they had come up the night before was a good deal narrower than they had thought. At several points she must have been almost scraping her sides along the rapidly shelving bottom. When he was up and awake he would put Marston into the sea boat to take sight lines on the channel out, so when time came to go they could do it in darkness if they had to.

Getting her round meant warping – locating something which they could attach mooring lines to ashore – and to do that would mean moving her out of the fast-flowing water in the centre of the pool towards the southern bank to secure her there. The how was the problem.

Heraklion Blue

The morning papers all covered the story in depth, but the *Telegraph*, with Perrin Dalton on the ground, had stolen a march on the others, and with their multi-page spread of his photographs, they were being swept off the stands in record numbers.

In addition to his material there were big background pieces on the DRC, other West African conflicts, and the MoD briefings in detail. There were graphics, little schematics of how Britain might support the small band of Royal Marines and their civilian charges. Coloured arrows showed airlifts to Ascension Island, the Congo or Zambia.

Henri Lefage bought both the *Telegraph* and *The Times*, and then walked down to his newsagent, who had copies of *Le Monde*. He read every story at least twice, and each paper mentioned Sister Mary among the dead.

He made a note of the sketchy details given by the Unita legation in Lisbon, details of the unit that had gone rogue, and its commander. He also noted other things. The details of the Royal Marines unit and where they were based. He wrote down the names of the officers, the nuns, the Médecins sans Frontières doctor, and the journalist who had written the story, and then sat back and – one hand touching the little gold cross around his neck – he looked away into space.

He didn't go into his office that day, but sat at home and looked out of the study windows at the grey, leaden English sky, so different to that of Africa, where he had spent so many years of his life. The memories were strong, vivid, in technicolour hues undulled by time – the browns and greens of the bush, dawn sky so blue it seemed unreal, and at midday – pale and hot – the smell of cordite, gun oil, petrol fumes, tobacco – the smell of fear and of death. He thought about John Peters: where was he now? he wondered. And Mary. He thought about Mary as he had done every day for forty years.

Western DRC

At eleven a.m., the sun high and hot in the sky above them, McLean called a halt. They were within half a mile of RV Alpha. He would let everyone settle, eat and get some rest somewhere up the rocky, sparsely wooded slope ahead of them, but first he wanted to know it was safe. With a sniper settled in, covering the slopes with his rifle, the lead fire team moved forward on a recce.

Sloth, Furby, and the fire team moved out in silence. Penny Carter watched them go and was suddenly aware of how much they had changed in appearance in the last twenty-four hours. When they had arrived at the mission they were in clean clothing, uniform in appearance. Watching the group of men move silently into the bush, each was now much more an individual. None were wearing helmets, some had floppy bush hats, many wore nothing on their heads, all wore long-sleeved shirts, but some, contrary to procedure, had rolled up their sleeves. Many had leaves, small branches, tufts of grass stuffed into their webbing and kit, and when they went to ground they were invisible. Everything was in whispers, or by hand signal, the marines using facial expressions like mime artists. All wore dark-coloured face cream on all exposed skin, and wearing bandoleers of ammunition, they looked like something out of a film. But this was real. They were real, and they weren't doing it for effect.

It was an hour before McLean signalled the group to its feet and the marines fanned out in their moving formation and began to move up the slope. Twenty minutes later they arrived in a small, dish-shaped plateau three-quarters of the way up. Biscuit, Kevin and Jock were there to meet them.

Furby and Sloth were up on the summit with the sniper, the first watch where they could see around them three hundred and sixty degrees. This was almost hard routine – no fires, no smoke. Hexy was smokeless but it did have a smell, so when Sloth broke out the makings for a wet he hunched over the little chemical burner, instinctively wafting away the haze that came off it. The chances that a few hexy blocks would be smelt were extremely remote, but he did it anyway. Above him the sniper swept the horizon through his telescopic sight. He also had a big pair of powerful binoculars for a spotter, and these he had given to Furby.

Down in the dish, as people flopped down, McLean thought, this might be their last chance for something hot, and the civvies were looking rough. They were sweating, tired, dirty, waving flies away and settling under what shade they could find. A couple of them were limping, feet blistered, and the LMA dolled out blister tape. It was hot, but that didn't mean that people didn't want a hot drink. Good for morale. The wind was from the east, so they were downwind from the enemy, but it was dry up here, and there was a chance of starting a fire, so he would have to limit the use of burners and work communally.

It was time to report in, get a sitrep from both 3 Troop and HMS *Winchester*. As the signals sergeant was setting up Dalton's satellite phone, he looked across at the two senior men.

'Mr Harvey, Sergeant Willis. Hexy or gas only. Be aware of the risks, please. A hot wet for anyone who wants one, but no food cooking. I want it all over in half an hour. Get the civvies sorted and then rotate your perimeter. Make sure everyone gets a chance of some rest. We'll move out two hours before nightfall.'

The CSM began to move people into groups, one marine manning a burner, and Willis went out to check his perimeter, while McLean made contact with the outside world. First priority was *Winchester*. If they were the only successful contact they could always pass word on, and he needed to know about the helicopter.

When he looked round, Penny Carter, da Silva and one of the nuns were settling down in the shade of the tree where the signals sergeant, McLean's bivvy partner, was brewing up.

Twenty feet away Dalton walked over to where Sister

Marie-Claire had sat down. The nun was wearing a pair of baggy, black trousers, a loose shift top, and a floppy hat, looking for all the world like an eccentric artist in some 1960s New Mexico commune. He wanted to follow up on Sister Mary, learn more about her. This was the human interest part of the story. He talked with Sister Marie-Claire for a while and then turned the topic to Sister Mary.

'You knew her a long time. Tell me about her.'

They talked for fifteen or twenty minutes, Sister Marie-Claire recalling her old friend, the time they had spent together, and what she had known of Sister Mary's past. They were speaking in French, one of four languages that Dalton was fluent in.

'Who was Henri?'

Sister Marie-Claire smiled. 'Her great love, although she only ever knew him a few hours. She used to talk to me about it, feeling like she was betraying her calling. God loves those who love. He was a young soldier. He was one of the men who came to the mission when they were attacked. She felt – she felt she was wrong to feel that level of emotion for a man when she had given herself to God. She felt it was childish – after all, she had only known him a few hours and never saw him again, never consummated the love.'

'And you said?'

'Love is pure, and pure love is the best kind of all. She had not betrayed her calling, just loved someone.' She looked at him. 'I am a pragmatist, Mr Dalton. If a nun is incapable of love, then she has no business in the cloth. She loved God no less, the people we looked after no less.'

'And she never saw him again?'

'No,' she replied. 'She saw a newspaper article once, about mercenaries. He was mentioned, there was a photo, his face was blacked out. This was at the time of the Seychelles incident. He was called Lucky then.'

'Lucky?'

'Yes.'

The bits suddenly fell into place. Henri. Henri 'Lucky' Lefage. 'Is this Lucky Lefage we are talking about?'

'That is him.' She looked at him. 'Have you met him?'

'No,' he replied. 'No, I haven't. Heard about him.'

A mercenary who began with Hoare, then worked the conflicts for the next two decades. Never a senior commander, never a planner, kept a low profile. Stayed out of the media's eyes on the whole. Solid soldier, commanded to platoon level, very good at it, and a romantic who seemed to lead a charmed existence. He was a talisman for the men he fought with, a lucky charm. Wounded but never badly, in and out of incredible scrapes, used up his nine lives many times over. If Henri Lefage was on the payroll, then others would join. He brought good luck. Dalton had met a man, a South African who had fought with him many times. Said he was lucky, but unhappy. A man who had left something or lost something he would never replace.

Dalton now knew what it was. Something touched his arm and brought him back to reality. The marine with them passed him a metal mug of tea and he took it and smiled his thanks.

He was dirty, grubby, covered in scratches and insect bites, tired and thirsty, and the tea was delicious.

Above them at the summit, Furby, Sloth and Kevin sat a few feet below the sniper who still had the watch. They could see miles in most directions, miles of the African savannah, with the darker green of the forest near the river away to the north. It was spectacular, beautiful.

'Whaddya reckon?' Furby asked them.

'It looks good from up here, very Wilbur Smith. But—' Sloth began

'Its a fucking shithole,' Kevin finished. 'It is. Let's face it. Would you choose this place to go on holiday? Would you fuck!'

'It is beautiful,' Dave Hobson said. He had come up, pissed-off with making tea for civvies. Dave had a silver-foil compo pack out. He had given it a rev with a big dollop of Tabasco sauce and was spooning cold pasta and chicken into his mouth.

'Bollocks,' Kevin grunted. He had his boots off and was changing his socks, rubbing powder on to his feet, looking like Popeye again, his little jaw thrust out. 'Fuckin' Michelle Pfeiffer is beautiful. Penny Smith, that bird on GMTV, is beautiful, a Tottenham penalty is beautiful. This' – he swung an arm expansively – 'is not beautiful. It's full of snakes and mosquitoes and has got more hostile fucking natives than an old Michael Caine movie. Get me to the old *Winch*, my son. I'll be glad to see the back of this fuckin' place. Gives me the creeps.'

'This is beautiful,' Jock muttered. 'See this moth?' He was pointing down at a piece of bark. 'I wonder what it is. Haven't seen this type before.'

'You got no soul,' Sloth said, looking back at Kevin.

'I like it,' Furby said. 'It's nature. It's—'

Sloth looked at him and smiled, but it was Hobson who spoke. 'You're a predator, mate,' he said. 'That's why you like it.'

'Bollocks,' Kevin muttered, pulling his boot on. 'Even the predators get killed out here. I am a predator and I want to die in my kip, mate. My head cradled on some bird's breasts.'

'You?' Sloth said. 'A predator? You're about as predatory as Winnie the Pooh.'

'Yeah, well. That is one fucking hardcore salty pusser's bear. Well 'ard he is, like me. Cor,' he said, changing the subject. 'That doctor. Major Mac's ex bit of fluff? Wouldn't mind a bit of that.'

'See its wings there, sort of velvety,' Jock said with reverence.

'Velvet? They are stupid. They fly into light bulbs,' Kevin said, exasperated.

'What the fuck would she want you for?' Sloth continued the conversation. 'She's a doctor, he's an officer. That's the sort she goes for. They may be over but—'

'That's just it, innit? She'll be wanting a bit of rough now,' Kevin replied, convincing himself as he spoke. 'Gagging for it.'

'I remember when it went wrong,' Hobson said. 'He was fucking gutted. Saw him what must have been the next day. Went into the company offices. Looked like a truck had driven over him.'

'Caught her out, didn't he? Fucking women. Can't live with them, can't live without them,' Kevin muttered, chucking another cliché into the mix.

'I would have slotted the bastard,' Furby said.

'Not his fault,' Sloth said. 'Women do the selecting. The good-lookers have always got blokes sniffing around. It's up to them to say no.'

'I still would have slotted the bastard. Then I would have given the bitch a fucking hiding she would never forget. Can't stand deceitful women.'

'Yeah, but of all the places to bump into your ex, you wouldn't have said it would have been here in a million years, would you? Love to have seen her face.'

I did, Hobson thought. I did. She was terrified – wild-eyed, animal fear. He looked back down at his compo pack and squeezed the bottom to get the gunky mix further up.

The sniper was still up on the summit. 'I've got movement,' he called.

'Three Troop?' Furby asked, going up with the binoculars, careful not to skyline himself.

'Can't tell yet,' he pointed out 'Three groups of trees at eleven o'clock. Maybe a klick out. Behind the left group of trees.'

Furby swung the glasses until he could see the trees. 'Can't see shit – oh, yeah. Got 'em!'

He watched for two minutes, looking for movement, and finally picked out the various elements of the group. Platoon or troop-size, they were moving in formation, a loose arrowhead, staying in the cover of the trees. Moving and covering each other's teams. Looked like 3 Troop, but it wasn't just Western soldiers who moved like that through open country. Know soon enough.

'Get Mufti up here,' he said.

The sniper touched his throat mic.

279

*　　*　　*

Seventy feet below them in the depression, McLean had just put down the satellite phone and reached for the tea that his sergeant had made. Da Silva had wandered off, leaving just the three of them, and the sergeant could feel the mood between the boss and his ex, and made himself scarce. Everyone knew now. Went round like wildfire.

McLean was preoccupied. *Winchester* were still trying to fix their helicopter and said, although they could not get the helo away and back by dark today, they might be able to do a pickup in the morning. He understood. Unless they needed an immediate casevac, the crew didn't want to be flying without most of their instruments, and couldn't in the dark. Penny looked over at him.

'Problems?'

He looked up. 'No. We'll be OK,' he replied briskly. He spread out a map on the ground and sipped tea while he looked at it.

She shook her head to herself. 'Look, Doug, can't we put this behind us? I know it's not the time and place but I understand how you feel. I was wrong. OK? I behaved appallingly. Please, Doug, I still love you. Please can't we—' She stopped speaking as he tilted his head to one side, a habit she now knew meant he was listening to his radio earpiece.

'Excuse me,' he said briskly, coming to his feet. He began to walk away, but then stopped and turned and looked at her. Through the cam cream she could see his expression soften, a half-smile played on his lips and his fair hair blew in the hot breeze. For a few seconds it was the old Doug, the one she loved, the one who once loved her, but then something washed over him and his face hardened again.

'I'm sorry. I have to go.'

Thirty feet away the Padre saw the exchange and excused himself from the people he was with. He stood up and walked over to her as McLean clambered up the last few feet to the summit, where Sergeant Willis had joined his lads.

'I've got 'em,' McLean said. Looked like it could be 3

Troop, but you could never tell. They were heavily camouflaged with leaves and grass, and the cam cream covering
their faces made them unidentifiable as Caucasians. It was
only the occasional movement that allowed him to see them
at all. The sniper or whoever had spotted them had eyes like
a bloody hawk, he thought As they got closer he was able to
recognise SA80s. He thumbed his throat mic button.

'Hotel Three Zero. Hotel Three Zero, Zero Alpha.'

The response was immediate.

'Three Alpha, think we have you visual. Confirm you are
moving west two hundred metres to the left of a rocky
outcrop. Over.'

'Roger, Zero Alpha.'

'Three Zero' – McLean grinned. 'We have you visual. See
you in a few minutes.'

There were muffled cheers and groans from the 2-Troop
lads as a grinning but tired 3 Troop arrived and moved
through their defensive positions. The civilian delight was
obvious, the sight of the rest of the marines wandering in
as casually as if they had had a day out on Salisbury Plain,
a boost to morale and confidence. Only they didn't look like
they had been on Salisbury Plain. They were covered with
dust, and dirt was crusted to their uniforms where they had
got wet crossing the river. From a few feet they would have
been invisible.

'You can relax now, you girlies. The professionals are here,'
one of them called softly.

'Yeah, so professional a bunch of spear-chuckers surprised
you,' someone retaliated.

'Yeah, well they learnt the lesson—'

'And what's that then, you tosser?'

The marine opened his arms expansively, like it was obvious. 'You fuck with the best, you die like the rest. 3 Troop –
the Saints. You are looking,' he said, 'at the fighting elite.'

There were muffled giggles and groans, and several circled
fingers and thumbs with the wanking wrist motion.

'Now, you fellas stay here,' another 3-Troop man said, 'and

keep a lookout for the fuzzy-wuzzies – and if you see them and get scared, come get us. We are going to get some rays.'

Captain Lowry immediately had his sergeant get the troop in position and moved to find McLean.

Dalton, as part of his agreement with McLean, got his phone back twice a day, for a single ten-minute conversation or transmission. There was still battery life in the set and his laptop battery was still looking OK.

He typed a new story, emotive personal observations mixed with hard reporting. When he had finished, he carefully checked the piece to make sure he compromised no one, not least himself, and then uploaded pictures from the digital camera. There were images of marines in formation, of the civilians, one of a marine carrying a civilian, others of them on the move and resting, marines bent over machine guns – and one picture that spoke of the loneliness of command. A photograph taken up close, of McLean. His beret was off, his fair hair light against a face filthy with dust and cam cream and his brow furrowed in concentration as he looked at a map. A radio handset was in his hand as he spoke to someone, and, out of focus behind him, was the wide rolling bush of Africa.

The last thing he sent was a request for a researcher. Someone to start pulling background references to one Henri 'Lucky' Lefage, mercenary working in Africa in the 1960s – see if he was still alive and to try and track him down – and someone to pull background on Heraklion.

Downriver in the pool below the rapids above Matadi, Commander Channing had turned the *Winchester*, and she was now facing downstream. It had been a complex piece of seamanship. Now moored nearer the southern bank, out of the ten-knot current, it was nearer six in where she was, but the mud was barely two feet under her keel and the MEO wasn't happy. His water intakes were clogging at the filter points, but Channing considered that the lesser of the evils. With two anchors out at the stern, she was holding in the six-knot current but she would have had trouble in ten. They had warped her round, on anchors and warps to a massive tree on the shoreline, the sea boats buzzing back and forth and the big winch aft taking the strain to line her up in the current, engines running, while the anchor lines were secured. Now she lay stern-on to the flow, a position from which he could shear the cables and be under way downriver very quickly if the risk profile demanded it.

The northern side of the pool was a wall of rock. Cliffs eight hundred feet high made approach from that side impossible, and Channing had dismissed any threat from there. The trouble was from the west and his marines – he was thinking that way now – would come in from the southern riverbank.

A marine patrol was out, Sergeant Connors with his ten-man section working in two fire teams on a recce right round the southern shoreline. Already, locals had gathered, people who had never seen a warship, or anything this size before. Connors had worked in Africa before and had always been amazed just where people would appear. He had had a puncture once in Zambia, and in the middle of nowhere, he had stopped to fix the tyre, and within ten minutes there were six or seven people standing watching him. This was the same. People just seemed to appear from nowhere. The good news was none of them were armed with anything other than machetes, and there was no overt hostility. Connors and his team of marines would remain on the bank overnight, a sentry post, with communications and a sea boat. Their weapons would be discreetly within reach, but Channing's orders were that there was to be no overt warlike intent, nothing, as he said, 'to stir up the natives'.

On board, the XO was working up to secure the ship for nightfall, while down aft the aviation engineers were still trying to get the Lynx's instruments working. Many of them were beyond repair, but the P1 had listed his minimum requirement, and they were trying to get him ready for ops by dawn.

Mike Lunnon-Wood

1530 hrs

McLean began moving among the company, getting them ready to move. They could have been up and moving within moments if needed, but time to mentally prepare was good, and the civilians needed that time.

He had Captain Lowry and Willis for an O group meeting and they worked out a new two-troop ORBAT – their order of battle – the formation they would move in to best defend the civilians and best react to tactical needs. Maneru sat to one side.

An advance patrol, a recce group, moved out twenty minutes ahead of them, down the slope to the west to ensure the way out was clear. At exactly 1600 hours, the main formation began to move silently down the hill for what they all knew would be an all-night march. The OP on the hilltop had seen no movement in the east since halting for the RV, and hopefully they had thrown their pursuers off the track. Time now to put some more distance between them and any possible followers, and get another leap nearer the ship.

Just over an hour and a half later they were off and moving. After half an hour in the savannah, Biscuit's fire team was out on the left flank, as they had been on point all night and were being given something of a rest away from the intense pressure and stress of the point position, the most exposed to contact with the enemy. Sloth moved along on the far left. The only man further out was the sniper, but he was well behind. Inside him were Furby, Jock and Kevin on the gun, and Dave Hobson. Biscuit was a few feet in front of him to his right.

Where's Shagger? he was thinking. C'mon boy, where are you? When they had moved out, the dog had been a little confused, because his master was no longer walking in front, but he had soon settled and swung back, sweeping just ahead of Sloth, up to the point team and back again, relaxed and panting.

One hundred and fifty yards back and away to the right

284

was the main element, the gaggle of civilians. They weren't ambling along. They were being pushed, pushed hard to keep up, and this was only half the marines' usual march pace, a speed set at six miles an hour. Trouble was, at six miles an hour you were almost jogging, and that was tactical suicide. You could see nothing, hear nothing. This was nice and slow. Tactical speed.

Out on the left flank Sloth was still looking for Shagger. Then he saw him. Away to the left. Now he wasn't relaxed. He had seen something, was hunching over, hackles coming up. Oh fuckfuckfuck. Sloth clicked his fingers and hissed. Furby swung and he pointed at the dog, sixty yards out ahead of them. Shagger looking into the bush on the forward left axis, growling.

From there on everything seemed to go into slow motion. Sloth and Furby went to ground at the same moment. Biscuit, ten feet to their right, was coming round, signalling to Jock, who was looking down at something, touching his mic switch, trusting Sloth's instincts and his mega-fucking-Gucci dog. Kevin and Dave Hobson out to his right turned and went down, but Jock was the last to move.Then from the bush a hail of automatic weapons fire. Noise, smoke, acrid bird-shit taste of cordite, muzzle flash, dust kicking up as rounds hit, flying steel tearing grass – Sloth and Furby engaging, returning fire, bullets snapping past, the whine, snap and buzz of ricochet, liquid fear, someone yelling, Dave Hobson crawling over to where Jock was down, and Kevin struggling to get the gun up and lay down covering fire, the flat crack of a grenade, smoke.

'Contact, wait, out!'

Fire ripping out at them, bullets snatching at grass and leaves, whirring, snapping past, heart pounding, hitting the ground, weapons up, fire returned now.

'Contact left. Two Alpha, Two Alpha, two two, we have a contact on our left. Unknown number of enemy in the bush at ten o'clock, we are engaging. I have a man down.'

Biscuit was up then, skirmishing forward into better cover, calling to Sloth, shouting for Kevin to get the gun up and

working. 'Lots of fire, Two Alpha. I say again, lots of fire.
We need support, over.'

He engaged himself, picking targets in the trees, firing at
concealed positions. Behind him the troop was down in cover
and Willis was already swinging the point fire team on to the
new axis, and bringing up the other section. They were moving
fast now under the covering fire of their snipers, and the troop's
other GPMG began hammering out, its deeper heavier note
different, satisfying.

Biscuit heard an LSW rip into fire and knew the point team
had turned and engaged. He looked out over his shoulder as
Kevin finally got the GPMG firing, Dave Hobson with him,
feeding the belt into the gun's workings.

He could see the Love Machine on the move now, two
sections skirmishing round behind them to their left to open
a new flank, and a few moments later, further back, he
heard the old familiar thump of a 51-mill. leaving the tube.
Troop mortar had opened up – sweet Jesus, that's fast –
and a second or two later the first bomb landed in the
trees and exploded. The concussion wave followed with a
shower of clods of earth and dirt and leaves, the smoke
blowing in through the bush. Someone in there was screaming now.

He was up and moving again to clear the fire arc for the
GPMG, and dived over to where Sloth and Furby were. As
he went down again something tugged at his pack, then again
and a burning sensation seared through his upper back.

The Love Machine was up again, Willis and the boss on
the net, calling for him to hold fire as the Love Machine
skirmished through on their new axis of attack and went
into cover, pouring fire into the enemy's unprotected flank.
Rounds hitting all around them, kicking up dust, one up close
– the kick of his rifle in his shoulder – one goes down, another
– aimed at a third, a face through the trees, fired, head snapped
back – die, you fucker.

Another bomb, then a third. Someone threw a white phos,
pretty white trails of smoke showering the air, and the fire

started, the wind catching it, fanning it, crackling and roaring into the enemy positions.

'As they rise!' someone yelled. Familiar. Mufti Willis. He was up. No tactical bound here. He was in the thick of it. The enemy were up, forced up by the flames, and as they were taking rounds, their retreat turned into a rout, the marines targeting the fleeing men as Willis yelled, 'Hit 'em!' There seemed to be dozens of them, over a hundred even, large groups running away through the bush, the GPMG cutting into them like a scythe. Take the fight to them – he was up, Furby and Sloth up and advancing. A few moments later it was over. The Love Machine skirmished through rocky grass and trees, but the enemy were gone, leaving their dead and wounded scattered across fifty yards of bush. There were cries of the wounded, men whose clothes were on fire, and ammunition cooked off somewhere and began to explode, and everyone went to ground.

Sheer focused firepower had won the day here, professional soldiers against irregulars. But they had paid a price.

'Jock's down!' Kevin called.

A marine, a 3-Troop man, well back with the reserves, had taken a bullet in the head and was dead, and McLean was now up with 2 Troop, kneeling down with Big Jock, who was lying on ground, the dirt beneath him wet with his blood and urine.

'Hang on, Jock,' McLean said, taking his hand. 'Medic's here. We'll get you sorted.'

'Naa, boss – aaaah – fuckfuckfuck! I'm gutshot. Never make it.' Jock looked up through the pain and the shock. 'Fuckers have shot me.'

Gubby hit him with a syrette of morphine and went to work, stripping off the business end of a saline drip, looking down at the entry wounds. Two bullets had hit him, both in through the side of the hip, one through the bone, one just above. Gubby didn't like this. This was serious. A bullet in at that point could mean structural damage to the pelvic bone, and then the liver, kidneys, spleen, lower intestine were all in that area. He spat out the needle cover on to the ground and looked at McLean.

'Doc Carter, please, sir?'

Kevin didn't wait for McLean's nod, but was away to find Penny and bring her up.

'Biscuit – Corp' Barton caught one too, sir,' Sloth said. 'Upper back, sort of under the shoulder. Gone straight through, but Furby got the bleeding stopped.'

McLean looked up. 'Where is he?' His boys – his boys were wounded and dead. Their luck had turned. Barton wounded, his gunner down, a fire team now no longer an effective fighting force. The Padre dropped down beside them and took Jock's hand, and gently brushed dust from his face. 'Oh, dear! It's back to Scotland for you then,' he said to Jock in his soft island burr. Sloth looked back at McLean and pointed. 'That tree.'

Five minutes later, McLean had 3 Troop move ahead with the civilians and agreed where they should stop, a stand of trees a mile way, while they got 2-Troop wounded sorted, Penny Carter the only civilian remaining.

'Prognosis?' McLean asked.

'Internal organ damage is considerable. From the look of him, liver, kidneys, spleen could have all been damaged. If we can get a helicopter tonight, and then I can open him up on the ship – have a look – I'll know more then. For now, there's a certain shattered pelvis. Every step will be agony, every bounce of the stretcher. I don't have the correct analgesic for this sort of injury. Morphine will help, but it wears off, and we only have a little.'

'How long will he last without casevac?'

'He won't,' she said. 'Even once we get him back, he will need hospitalisation, possibly a dialysis machine.'

McLean moved back to where Jock was lying. He opened his eyes and looked up at his officer. 'Major Mac, I'm staying.'

'Naa, we'll get you away. Everyone goes home, Jock.'

'No, sir. Let me stay. My call, sir—' His eyes closed as he dealt with a wave of pain. 'I'm too heavy – just hold the

288

lads back and any movement is – Hide me. I'll hold them here.
When you get back, send a helo.'

'You're sure?'

'Aye, sir.' He closed his eyes again, relaxing as the first
shot of morphine worked its magic.

McLean smiled down at him and then moved back to where
Penny was waiting.

'Penny, there won't be a helo tonight. It's going to be dark
in ten minutes. They can't find us or land.'

'Surely they can—'

'No,' he replied. 'Anyway. He wants to stay here. Wants
us to come back.'

'You can't! God, Doug, you can't just leave him!'

'We must.'

'You can't! He'll have no chance!'

'I'm sorry.'

'You bastard!' she hissed. 'He'll die for sure if you leave
him. Or they will find him and – Jesus, Doug – you can't!'

'I must,' he said standing.

'Leave him here to die?'

'No. Hide him, and leave him here till we can get back.
He wants to fight. His decision, and a brave one,' he said,
knowing the truth, knowing that Jock would never survive
the night, so they wouldn't be coming back unless it was to
recover his body.

He walked away, his back to her, so she never saw the tears
forming in his eyes.

'You're a prize bastard!' she snapped at his retreating back.
'You don't deserve them, you know. Their loyalty, their bravery. You don't deserve them if that's the way you treat them.'

The CSM walked over the few feet from where he was.
'Doctor?'

'Yes?'

He was getting closer, just feet away now. 'Shut it!' he
rasped.

Jock would be armed, but they couldn't leave him the GPMG.

They moved him into a thicket and made him as comfortable as they could. Sergeant Willis produced an AK47, inserted a new magazine into the rifle and then produced a fragmentation grenade from his belt kit. They both knew what it was for, neither needing to say it. 'Do you want the pin out, then, or can you manage?'

The fast-weakening man smiled. 'Never do it, Sarge. Not brave enough. You better do it for me, eh?'

Willis looked down at him. Big Jock had always been a ridiculously strong young man, but now he was wan, pale, going into traumatic shock in spite of the drip in his arm. The life force was fading. 'Right you are, son. That morph working, then?'

'Aye, it's better now.'

'Yeah, well, not too much now. You'll get addicted,' Willis joked. Jock laughed softly. A silly joke really. 'Then your bird Tracy would give me a load of shit.'

'Aye. She would at that.' He looked up at Willis. 'You know her name,' he said, surprised. 'Never knew you knew that.'

'Course I fucking do! Right then, you sorry bastard, see you tomorrow.' Willis smiled. He knew much more about all of them then they would ever realise, until they wore the stripes.

'Aye, tomorrow,' he agreed, playing the game. 'Tell her – tell her – You ken? You'll know what to say.'

'Bullshit. We'll come back for you with the helo. We've got a GPS mark.'

'Yeah, OK. But you tell her.'

'Aye. I'll tell her.'

Two minutes later, Biscuit Barton, with a big shell dressing covering the wound under his pack straps, was the last man up. The bullet had run under the skin, through the muscle and exited seven inches across his back. An inch to the right and it would have hit his spine.

They were ready to go, and as McLean looked over, one of the 2-Troop snipers was hanging back talking with Willis. McLean had already said no to the Padre. The Padre had wanted to stay with him in case he was found by the Unita men, to talk to them, appeal to them, but McLean had refused outright. The Padre had pleaded his case, and McLean had finished by looking at him and saying, 'Rory, don't make me order you to rejoin the column.'

He walked over. Sloth and Furby were also holding back. He knew why. Jock was a mate, a popular man. They understood the need to leave him, they all knew that it could be them one day. Always had done. But with an enemy like this, where there was no Geneva convention, no medical care, just the prospect of a brutal, painful last few hours, maybe even torture, they would do what they had to do. None of them wanted to be taken alive, not by these bastards.

'Thought I'd drop back a bit, sir,' the sniper said innocuously. It was in his eyes. He didn't want to do it, but he would if he had too. You do what you have to do. Sloth had offered to take the sniper's L96 rifle, but the sniper shook his head. Willis looked at McLean, his expression saying, leave this to us. We know what has to be done.

It was Maneru who made the last gesture. As they moved out, now at the marines' pace of six miles an hour to catch up with 3 Troop, he turned and looked back at the stand of trees where they had left Jock and raised his stick in salute.

Eleven

Furby, Sloth and the sniper settled themselves in six hundred yards from Jock on a bit of rising ground. The light was dying now, and they had maybe ten minutes, fifteen at the most, with enough light for him to do his work. They were tense, edgy, hating the task they had set themselves, watching the light fade, knowing their colleagues were further away every minute, knowing they were about to see a friend die down below them.

'Stupid little Scots shit. Why didn't he go down with the rest of us?' Sloth said fondly, wiping a tear from his eye.

'He was probably looking at a fucking butterfly,' Furby replied. 'Couldn't resist, could he?'

They didn't have to wait that long.

The Unita men were sweeping through the bush over the contact scene looking for tracks to follow. Sloth watched through binoculars, seeing their tracker at work. He pointed him out to the sniper. He would have to go, but even as Sloth got the nod from the man with the long rifle, he knew that it wouldn't take a tracker to follow them. Seventy-five people leave a lot of footprints. A child could do it. But if they were relying on tracks, then they would halt here for the night, until they could follow spoor again at dawn. The OC needed to know that.

The sniper was trying to identify the cadre leader, see who was giving orders. He would be the first target, and he could zero and take out the tracker before the sound of the first shot reached them. He didn't need to. Furby had his rifle up, looking down at the scene through his 4x SUSAT sight.

'I've got the tracker,' he said.

'I've got the officer,' the sniper murmured, steadying his breathing, watching the wind. He was shooting directly into wind, had chosen this spot for that reason. 'Wait for it, wait for it . . .' he said.

'They've found Jock.' From Sloth.

'After me . . .' Breathe out, pause, squeeze gently, hair trigger.

From six hundred yards the bullet took the Unita cadre leader squarely in the temple, exiting on the other side in a mist of blood, bone fragments and brain matter. Furby's shot, harder with the shorter barrel and less powerful scope, was aimed dead centre of the tracker, the middle of his torso. It hit low, ironically into the same area as the bullets that had hit Jock, into the pelvis. As the man was going down, Sloth snapped off five rounds, all of them waiting for the distant, flat crack that would be Jock's grenade, hoping he would do it himself. There was gunfire from the thicket – wild erratic fire, some of it going up in the air – so they had to assume that Jock was conscious and fighting. Then the flat crack of a grenade and a few seconds later all firing ceased.

In thirty seconds they were up and moving. They had ten minutes of light and they would cover the better part of two miles in that time, running to catch up, but foregoing silence and time to see danger for the sake of speed. They moved in the classic arrowhead formation, the leader Furby – lean and super-fit – in front by ten yards, one either side of him, jogging steadily. If they got into trouble each was out of the first contact killing ground, but close enough to support the others.

Ahead with the main body, the CSM was pushing them hard. In the centre with the civvies, the two drivers trailing them, they seemed alone. They weren't. The rest of the marines were extended around them moving hard in the dying light. Once it was dark, the ORBAT would change, close up considerably, but now he was driving them, pleading, cajoling, motivating them, using threats when he had to.

They had heard the rear patrol engage, knew that what had

293

needed to be done was done, and the tail-end Charlies were now keeping an eyes out for the patrol's return.

A couple of powerful analgesics and Biscuit was on top of it. He hadn't used his morphine syrettes, he was saving those, but even through the painkillers the wound in his back was throbbing and pounding like a bastard, every movement of the pack on his back making it worse. He shut out the pain and pushed on, the section light till Furby and Sloth got back. Little Kevin, Popeye, was now humping the gimmpy.

Biscuit looked back. The Portuguese engineer had broken from the main civvy pack and moved up, the rifle he had taken from the stack back at the mission now held purposefully. He was now just behind Biscuit's team, so he dropped back to talk to him.

'What are you doing?' he asked.

'Fuckall good back there.'

'You know how to use that?' Biscuit asked bluntly.

'Since you were trying to ride a bike,' da Silva replied. 'Two year Portuguese Army in Angola against these same peoples.'

'When?'

'Mid-seventies. I was a sergeant,' he added pointedly.

'On the inside, then, and don't shoot till I say you can. Understand?'

Da Silva nodded, moved inside Kevin and a few steps ahead.

The three-man patrol rejoined them as the last light faded, calling a password and then pounding through the tail-end Charlies without a change of pace. Sloth swung over to where Major McLean and his signals sergeant were, to let him know they were being tracked, and Furby and the sniper dropped into the formation, breathing hard but not unduly, the sweat flowing freely.

As Furby rejoined, Sergeant Willis and Lt Lowry took the command call, and the formation – some hundred and fifty yards across at its widest point – began to close in towards the centre. Night falls quickly in the tropics, and by the time they were closed up and organised it was dark, a moon rising over the trees.

McLean was pleased. Moonlight meant they could keep moving without too much danger of people tripping, or getting separated from the main body. A Royal Marines night yomp could be done in complete darkness, each man wearing a tiny dull light on the back of his bergen for the man behind to follow, but in real terms no one ever used them. Good aiming points, as someone remarked. Here the discipline was tight. The last thing you wanted people doing, and the thing they most wanted to do, was turn on even hooded or red-filtered torches. Otherwise it became a clusterfuck.

Tonight, in the moonlight, moving alongside the treeline but through grass, they would have the best of both worlds. A black-as-pitch backdrop, so no silhouettes, and light enough on the grass to see where the others were.

The problem was the river. The Lufu. It would have to be forded, and Maneru out front was leading them towards one of the few villages on this side of the river, so they could buy, borrow, beg or steal boats.

He looked across at the civilian party. They were straggled out, walking in pairs, some helping each other. Terry, the oldest of the three men kidnapped from Yetwene, was in a shit state. He had dysentery and was being supported. He was weakening, and although Penny tried to keep him rehydrated, as fast as fluid was going in it was coming out, almost clear, and he had stopped asking for the column to halt for him to find a bush. He just keep moving, his system evacuating his bowels as he staggered along. CSM Harvey had clocked this, and had the makings for a stretcher, two poles and a bivvy bag, ready. He wasn't going to tire his men till needed, but when the miner could no longer go on, the lads would carry him.

He would be out on the chopper if and when it came back. The nuns were coping well, all things considered. Sister Marie-Claire, now the oldest in the group by some ten years, was still going strong, but McLean wondered for how long. Two of the others, both in their fifties, were not going so well. One was being helped by one of the younger ones – Sister Jo – who seemed strong and walked with her head held high, and the other was now holding on to the pack straps of one of the marines as he walked. Whenever she stumbled, he took her weight like a packhorse, leaning to pull her up. McLean smiled to himself. This marine wasn't the most socially aware bloke in the world, not the sort who would have time for the old, the sick or the weak, but there he was. It was him, appalled at the atrocities they had witnessed back at the mission, that had looked down at a dying Unita fighter and said, 'Oh dear – What have we got here? You've got a sucking chest wound. Silly boy!' He had leaned closer. 'You just met the Saints, the best of 40 Commando. Have a nice day, shithead,' he'd hissed.

Gubby, the, gap-toothed LMA who pretended to be hard as nails but was so deeply compassionate that no one even bothered mentioning it, was in helping them, as was the Padre. They pushed on, the pace relentless. When they got to the dirt road that ran from Lufu down to the river, he had them crossing quickly. Makuma's men would be trying to get ahead of them. He had stopped thinking of them as a Unita force, they were rogue – rebels, bandits and murderers.

'Major,' one of the nuns called as he roamed past, 'we must stop. Rest.'

'We stop at the river. Not before.'

'We must.'

'We can't. Keep going.'

It was about then that the point element reported that they thought they had heard an engine.

'Engine whine. A fair way off, but it was a truck,' the marine said.

'Anyone else hear it?' Lowry asked.

The others shook their heads.

'Well, I did, sir.' He pointed out into the dark. 'Out there.'

Lowry reported it to Mclean and they kept moving, but now the point element were listening out for it.

*   *   *

Makuma felt he was closing in. Since the first sighting that morning he had swung his men west, moved others of them back round on the road in the trucks, dropping them off in groups. As they passed his positions back at the main highway they had collected others, and now he had fifteen hundred men on the pursuit. To be running like this he thought, they must have the diamonds with them.

He was in his Land Cruiser as it was slowly grinding its way across the bush, followed by three trucks, big Mercedes heavies that could take the punishment. News had reached him of a third strike, where they had killed some of the foreigners, and the tracks showed them to be heading this way.

He swung his massive head to watch as lights bounced their way across the bush towards them. He had vehicle patrols out, and this was one returning. They halted while the Toyota pickup picked its way over to them and the driver jumped out to report. They had found several villages on the riverbank. Makuma told them to lead him into the first, and he split his men up, sending groups on to the other villages. He wanted silence, didn't want to scare them off with too much noise. Maybe they could prevent them crossing here. If there were no boats, then it would take them hours, maybe into tomorrow, to find a ford and get across, and he would have them.

They parked up and walked the last five hundred yards into the village, weapons slung, knives and machetes out, Makuma out front. He heard voices. Women talking. He hefted the machete in his hand and a smile crossed his lips.

As they entered the village a dog began to bark and a man sitting at the door to his hut came to his feet. Makuma said nothing, just swung the machete – a powerful blow – and took the man's head from his shoulders. A woman screamed, and his men were on them, running through the huts, killing as they went. They found the boats on the riverbank, and turning them over, holed them with adzes and mattocks, whatever tools they could find. Makuma moved his men straight on, but at the next village up, the one where Ndube had been in charge, the dry thatched roof of a hut had caught fire and spread to others. Furious, he lashed out at the man who had allowed it to happen, then moved them on.

It was just before eleven that night when Maneru called a halt. As McLean moved up to him he pointed to the south-west a few degrees off their track. There was a glow in the sky.

'What is it?'

'Fire,' the old man answered. 'The village. It burns.'

Oh, Jesus, McLean thought. The implications were two-fold. Not only were they now ahead of his party, but his fears were confirmed. The point man was right. They were using transport. They had to be. They have driven round and dropped stop groups, but they were burning and attacking villages. This could only be to prevent them helping, or deny them boats, food and shelter. He wanted a recce patrol in there now. 'How far is it?'

Maneru shrugged in the darkness. 'Your soldiers, maybe the time it takes to smoke two or three cigarettes. The women, an hour or more.'

'Will you go with my men. Speak for them? Let us see what they have done? What is left?'

Maneru nodded.

Five minutes later the 3-Troop sergeant and a fire team moved out, and just over an hour later, some pre-agreed recognition procedures used, they met the main party a quarter of a mile from the village. Maneru was silent, stoic – the way he always was when life's brutality surfaced. The sergeant was clear and concise in his report.

'Torched the village, sir. Did the place and pissed off heading north, they said. Most of the villagers took off into the bush, but there's a few dead and injured. They killed some women, did the job on them, a couple of kids too. There's some badly hurt, too. We found some boats. They're fucked. Bottoms stove in.' He went quiet. 'They killed a baby. Threw it on the fire.'

'They did what?'

'A baby, sir. Threw a baby on to a fire. The mother saw them do it. She's hysterical.'

'Thank you, Sergeant,' McLean replied, not knowing what else to say. 'Captain Lowry, Sergeant Willis . . .' He told them what he wanted to do and they moved out, and ten minutes later moved into the village, fire teams flanking either side and setting up defensive perimeters. That done, the main party moved into the village, Maneru calling out to whoever was there that he was back, with friends, moving through the still-burning remains of the simple dwellings and the basic possessions of poor people on a poor continent. There were people, some hurt, crying, weeping for their dead – others stunned, wandering around, trying to take it in, sifting through still-simmering embers.

'Fucking 'ell!' one of the marines muttered. 'They've got little enough. They did nothing to deserve this.'

Penny Carter and Gubby moved in to do their work, and McLean looked at Willis. 'While they are doing that, find us something that will cross the river, please. I want to be over there and on the move again in one hour.'

Da Silva walked over to him. 'This was to stop us crossing here?'

'They might have looted and burned the place anyway, but I suspect so,' McLean answered, his voice with a hard edge. A marine bent down and picked up a little toddler, standing over the body of what was its mother, tears streaming down its face. McLean looked across at the journalist. 'Get some pictures if you like, Mr Dalton. Let the world see this.' As he watched, a nun – Sister Jo – took the child from the marine, swept it into her arms. Unlike the other nuns whose expressions were passive, peaceful – even at the worst of times – her face in the firelight showed anger, furious that anyone could do this.

'Don't take this personally,' Dalton said softly to McLean. 'This may have been to destroy the boats and deliver a message to anyone thinking of helping us.' Something at his feet flickered in the firelight and he bent down and picked it up. It was an enamelled metal cup, covered in blood. He grimaced, dropped it and wiped his hands on his trousers. 'But they would have done it anyway. This' – he swept an arm –

'is Africa. Where life is cheap. I have been here all my adult life. It still shocks me. Appals me. Just when you think there is no horror undone, nothing you haven't seen. You never get used to it. Will they be back?'

'I don't know. I hate to leave these people like this but we have to keep moving.'

Dalton's words weren't much comfort. He did feel guilty. He felt that, had they not been coming this way, then Makuma wouldn't have, and these people would not have had their world destroyed in minutes. 'I'd like to find this Makuma,' he said.

Dalton smiled bleakly. He knew McLean meant it. Knew there would be no rules of engagement, no rules at all, and he suspected it was the same for all of the marines. The first chance they got they would take him out. What was it? Dalton thought. The first rule of the warrior? Protect the weak. Even if they caught him alive these men were so incensed by what they had seen, he would be lucky to make a trial.

Willis was back a few minutes later. 'Sir, all the boats are holed, but I reckon we can raft them together, and they will float enough to be paddled across. It won't be fast, but it'll work.'

'Very well. Get started. Your troop across first, secure the far bank and get a recce out ahead. Find the track.'

His headset hissed into life and he put one hand up to the headphone and tilted his head to listen. Willis did the same. Two-Troop marines on their sector of the perimeter had seen a vehicle's headlights heading towards them.

'That was inevitable,' he snapped bitterly. 'CSM, get one of your men to quieten everyone down here. No noise at all. And start on your boat, Sergeant. Quietly!' He moved off at a run.

Sloth and Furby skittered into the bush where Kevin and Dave Hobson had spotted the vehicle. It was a lightweight, a 4x4 utility pickup, and was still approaching them, picking its way down the path normally just used by people on foot.

'Here we fucking go, then,' Furby said. Biscuit slithered into the position and passed Furby an LAW. 'Just one, right?'

'Right. Listen up. Let it pass you, then close the track off. That's only for if they suss us. We'll take it further down when they debus.'

They settled in, Kevin and Dave on the GPMG, Sloth a few feet to one side. Furby moved another ten or twelve feet to a tree where heavy vegetation would conceal him and waited. The vehicle was now about a hundred yards away, bumping and grinding its way nearer. They could hear voices now, the shouting of men on the back, cocky, overconfident. It got closer, closer and then inexplicably it stopped – right beside the four marines secreted in the bushes on the side of the track. The driver shouted something and got out, leaving his door open, the engine running, and there was laughter from the others. He walked a few feet to the right – they could see his uniform clearly in the cab lights – stopped and undid his fly buttons.

As the vehicle stopped, Furby had thought about sheath knife, but it wasn't sharp enough. His Leatherman was. The blade on the little American multi-purpose tool was razor sharp. As the door opened, Furby – not eight feet way – silently put his rifle down against the tree trunk, pulled out the Leatherman and opened the blade, and then slid it into his belt order within reach before picking up his rifle again.

The driver lazily swung his hips left and right, directing the stream of urine across a big, broad-leafed plant. The man was only two feet from Furby, who was standing stock still against the tree trunk immediately to his right. Furby knew one more exaggerated swing to piss to the right and he could see him, so as he looked left, he put his rifle down between his legs and took out the Leatherman. The men on the back of the pickup jabbered and talked amongst themselves and never saw what happened next. The man looked round, and as his head turned Furby didn't wait. With one hand round his face and mouth he pulled him backwards and to the right and in one sweeping blur cut his throat from ear to ear, the razor-sharp blade severing

his windpipe and both carotid arteries. There was a moment's
pause and then blood fountained out, a gurgling noise and
a soft sigh from his severed trachea as the man died. Furby
lowered him to the ground and got his rifle up, the men on
the truck still talking to each other not ten feet way.

Sloth and Kevin knew him well, and settled down deeper
into cover, pulling Hobson with them. They knew what he
would do next.

He took a grenade from his belt kit, pulled the pin, eased
the spoon off, quietly counted to three and lobbed it straight
into the back of the pickup. As it landed on the floor amongst
the legs and feet of the men in the truck he darted back behind
the tree and it exploded, a flash of orange-white light and a
nasty, flat B-L-A-M. As it did so, he was round the tree trunk
firing into the cab. Everyone in the vehicle was hurt in some
manner by the grenade, so there was no return fire, and when
the other three marines popped up and opened fire it was all
over. There was only one man still alive.

McLean was there a minute later, and they told him what
had happened.

'Well done. Right, disable the vehicle, take the rotor arm
and plug leads. If that one can talk, I'll send da Silva up. Find
out what their orders were. Don't hang about. They may have
heard your gunfire.'

'What shall we do with this one, sir?' Kevin asked.

'Leave him.'

Da Silva was there a few minutes later, but the Unita man
was too far gone to answer questions, and while he was trying,
the Padre arrived. Da Silva stood up and shook his head. 'I
done think he can hear me.'

'Fair enough,' Biscuit replied and then he looked down. The
Padre had his little bag out and was fossicking for something
in the dark. He gave up, closed it, put it down, then – in an
act that surprised everyone but no one – he began to give the
dying Unita man the last rights. The others moved away back
into their positions, and when he finished only Furby was still
standing over them.

'You'd do that, for one of them? Ask God to forgive them?' Furby asked. The Padre was surprised – pleased but surprised. This man had never spoken to him, not ever.

'Yes. Yes, I would,' the Padre answered.

'And what about you, Padre? Do you forgive them?'

'I'm trying, but seeing what they did, it's – it's diffi-cult. In time – tomorrow maybe, in the light of a new day – I will, I am sure.' The gentle Hebridean priest paused and looked up at Furby. 'And you? Can you ever forgive them?'

'No. I'd just kill the fuckers,' Furby said. 'Then, if he's up there, let 'em look God in the eye and ask for forgiveness in person.'

'You're not sure he is up there?'

'Is anyone?'

'Yes. I am. The sisters from the mission are.'

Furby pointed down at the village. 'So, where was he tonight, then, Padre? 'Cos he wasn't here.' Rory Chisholm didn't know what to say to that, and the big marine turned and walked away.

England

Back in Taunton, the Ace of Spades – the nightclub the Love Machine lads usually went to – was about to open for the evening. One of the doormen, Big Eddie, had been flipping through the *Sun*, had seen some of the unfolding story and put two and two together. He had had trouble over the years with booties, but it wasn't often, and he had never had a squeak from the lads he was thinking about. In fact, one night they had come to his assistance when a bunch travelling back from a night out in Bristol thought they could get the better of him and get in the back doors.

These booties were like any other young blokes. They came in, had some fun, drank a few pints, danced, tried to pull and went home. This was their big night out. In Taunton there wasn't much else on offer. There were only a couple of other clubs. He walked over to where Sandra, the ticket girl, was loading the float into her cash drawer.

'You know those lads from the camp. Norton Manor. Usually come in Friday and Saturdays?'

'Loads do,' she challenged.

'Naa. The young ones. Eight or nine of 'em, always together. Sit over there in the corner?'

'Oh. Yeah. What Paul and Boff 'n them?' She smiled, images of bootie haircuts, acne, tight trousers, trying way too hard – earnest glances, nudges and awful dancing, buying girls huge drinks with umbrellas. The DJ knew they would always ask him to play Verve and it pissed him off, because it wasn't dance music.

'Bless 'em,' she said. 'They ain't been in for ages, 'ave they?'

'Yeah. 'Cos they're in umbungo land,' Big Eddie replied.

'What?'

'We'll that's them in the shit in Africa, innit?' He showed her the pages from the *Sun*. 'So, they won't be in tonight either.'

'What?' She took the pages. 'Shit! Poor little buggers,' she exclaimed, spitting her chewing gum into the bin and looking at the text. One had even asked her out once, her at least ten years older than him. He was sweet, and if her fella wasn't the jealous, I'll-kick-their-friggin'-heads-in type she would have gone out with him. Because he was nice and he would do anything to please her, she just knew it. The pieces suddenly fell into place. It had been on the local radio all day. The lads from 40 Commando at Norton Manor doing something that had been on the news, and the DJs had been talking to people 'n that.

'Hey, Paula,' she called to one of the bar staff. 'Come and see this.'

Later that evening, when Big Eddie did one of his regular sweeps through the crowded club, he saw that the corner table was empty. Someone had put a reserved sign on it. Silly tart, he thought, but fair enough. Just then two lads fell into the booth seats of the table and he walked over.

'Sorry, lads. Table's reserved.'

'Well, where are they then? Been empty all night,' one of them challenged. He was knocking back a big bottle of water, sweating like a pig. E, Big Eddie thought. He's zonked on E. 'They aren't here.' He leaned forward. 'But when they do get here, it's reserved for them. So hop it.'

Once across the river, McLean pushed them hard. They were all wet from the half-submerged hulls of the canoes they had rafted together. Once on the other side, moving in single file along the jungle track, he had the point and tail elements set a gruelling pace. Till they were clear of the thick forest, the half-mile that edged on the river, he was trusting to fate. If Makuma's men had crossed, then they might have mined the path, or set up an ambush, but speed was vital. There was no way they could get their vehicles across the Lufu, not this far down, and this was their chance to outdistance their pursuers.

Once out in the open, back on the stretches of savannah grassland and rolling terrain, he kept the pace going. Ahead in the moonlight he could see the ground rising. On the other side of that, just twenty-two miles away, was the *Winchester*.

At one point he halted and let the group of civilians catch him up. CSM Harvey was pulling a travois with someone on it, and behind that the two VMs had shouldered their weapons and were carrying someone on a makeshift stretcher.

He moved across. On the travois – two poles from hip height down to the ground attached with a rope that ran round the CSM's shoulders – was Terry. Weakened by the dysentery, he had finally collapsed.

'You OK with that, Don?' McLean asked Harvey.

'Yeah.'

'OK. Half an hour on, then rotate.'

On the stretcher was one of the nuns. She had fallen, twisting her ankle very badly, and it was now swollen with fluid. As they carried her she kept saying she could manage, and to put her down, but they didn't because it was faster this way. The pace was beginning to tell now, even on his blokes. He noticed that they had been giving their composite rations to the civvies. The 24-hour ration packs were enough to keep a man fighting in the field for that time, but no longer.

Ammunition was another problem. The resupply from *Winchester* hadn't gone far enough, and there were now eighteen men using captured kit, none of which had SUSAT sights. He kept them moving – roving back and forth, up and down the formation, encouraging, cajoling, praising, pushing them – while out in the dark the two troops formed a silent, deadly, ever-moving defensive cordon.

Just before dawn he called a halt. He knew if he kept them going any longer, he would have more people going down than they could carry and still fight, and it was time to rest briefly, see what the sitrep was with the Lynx, find an LUP, a lying-up point, one they could defend. Three Troop formed a perimeter and McLean moved round. 'Right. Half an hour here. Get a wet on for everyone. Scran for everyone. If they can't eat, make 'em. But after the wet is boiled, back to hard routine.'

That done and Dalton's satellite phone ready to go, the signals sergeant did what he did every time they stopped, he tried the 320 Clansman, and this time he got through.

'Got comms with *Winchester*, sir,' he said with a grin. It was the first break they had had in days.

The news was good. The Lynx was operable in clear visibility, the met was good and they were ready to lift off in the dawn light. Where did OC Operation Heraklion want his casevac uplift? McLean said he'd get back to them, and squatting down over a hooded, red-filtered torch beam and the GPS with Captain Lowry and Willis, they planned the next hour. They had only covered fourteen miles and he wanted at least another two before they stopped. They would need a map reference for the helo to come into, it had to be safe, and it had to be far enough from the others and the daylight LUP so as not to lead the Unita forces in on their position.

'They can take eight, right?'

'Corp' Barton will—'

'He won't go, sir. Not while there is one civvy on the ground,' Willis said firmly. 'He can make it.'

'Give him the option. After that, I want the fittest four left. Terry will have to go, but that young bloke looks OK. Penny – Dr Carter – is OK, the young English nun—'

'Jo,' Lowry offered.

'—Jo, and one other, stay. Everyone else is on that helo. With a bit of luck it can come straight back and the rest, including Corp' Barton, *will* go. Understood!'

'Sir!'

'Right, let's do it.' And as they stood to go McLean looked at the 2-Troop temporary commander. 'Sergeant Willis.'

The man turned round. 'For the record, there are troop officers who would have been under pressure with this task. Your conduct and your command have been exemplary. In case I haven't said it before, you are doing an outstanding job.'

'Thanks, boss.' He gave one of his rare grins, and the CSM raised a thumb at him.

They found a stand of forest that closed in on three sides round a grassy knoll, and McLean called in the satnav reference. The *Winchester*'s Lynx was already airborne, and with them now just a handful of miles from the ship, it would be there in minutes.

The two troops were deployed to protect the LZ, and as the Lynx touched down, the door gunner kicked out bottled water and food. The packs were as McLean had requested, each small enough to go in a day sack, they could be divvied up later, and with the eight people crammed in, the Lynx – technically overloaded – struggled upward and immediately turned north to get back over the other side of the river and make its longer, curving return run.

As it disappeared over the treetops the food and water were bundled into various day sacks, the CSM hurrying them. McLean wanted to put territory between him and the LZ because anyone within a couple of miles would have pin-pointed their position. They were just hefting their packs again, within thirty or forty seconds of the helo lifting off, when there was sustained and heavy weapons fire to the north, the direction the Lynx had flown in. On the headphones of the 320 the signals sergeant heard the call.

'*Winchester, Winchester*, 33, we are taking ground fire and we are hit, I say again, we are hit.'

'Roger, 33. Your status, over?'

'Fire has stopped. We are still airborne. I have falling hydraulic pressure, engine temp is rising and we are trailing smoke. We'll try and make the ship. We took rounds into the cabin and I now have wounded on board.'

'Roger, 33.' This was Channing. 'Come straight in. We are tracking your course. You are now – eight minutes out. If you have to land, do so, and we will put a party out to meet you.'

'Roger, *Winchester*. For the record, we have eleven souls on board.'

The use of the word souls was ominous. This pilot didn't think they would make it, and on *Winchester* Channing looked at the XO. 'Get Sergeant Connors on the radio. They reckon they can cover country. How long for them to get to the Lynx if she goes in now?'

'She's, what, eighteen miles away?'

'Less by the minute. OOW?'

'Sir?'

'Main broadcast, please. Thirty-three emergency landing. ETA six minutes. Get 'em ready in four minutes.'

Twenty seconds later the XO, the VHF microphone in his hand, looked across at Channing.

'He says, this side of the river, it's clear going a hundred yards off the bank. If it's that clear all the way, in light order, they could cover ten miles in an hour.'

'They are still airborne, they might just make it. Tell Connors to get light order, whatever that is, and be ready to go. If they do make it, then the landing will be the tricky part.' It would entail emergency recovery drills on the flight deck, fire and damage-control parties closed up, sea boats away in case she hit short or went over the side, ship's swimmers ready and the sickbay alerted.

'Do you hear, there? Do you hear, there? Thirty-three emergency, 33 emergency.' The officer of the watch was reading from a standard procedure laid out under perspex at the comms station on the port side of the bridge. 'Helo is damaged and inbound in four minutes. Special duty seamen close up, damage-control parties close up, aft fire parties close up . . .'

From all over the ship men and women began to run to quarters. Channing was thinking fast. He knew the pilot wanted more space to put down if he had hydraulic problems – certainly a bigger area than the landing deck aft, and for his part he would rather not have a damaged aircraft crashing on the ship. She was old and vulnerable to fire.

'Get on to Connors. See if he can get out where it's clear beyond the trees and find a space where the Lynx can be put down. If he can, mark it.'

Down below fire parties suited up in fearnot suits, rolled out hoses and foam, and personnel mustered in damage-control areas. The sea boat – alongside and in the water already – fired up its engine, and with two ship's swimmers on board, cleared away from the side while, below, the sickbay broke out trauma and burns treatment equipment – the trauma for the wounded, and burns in case the helo crashed on landing. Saline was put up on stands and the PO ship's writer was pulling blood donor information.

Ashore, Connors and two of his marines raced inland, away from the river bank to a clearing they had found the night before. Connors was a very organised fellow, very professional, and in his day sack he had two smoke grenades intended to provide cover for his men to withdraw if attacked while on the shore. One of the two marines with him was packing the Clansman and as they ran into the clearing Connors called it. 'Good enough. Let 'em know. Purple smoke!' The marine dropped to one knee and without waiting for protocol called the inbound Lynx.

'Thirty-three, Thirty-three, Whisky Romeo Mike. Lima Zulu in clearing one hundred yards south of ship. Port side of the ship in the bush, look for purple smoke, I say, purple smoke, over.'

'Roger, Romeo Mike. Thanks. Pop the smoke, pop the smoke, I should have you visual any time.'

On *Winchester* Channing overheard and grinned hugely. 'They're gonna make it! XO get a party ashore right now. Take the LMA.'

It was a difficult landing. The pilot had lost virtually all of his hydraulic power and had only limited control over the disc – the main rotor angle. They could see it from the *Winchester*.

It came in fast, trailing oily, black smoke, sounding all wrong, veering to the left, and then it dropped below the level of the trees. At the clearing, Connors and his two marines were there when it touched the ground and tipped over, the rotors almost striking the ground. The three marines rushed forward and began pulling people clear as gently as they could, as the pilot baled out of his door and ran round to the other side.

By the time the XO and his party were ashore and on the scene, the marines had shell dressings on three wounded people. One of the nuns had taken a bullet through her left thigh, the bullet exiting her and entering Terry's upper arm and lodging against the bone. The door gunner was in a bad condition, wounded in the pelvis, but the observer, a twenty-six-year-old lieutenant aviator, was dead, hit by two bullets, one up through the side of his neck into his brain.

McLean's signals sergeant had kept a listening watch, and when the aircraft was on the ground next to the ship, he was able to advise McLean on the company net. They didn't stop. Almost running, he had them moving away from the gunfire that had hit the Lynx. By the volume, there must have been thirty weapons at least firing, and it could have been a much larger force. Three miles from the landing zone, on a rise, he drew them to a halt. Not because he wanted to, but because he had to. The women couldn't go on, they were being virtually dragged and carried by his men, and Dalton and the young English fellow were barely keeping up. Only da Silva, the lean, sinewy Portuguese engineer, was able to keep up with the marines. It was also now broad daylight and the risks to keep moving were extreme. Time to lie up in a defensive position, a proper defensive position for the first time since leaving the mission. This place was as good as it was going to get. High ground, gently sloping away, clear on two sides for over a hundred yards, acceptable on the other two sides. Thick forest further out.

'Raise the ship. Give them this location. We're lying up here till dark. And get a sitrep on the helo if you can. See if anyone was hurt.'

The marines went to work. The helo wouldn't be back, that much was certain, so now he needed a place they could lie and rest till nightfall, but a place he could defend. He opted for a reinforced, single-troop defensive position.

For any infantryman, happiness is many things. It's fire support, artillery, close air, hot food, smokes, a wet. But at its most basic level it's a good deep hole and interlocking fields of fire. They formed in a triangle, on a bit of rising ground with clear visibility. At its centre was a rocky depression. There were acacia trees, thorn bushes and grass but they could see out some distance.

A GPMG team was placed at each of the three corners and each gun had a 270° arc of fire, in theory able to control and dominate the ground out to a thousand metres. Marines in fire teams with light section weapons were dug in down each of the three sides and a machine gun and a support section of ten men were in the centre near the company TAC HQ, able to react and support any side that came under attack. They silently dug, sweating in the sun, deeper and deeper into the red earth. Each marine carried one sandbag as standard kit, and these were filled and lined their holes, and they piled up earth and concealed the traces with grass and leaves.

'This digging shit,' Kevin muttered. 'This is what pongos do. I am a marine. A commando. Stealth is my way. In, attack, out again.' He threw another spade full of dirt out. 'Men of the hunter-killer class. And here we are. Digging fucking holes like pongos.' He was smeared with dirt, it was ingrained into his skin, and the sweat lifted it and made little streaks down his tattoos, and the cam cream on his face was smudged and worn.

'That and helmets,' Dave joined in.

'It's a diabolical liberty,' Kevin went on.

'Write to your MP,' Sloth suggested.

'That bastard? Naa.'

'You don't even know his name.' From Furby, who had the watch and was peering out at the bush through his sight. 'And anyway, you can't write.'

'Don't need to know his name to know he's an arsehole, do I? It should be him here digging holes. Fucking slimy little shit, an' all, he is.'

'They all are,' Sloth agreed.

'And then, to cap it off,' Kevin continued, 'four million nignogs are gonna come out of those bushes. All with shooters.'

'They heard about your sister, then,' Dave muttered.

'Sounds like Clapham Common on a Saturday night.'

'Your MP like that Welsh poof, then?' Sloth asked.

The civvies – Dalton, da Silva, the young English miner, Penny and the two nuns – gathered rocks in the centre under the CSM's whispered directions. He couldn't make them dig, but he could use the two VMs and they dug shell scraps and moved rocks to give the civvies a small, low redoubt to shelter in, each hole and the main redoubt at the centre camouflaged with branches and vegetation.

The two combat engineers were now at last allowed to work their black art. They were placing Claymore mines and their various improvised devices out beyond the position, everything from booby traps to incendiaries, some of them very lethal indeed. It was two hours later before McLean, happy with what was happening, relaxed the pace and let members of the fire teams get some scran and a wet.

312

The array had a seven-man fire team at each corner and then ten two-man holes down each side, and the support section with the 2-Troop mortars in the redoubt.

Two Troop had two sides, and at their corner Sloth, Furby, Kevin, Dave and Biscuit were as ready as they were going to be. Sloth and Furby doing last-minute alterations to their camouflage and then walking back to see if it could be seen. Down in the bottom of the hole Kevin, filthy and sweating, sat over three hexy burners brewing up a wet. He peeled back the clingfilm wrapping from the food packages made up on *Winchester*. There were bacon-and-egg sandwiches, cold sausages, tea bags, sugar sachets, and cartons of long-life milk. He split up the food in their parcel exactly evenly. 'That chopper only just made it back,' someone said. 'It landed in the bush beside the ship.'

'Don't blame the bastard,' Biscuit muttered. 'Landing deck is fucking small even in a good one.' He paused. 'The observer didn't make it,' he confirmed.

Dave Hobson, who was stood to, looked back at hearing the news. 'Poor bastard. Anyone else hit?'

'Three others. Dunno who.'

'Fucking 'ell. Must have riddled it,' Kevin said, looking up from his burners. He was stripped to the waist, sweating freely, so he leant against the cool earth of the wall, while the thought of a hot cup of tea kept him down there guarding the little burners from an errant foot.

'Dave, stand to, lad. Watch the front,' Biscuit said. 'Kevin, your turn when you have finished down there.'

'Sure. How far, now?' Kevin asked, looking up. Sloth and Furby were back, and dropped into the hole carefully.

'Fifteen miles, maybe sixteen,' Biscuit said, wincing as he raised an arm to point. 'Thataway.'

'Fifteen. Shit we could have been there for elevenses. Cucumber sandwiches and tea cakes on the bridge, regaling them with tales of high adventure.'

'Civvies are in a shit state,' Hobson reminded him.

'So?' Kevin argued. 'They'd just be a bit shitter.'

'The old bird? The mother superior or whatever she is? She's a one,' Sloth said fondly. 'She's as tough as old leather. Like my granny. I like the young one. The Londoner. She's different, you know. Not plodding like the others. She's like a spirited filly.'

'Cut the romantic shit. You want to shag her,' Furby muttered. 'Me too. She's fucking wasted as a nun.'

'Yes! You fucking beauty!' Kevin muttered, looking at the bubbles coming up from the now gently boiling water in two of the three containers. 'Main galley's open, lads. Scran's there, and a wet in a mo'. Flasks?' he called, holding out a hand. This was marine thinking. Fill a flask with hot tea or coffee, and later, when you couldn't light even a smokeless hexy block or had no time, you still had a hot drink available to you.

'Reckon they'll find us here?'

'Yeah. They are tracking,' Sloth replied. 'Just a question of how many there are and are they brave enough to have a go?'

'They will be more cautious now,' Biscuit said. 'Wait for reinforcements. With a bit of luck by the time they get word back to wherever their mates are, we'll be out of here.'

'Breakfast on the ship,' Kevin said. 'Fried eggs, bacon, black puddin'.'

'That's all you ever want,' Hobson responded. 'Fry-ups. What about an omelette with chives and cream cheese, or eggs benedict?'

'Eggs who?'

The heat of the day was beginning to really bite. The only sounds were the emerald doves in the trees and the sound of flies buzzing round, drinking from sweat droplets. Other than that it was hot and still. Shagger, bored with lying on the earth beside Sloth's hole, got up and walked stiff-legged towards the redoubt where the CSM was in his shell scrape, eating. Shagger looked at him, then at the food, then back at him.

'Piss off!' Harvey said unconvincingly. 'You've had mine before.'

314

Shagger wagged his tail and did a grin-like yawn and stared back at Harvey through huge, appealing eyes.

'No.'

The eyes didn't waver and finally the Company Sergeant Major gave in.

'Oh, all right, you ugly bugger!' He gave him a sausage and then another – there were plenty of them.

'Only because you spotted that ambush. Otherwise you are still a thieving, gypsy bastard.' Shagger moved closer and sat down with him and Harvey stroked his big yellow head. From his hole Sloth watched this with Kevin, who couldn't believe what he was seeing.

'That bloody dog has got the CSM hand-feeding him,' he said incredulously.

Down one side from them the Love Machine was dug into five holes, everyone sweating. The lads had pulled foliage over the tops of their holes. They wouldn't be surprised. The snipers were out there somewhere with their big scopes, and anyway, they were now well enough camouflaged that people could walk by within fifteen feet and not see them. They slept, the troop's babies – acne, what trainers were cool and music forgotten. It would be their last.

The government of the Democratic Republic of Congo had at last reacted to the incursion and the closure of the road and railway line from Kinshasa down to the country's only port at Matadi. They could no longer ignore the situation in the west because the Unita troops had not only closed the road and railway line, but Makuma in a fit of rage had ordered the power lines to be taken down. They had a couple of ex-miners amongst the cadre and with the explosives from the mine they had finally dropped one of the pylons. It was not too efficient. It never occurred to them to simply climb up and blow up the much less robust insulator assembly at the top of the pylon, and it had taken them almost two days, four attempts, some digging and use of fires to heat the steel, before the whole pylon came crashing down.

With whole suburbs of Kinshasa without electricity the DRC government had redeployed an army unit from the east and they were making their way towards the area. With huge distances involved, though, it would be two days before they arrived, and so Makuma had absolute if temporary control over a huge tract of country and he sat like a huge black bullfrog in his Land Cruiser.

It was just approaching noon when a vehicle came bouncing along and a man jumped out with news. Their advance elements in the stop groups near Matadi had seen the grey helicopter crash and had gone to investigate. They had found a ship on the river, twenty-five kilometres away. A big one, grey like the helicopter, with a big gun. A warship.

Things began to fall into place for Makuma. So this was where they were running to.

That got him thinking. It made it easier to cut them off, but a ship? A whole ship?

Diamonds were one thing, but a whole ship? Now that was valuable. With all those white people. For that there would be a price paid.

All they would have to do was get it further down the river, out of DRC territory to where Angola bordered the river on the southern side. Hide it somewhere. He imagined himself steering it, firing the gun, yelling orders at people. He turned and looked at the runner, his presence huge, glowering, and quite deranged.

'Where is it?'

1200 hrs local

It was hot, baking hot, the bush silent but for bird calls. Away down the slope the heat shimmered. In the LUP everyone was quiet, most people sleeping. The sentries were out, the snipers were out, all maintaining radio comms with the CSM, who silently roamed the position.

Penny crept the few feet over to where McLean – who had been roving, never resting for more than a minute – was down on one knee in his scrape, looking at a map. She had never seen him like this, this relentless, charged, committed, motivated commander who did nothing for himself till his men had eaten, rested, had their wet, slept – nothing. His hair was matted and filthy, he had three days' growth in his beard, he was covered in grime and dust. His blouse was gone – she was wearing it – and he was just wearing a green T-shirt. His arms were brown from the sun and he had lost weight, lost some of the stockiness and looked leaner and sinewy, but there were bags under his eyes and the eyes themselves were red-rimmed. He looked tired, exhausted even, but then they all did.

'As your physician, take some advice. Stop. Sit down. Rest.'

He just looked at her and then back at the map he was reading. 'Time for that when we are clear of here.'

'I'm sorry about what I said back at – where—'

'Jock,' he said, without looking up. 'His name was Jock.' Images flashed through his mind of the big, light-skinned Celt, as he played good rugby. He had a girlfriend called Janice, she always wore those boots with the big clumpy heels and would totter up and down the touchline. Jock was a Van Morrison fan big time, was all he ever played in his quarters. You could hear it as you walked past.

'Well, I'm sorry about what I said where Jock—' She had trouble saying it, saying 'was left' or 'killed'. 'I'm sorry about everything. The way I behaved. I never understood what you did. It was mess dinners, and uniforms, and bloody training and deployments – all toy soldiers, big kiddies playing bang bang. I never knew. Now I do. I'm sorry. About everything. You have got us this far. No one else could have. And you do deserve them and their loyalty.'

He looked up finally and shook his head. She was wearing one of his shirts, her trousers were torn, her hair was tied back in a ponytail, and was matted with bits of grass and dust. She had a smudge down her cheek and across her forehead where she had wiped sweat away. Even looking like that, her eyes were clear and bright and she was, he still thought, quite beautiful.

'Officers come and go, their loyalty is to the Corps and their mates and this mission. Anyone could have got us this far. The greenest troop commander could have done this, and probably without losing a man.'

'Bullshit,' she replied, pushing a lock of her hair back behind her ear. 'I remember Nick Webber saying you were probably the best company commander in the Corps.' She paused. 'Some accolade.'

'Nick said that?' He grinned ruefully, putting the map down. 'He always was a crap judge of people.'

'I don't know about Nick,' she said softly, taking advantage of the moment – or the first eye contact in what seemed like days. 'But I am. I lied to you, I deceived you, I hurt you deeply. I'm sorry. I have had time to think here. If you could ever forgive me, then I'd like to come back to you. I still love you and—' He put one hand up to his earphone and cocked his head to listen to his radio, and suddenly he was up on his feet and moving. 'If you'll . . .' She trailed off, an overwhelming feeling of frustration welling up in her – that and anger – like even fate was trying to make sure she couldn't have time with him. She went to stand up and a hand pulled her back down and covered her mouth.

'Stay here. Lie down. Be very quiet,' a marine whispered.

Twelve

The marines weren't happy about their predicament, no one would be, but they were confident. Unlike the high-risk, knee-jerk rescue raid on the mission and the previous contacts, they had chosen their ground here and had had time to prepare defensive positions.

So, when the 2-Troop fire team saw their company commander skitter across the ground and drop into his TAC, and saw the CSM pointing outward, they knew it was going down, and they were ready.

This first group would be recce. No way on God's earth could they effectively assault this position. That would come later. Kevin saw Major McLean lift his binoculars.

'Here we fucking go, then. The first remake of *Platoon*,' he whispered. 'Tell you what. The first cunt who says "lock and load" or "let's rock and roll" is going to get a good slapping.'

'Lock and load,' Furby called softly.

'Let's rock and roll,' from Sloth.

'Keep your pecker hard and your powder dry, and the world *will* turn,' Dave Hobson offered, another memorable quote from the film.

'Fuck the lot of ya,' Kevin finished, thrusting his jaw out. Hobson was chuckling to himself but looking out at the heat shimmer through the bush. Biscuit raised a finger to his lips while he listened to the comms through his headphones.

'Have I told you bastards about big Mandy? The bird from Bournemouth? She was very appreciative. Gagging for it, she was,' Kevin began again. 'Trouble was, she is such a big girl

– you know, rolls of her everywhere. Well, how do you know which crack to get into? You know?' he grinned. 'You sprinkle on some Enos and fuck the one that bubbles!' he finished triumphant.

'You're a slimy bastard,' Hobson replied. He liked women. Respected them, but he was still trying to keep the smile off his face.

'Yeah. A fucking lowlife.' From Biscuit.

'Well,' Kevin responded, leaning forward into the GPMG stock. 'Eagles may soar, but on the other hand, weasels don't get sucked into jet engines.'

Sixty yards away McLean was in the hole that was the TAC HQ. 'Ericks has movement,' the CSM said. 'He's out there.' He pointed away to the right. 'Two hundred yards out and they are about five hundred yards away, moving diagonally across our front. He reckons if they keep moving on that axis, their left flank could swing into us.' Ericks was in 3 Troop, a sniper. He was watching them through his scope. They were tracking. McLean knew it. 'No. They are on our tracks. How many?'

'He is watching about twenty.'

Could be more, many more, McLean realised. A contact was inevitable. It was too late to move out and when the patrol stumbled into the LUP, they would have to be taken out. He didn't want them in that close, and he didn't want to waste his Claymores either.

'Three Five, Zero Alpha. Can you engage, over?'

'Roger, Zero Alpha. Three Six might also have them by now, over.'

Three Six was the other 3-Troop sniper two hundred yards way on the north-eastern corner. McLean called him and a few seconds later, after turning his body ninety degrees and settling back in again, he had them in his scope, eight hundred yards out. In open bush country like this, two snipers from two stands could hold down an entire company all day. It had been done, in Vietnam, by Gunnery Sergeant Carlos 'White Feather' Hathcock, the legendary US Marine sniper. He had held down almost a battalion from dawn till dark.

In this situation snipers were a tactical weapon, one that could reach out a thousand yards, and the effect on morale was devastating. Bullets that came from nowhere killing anyone who tried to stand or became visible. It also meant he wasn't betraying his other weapons or actual position.

'I'm ready,' Three Six said.

'Three Five and Six, Zero Alpha. Hold them there. Your objective is to halt the advance. Pin them down.' They both understood.

'Acknowledge, Three Alpha and Two Alpha?'

Both troop commanders responded.

'Three Five and Six, Zero Alpha. Fire at will,' McLean finished.

It was up to the snipers now. They would fire the first shot when they had drawn the enemy into whatever killing ground they had found.

McLean sat back and waited.

Twenty feet away da Silva and Dalton were in the main shell scrape with the two nuns. It was hot, still and the tension was building, almost palpable. The Portuguese engineer looked at Dalton, the man he had met playing poker at the hotel in Kinshasa only four nights ago. He was tapping a story into his PC, the satellite phone at his feet. Just four nights ago, da Silva thought again – the sequence of events flashing through his mind on fast forward – the Ambassador, and the cold drink in his office. The cold drink, condensation on the glass, the ice clinking against the side, the taste, the coolness. He looked at the journalist, and then at Sister Marie-Claire, then at the Padre.

'Ever had a rock shandy?' he asked.

'A what?' the Padre whispered back.

'A rock shandy, I think it was. Your Ambassador gave me one. Pink,' he explained, his mouth salivating at the thought. 'It was pink and cold with lots of ice. That what I want now. Not cold beer, not champagne, not even a Blinis from Harry's Bar in Venice. I want a rock shandy. You ever had one?'

The Padre shook his head. 'No, I don't think I have.'

'When we get out of here,' da Silva muttered, 'I get you one, Padre.'

'That's very kind of you, but I'm a malt whisky man.'

'Now you're talking,' Dalton said, looking up from his keyboard. He reckoned he had batteries for another hour or so and then it was over for him, filing stories from the scene. He looked at Sister Marie-Claire. 'And what about you, Sister? What would you like?'

She looked at him and smiled. 'A bath, Mr Dalton. A hot bath, with some bubbles and—' There was a long, echoing report of a rifle shot some way off. It came off the hills in the distance, rolled back over them, and was quickly followed by another.

The battle had begun.

Two hundred metres out from the marine's position, and six hundred yards off the approaching Unita force, Ericks was in his stand. He had camouflaged himself with grass and leaves, filled a sandbag to rest his L96 rifle on and laid out his ammunition to the right.He had a spotting scope to hand and he was wearing his lucky hat – a battered old Australian Akubra with fishing flies in the brim. It was wearing this hat that he had beaten the last Queen's medallist at Bisley the previous summer.

The air was still, hot, almost breathless, so nothing to bother him. The sun was high in the sky. Later it would drop down behind his targets and be in his eyes, but he had several hours yet. From this range – six hundred yards – with no windage, in good light, he could put a round into a tea cup ninety-nine times out of a hundred without any real effort. He had seventy-four rounds of Green Spot 7.62 ammunition. Each time he fired, his number two would replace the round so there were always five on the clean handkerchief laid out on the sandbag.

Out in the bush, Makuma's men were trapped. They had taken two killed up at the head of the cadre, three more men were down at the rear, and there was only forty yards between them. The older ones among them were veterans and they knew that the shots had obviously come from two different positions, one to the front and left, and one to the rear and the left. The ground was flat. Down on the ground they were concealed by the grass, but anyone rising up more than fifteen inches or so would be out of cover and a target. Men lay on the ground and pulled stones towards themselves to try and form small barricades, calling to each other, asking if anyone could see where the fire was coming from.

Someone called out a comrade's name and he rose up to answer and his head snapped back. He fell back down again, dead before the sound of the shot reached them. The others got lower down, lying flat against the ground, not moving lest they be seen and singled out by whoever was out there. An officer shouted that that was what happened when someone was that baboon stupid and to lie still until he worked out what to do.

Ericks worked the scope slowly across the scene, looking for movement, looking for a target. There. A leg. He swung the scope left up the body and found the hip, then the mid torso. There were dead down there. He knew that. He had capped two and Phillips the other 3-Troop sniper had capped three. They were trapped, pinned down. Now put on the pressure and see if he could further debilitate their capability. So far these people had cared little for their own wounded comrades, but it was worth a try, he thought.

He swung the scope back down to the mid-point of the man and, breathing out gently, touched the hair trigger. The bullet hit Makuma's man just below the hip, shattering his thigh bone. Ericks knew he would soon be in real pain, and even if his mates didn't care about him or each other, his cries would grind them down, strip any morale they had left. If anyone was brave enough to go to his aid then he wouldn't shoot, not at a man going to help another, and that was what he hoped would happen. No one moved, not to help their mate, not to move forward, not to retreat.

The advance had just stopped dead.

*   *   *

Sixteen miles away in the pool below the rapids, *Winchester* trembled gently and tugged on her mooring line and anchor cables. The survivors from the damaged Lynx were now aboard ship down in the sickbay with the LMA and the Australian lieutenant dentist, who was the nearest they had to an anaesthetist.

Connors was back ashore with his detachment, in two fire teams, fifty yards apart, each dug into a fortified position, a sangar. Earlier he had them in pairs in observation posts further out, but as the day wore on, and growing increasingly wary, he had drawn them in closer and re-formed them into their fire teams. His corporal had one OP directly out ahead of them. One marine half a mile away, high in a tree with a pair of binoculars, could see a fair distance. What Connors was concerned about now was the lack of locals. They had got used to seeing the gawkers on the bank, the small knots of villagers, local people standing looking at this strange foreign ship, but now they were gone. There were none of them. In broad daylight, lunch time, there was no one on the southern bank. So where were they? The high green walls of the rainforest seemed silent, brooding, hiding something.

'It's too fucking quiet,' the corporal muttered. 'Even the birds have gone shtum.'

'I know,' Connors said. 'We're being watched. Not us specifically, but the ship is. I can feel it in me Irish blood.' He was looking into the trees, up into the branches, out along the trails coming in towards them. 'Keep your lads alert. I'm going back to the other team. Get the OP in. I'm not sure he can see enough to make the risk of separation worthwhile. OK?'

'Sarge? Whaddya reckon the forty lads are gonna do?' one of the youngsters asked.

'Lie up, then move again tonight. They are sixteen miles' – he pointed – 'thataway.'

'But if we are being watched, like if the boongs are already here, then they could be behind every bloody bush all the way in.'

324

Connors looked at him. The lads were feeling exposed here on the bank. Just ten of them. It was build morale time. 'That's Alpha out there. Not as good as Zulu, obviously' – there were grins in the sangar – 'but I'll tell you what, you wouldn't want to mix it with them. They'll fight their way in if they have to and they'll leave the enemy dead behind them every inch of the way. Our job is the ship. Keep your mind on that and let the forty lads come in when they are ready. OK? And when they get here, we'll have a boat for them.'

Five minutes later the marine from the observation post, now down from his tree-top vantage point and making his way back to the sangar, saw a group of armed men, a large group.

Connors didn't wait to verify it. He radioed the ship and advised what they had seen.

Commander Channing, on the bridge, took the message, spoke to Connors on the VHF and looked across at the XO.

'Bring the ship to action stations. Gun crews closed up. Special duty seamen and boarding parties closed up. Chops M's reaction party in the main mess. Quietly, Mr Selby. Nothing to frighten the horses, eh?'

They had drilled this. A silent change in posture. One phone call down to the main control room where the ship's main electrical circuits were all controlled, and a few seconds later the lights went off and then on three times, and people began moving for their stations, very casually, very calmly. Disguised intent.

In the Phalanx control office, Chief Petty Officer Davies sat at his console and tapped a few codes into his keyboard. The port side Phalanx jerked once as it went live and its circuits powered up.

In the old days it would have been solid rounds, solid 20-millimetre chunks of depleted uranium, but now they could load standard 20-mill. ammunition, each shell with an exploding head that could take out an aircraft, a car, an armoured personnel carrier. The gun's stubby snout seemed to sniff at whatever was out there on the dark, forested riverbank.

Mike Lunnon-Wood

Below the main deck gun in the gun bay, ammunition for the 4.5-inch gun was already in the feed ring, and a hoist began to bring up more from the main magazines. On the decks the 20-mill. Oerlikons, the gambos, had belts in the feed tray, and the GPMGs had rounds in the breeches and steel boxes of ammunition already in place.

Nellie Tusker arrived up on the gun-controller's platform behind the bridge, his flash gear under his arm, gave the brooding trees along the shore a nonchalant look and moved towards the four lads by the port gambo.

'So, whaddya reckon, Nellie? They watching us?' He smiled quickly. Ships were small places, where rumour and scuttlebutt raced round in no time at all.

'You know what they say,' he replied in a John Wayne drawl. 'If you can see 'em, they ain't Apaches.' One lit a cigarette and Nellie noticed his hand was shaking.

'You lads ready, then?' They nodded, and he quickly ran them through their instructions and checks before sending two of them up to the GPMG on the bridge wing. The pair got there, turned into the bridge, then dropped out of sight and crawled back out to sit behind the screen within reach of their machine gun. They were ready and Nellie plugged in his comms line. 'Ops, Gun Controller. Port crews closed up.'

Makuma had come to see for himself. He had been driven up as far as the Land Cruiser would go and walked the last half mile, and now he was on the bank, some four hundred yards downstream of the *Winchester*, looking up at her sharp bows. He was confident. He had three hundred of his men either here or closing on this pool and he stood just inside the trees overlooking the wide waters like he owned the place.

How to get to it, and when they got there, would it be guarded? He could see figures moving around, so there would be some resistance, but he had hundreds of men and could lose a few. There had to be a boat somewhere nearby, maybe several. He called out orders, and looked down at his watch. By now Ndube should have closed on the nuns, they had been

326

following spoor since morning. He would leave a large cadre here to find boats, and go back to where the nuns were with the diamonds.

A few hundred yards along the bank one of the Royal Marines looked back out of the sangar with very mixed feelings. He was very pleased there was a big 'fuck-off warship', as his mate had articulately called it, up close ready to support them, but he was also aware that meant there were sailors with GPMGs, SA80s and, fucksakes, a 20-mill. cannon and they were in the middle.

'Hope those bastards can shoot,' he muttered.

'Me too,' someone added.

'Don't be fucking stupid,' his mate said. 'There's nothing more dangerous than a jack with a weapon. The only safe place to be is in behind them.'

'Yeah, a long way behind them. In Brighton.'

'Or New Zealand,' someone added.

'The only good news is that the other cunts probably shoot worse.'

'Yeah and the other good news is there's only a couple of hundred of them.'

'And a couple of hundred sailors.'

'So, to recap, that's four hundred wankers with guns, none of whom can shoot, squaring up against each other, and we are in the middle.' They began laughing. It was a very Royal Marines thing to do. The worse it got, the more they made light of it.

'There's every chance nothing will happen,' the corporal said. 'But, whatever happens, remember the ROE. We don't initiate fire.'

Sixteen miles away at the Alpha Company position the two snipers on the western flank held Makuma's men pinned down. There was a shot every few minutes from one stand or the other and every now and then one of the Unita men, fear or anger getting the better of prudence, would fire an ineffectual burst in the general direction of where they thought the fire was coming from.

In the centre area where the civilians were gathered in the shell scrape behind their small redoubt of stones, the emotions were mixed. Sister Marie-Claire was praying, but Sister Jo, the youngest, was just staring at the ground, angry, upset, disappointed – mostly at herself. From the start the others had been sharing the anguish with each other, praying, supporting each other, but she had found herself more and more on the periphery – but there by her own choice. She had never doubted her calling before now, not seriously. But now, for the first time, she was questioning the passivity of her own faith. She looked up at them and realised she had also unconsciously distanced herself physically. What is happening to me? she thought. She was full of fear, hurt, anger, she wanted to hit out at the people hunting them. She felt no forgiveness, no compassion for them, not like she should have done. Suddenly after days of confusion and doubt, the anger brought clarity. She wasn't going to roll over and give in, stand bovine-like and die, that wasn't what God wanted. There's a time to fight. She thought about Sister Sarah, her friend – the rape, the men on her, the smell, the stench of them, the vileness, the evil, the others who had died, the child at the village, its mother hacked to death, the people with their hands chopped off.

She rubbed her face, the big, blue swelling where she had been hit with the rifle butt at the mission. If God wanted her to die, then she would have died at the mission, so he didn't. He wanted her to stand up. Look it in the eye. Fight in his name. She looked across at Penny. She had grown to like the doctor in the last few weeks and had seen the interaction between her and McLean. They obviously knew each other and there was something between them, and now she wanted him back, but by all the signs he wasn't having it. She envied them, though – envied them the passion, the richness, the texture of it. The reality. Penny would fight. Fight for what she wanted. She was now. She looked across at da Silva. He had a gun. A big long one. She didn't want to be with him, she wanted to be with

Sloth, but he wasn't here and da Silva was. She crawled over to where he sat.

A few feet away the Padre watched her and then looked back at Dalton to answer his question. 'I'm not sure really. I did the all-arms course but I'm not a soldier really. I think our chaps just hold them there till dark and then we slip out again.'

Rory Chisholm may not have been a soldier but he got it exactly right. That was just what McLean was hoping to do. Pin down the Unita patrol until nightfall and then slip out and make the run for the ship. His marines were good at night, better than any soldiers on this continent, that was for sure, and certainly better than irregulars. Webber used to say he had never met an African soldier below staff level who could read a map worth a damn, and they just didn't like fighting at night. So far the latter had been proven enough for him to prefer the night march option and they could do sixteen miles in one push.

He was looking at his map, the crap 1:500 000 aviators' chart that showed bugger-all on the ground, but major water courses and high ground, the things that pilots need to do pinpoint navigation and not fly into things. So, what will they expect us to do? he wondered. Swing north and round, south and then up to the ship, or a short dog-leg? They certainly won't expect a straight march. He looked at his watch. It was 1320 hours. The snipers had been at work for over an hour now, covering an area a kilometre deep and almost one and a half wide. Break out at 1800.

'Pass the word,' he said to the CSM. 'They know we are here. Anyone with scran can come off hard routine. Tell 'em to get some hot food down while they can.'

Back at the river the marines in the sangars were settled in, two looking out watching the trails, three down resting in the bottom of the hole. In the western sangar, fifty yards downstream from the other, the marine looking west never took his eyes from the forest track, just moved his boot and tapped the bloke nearest him.

Mike Lunnon-Wood

'Sergeant. I have visual. Armed and heading this way.'

Connors was up on his feet in a second, the radio handset in his hand, and as he looked out of the camouflaged sangar, he was already talking to the ship.

This was the hairy bit. Their rules of engagement, meant they couldn't fire unless fired upon, but if these men were hostile, then every step closer they became more of a threat, harder to contain, harder to repulse. So, stay in cover, issue a challenge, wave in a friendly manner, dig like fuck, hope they walk past, or shoot the shit out of them? He knew what he wanted to do. Come on, Channing. Earn your rank. Make a decision, man, it's getting hairy down here. Fifty yards and closer, at least thirty in this group. How many others nearby? Come on, come on. Forty yards, right in the improvised anti-personnel mine's arc.

'Tosh on the clackers,' he called softly. Come on, come on, say something. Then he did it. Did what he had to do.

'I'm gonna challenge. The first cunt that raises a weapon, engage!' He stuck his head up out of the top of the slit and waved a hand in the air at the approaching men.

'Hello! We are British forces. We are friendly!' he called. *'Anglaise! Britannie! Vous—'* There were weapons coming up from at least four men in the front bunch and he dropped back as a burst of fire hammered out above their heads.

'Open fire,' he snapped. 'Hit 'em!'

The marine holding the mine-initiator hit the electrical detonator and it went off.

It was spectacular. It was a kilogram of torpex – an explosive removed from a torpedo – packed into a convex piece of steel removed from a pump housing and embedded with three kilos of iron filings, nails, screws and other assorted crap and debris from the depths of the MEO's world.

The blast shook the earth, the shrapnel flying outwards with a concussion wave that ripped leaves from trees and shook dust up from the ground. In the sangar they were deafened for a moment, their ears ringing, and when they looked out, no one was standing on the track. Whoever had survived the lethal shrapnel had been knocked down by the blast wave and hadn't got up, if they ever would.

Not one of the marines had even got a single shot away.

'Fuckin' 'ell!' Tosh muttered. 'I think we got them, Sarge.'

'Romeo Mike, *Winchester*. Are you OK? Was that you?' It was Channing. He must have had the mic in his hand when it went off.

'Aah – roger, *Winchester*. That was us. They presented weapons and fired on us, over,' Connors replied. As he spoke there was another burst of fire, this one from further down the shore, and aimed at the ship, but even inside the sangar they all instinctively ducked. It was followed by more as other weapons opened up, some at them, some out over the water at the *Winchester* and the heavier beat of a GPMG opening up on the ship. 'Here we go then,' Connors muttered.

On *Winchester*, up on the gun controller's platform the voice crackled in Nellie's headphones. 'Gun Controller, Ops.'

Nellie thumbed his mic switch, not taking his eyes from the bank. 'Ops, Gun Controller. Go.'

'Do you have a visual on where the fire is coming from, over?' As he asked the question, the rating on the gambo, the 20-mill., turned and look at him and raised a thumb. He had visual. Twenty feet further along, a GPMG opened up, returning fire at the shoreline.

'Ops, Gun Controller. We have visual.'

'Take it with 20-mill.,' came the command. This was Channing on the bridge. Nellie gave the command and the 20-millimetre Oerlikon anti-aircraft gun began to fire, short bursts of two or three rounds, the bank so close they could see the strikes as the exploding ammunition hit. The rhythm was one-second bursts, broken by breaks of one second, and with the gun designed to deliver fire accurately 8000 yards, this was point-blank range. The firing from that spot died away but started from another.

Channing had a pair of binoculars up, as did both Selby and Sally Wallace.

331

'Shit,' Selby muttered. 'Hit one and it comes from somewhere else.'

Wallace had seen something. She looked again and then stepped back to take a bearing.

'Rocket launcher. I can see a rocket launcher,' she called.

'Where away?' Channing snapped.

'Red 43 degrees, it's on 234 degrees! On the bank above the waterline.'

'Gun Controller, bridge, red 43 degrees, range two hundred metres, a party with a rocket launcher! Can you see 'em?' Channing paused and looked at Selby. 'Get some snipers for'ard!'

Further back in his hutch, the Chief Petty Officer heard the call.

'Bridge, Phalanx. I have the bearing for PAC. Give me an elevation and someone spotting and I can take it.'

Channing, who prided himself on encouraging initiative in his crew, wasn't changing now. Bullets were hitting the ship and a rocket or rocket-propelled grenade would do real damage.

'Gun Controller, Captain,' he said as Selby darted off the bridge. 'Correct fire for port Phalanx.' There was no time for drills, no time for the book. If PO Davies said he could do it, let him have a go.

'Phalanx, Captain. Stand to!'

'GDC clear visual?'

'Clear visual,' Nellie reported.

'Port Phalanx, engage!'

In the cramped hutch, PO Davies – who had entered the bearing as a pre-action calibration test – armed the gun from his LCP – the local control panel – removed the 'hold fire' from his console, and now effectively with a manual override, he moved his finger two inches to the right and pressed the 'fire' button. He had loaded enough solid rounds – the depleted uranium type – for sighting bursts, and could do three before he reached the exploding head in the feed belts. The Phalanx – like a big, white, dome-topped telephone box – flicked on to the bearing, the stubby barrels pointing at the bank on zero elevation, and fired a sighting burst. The rounds hammered into the trees above the spot where the Unita men were settling in.

'Down thirty feet,' Nellie called.

Thirty feet, thirty feet. Come on, what the fuck's thirty feet at two hundred yards? He tapped in an elevation shift in degrees and fired again.

'Down ten. Fire for effect!'

The Phalanx could fire 4500 rounds a minute, and this time he hit them with a full ninety-round burst, the first ten DU rounds, but the next all high explosive with contact detonators.

It was like a second-long explosion on the bank. Trees fell, cut down by the burst, and when the smoke had cleared, there was no vegetation, no undergrowth, nothing was left across an area five metres square. Just blackened smoking earth. Along the bank, all fire had stopped. There was a deathly silence.

'Jesus,' Channing muttered softly.

'And the lads in the Falklands thought that Milan was the ultimate trench-clearing weapon,' Selby added.

'Phalanx, relax!' Channing called. 'Well done, PO.'

PO Davies responded and went back to his calculations. He needed a ready reckoner for elevation and range and when that was done and only then would he pop his head out and see what he had achieved. He began working away, smiling to himself, when the Captain arrived in the doorway, followed by Selby.

'Bloody outstanding!' the Captain snapped, a big grin on his face.

'Thanks, sir!' He beamed.

'How much control have you wrestled away from the computer, then?'

'Quite a lot, sir. Give me the range and the bearing and a rough elevation and I can adjust on the second burst.'

'Can you see if you can support the RM positions? Pre-plan it?'

'I don't see why not, sir. We'll need some more 20-mill. up here, and a couple of lads to reload for me.'

'Done. Anything else?'

'Someone numerate? I'm working a ready reckoner for elevations, but if someone else can do that, then I can get back into the software and preprogramme the increments.'

Channing looked at Selby and it was the XO who said it.

'Teller?' he suggested. Jenny Teller, the girl who said numbers were her thing.

'You got it. Make it happen. If she can't hack it, get a watch-keeping officer here. Anything this man needs up here.'

'Aye aye.'

Ashore, Connors was wondering what it was. He had never heard Phalanx engage before. It just sounded like a loud second-long fart – a B-R-R-R-R-P, and a chunk of the bank had been reduced to cinders. The effect was that all the firing on the bank had ceased, for the time being at least.

'Baaaluddy 'ell!' one of his lads said. 'What the fuck was that?'

'Phalanx,' another replied. 'Saw it in Nottingham once.'

'Phalanx! But that's for missiles 'n shit. They supposed to use it on shore targets?'

'Who cares? Works a treat.'

'Yeah, fuck 'em!' the fourth added, chuckling. 'Now that is what I call an anti-personnel weapon.'

'We'll have some more of that.'

'Settle down, lads, and stand to,' Connors said. 'They'll be back.'

On board *Winchester*, the senior rating down in the MCO put the phone back on the hook and looked at Teller. 'You. Phalanx control. Go!'

'Me?'

'You. That was the Jimmy. He's waiting up there for you.'

When she arrived – she had taken the ladders at a run – Selby just pointed at PO Davies and walked away.

'You said you liked numbers?' Davies said. 'You any good?'

She looked him in the eye. 'Maths and Physics A levels.'

Heraklion Blue*

'A levels!' he raised an eyebrow and pointed to an old swivel chair in the corner of the tiny, cramped station. 'Right,' he said. 'The barrels are' – he jotted down a figure – 'above the water here at point A. Can you work out how far they need to be depressed, in one-degree increments, at differing ranges, say between one hundred and four hundred metres?'

'Easy.' She took the piece of paper, and quickly worked out a formula. 'Four ranges, that's four variables on X, and with maximum downward elevation spread of, what, thirty degrees, but we would only use maybe twelve or thirteen of those—'

'Don't give me formula. I want a chart. Can you do it?'

'Sure.'

He looked at her. 'Can I ask something?'

She looked up at him, no longer the shy, angry girl she was three days ago. She was in her element, confident, it was coming off her in force.

'Two science As. What the hell are you doing on the lower decks?'

Ashore, Connors looked down at his watch. It was just coming up for two p.m. Four hours of daylight left.

They would come soon, not along the bank as they had done, but through the bush, out of sight of *Winchester*'s guns.

Back at the place where his men were pinned down, Makuma strode through the bush like an angry elephant. He fumed, the anger flowing from him, his acolytes having a job to keep up, but keeping a distance in case he lashed out. Ahead of him in three large cadres were almost five hundred of his men, and they had stopped. They knew where the nuns were. They had found them and then stopped. Baboons. They were stupid, frightened baboons and he knew how to get them moving. It was simple. Remind them about the diamonds and the bigger prize on the water, and finally just be the more frightening of the two alternatives.

He could hear the long, rolling report of a rifle every now and then, a flat whiplash crack that echoed round the hills.

So, that's it, he thought. His men were highly respectful,

335

fearful even of a man who could use a long rifle. The older ones, when working with South African troops in the eighties, had seen their snipers perform, and they had an almost unreasoning fear of white men with scope-mounted weapons. In Makuma's experience he had never met a Unita fighter who could hit anything much over a hundred yards away, and they never had the training to do long shots.

'Send a runner,' he snapped, 'Tell them if they all shoot at once the sniper will have to duck and then they can move. Hurry! If they are still there when I get there, there will be trouble!'

Inside the Royal Marines' position they were stood to, but resting.

'Why haven't they swung round this side, then? All the tactical nous of a bunch of schoolgirls,' Kevin muttered. As far as he was concerned, any green, pongo squaddie knew that much. If your advance is pinned down at one point you try another.

'Who cares?' Sloth responded. 'They can sit there all afternoon for all I care.'

Hobson, down in the bottom of the hole, was repacking his day sack and the tin was out. He had found it earlier, a treat his mother had given him months before. He had been rooting around in his pack, sifting through the goodies, the little extras one added to make half-edible scran. Down below the curry powder, the Tabasco sauce, the garlic, the fresh onion and the little bell peppers of a kind he hadn't seen before, was the little orange tin. He held it up and looked at it.

'Fuckin' 'ell, Dave. You still got that? You had that on Bodmin, didn't you?'

'Yeah, been saving it.'

'Crack it open, then,' Furby said. 'I fancy a bit of something nice. What is it?' Hobson looked at the small tin again. It came from a Fortnum and Mason hamper that his mum had won in the local church hall raffle, a small tin containing 'Sir, Nigel's Vintage Orange Marmalade cake'. He had never eaten one, and in spite of having humped it for months, waiting for the day that he would really appreciate it, he looked across the rocky grassy position into the redoubt and saw one of the VMs handing a wet round the women. He knew who would appreciate it more.

'Naa. Let's give it to the women,' he said. He scuttled over to the group and gave it to the Padre. 'For the girlies, Padre. Can't have tea without cake, now, can we?' And he was gone back to his hole.

'Oi,' Kevin muttered, with mock indignation. 'Fuck us, right? Fuck your mates. What else you got secreted in there, then?'

'This,' he said with a grin.

'What?'

'Hobnobs.'

'Oh yes! Give the totty the bloody cake then. We'll have the bikkies.' They all piled into them, Sloth throwing two up to Furby, who remained stood to, watching the bush.

'What a kind young man,' Sister Marie-Claire said. She took off the floppy hat she had been wearing and wiped sweat from her brow.

'Yes,' the Padre smiled. 'He is.'

'I think we should save this,' Sister Marie-Claire said, taking the tin and looking at it. 'It's early for afternoon tea. What do you think, *girlies*?' she asked, using Hobson's word with a smile. Penny nodded, but not Sister Jo, who had changed in the last hours, almost like she had begun to deal with what had happened to them in some form. She had said no to tea, and was sipping water from a bottle, small sips like she had seen the soldiers taking, her look somewhere distant, her expression hard, resolute. Time for that later, Sister Marie-Claire thought. She looked at Maneru, and knowing he had every African's love of sweet things, thinking how he would enjoy some of the cake when they opened the tin. He was now many miles from his village and twice she had heard Major McLean ask him if he wanted to go home, releasing him from any obligation, but he had declined.

Dalton was just finishing a piece, an emotive first person account, which began, 'We are now lying up, as the marines call it, in a defensive position, awaiting nightfall, when we can move again. Out there, somewhere in the hot, dry bush, maybe all around us already, are two thousand men, no longer just a rogue, Angolan rebel unit, but a warring army, who want to kill us and we don't know why. We just run and hide, all the time trying to get closer to safety, closer to HMS *Winchester*, now just sixteen miles away. The marines could do that at a jog – be there in two hours – but they are here to help us to safety, and so our slowest pace determines theirs. Their presence, their quiet confidence, their sheer professionalism, leaves us less fearful, and their unfailing good humour carries our morale. Without them the nuns and staff from Tenta mission would all surely be dead by now. At dawn – as we finished our night march, exhausted – I watched a Royal Marine pick up and carry one of our party who simply couldn't go on, as gently as he would have a baby. This from a man who had been in the thick of the fighting just hours earlier. Now here, on this small hill in the middle of nowhere on this huge, sprawling, violent continent, we wait for dark, wait in silence, wait in the heat, while the Royal Marine snipers hold back the advancing patrols who have been tracking us since first light.

'I am frightened. I admit it. We all are – those of us left – from England and Belgium. Mr da Silva, the Portuguese engineer, a road builder here on an aid programme, shows it least . . .'

Maneru was squatting, watching the journalist, fascinated with the laptop computer. Dalton smiled, stopped what he was doing and opened a graphics package, this one a screen saver with a leopard moving. The old man's eyes widened in wonder, one long bony finger reaching out and touching the screen.

Dalton looked across at him and noticed something for the first time. A scar, healed long ago, but its shape was unmistakable. A small cross on his forehead. The ritual scarring of the Simbas, who had terrorised Katanga back in the sixties.

'I see you have the mark, old one,' Dalton said softly, the pieces falling into place. 'You were there?'

Maneru nodded. 'I was young and foolish. I should have left, but I stayed. You joined them or you died.' Sister Marie-Claire said that Sister Mary had known him a long time back, in the sixties.

'Isangi? Were you at Isangi?'

Maneru nodded, his eyes clouding over as the memories bit into the present, and he seemed to recoil at what he saw. 'It was a time of death. Of killing. When they went to the mission to take the whites, I knew them and I ran away.' He went silent for a second or two, but the need to say something was strong, the guilt still strong, undulled by the thirty-five years that had passed. 'I should have tried to help them, but I was fearful.'

'So, this time you do,' Dalton finished for him.

Sister Marie-Claire watched them – two generations, two worlds, two cultures meeting – when suddenly the shooting seemed to increase and she looked across at the Major.

McLean was crouching down, listening to someone in his headphones.

They had dug in, prepared their position. Which way would they come? he was thinking. This was important, because that would have an impact on where they held them. They only had enough explosives and mines for two-thirds of the perimeter and the bulk of those were in a channel heading north-west, the route he had chosen for them when they moved out. He looked out that way. A large old baobab tree formed one side, the two msasas the other. Claymore mines, real and improvised, lined that avenue, and tonight after dark they would leave by that route. Anyone either side of that channel for one hundred yards either way would be taken out by the mines. Anyone inside the channel would have his fire teams advancing on them. If Makuma positioned men there they could be dealt with, unless, for some reason, they were there in concentrated strength. But there was no reason for him to do that. They could break out in any direction and there was no reason to suppose that any, other than directly west, was a preference.

'Zero Alpha, sitrep. They are moving. Lots of fire from them and they have split up. I say again, split up into two forces, one moving north, the other south. The group moving north – company strength – I can keep an eye on and re-engage in a couple of minutes, over.'

'Three Five, Zero Alpha. Roger, thank you. Re-engage when you can. Three Six, acknowledge, over?'

Zero Alpha, roger.'

'Three Six, can you get a visual on the group heading south, over?'

'Not yet. I have a thick stand of trees in my way maybe four hundred metres out. If they pass behind them— Wait.'

McLean waited and a second later there was a gunshot from his right.

'Sorry, Zero. Saw one and took him out. I'll advise if I see the big party again, over.'

'Roger, Six,' McLean finished. 'Mind your right. I say, mind your right flank.'

Over in their hole, Furby looked down at Biscuit, who lay in the bottom of the dugout. He was pale and breathing in short breaths. The wound in his back was obviously giving him trouble. He looked across at Sloth and pointed down. Sloth nodded, and took a decision. He slipped out of the hole and slithered over to where Willis was about twenty feet further back.

'Boss? Biscuit. That wound in his back? He looks like shit.'

Willis nodded, followed Sloth back to the hole, and took one look. One man down already with Jock gone, and now Barton in real pain. It was barely a functioning fire team. He spoke into his throat mic and a few moments later looked up. 'You lot will move into the redoubt. Now. You are in the support team.'

They picked up packs and weapons and, gathering up their corporal, who had come out of his fitful sleep, they all slithered back towards the centre, Barton complaining that he was OK, he could cuff it.

'Shaddup, Biscuit,' Willis said tiredly. 'You *will* use a

syrette! Understand. None of this hero shit. If I need your blokes, then you better be able to lead them.'

Barton nodded, and they slipped into the redoubt past the team that would be relieving them, Sloth dropping his pack and helping Barton to get his blouse off, Shagger dropping down in the bottom of the shell scrape and going back to sleep.

'Fucking 'ell,' he muttered. The wound had been bleeding, and Barton's shirt was saturated with blood. 'If that was meant to make me feel better, it doesn't,' he said through the pain as Sloth stripped the dressing away.

A pair of hands pushed Sloth's away and Gubby took over. He didn't like what he was seeing, and in a moment or two had morphine out, not with a disposable morphine syrette, but the full-monty syringe and a little bottle he was filling it from.

'I hate needles,' Biscuit said, looking at it.

'Yeah, well. It's the first of two, sport,' Gubby replied through his missing teeth. 'You're getting morph and anti-biotics, like it or not.' Someone had woken Penny by then and she slipped in beside him. 'Then the doc is going to redo the sutures you have pulled out, so be a good boy. If you're not, then I'll do 'em myself, and you wouldn't like that. Now relax, because when I have got this shit' – he grinned again – 'I am Doctor Feelgood.'

Sloth, Furby, Kevin and Dave Hobson sat back and let the medics do their stuff, while the Three-Troop sergeant in command of the support team and mortars, briefed them. Behind him Sloth could see the civvies – and the girl, Sister Jo. She was looking at him and smiling.

He looked away from her, back to the sergeant, concentrating on what he was saying.

'Two groups, now, one moving north.' He swung his arm round to show the way they were moving. 'The others swinging the other way. We still have four snipers out there, so it's wait-and-see time. If they come at us, our job is to support any breach in the line. Any questions?'

'We fight as a team?' Kevin asked, pointing round the group, his question including Biscuit, who was now bent over with the doctor putting stitches into his back.

'Yes. Your call sign stands.' The sergeant grinned. 'You are not part of my troop, you are mere wannabes.'

'You wish!' Kevin replied, thrusting his jaw out.

There was a rattle of gunfire from the south, automatic weapons. They all knew what it was. Frightened, tense men, doing what the Americans in Vietnam termed 'reconnaissance by fire' – a grand expression for, if you aren't sure, shoot the shit out of it and see if anything shoots back. After being pinned down by sniper fire for so long they would be seeing snipers behind every rock. Sloth looked over that way and said nothing. He had done the sniper's course, knew what they were capable of, knew that a sniper was an effective weapon, even against well-trained troops, because often all you could fight a sniper with was another sniper, and if you didn't have one, you were in trouble. This Two-Troop detachment had four.

'Listen to that,' Kevin sneered. 'No fucking discipline.'

'They're shitting themselves,' Furby muttered.

'I would, too,' Sloth said quietly. In fact, he admitted to himself, he *was*. Two thousand of them, sixty of us, with a bunch of civilians in a shit state, and sixteen miles away from our ship. He had begun to think like that. That *Winchester* was their ship. And the girl, Jo. He didn't want her in this. He didn't want any of them in this, but not her, not now. He looked across at where she was, just twenty feet way, and his heart began to pound in his chest. He hadn't grumbled when they were moved in here. In any normal circumstances he would have, but she was here. He felt closer. Nearer. She smiled at him and for a second there was no one else in the world but them.

'Incoming!' someone called. There was a, tearing sound and a rocket-propelled grenade seared overhead, a grey-white smoke trail behind it, before it hit some trees on the other side and exploded. 'And another!'

'Cover!' This one was aimed better, lower, because it hit a few feet from the high, rock-lined side of the shell scrape with a bang that left people's ears ringing, and dust, earth, leaves and grass raining down on them. Bullets began hitting around them, some going past like angry, whirring, buzzing insects, the sounds of the guns reaching them moments later.

It had started.

Thirteen

Half a mile away, Makuma had arrived with his men and joined the group swinging south. Other reinforcements had arrived – many of them – and he had them split to flank the whites and be able to come from two places at once. Comms was his problem and always had been. What radios they had once had, supplied by the Americans and South Africans years before, were now largely unserviceable, and he only had three working in the entire formation of two thousand men. For the last few years he had reverted to the old way – runners.

One radio was with the cadre down at the river, one he had with his vehicle, and the other was with one of the two groups here. Trouble was, it was with the group he was with, not the ones on the far side, so he called for a runner, and it occurred to him that when they got the diamonds and stripped the dead, he would also get working radios, new ones, the latest type. The fact that none of his men would know how to use them was irrelevant.

The men this side had started. From this position on this rising ground they were on the same level as the whites and south-east of them, and from some points they could see where the nuns' camp was positioned. Urged on by him, and at last in sight of the whites they had begun to fight, Ndube and his vicious henchmen darted around them to remind them of their duty to the cause.

Makuma moved forward, bull-like, rampaging among his men, exhorting their efforts, threatening those who lingered before moving forward. He had a pistol and occasionally fired a shot towards the nuns' camp, before looking at whatever group was nearest, the pistol in his hand, the madness in his single functioning eye, and they would move forward. Rural Africans have great fear of the insane. They see them as possessed by demons, as not entirely human, something not to be understood and dealt with, but instead to be feared and in awe of. They were terrified of their commander. Terrified not only of his huge bulk and imposing strength, but his violence. He was brutal, sadistic and, with a complete lack of any compunction, remorse or empathy, he would single out and kill anyone who disobeyed him.

Their fear of him was unreasoning. They were all armed. Any of them could have turned on him and killed him, but so deep was the ingrained fear, and the aura that surrounded him, that no one dared, and some even said he was protected by evil spirits.

He called for a runner to find Ndube and when the ferrety little acolyte arrived Makuma sent him round the other side, to personally take command of the other cadre and to meet him in the middle. He explained what he wanted done, and Ndube left with three of his immediate cohort – young men, impressionable, brutalised by bush warfare, who knew no other way and who were as merciless as their master.

Eight hundred yards away, one of the 2-Troop snipers, Tino Dallaglio, who had been facing south-west, could now see the Unita troops in the bush on his left flank. He turned his stand fifty degrees, got settled, and raised his rifle to look through the powerful telescopic sight.

'Got 'em?' his spotter asked.

'Yeah. I got 'em.' He touched his throat mic, 'Two Alpha, Two Five.'

'Two Five, Two Alpha. Go!'

'Two Alpha, I have the enemy firing on you visual from my loc, they are company strength, advancing from the south-east. Permission to engage, over?'

Willis never got a chance to respond. McLean came in then. 'Two Five, Zero Alpha. Fire at will!'

Tino was a twenty-two-year-old, swarthy kid, whose parents

had come to Bournemouth from Italy in the sixties and owned a fish-and-chip shop. He preferred London, always had done. His auntie had a flower shop near the hospital in Roehampton, and he used to work there as a kid. He wondered what all the old dears would think of what he was doing now. 'Here we go, then,' he said. 'Just make sure no one gets in behind us, OK?'

He pulled his floppy hat forward – the one his mum had bought in Benidorm, and he had dyed green and brown – and then he adjusted the face veil, so that lay across his hat and then down over the scope and workings. The number two lying beside him could see remnants of the words '*Buenos Dias*' through the veil and dye, but from anything more than six feet away he was invisible.

Tino closed the bolt on his rifle and sighted on one of the Unita men moving forward through the scrub and trees, and holding his breath, touched the hair trigger. The man was wearing cut-down jeans, what looked like a tea cosy on his head, a DPM shirt, and carried an AKM, a folding-stock Kalashnikov. The L96 7.62-calibre rifle kicked back into his shoulder and the man he had sighted on dropped dead before the sound of the shot reached them. By then Tino had a second round into the breech and sighted on the next man. He fired again and as the second man went down like a rag roll, everyone vanished into cover.

'Move!' Makuma bellowed, moving up. 'Up, you cowards! Shoot at him. If you all shoot, he can't.' Some of them moved, some didn't. One man stood, began to run forward and died, and the Royal Marine found his mark again.

Makuma stopped over one man, 'Get up!'

The man didn't. He was frightened of Makuma, but more frightened of the sniper. As Makuma stood over him and swung a foot, the Royal Marine sniper saw him through the trees and swung the barrel of his rifle.

Makuma kicked the man, and then bent down to pull him to his feet, and as he bent from the waist, a bullet thunked into the tree trunk behind him, wood chips and bits of bark hitting him.

In their stand, the number two was watching through his binoculars. 'Where's the big fat git gone? D'you get 'im?'

'No.'

'That's the one, isn't it? Their CO?' he said dropping his binoculars. The description had been clear. Big man – huge – baseball cap, women's sunglasses, red T-shirt under a DPM shirt.

'Yeah, I had him. He ducked.' Where are you, you great, fat, fucking tub of lard? he was thinking. This is Pissed-off of Bournemouth and I've got your fucking number! But nothing moved in the trees.

Makuma glowered, the rage burning deep within him, so deep it was cold, evil. He had crawled away from the tree the sniper had hit, knowing he had only just survived. It was sheer luck he had bent over at the right moment, or he would now be as dead as the others. He looked out in the direction the shot had come from, his one working eye black and flat like that of a snake, trying to work out what to do next. He needed to get men round that side, to find the man with the gun. He wanted him alive. He wanted to make him pay for what he had done. Pay for the audacity he had shown. He had shot at him. Aimed at him. At him! Paul Makuma. No one did that and lived. No one! He would skin him alive. Cut his testicles off, gut him and let the ants feed off his still-living body.

He called an order to be passed to a runner and then began to crawl backwards through the men around him. They watched him go, men who had never seen him defer to anyone, let alone crawl away on his belly. Some, the younger ones, were confused. This was their leader, their commanding officer. But more than that. He was their warlord – fearless, some even said unkillable like a chimera, and here he was down on his belly with the rest of them. The older ones were more practical, and one or two, pleased to see him humbled, even looked away and smiled.

On the far side, Ndube arrived with his acolytes and immediately set about galvanising the men cowering in the bush. They had found a position where they were out of sight of the snipers and had settled in.

McLean looked at his watch. It was now coming up for 1500 hours. The enemy were on two flanks – north-east and south-east – by now at least four companies in strength and increasing. In classical tactical thinking they now had the numerical superiority, the better than 3:1 ratio, to mount an assault on a prepared position, although he doubted they saw in those absolute terms. They just knew there were lots of them, many more than the defenders, and it would – should – be enough.

He looked back into the centre redoubt at the clutch of people, the women tired, filthy, grimy, some hurt, all frightened. Sister Marie-Claire was fanning her face with her hat, Dalton writing notes, da Silva asleep, his rifle in his arms lying next to the last of the three fellows taken at Yetwene. Maneru, the local man who had guided them, was still there with them. His job was done, but he wouldn't leave them.

Sister Jo was sitting with Penny, who had finished patching up Corporal Barton, and the two of them were talking softly. McLean had seen the change. There was anger there, righteous anger, a fighting spirit, a resoluteness. Less of *God's will be done* and more *He helps those who help themselves*. Go for it, girl, he was thinking.

They were looking rough.

He was questioning his judgement in stopping for the hundredth time, but knowing that he had had no alternative. The civvies were going down. Exhausted, some with injuries. If they had kept going they would have slowed down and would eventually have been run down by Makuma's men out in the open. The fact was they would not have been able to go on. Although he could have put them all into litters if he had to, it would have taken half of his men to carry them. It would have been slow and, without the fighting integrity and order of battle he needed, they would have been in deep shit. Out there, with no prepared positions, nowhere to fight from, his two troops would eventually have been overrun by sheer numbers. That would have been very unprofessional. At least here, on rising ground, they could rest till dark, and with mines out and with interlocking fields of fire, they had a chance if the enemy came.

But it was time to pull his snipers in. They had done their job, held the advance; and the chances of them being flanked, cut off from their exit route, and killed were increasing by the minute. They could now perform their black art from the defensive perimeter.

'Three Five and Six, Zero Alpha. Withdraw to the perimeter. I say, withdraw to the perimeter. Two Five and Six, hold in position till advised or situation requires withdrawal, over.'

Everyone responded, and a couple of minutes later the two snipers with their number twos slipped in through the defensive line, pleased to be back in with their mates.

It was ten minutes before Ndube figured it out. The sniper fire had stopped and four times now someone had darted forward without attracting a shot. They had gone, slipped away into the bush, back to their camp, maybe, or somewhere else? One way to find out.

'You.' He pointed at a section leader. 'Take your men forward. The sniper has gone.'

The man lying on the ground a few feet away, looked at him with mounting horror.

'He could still be there. Fooling us,' he replied. 'We should wait longer—'

Ndube, also lying on the ground, pointed his rifle at him. 'Move,' he said, his eyes glittering, an evil grin across his face.

The man's expression changed to one of resignation, acceptance of his own death, and he rose and began to move forward, darting from cover to cover, gaining confidence as he ran. Nothing happened to him and his section rose and followed in the same manner, careful not to expose themselves for any longer than was absolutely necessary. Finally, Ndube got up as well and moved down the stalled advance line, kicking men to their feet with threats and a pointed gun. Within a minute he had the advance moving again. The nuns and the whites were just four hundred yards away now, and he had the better part of three hundred men closing on them. He grinned and followed the first wave of fighters, urging on those around him.

Penny Carter and Sister Jo were sitting together against the sloping side of the redoubt. More rectangular than oval in shape, it was fifteen metres long, and McLean had his company command post in a fighting hole dug in a few yards out from the south-eastern end. Filthy, dusty, bareheaded, he was crouched over, a radio handset in his hand, talking to two of his men, the conversation intense, the faces serious.

The shooting had stopped now, and it was quiet, just the sound of emerald doves in the trees, and the buzzing of flies. Sister Jo looked past the group of marines at him. 'You and the Major. You were – friends before, weren't you?'

'Is it that obvious?' Penny said with a little, bitter smile. She wiped sweat from her forehead with the back of her arm. 'Yes. Yes, we were. Not just friends, either.' She looked down over the heads of the marines at him. 'I had never seen him work before. It was just the camp, and parties and mess dinners and lots of social things. He would disappear off to Dartmoor or Salisbury Plain training and come back with piles of filthy kit, but I had never seen what they do.' She paused. 'Look at him. He is in his element. I'm told he is very good at it. Nick Webber, who is the ops officer, says he is the best company commander in the corps.' She smiled. 'Actually, he looks like a naughty schoolboy.'

Jo smiled at that. 'You going to get him back, then?' she asked.

'If I can.'

'What happened? Did he leave you?'

'No.' She paused and looked down at the ground. 'I was, I dunno – bored, something. I met someone else. We, you know – anyway, Doug found out. Drove over to my place and found him there. He sat outside all night.' She looked at Jo, wondering why she was telling anyone this. She had spoken to no third party about it since Teddy. 'I broke his heart. I lied to him. I deceived him. So, I'm not even sure he wants me back.' Shagger had wandered up the depression and stopped beside Sister Jo, and let her scratch his ears. Having found a new friend, he flopped down beside her. 'We are all weak,' Jo said softly, stroking his head. 'Ask for forgiveness and pray for what you want, for what you love.'

'And you?' Penny asked, changing the subject. 'What do you want?'

Sister Jo smiled. 'I used to think I knew.'

A few feet away the marines who formed the support team were supposedly resting, but Barton, with a shot of morphine in him, was playing catch-up, field stripping his weapon, cleaning the working parts, checking magazine loadings. He rubbed his camouflage face veil over the glass of the SUSAT sight and looked through it. That done, he took out his other ordnance and began on that, checking the pins and fuses in his grenades, clearing dust and plant debris from the link ammunition he was carrying. Finally, he broke open his little gaz cooker and put some water on to boil a wet, humming softy to himself. Kevin and the Padre were sitting opposite Sloth, Furby and Hobson, who was rolling himself a smoke, the makings bummed from Sloth. His first since he had given up three years before.

'Look at that, sir,' Kevin said to the Padre, mildly amused. 'We're here in this shithole, stinking hot, flies everywhere, being chased by hundreds of fuzzy-wuzzies, and there is a Royal Marines corporal. Look at him. A clean rifle, a wet going and he's happy as a pig in shit.'

'Bollocks!' Biscuit replied. 'Happiness would be a double cheeseburger, a cold pint of lager – real cold, condensation on the glass – and a bird with huge bazoombas serving them. But I ain't got that, so I make do. Have some respect. Remember Hitler was a corporal.'

'Hitler had the bird with the bazoombas,' Kevin responded.

'And the beer.' From Furby

'So, Biscuit?' Dave Hobson asked. 'Where did you go wrong, my son? Karmic debt, perhaps?'

'I got stuck with you wankers, so it must be.'

'Waddya reckon, Padre?' from Kevin, eagerly stirring it up.

'It's possible,' Rory replied in his soft Hebridian burr, his expression deadpan. 'To pay for one's sins is a common principle of many religions, but they must have been terrible sins for such a fine man to be saddled with you lot.' He tipped his hip flask up and took a tiny sip, just wetting his lips, and passed it along the line.

'There you go,' Kevin said. 'Biscuit, I am – we are,' he corrected, 'instruments of God's will. Inextricably linked to your destiny. We' – he swung his arm to include the fire team – 'are your cross to bear – with humour, with dignity, with wisdom and great forbearance.'

'Get fucked,' Biscuit responded, then looked up from his steaming cup. 'No offence, Padre.'

'None taken.'

Biscuit dropped his head and listened to his earpiece.

Sloth had ignored the banter. She was back in his sightline again and he wanted to enjoy the moment, savour it, remember it. Short dark hair, skin like cream, green, green eyes, behind the bruises the face of an angel, sitting there not twenty feet away, stroking Shagger. That made him feel better. She was stroking his dog.

She caught his eye and held the look for a second, then two, then demurely looked away, and his heart pounded in his chest. What was it his sister said? If they hold the look for two seconds – was it two or twenty? Couldn't be twenty, that's a fucking lifetime in a crowded pub. Must be two. If they hold the look for two, they are interested. But she's a nun. This can't be. She won't let it. Anywhere else – another time, another life choice, it would be on, he knew it. Elated, chuffed, feeling wonderful – and gutted, disappointed and confused all at once.

'Stand to,' Biscuit said.

*   *   *

'Two Alpha, Zero Alpha. Send.'

'Zero, we have movement. Three hundred and fifty metres out, enemy at troop strength, advancing into sector Foxtrot Five, over.'

McLean swung his binoculars but could see nothing from his position. He didn't doubt Sergeant Willis, he just wanted to see them. They had marked out the perimeter that morning, breaking it into grid squares, much easier to describe, much easier to manage.

'Two Alpha, can your gun teams see them, over?' Three hundred and fifty yards was pushing it for accurate fire from an SA80, and he didn't have the ammunition to waste, but the heavier GPMGs on bipod legs could be fired accurately out the better part of 800 yards.

'No, Zero. Both out of sightline in the trees. My view is directly through the bush, still visual.'

'Two Alpha, your snipers?'

'Roger that. One sniper can get visual, over.'

He turned his head and looked across at the 3-Troop sergeant with the support section and the mortars. Advancing at troop strength. 'Prepare two 51-mills. for a sighting round, one only into the centre of Foxtrot Five, on the command, then get ready to fire for effect. Engineers?'

'Sir?'

'Whatever you have got out this side. Get it ready to go.'

'Sir.'

McLean went back to his radio. 'Two Alpha, once they hit the middle of Foxtrot Five, advise and have your sniper open fire at will. When they go to cover, we support you with company weapons, over.'

In the centre of the redoubt, the 2-Troop mortar men lined up their light 51-mill. tubes, helped by the VMs. A few feet away, the combat engineers, limited with equipment, were wiring up their clackers and other electrical initiators for that sector.

The attack was coming from two directions. Ndube had split his force, one force coming from the north-east, and another equal in size directly from the north. Both of these were to support Makuma's advance from the south-east, which had stalled under Tino Dallaglio's sights, but Ndube didn't know this, just knew he had to get his group in among the whites by the time the group with Makuma arrived.

The group coming in from the north were moving slowly but steadily, doing what they did best. Daylight manoeuvring through thick dry bush, with plenty of cover. They moved at a steady pace in an easy fluid formation, men with AK47s, AKMs, some heavy-barrelled versions with drum magazines, and a few had RPG7s.

The bush was thick here, and their leader was pleased. His recce had reported back and told him they could advance to within maybe sixty yards of the whites. He, like most of them, disliked fighting in big formations. Their ethos, their experience, their culture, was that of the irregular, and this, a controlled, quick attack, was what they did best. Surprise, then away. This was more like it. They moved silently through the bush, gathering pace, watching for the signals from the leader elements that they had reached the scouts who were lying in cover, watching the whites.

The marines' defensive position was a classic layout, a tried and tested troop or platoon array that McLean had adapted for two troops. Triangular in shape, a machine gun was positioned at each point and the three lines that joined them were pairs of marines in fighting holes. From each point the machine guns had a 270° arc of fire and could overlap each other, making any point sixty yards out coverable by at least two guns. Any point, that is, except directly at one of the corners. Neither of the other two guns could traverse that far for fear of killing their own men, so in case the gunner was hit, or they had a stoppage, each GPMG had supporting rifles covering the ground directly in front of it.

The Unita scout eventually saw the machine gun and the line of holes leading back away from it, and he knew what he was looking at. It had taken some time, the positions camouflaged well, but he had been in the bush all his life and knew what to look for. Movement.

The Unita fighters had never attacked a Western-type, pre-pared position before. They had come across and attacked the MPLA, Cuban-trained and using the Russian doctrine, but never one like this. However, they had seen them, used them for a short while with the South Africans back in the seventies and early eighties, and they knew the weak points.

What they had been taught to defend against by the South Africans was the crew on the gun being taken out and then a rush forward, before they could re-man the position. That was the theory. Once the attacker was on the inside, sheer weight of numbers would carry the day.

But he wasn't overly concerned, because this was just a feint. This was the diversionary attack. The real attack was coming from the other side.

He waited for the unit to reach him.

The northern corner had been a 2-Troop position, but when Biscuit's fire team had moved into the redoubt with him, a 3-Troop fire team had relieved them. Down their right flank was a 2-Troop section, the Love Machine. Their section commander, Corporal 'Grandad' Phillips, was the only combat veteran in the company other than the CSM. Phillips was in the centre of the line in a hole with the section's LSW team, the others in the section in four two-man holes, three to his left, one to his right. Just down from him, Sergeant Willis was watching the enemy approach. Phillips could see the sniper next to him, all attention now on the eastern flank. He looked back over to his left. Even the 3-Troop lads at the top end were watching this way. Eyes to your front, he thought. Suddenly, almost as if on cue, there was heavy fire coming out of the bush, all of it ripping into the northern position. Fuck me! he thought.

'Watch your fronts,' he yelled, 'Boff, Tuppy, the left!' The two marines turned ninety degrees to support the northernmost 2-Troop hole, whose occupants had wisely dropped down deep. Fire was still pouring in on to the GPMG position, the lads down deep, but someone got a hand up on to the trigger and began to fire the gun sweeping it left and right to suppress the enemy fire long enough to get organised. Other holes on the western flank had turned their weapons to support the north. 'Stand fast!' Willis yelled. 'Watch your fronts!' He pulled a rifle grenade from his kit and a few seconds later fired it expertly over the heads of the beleaguered fire team into the bush beyond them. In the redoubt, anticipating the Captain's next command to them, the engineers were quickly changing wiring on their initiators, the civilians cowering down deeper, only da Silva up, swinging his heavy 7.62 SLR round.

'Hold that,' McLean yelled at the engineers. 'Mortars, turn one tube. Sector Delta Two. Two rounds for effect. Corp Barton' – there were enemy running through the bush towards the northern end and the gun team were just coming up as a hail of suppression fire reached out from the sections either side – 'half your section up!'

Biscuit didn't wait. 'Let's go!' he yelled, and was up and moving – Sloth, Furby, Kevin and Dave Hobson behind him, running, dropping, firing, and coming up, as they crossed the ground to the north. Kevin and Hobson dropped into a hole and got their GPMG up and engaged, the big gun's withering fire chopping into the bush where the Unita men advanced.

The mortarmen, who had their range and bearings for each sector all jotted down on paper, finally made the last calibration and began. There was the characteristic 'whump' of a bomb leaving the tube and then another. A few seconds later they dropped into the bush in Delta Two, even a small mortar bomb landing with deafening blasts, the concussion waves shaking trees and leaves before dust rose in the air.

The two GPMGs, the queens of any infantry battle, were in command now, supported by rifles either side.

McLean, in his CP, could see the action sixty yards away and cut through the command structure again, as he had done consistently over the last few days, and talked direct to the marines he wanted – Biscuit's fire team, in support of the northern corner.

Their position was good, and they could easily turn their guns to put an arc of fire down the eastern flank.

'Two Two, Zero Alpha. Hold there, I say, hold there.'

'Three Alpha, Three Four. Sitrep – advance has stopped but we still have mega movement in the trees there, over.'

'Roger, Three Four.'

Furious fire was now coming back into the position from the north, bullets crackling overhead, others better aimed, hitting the ground and kicking up dirt and dust behind the marines' positions.

'Lie down low!' the CSM, now back with the mortar team and engineers, yelled at those in the redoubt. 'Low as you can!'

'Three Alpha, Three Four. They're coming again!'

'Zero Alpha, Three Alpha. Need mortar support 50 metres north of twelve o'clock.'

'You got it, Three,' McLean responded. He looked across at the engineers. 'Sector Delta. Hit it!' The two engineers were bent over, moving wires on to initiators, and a few seconds later, one raised a thumb. 'Tell 'em, heads down in five! One – two – three—'

The defensive array wasn't sophisticated. With their limited technology, they didn't have many real Claymore mines out there; the rest of their nasty things were improvised. Much of it would be detonated by the same electrical impulse that would trigger the Claymores.

A Claymore mine is an anti-personnel, defensive weapon. It is the size of a breadboard, concave in shape, and has seven hundred ball bearings packed into military explosive. When fired, the explosive blasts the ball bearings outward in a 70° arc. It is lethal if advancing enemy are caught at close range. The mine went off, its charge stripped leaves from trees, and was followed by a sequence that included two RPG7 grenades and two white phosphorous grenades, good incendiaries.

The grenades all went off within seconds of the Claymore mine, a sequence of explosions, leaving dust and smoke rising; and pretty white-grey smoke trails left by burning phosphorus as it went up in the air and dropped back to earth, lighting the bush where it fell.

The marines could see little of the effect other than that the movement seemed to have stopped again, and smoke was rising from fires started by the phosphorus, but they drove home the advantage gained, and raked the trees with machine-gun fire. Understandably, almost all eyes were on the furious firefight at the northern point of the triangle, all except Willis's, the 2-Troop commander. He had, with incredible discipline, not taken his eyes off his sector for more than a few moments at any time. He was facing directly east, Grandad's Love Machine either side of him, when he saw them. Advancing fast through the trees, running at them, were dozens, maybe many dozens of Unita men, some of whom had obviously crept closer during the firefight at the northern end.

'Face your fronts! Stand to!' he yelled, and opened fire. McLean in the CP turned to face them, to assess the new threat.

Christ, he thought. There must be a couple of hundred of them. 'Two Two, Zero Alpha. Turn your gun east. I say again, turn your gun east. Support Two One. Mortars, fire for effect, sector Charlie Two. Quick as you can. Engineers, fire, sector Charlie Two!' they were still coming, even with the gimmpy hammering out at them, but they were spread through the bush, no concentrations, no groups, firing as they advanced at the run. McLean looked across at the redoubt. 'Support section up!'

The engineers were trying to rewire their initiators, but it was taking time, and from their position up near the northern gun team, Biscuit, Sloth and Furby watched with mounting horror as the fusillade of fire from the marine line seemed to do little to halt the rush. There were only eighteen marines down that side, with the babies, the Love Machine, in the centre. They saw Willis come up and throw a grenade and drop down again. If they were close enough to be throwing grenades at them, the lads were in the shit. Their lads. Two

Troop. Suddenly, a group had broken through, and were on the line, the Love-Machine lads firing up at them as they passed.

'Come on!' Furby yelled, and he was up and away, running past Kevin and Dave Hobson who had got their gun swivelled on a new arc and were engaging. Sloth and Biscuit took off after him, bullets buzzing and snapping past them.

In the redoubt, Penny, like all the civvies except da Silva, huddled down closer to the ground, all thoughts of Doug driven from her mind as burst after burst of fire plucked at the leaves in the tree overhead. Bullets, one hit a rock ten feet from her and chippings flew out, one grazing her neck. Oh, Jesus! That was close. I'll change. I'll be better. If we live through this, I will be a better person. Please, God? Please, Doug? Please. The sounds of the fighting got closer, not just gunfire – and then it was there. With them in the redoubt, the grunts, cries and screams of men fighting hand to hand. The clash of steel on steel, the wet thump and grunt of steel on bone, da Silva up opposite her, shooting at someone. Bodies falling, death, blood, a man dropping in with them, then another – black men. Maneru coming up, his stick in his hand, the man above her, gouts of blood as his body flicked backward, punched by bullets, screams, a boot beside her face. Someone grunting, 'Get the cunt!' A knife flashed past her, blood fountaining over her. Shooting beside her, level shooting – bang, bang, bang, like a metronome. From the corner of her eye she saw a man, filthy, with short dreadlocks, eyes wild with *dagga*, standing over Sister Marie-Claire, his rifle jammed – the signals sergeant covered the ground from the CP like a leopard and took him down, his fifteen stone weight behind the swing of a machete he had picked up. The scything blow took the Unita bandit in the stomach and almost cut him in half and as he fell, guts and intestines spilled out. The signaller got another mag in his weapon, Dalton kicking up at another man before he too was killed by the signaller.

Furby was in the redoubt, firing till he was out of ammo, then on, knife in one hand – a killing machine – a trenching tool in the other hand, Sloth beside him, aimed shots. Sloth

359

kneeling over Sister Jo, firing, cool as a cucumber, every shot taking someone down. Biscuit with a light section weapon on automatic, chopping into the enemy. He turned.

A man was on Sister Jo and she was squirming, kicking, biting and shrieking. He peeled the man off and put a burst into him, then clubbed his head with the rifle butt. Sister Jo, sitting up now, screaming in anger, fired a pistol she had got from da Silva, expending eight rounds from the Tokarov into two men, men already shot by Sloth. He stepped back to give her room to shoot, the redoubt and CP littered with bodies, dead and dying, and more were coming. Da Silva lay prone, firing his rifle, McLean now in with them, hand to hand. The Padre was there, unarmed, going to help Sister Marie-Claire, when suddenly a Unita man, wild-eyed and panting, stood over him. Furby, splattered in blood, now a berserker, crossed the ground and killed him with the trenching tool, hacked his head from his shoulders with three blows.

Ndube followed his men in through the fighting, looking for the nuns. They had to die. The old ones anyway. He dropped into the hole where men were fighting hand to hand and found himself just feet from one of them. He came up over her.

Furby turned and there was another slithering up, going for Sister Marie-Claire. He dropped the tool and took him by the throat with one huge hand, his weight holding the man's gun down flat against his chest. Shagger was in there with him, protecting his new pack under his own instincts, tearing at the man's ear.

Makuma's right-hand man had just met his nemesis. Furby held the wiry little man as Shagger savaged him and then drove his knife into his eye, piercing the brain till the heavy point hit the skull at the back, killing him like a cockroach before coming up, changing magazines and getting back into the fight.

Then Kevin and Dave Hobson were there, little Kevin – Popeye – with the GPMG blasting out.

With Ndube dead, the Unita men fell back, back into the now ready minefield, and as they ran, the engineers fired their initiators, phos grenades going off and two Claymore mines cutting through them as they ran into the now burning bush.

'Support section, secure the redoubt! Secure your positions! Face your fronts,' McLean yelled. As some form of order returned, McLean surveyed the scene. It was dreadful, a Dantean horror scene of dead and dying, of blood and guts and intestines, bodies everywhere, the wounded moaning and writhing. Hobson, a consummate professional and oblivious to it all, a pair of gloves on his hands, changed barrels on the GPMG, dropping the almost red-hot one to the ground. Black smoke wreathed the sky, rising from fires set off by the incendiaries the engineers had laid. The westerly wind was blowing it back into the bush to the east, but cinder and ash fell down on them. The 2-Troop section that had taken the brunt of the attack and been overrun was in a bad way.

'Three Alpha, Zero Alpha. One section from your troop over to support the eastern line asap. Two Alpha, Zero Alpha. Sitrep and ammo caz.' Tactical training and the doctrine said, keep the tactical bound at all times, but not now, not with his lads in this state. Fuck it.

'Move the TAC HQ in here,' he said to the signals sergeant, his eyes looking for Penny, looking to see if she was alright, safe. 'Mr Harvey, take the top end, see how we are doing, move back towards me. There's a section from 3 Troop coming across to support. As soon as they are in position, get the wounded back in here.' McLean looked at Furby – who was panting, splattered in blood and gore, but otherwise seemed unhurt – and Sloth, who was loading loose ammunition into his empty magazines. The young nun, sitting beside Sloth, was also helping, filling mags.

'You blokes get this shit out of here,' he said, pointing at the dead and wounded Unita men lying on the bottom of the redoubt. 'And then help your mates back in, OK? Popeye, you on the gun. Cover this sector while we get sorted out.'

It was five o'clock and they hadn't been back. Dark in an hour, McLean knew, and they could move again. It had taken them half an hour to get sorted out and reorganised. The CSM had done his job fast, resupplying those he could, moving what ammunition he could from the men who hadn't engaged to those who had and needed more. Each man was made up to one hundred rounds, and when they ran out of ammo for the SA80s he issued enemy rifles to those left, moving among them, encouraging them to eat, brew up a wet, clean and repair their kit. The line was now smaller, drawn into secondary fighting positions needing fewer men. Because there were fewer. Two Troop had taken a hammering. The fourteen men of one section – the barely-out-of-adolescence, spotty-faced, incredibly tight, inseparable lads of the Love Machine – were now just eight, and all of them except one were wounded in some form, four badly.

Their defence of their sector had been exemplary. Enemy bodies were littering the ground in front of them and in their holes. They had taken down dozens – sixty-one in front of their holes – and then fought hand to hand, close enough to see into a man's eyes, smell his breath, see his life force fade – and they fought on.

Willis, their SBS sergeant, who had been in the thick of the fight, was miraculously unscathed, but no one else was.

The survivors were back in the redoubt with Gubby and Penny and the Padre, where Kevin – gashed on the head – sat with his machine gun and watched the bush. Sloth and Furby had reloaded, cleared up, and finally found Biscuit's body.

When they had rallied to the redoubt, Biscuit had kept going to support the Love-Machine lads and had died in one of their holes. The Unita dead were piled up around him and on top of him which was why it took them time to find him.

They carried him back and laid him out with the others. Furby found some smokes in his pocket and lit one and sat down with him for a while.

The original thirty-two men of 2 Troop were now just twenty-two, and seven of those were wounded, four of them badly. Fighting strength was fifteen.

They had prisoners and many more wounded than they could

deal with. It was one of the wounded who pointed out Ndube's body and told da Silva that he was their leader, number two only to Makuma himself.

Maneru, himself bleeding from a wound to his arm, translated. He said they called him the snake, he was like a puff adder, would strike without warning. Furby looked at the man and remembered killing him and thought, not any more he doesn't. He felt nothing – not shame, not remorse, not pride, not loathing – he felt nothing. He moved on, looked down at one of the bodies. The man was wearing a newish-looking woman's watch. Thieving cunt, he thought. And from feeling nothing, the anger welled up and he swung a boot into the body and then bent over and pulled the watch off.

Futher along, down in the redoubt, Sloth and Grandad sat with the last of the Love Machine. The doctor had got them stable enough, filled them full of painkillers – but these lads weren't going anywhere, not under their own steam. One was in traumatic shock already, the other three hanging in there, with weak jokes and weaker smiles, just wanting to go home now, back to Taunton, maybe even back to their mums. Grandad, their section corporal, his eyes moist, gently brushed dirt from one's face like it was his own son. Penny was still working on the last, getting him sitting up on his left side to get him comfortable – as comfortable as she could get anyone with a sucking chest wound. Every now and then she looked down at McLean, thanking God that he was safe, that she was, that they had survived.

Further along, Gubby moved among the wounded in the redoubt and looked at the ground. There was something orange and soft squashed into the red earth, and for a moment it looked like cake, but he thought, naaa – cake? Out here? Naaa.

At the far end, McLean squatted down looking at Willis and Lowry, his two troop commanders. All of them were tired, exhausted – but so was everyone, and it was up to them to keep the momentum going. This was what they hoped was their last, full O group meeting. This next stage was go for broke – make the ship or go down trying. This position was a butcher's yard, but there were many more of them out there. The CSM had got stuck in. Food and water, what they had left was on the hexy burners, no point doing hard routine, every gook in miles knew where they were, and everyone had been sorted and resupplied as best they could manage. There was only enough 5.56mm for seven SA80s, and the rest of the men were now using captured kit – AK47s and 74s.

'Dark in half an hour. Here's what I want to do. ORBAT' – he looked round the remnants of his force – 'changes, obviously, and . . .'

On the riverbank, Sergeant Connors and his men had fought off three light attacks. The Unita fighters probed his position and tried to clear the riverbank, so they could attack the ship at leisure without flank fire from the men in the sangar, but they knew nightfall wasn't far away and they would be back for a serious crack at it before then.

In each of the firefights, the *Winchester*'s 20-mill. Oerlikon had opened up and been absolutely decisive, and Chops M's anti-boarding group were now along the superstructure behind pillow cases filled with dirt, adding their fire, something the marines were less happy with. In the Phalanx local control room, Jenny Teller had long since finished her calculations and given the Chief his ready reckoner. It was a complex series of bisecting lines, to match the topography at various distances, and he had programmed the increments into the computer, calling out to her his code number to annotate the chart.

Commander Channing, who had been listening to the radio traffic all afternoon, wasn't prepared to order the marines to stay, but asked for Connors to make his call. They would wait out the night here, and defend this position. Without a foothold – a beachhead – they might even have trouble getting ashore to meet the incoming 40 Commando lads without a major fight, so this was the better option.

After the last sitrep from OC Heraklion there was now some considerable doubt about how many of them would even make it back, and he knew that in London, at Northwood and at RMHQ, where they were awaiting relayed reports, the atmosphere was gloomy.

Ashore, one of Connors' marines saw movement again.

'Here we go,' he muttered to himself before calling, 'Sergeant, they're coming!'

Connors was up in a flash. He now had both his fire teams close to each other, just twenty feet between the holes so they could support each other. With two GPMGs and two section weapons they could put out some fire, but nevertheless he called it in.

'*Winchester*, Romeo Mike. Movement in the bush to our right, sixty yards, over.'

'And the left!' one of his men yelled, bringing his rifle up. Fire began to hit the sangars.

'RPG on the left!'

'Hit the cunt!' someone yelled back.

'*Winchester*, be advised RPG on the left. I say again, RPG on the left, fifty yards,' Connors called, looking out that side. 'At the base of the flame tree.'

Fire was tearing into them now and the marines' guns were returning it, with measured bursts. On *Winchester*, the Oerlikon began to hammer out, one second on, one second off. Up on the superstructure, Chops M's lads began to fire, their vantage point much higher.

'Face the right!' the corporal yelled to his three.

'Take the RPG with Phalanx!' Channing called.

The rating on the port TDS called the bearing and the distance up the bank to CPO Davies in the Phalanx Local Control hutch. Bullets were hitting the ship, thumping into it, clanging off hard steel, but penetrating in many places. Up on the gun controller's platform, a burst stitched its way across the superstructure, the last two bullets hitting Nellie Tusker. He staggered, found his feet, and then just slowly crumpled to the deck.

'Bearing 184, range 150 yards, 40 feet up the bank!' the rating on the TDS shouted.

Jenny looked at her annotated chart. '304!' she called back. He keyed in the digits and hit the fire button.

The Phalanx jerked round, dropped its six-barrelled snout and fired a ninety-round burst. The flame tree and the entire area around it disappeared in a fireball of explosions, each a nanosecond apart.

'Phalanx, traverse right. Bearing—'

'276!' she called.

It burped again, swung right, burped, swung right, then burped again. Four seconds later the entire edge of the riverbank from the marines' sangar for sixty yards was a smoking strip of churned-up earth, branches, bits of tree trunk, stumps. It looked like a tornado had ripped through it – a fiery tornado out of hell itself.

'Phalanx, relax!'

The TDS rating looked round to raise a thumb at his mate. He wasn't there. Just a pile of dark-blue denim. Someone's down. Oh, Jesus. No. Not Nellie.

'Ops, Port TDS. Gun Controller is down. He's hit. Nellie's hit. We need the medic up here!'

In the Phalanx hutch, just thirty feet away, Jenny Teller heard the call. So did CPO Davies, and as she stood up and moved to the door, he shook his head.

'Remain at your station!' But he had seen her eyes and softened. 'I need you here. Don't worry. The lads will get him below.'

Dark was falling, and they were ready to go. McLean had just made the toughest decision of his career, not on his own – the consensus grew and everyone just knew – but he could have countermanded it. The four badly wounded marines would be staying behind. They knew they couldn't go on, they knew they would just hold the others back, so they volunteered to stay and to fight. They would defend the redoubt and give the others time to melt into the darkness.

The signals sergeant had listened to their request and set them up with spare batteries dropped from *Winchester* that morning. The ghetto blaster, humped all the way from the Manor and all the way from Brazzaville, was dragged out and connected to the batteries and left under their daysacks. Some food was left for them, plenty of ammo, a small Clansman radio, and optimistically, some morphine 'for tomorrow'.

'We'll get these civvvies aboard and come back, right?' Grandad had said. 'Be mid-morning.' They smiled and nodded and knew he was just saying it because it was good form. McLean said a few words to them, as did the two nuns, and Sloth and Furby and Kevin made silly jokes. The Padre was the last with them as the formation moved off.

'They are just boys. Little more than children,' the Padre said to someone beside him in the darkness, thinking it was Grandad. He lowered his head, and tears welled in his eyes. He began to pray for their souls. It wasn't Grandad. It was Furby – Furby who saw all priests as opportunistic perverts. 'You're alright,' he said. 'For one of them. C'mon, Padre. Time to go.'

Grandad, down with his lads, came to his feet. Willis had given him Biscuit's fire team. He looked at Sloth and Furby.

'I'll not be coming, lads,' he said softly. 'Don't say anything, or I'll kick the fuck out of you.'

'You and whose army, you soft old git,' Furby replied. He put his hand out. Grandad – who had seen his first action in the Falklands, and was about to see his last – took it.

'Teach 'em to dance while you're waiting,' Furby said. He unhooked both his grenades and gave them to Grandad, nodded just the once to them all, and without another word, he walked way.

Trying for complete silence, they moved out to follow the small point unit that already scouted the channel, set up as their egress route that morning. Maneru was with them. It was clear. There was a large gang directly west, and what was left of the attacking groups to the north-east, but their route seemed clear.

If they could cover the next five miles without a serious contact, then they would be within range of *Winchester*'s main gun.

Grandad waited for a few minutes and then moved back to the redoubt with his lads.

'What the fuck you doing here?' one of them, shot through both legs, asked.

'Sick of this yomping-in-the-dark shit. Reckon I'll wait a bit,' he replied.

'Bollocks, Grandad,' one of them responded. 'Nice thought, but not smart.'

'If I was smart, would I still be a corporal? Cunts know we're here.' He pulled out a hip flask given him by the Padre. 'Let's have some music then.' He lifted the day sacks. There was a CD in the player and he turned it on.

A few minutes later, clear of the channel, the Padre stopped and turned. Sloth and Furby, the tail-end Charlies, caught him up.

'What?' Sloth whispered.

'Nothing. I thought I heard something. Music.'

'You did,' Sloth said.

The sound carried, echoing round the hills and the rocks. Acoustically, it was a natural auditorium. Maneru spoke then. He took some snuff from a tin, slowly, his arm bandaged. 'If one must die, then this is a good place.'

'Let's go,' Furby said.

As he finished speaking, they heard the GPMG open up, the rolling, hammering burst echoing round the hills with the strains of the Verve's 'Bitter Sweet Symphony' in the background.

It was the Love Machine's last night out.

Fourteen

Everyone heard it, but McLean kept them moving as fast as he could. It was now a single-troop arrowhead formation with an enlarged centre group, ten of Two Troop in there with the civvies, lifting, carrying, supporting, dragging, the last five as the tail-end-Charlie fire team. Every minute the Love Machine could keep the enemy thinking they were still there, they were closer to the ship. Every now and then when the wind shifted they could hear the firefight still going on, and it was half past seven when McLean swept back through the troop.

'Where's Grandad?' he asked the tail-end team. Furby and Sloth said nothing for a moment and Sloth was about to come out with some bullshit when the Padre spoke.

'He's with his section,' he replied.

McLean said nothing. There was no point in comment, no point saying someone should have noticed in time for him to intervene, that someone should have reported it. And anyway, he had a big lump in his throat. He just turned and walked away. He didn't want them to see the look in his eyes.

At 2000 hours local, he checked his GPS for the fourth time in twenty minutes and decided he was now ready to swing west again. They were nine and a half miles from the ship, within range of naval gunfire support from her 4.5-inch, rapid-firing Vickers Mark VIII deck gun.

With the ship now under sporadic fire from the shoreline, he and Commander Channing had looked at the other option, the encryption unit running hot. The suggestion – McLean's – was to cut back towards the road, get a vehicle and meet the ship west of Matadi, outrun Makuma's ability to move his people. But that would involve putting locals at risk on the route, and between here and the ship there were no major populations, only the odd small scattering of huts. It would also mean moving back out of *Winchester*'s reach, and Channing and McLean both knew the effect it would have on morale if they needed her support.

Ahead in the dark someone stumbled and went down, and when McLean got to them he found it was Sister Marie-Claire.

'She says she can't go on, boss,' the marine with her said. McLean knew they were exhausted. There had been no sleep during the day, and the battle had taken its toll on them – their nerves and confidence, their self-belief.

'The others are as bad,' the CSM said, sidling up. 'The young one is OK, but the others are going down any time now.'

Penny walked over. 'They can't go on at this pace, Doug. *I* can't.'

'The men?' McLean asked. Da Silva, Dalton and the last of the Yetwene hostages were still on their feet, but for how long?

'Other than da Silva, they're as knackered as the women.'

It was a race now. There were certainly Unita at the riverbank, but having swung this far north, he hoped he had avoided any stop groups on the more direct route. With luck, on this route it could be clear all the way to within a mile of the riverbank. There was bright moonlight, no clouds in the sky at all. This was the risk assessment, the trade-off between speed and stealth. He made his decision.

'Our ship is nine miles that way,' he said. 'I want to pick up the pace. A fast five miles, then we go in slow. Bin day sacks. Belt order only. Dump everything we don't need. The civvies we'll carry. Make litters out of ponchos. Four men on each, rotate them.'

Fifteen minutes later they were ready.

'But I can walk,' Sister Marie-Claire said when shown the makeshift stretcher.

'Barely, and you can't run. We can. Just get on it,' was the terse response, before the marine sighed. 'Come on, darlin', we just want to bloody get there now.'

As the marines got organised, Maneru approached McLean. 'You are close,' he said. 'There is little more for me to do. It is time for me to return to my family.' He had seen Sister Marie-Claire, made his farewells.

'I understand,' McLean said, shaking his hand. 'I thank you. My people owe you a debt. If there is anything we can do, you can contact me' – he wrote his name on a small piece of paper torn from his notebook, and into it he folded all the money he had – 'through the British Embassy in Kinshasa.' Maneru took the paper and put it in his pocket. 'It has been a pleasure,' McLean finished, 'to make this journey with you. Without you, it would have been very difficult.'

'It was something I had to do.' He pointed to Dalton. 'He understands. You would have made it anyway,' Maneru said simply. 'You are a soldier.' He paused and looked down before looking up. 'If you were to come back one day, we could hunt together.'

'I'd like that,' McLean said.

Maneru nodded, raised his stick in salute and disappeared into the darkness.

They jogged, walked when the ground got rough, jogged again. With a leaner arrowhead formation around the sweating, panting, pounding centre party, the marines moved at their forced-march pace of six miles an hour, carrying those who could not walk or keep up, dragging those that thought they could. Da Silva was fitter than he thought and kept up, but Dalton had the ignominy of being dragged by his belt every time he slowed.

McLean moved off to the left of them, where he could see his men but keep a tactical bound. He was now carrying his own radio and the PRC320 Clansman, which freed up his signals sergeant to help with the civvies. He had one side of a stretcher and the Padre had the other. The lads were working.

Hard. Most of them hadn't done 'phys' like this since they did the marines course, and they pounded through the bush with just the sounds of breathing and boots on the ground. Out beyond them in a protective screen were their mates, keeping in formation. Every few minutes someone tapped someone else on the shoulder and swapped roles, the men taking it in turns to carry the stretchers.

McLean felt enormous pride in them. Just youngsters, many of them, but professionals. For him, the best of the best. I'd put these lads head to head with any unit in the Corps and win, he said to himself. My lads. The Saints. Alpha Company, 40 Commando, Royal Marines. There were seventeen of them dead or left behind back along the route, and many of these men bore wounds, but the cohesion was tight, morale was good.

Suddenly, people watching those in front were going for cover, and off to his right several of the people on stretchers were unceremoniously dumped as the marines went for their weapons and dropped prone, ready to fight. He went down on to one knee.

'Zero Alpha, Three Alpha.' Lowry.

'Go, Three Alpha.'

'Zero Alpha, we have fires up ahead. Cooking fires by the look of it.'

'Roger, Three. I'm coming up to your location. Watch out for me and make yourself seen to me.'

The moment he said it, he wished Maneru was still with them. He would be able to look at the fires and tell what they were – a village, a travelling group, or – with their luck – something more threatening.

He made his decision as he arrived. Without the local knowledge, and without either the time or the resources to put out a recce patrol, he had the formation swing north. The next mile was a long, sweeping curve, and as they resumed their original track they picked up the pace again, the marines rotating on the stretchers, jogging through the moonlit bush, swearing, grunting, cursing, sweating, cajoling and encouraging each other.

'Boss?' His signals sergeant crossed over to him. 'The 320 has croaked.'

He had relieved McLean of the burden as they halted. 'How?'

'Dunno, sir. A couple of the lads have been humping it. It may have been dropped or maybe a board has gone, but it's fucked. In daylight I can tell you more.'

Makuma was back at the river. He was in his Land Cruiser parked on a track a mile from the ship, glowering, fuming – so filled with rage that he was beyond rational thought. The closeness of the bullet fired at him had unnerved him briefly and he had wanted to kill them, torture them, hear their screams. But after the whites had repelled his attack he recognised, somewhere back in his brain in an animal-cunning kind of way, that it was pointless attacking them in prepared positions. He had never fought men like these. Compared to his force they were just a handful, but they didn't run, they didn't waver. But they would scream once he had them.

He would do it the old way, the Unita way. Do it from ambush. The one place they had to go was the ship, and he would wait for them here. They would come. He had stop groups out and when they moved his men would follow them here.

In the meantime, he had sent some men into Matadi to find boats – steal them, take them, he didn't care. Once they had killed the nuns and got the diamonds, then they could take the ship. He had thought no more about it than that. Get boats.

Down near the water his men had pinned down the few on the riverbank. When the time came it would be good, the killing. The revenge. The thought of catching those who had eluded him for so long, who had made a fool of him in front of his men, overcame everything, more powerful even than the thought of the diamonds or the ship.

On the ship, the tracking radars on their endless sweep picked up three contacts leaving the dockside at Matadi just three miles or so downstream. Instead of heading downriver, the natural direction, they turned and headed upstream.

The operator on the radar, in his third hour watching the screen in the ops room, leant forward. And what the fuck are you up to, then? Nothing up here except us. Just the rapids. He watched the first boat joined by a second smaller trace and then a third.

In a hostile environment in the open sea there was a set of procedures that would have kicked in. He would have called, 'Slam-eye! Alarm! Contact bearing—' And as he did so the computers would have been allocating the contact a number, calculating the speed, and working out targeting solutions for a variety of weapon systems. The moment the probability was high, the computer having established those threat parameters, the PWO – the principle warfare officer – or the AWO – the air warfare officer – would manage the situation and fight the ship. The Royal Navy uses management by veto, so he could do this without the Captain's consent, until he could get to the ops room or a comms set and get involved. But up here it was different.

'Sir?' he called to the PWO, who was sitting behind him. 'You better have a look at this. Three contacts on the water moving our way, at three knots.'

The PWO, a lieutenant, was looking at his screen as the rating finished speaking.

'Ops, PWO.'

'PWO, Ops. Go.'

The ops officer was tired. He was monitoring the action outside, responsible for the effective use of all the ship's weapon systems. At this moment he had Phalanx in and out of the fight, and the Port 20-mill. in almost constant action. Bullets hit the ship every few seconds, but so far they had been lucky. Just two dead and just three injuries – one serious – and the damage done to the ship's wiring and systems had thankfully been minimised by the precautions taken earlier – filled pillowcases, moved internal bulkheads, shoring and thickening of external bulkheads.

'Ops, PWO. Boats, three of them, leaving Matadi port and heading our way.'

Eight or so feet away, the ops officer selected the surface radars on his screen and looked at the display. What were they? Rubberneckers? Locals out for a look? Transport for some village set back from the river that they hadn't seen? Or the enemy getting clever? 'Captain, Ops.'

At 2100 hours, McLean drew them to a halt. They were close to the river and in the dark they could hear the rumbling roar of rapids. Their ship was just one mile away, and he settled them into a thick stand of bush and asked Willis to send forward his two best scouts, but to let him brief them himself.

Willis protested mildly. As the only man in the company who had been with the SBS in Poole, he had done escape and evasion courses and was the best qualified by a long way, but McLean wouldn't hear of it. Willis was the troop commander and that was his job, not running dangerous two-man recce patrols.

Sloth and Furby moved up, and three or four minutes later they were making preparations to go, checking last-minute details – like anything that would rattle, or filling half-full canteens to stop them sloshing. Almost done, Sloth smeared cam cream on Furby's face and neck, and then sat still while Furby did his. There would be no reflection from white skin, not from these two, and Willis made bloody sure of it, standing over them, making sure everything was squared away and shipshape. As Furby finished, Sloth looked round and found that Sister Jo was kneeling beside him.

'You take care now,' she said.

'I will.' He grinned sheepishly and looked down and pointed at Shagger. 'Hang on to him, will you?'

The nun nodded and, holding the big, yellow dog round the neck, watched as the two marines melted into the dark. They moved as fast as they could. The enemy would be asleep with a bit of luck, but they simply didn't have the luxury of time. In full covert mode, in gillie suits, it could have taken them all night to cover three hundred yards, but the Unita units were sloppy and noisy and clearly hadn't been on hard routine in years. They moved, found enemy, moved again, found more, each time probing further along a perimeter that ran along the river. They were out and back in two hours.

'Sir, the place is thick with them,' Sloth said, pointing down at his drawing in the dirt by the light of a hooded, red-lensed torch. McLean nodded. 'We smelt fires, people all through here,' Sloth continued. 'There's an area in here, very wet and full of mosquitoes and shit.' He looked up at McLean with a grin. 'Furby and a croc scared each other shitless. Anyway, it seemed OK, but anywhere else the chances of running into them are high. Very high. I recommend we wait for first light.'

'Can we call in NGS? Beat a corridor?' Lowry asked. 'If the fire moves ahead of us that last four hundred yards or so, anyone who is still there is going to be in no state to engage us.'

'It's an option. I'm not sure how much they can offer.' He was thinking quickly, trying to work out how many 4.5-inch, high-explosive shells they would need to drop to beat an area that size. Although the big 320 was not working, they were close enough to use the much smaller, less powerful 351s to talk to the ship, and McLean began working out what he wanted to do. That contact with the ship completed, they settled in, one mile from the ship, huddled in the deep undergrowth to wait for the dawn.

It would be light enough to see by about 0540, and at 0500 McLean got them up and moving again, because at 0535 the NGS would begin and he wanted to creep the last yards into where the gun would beat their path to the ship. It would be a dog-leg. First stage into the river, then along the bank till they were in sight of the ship, and then the ship's other weapons would cover them.

The civvies were exhausted, and his men equally tired – now just running on fitness and stamina. They slept where they could, changing round the watch every half-hour – a touched shoulder, eyes opening, the butt of the rifle tight into the shoulder, and they had the watch.

CSM Harvey settled in beside McLean. 'Nearly there, sir. Just as well. I'm out of teabags,' he finished dryly.

'Yeah, but look at them,' McLean responded softly, pointing at the bodies sleeping around him, the five civilians. 'They're down. We will have to carry them in.'

'The lads will cuff it,' the CSM murmured. 'I've had nearly twenty years in and I've never seen a better bunch. When I was their age, down in the Falklands, I thought we were hard, but these kids? They'll take all the shit thrown and still come up punching. I'd never tell 'em, but I'm proud of the little bastards, every one of them.'

'I am too,' McLean said. 'They have fought like Spartans.'

They were both thinking the same thing. Who wouldn't make the last mile? The chances of getting everyone through were minimal, and 3 Troop, so far blessed by the gods of war and relatively intact, were out in the vanguard and along the left flank. They would take the brunt of it. Skirmishing and fighting running contacts to protect the main party to their right.

McLean woke them at 0500 and gathered the still-exhausted, sore civilians in a little, tight group.

'In a short while,' he said, 'we go the last few hundred yards. We will start slow, quietly – very quietly, please – and I'll warn you in time, but then they are going to use the main gun on the ship to protect us. That will mean shells landing very close to us. It will be frightening. You'll hear nothing else. Your ears may ring – they may even bleed if it's very close. You'll certainly feel the concussion waves, the ground shake under your feet. Those walking must keep going – do not stop, ever. As we move, the shells will drop ahead and around us. That young man over there' – he pointed to a corporal who had done the forward artillery observer course – 'a clever, well-trained young man, will be telling them where to drop the shells, and they will go exactly where we want them. OK? But don't stop. Only stop if the marine with you pulls you down, OK? If you are being carried, then stay on the stretcher.'

They nodded, and in the dark McLean thought he saw someone cross themselves.

Two miles away Makuma looked at the boats his men had found. They had stolen three, hijacking them at gunpoint, but this was the biggest, a heavy, flat-bottomed, iron boat with a little wheelhouse at the back, crewed by three very reluctant local men. They were at the narrow end of the pool, the boats pulled over to the bank under the overhanging undergrowth. He clambered aboard the biggest and moved ponderously down the side towards the flat aft section and the stubby little wheelhouse.

The skipper, older than the other two, silent until now, thought he recognised someone he could talk to, reason with, explain that riverboats could be chartered, arrangements could be made, that pointing guns was unnecessary and counter to the river culture. He had been on the river all his sixty years and had seen them come and go, and never, never had he been hijacked. It just wasn't done. You want a boat, you pay the boatmen. They don't care who you are, what your politics are. He didn't bother explaining that to the four men with the guns around him. They were just monkeys. He looked at Makuma approaching and began to gently remonstrate, to explain the way of it.

Makuma never even looked at him. He just kept moving, picked up an adze from a pile, and once near enough, swung it. The old man crumpled. There were another six blows, the last four when the old man was down on the steel deck – aimed, calculated to kill. Finished, his victim's dark blood pooling on the deck below the shattered face and skull, Makuma looked at the other two.

'Do as I say, or join him.'

Channing looked at the radar screen. The three contacts were stationary now, obviously pulled in to the bank. So, who were they and what was their intent?

The last thing he wanted was an incident with a local

Congolese boatman, someone going about his lawful business. They were perilously close to having breached their rules of engagement already.

They could sink 'em. Three rounds from the Vickers Mark VIII would do it, one each. At this range it was almost point-blank. Aimed by the radar it would be a certain direct hit each time. But what if they were locals? It was all about probability and there being no doubt of hostile intent. There was doubt here, in his mind, in anyone's mind.

'Keep an eye on 'em. If they get underway, let me know.'

'Then what, sir?' the ops officer asked. 'What if they have rockets or something mounted?'

'Normal ROE until they are within five hundred metres. We challenge,' Channing replied. 'But if so much as a rock is thrown our way, blow him out of the water.'

'Aye, aye.'

Channing looked at his watch. The NGS was due to start in three minutes. 'I'll be on the bridge.'

'Stand-by,' McLean called, and nodded to the marine who had done the forward observer's course with 148 battery. The man spoke into his throat mic, looking down at a piece of paper with his calculations on it in the light of a red-beamed and carefully hooded, tiny maglight torch, his own bit of Gucci kit.

'*Winchester*, Juliette Nine Alpha, requesting NGS, coordinates—'

The first 4.5-inch shell landed seventy yards in front of them, a bright light, a concussion wave, the ground shaking beneath their feet, all in half a second – and then the blast rolled over them. Another hit off to the right and a second later another to the left.

'Let's go!' McLean called. He didn't need to. These were professionals and they were up and moving as the third round hit. They ran into the beaten area, keeping going no matter what, moving behind the barrage, carrying all the civvies except da Silva now, brute strength, mind over matter. A burst of fire came from the left and the nearest 3-Troop section that side swung into the dark like tigers, pouring heavy fire into the Unita position and rolling through it, using weapons fire within inches, and grenades too close for comfort.

The signals sergeant, bearing an arm wound, had someone over his shoulder, pounding along, still carrying the big PRC320 Clansman on his back. McLean was with Penny – he had scooped her up as she had gone down. The Padre too was being carried. Too close to one of *Winchester*'s exploding shells, he was down on his knees, concussed, his nose bleeding, deafened by the blast, and Furby – huge, powerful – snatched him up like a child and slung him over his shoulder – Furby who days before wouldn't have given him the time of day.

'Come on, you Saints!' from CSM Harvey – brute, strong – Dalton over his shoulder. Dalton had gone down with two wounds in his lower legs.

'We're the Saints! The best of the best. Fucking move it!'

They moved, adrenalin coursing through their blood, pounding along – 2 Troop carrying the civvies any way they could, 3 Troop ahead and out on the left, skirmishing through the bush, a vicious, rolling firefight. Drop into a draw, into swamp – water – wading – the bank on the other side within reach.

The artillery stopped.

'Cover!' McLean yelled. Fuck! They were so close. A few hundred yards to the water, and then another few hundred along the bank. To the left, 3 Troop were still hammering out their fire, but the 2-Troop lads were going into cover, waist-deep in black, scummy water in some places. Off to the right, maybe one hundred and fifty yards away, they could hear the rapids, and this series of stagnant pools obviously flowed after rain. Beside him, up to her neck in water where McLean had dumped her – the safest place – Penny drank in deep breaths, her eyes wide.

'Wait for it,' he yelled again. 'We wait for the NGS! Sergeant Willis, cover the rear!'

McLean's radio, the only one tuned to the same frequency as the VHF sets on the ship, was now soaking wet, the water having entered through a crack in the casing. The other radios – fourteen of them, seven with each troop – were on the company net.

'Hoist from the magazine is jamming, sir. Gunner reckons he can jerry-rig it, says give him two minutes.'

'Get the WEO down there! Advise Heraklion to sit tight.'

'Can't raise them, sir.'

'Keep trying.' Outside, dawn was breaking. They were running out of darkness.

At that moment, a burst of fire from an automatic weapon on the shore raked the bridge and superstructure, and an RPG seared out from the bank. Attacked from less than a hundred yards away, with the Phalanx in manual mode, the ship's closer defence systems had no chance. The shooter, who stupidly stood to watch his rocket in flight, died in a hail of fire from Chops M's snipers.

Luckily, the rocket-propelled grenade went high, hitting the big, sweeping radar scanner high above the bridge, and no one was injured, but down in the ops room the surface threat and targeting radar screens went blank.

'Bridge, ops. Captain, please? Radar's gone down!'

Channing knew why, and touched his throat mic. 'Now we earn our money,' he muttered. 'Ops, Captain. What has happened to my radar, pray tell?'

On the bank in the undergrowth, something moved. Kevin spun and hoisted his gimmpy to his shoulder. It was a crocodile – small, maybe five feet long. He lowered the weapon and looked at it, still taking deep breaths. Just piss off, right! he thought. I'm tired, pissed-off, hungry, and I have a machine gun with real bullets, so just fuck off. He threw a rock at it and it slithered away. Beside him one of the nuns was sliding lower into the sludge. He reached out and grabbed her by the collar, holding the gimmpy up on the dry bit of bank above him. He looked back out at the night ahead. Down where the ship was, there was a furious firefight going on, with

381

some big grunty weapons in the battle, tracer lighting up the pinkening sky.

'Come one, come on,' McLean muttered almost to himself. 'We're fucking losing it here.' He looked to his right. One of the 2-Troop marines was holding Sister Marie-Claire up, keeping her upper body out of the water with one hand, and his weapon up and dry with the other, his feet scrabbling for purchase in the muddy glutinous mass beneath their feet. It was Kevin.

His eyes caught McLean's. 'Good 'ere, innit, sir?' He said casually.

'You alright?' McLean called.

'Marvellous, sir!' he replied with a grin. Kevin – Popeye to one and all – small, scrawny, but tough as old leather, was twenty years old, McLean remembered, and his mum ran a B&B in Salcombe. 'I'm going to book it again next year.'

McLean smiled. His marines.

'Bridge, Ops. Gun bay is ready!'

'Right, let's go!'

'Still can't raise 'em, sir.'

'Keep trying. We only have twenty rounds left. They must be ready to follow the fire in.'

The PO Yeoman was listening. The radio traffic, the gunfire – the marines were coming in and it was all going pearshaped because they couldn't talk them through the last three hundred yards. The Master at Arms, the one with the love of military music, took the tape he had found the day before. It was the band of the Royal Marines.

'We can use the tape,' he said to the Yeoman.

'What?'

'How about it, sir?' The Master at Arms turned and looked at the Captain. 'They'll know what this is.' And as he pressed play he turned up the volume on the main broadcast system.

Ashore, they could hear the drummers 'beating the retreat', the drum signal from the old Navy, now a ceremonial piece, once used by ships to signal their marines ashore, a signal which meant 'cease action and return to the ship'.

On board, Channing suddenly thought that if they could hear the music they could also hear voice, but so could everyone. The drumming at least was something only a marine, a musician or an anorak would know.

Three hundred yards away, they did. Mr Harvey could even tap it out with a knife and fork. 'That's them, boss. That's a signal,' he said to McLean.

Turning to the men. 'That's us, lads. The withdrawal,' the CSM bellowed, looking at McLean, who was trying to raise the ship on his radio and just looked up and nodded. 'On the command—' The shells began to fall out ahead, concussion waves blowing over them. 'Alpha Company will withdraw to the ship! Now, on me! Fucking move it!'

Over on the riverbank in the sangar, Connors flicked a look at his men. 'Right. Alpha lads are coming in! Covering fire, right flank!' The ten marines who had been fighting from the sangar off and on all night were stood to, anyway, the floor of the sangar deep in shell casings, remnants of whatever food they had taken and ammunition cases. Connors fired a flare out, and beside him a gimmpy began to sweep the jungle.

'Tonka, watch the back. When you see 'em, yell! Boats will be coming in.'

On the ship in the Phalanx hutch. PO Davies and Operator Maintainer Jenny Teller were ready. She had listed twenty sequential codes for the Phalanx gun, the software thinking it was calibration tests, but as before, the load was lethal high-explosive 20-mill. anti-aircraft ammunition. The XO was in there with them now. He had been roving the upper decks, the Captain's eyes and ears, moving from the bridge wing GPMG down to the 20-mill. gambo, back down to the Phalanx hutch, then down to where Chops M's people were playing at being snipers, firing at the shore.

'Port TDS is tracking,' PO Davies said. As soon as the marines were in sight on the bank, the TDS local area sight would track the area ahead of them and the Phalanx would do the rest. With Connors' marines facing the right, the incoming Alpha Company and their civilians would be inside a protective wall of fire.

Fire was arcing out from the bank, the odd round hitting the bridge, but Channing was up and moving around, and outside, the GPMG and the 20-mill. hammered out at the shore in reply.

'Port TDS has them in sight, sir!'

'Prepare to get underway. Aft parties ready to sever the warps. Anchor party close up.' Then softly, 'And if anyone knows the patron saint of marines, give him a call.' He would hold off moving as long as he could, because he knew that once he had the ship moving the Phalanx calculations would be amiss and they would have to cease fire on that weapon, but either way, it was now or never for the lads ashore.

'Mr Marston,' Channing called. 'Get us underway, but hold us here as near as you can.'

'Aye aye. Start Olympus.'

'Special duty anchor party, close up aft.' They were aft already, with the DMEO as safety officer, ready to snap the shackles that held the anchor chain out aft. Marker buoys had been rigged on a line, so a recovery was possible if they ever got a chance to come back, but for now they were going to leave one of their anchors behind.

'Anchor party ready!'

'Leggo aft,' Marston called. 'Shear the anchor pin! Cut the warps! Come up on Olympus. Astern both, thirty per cent.'

'I see them, Captain!' the Yeoman called.

Channing looked out.

There, running along a path on the bank, now just fifty yards from the marines' sangar, was what was left of Operation Heraklion. Exhausted men, carrying their weapons and the civilians, supporting each other. Inland of them, others, firing into the jungle. Come on, come on! Keep going. He was willing them in now, so near and yet so far, keep coming, lads. His ship was laying fire around them, a cacophony of noise, the Oerlikon 20-mill. and GPMGs hammering, the Phalanx roaring into fire every now and then, but it didn't seem enough. *Winchester* was a Type 42 destroyer and incredibly inadequate in this environment. No missiles, no aircraft, no ships or subs or things from her world she could engage and destroy, just the shadowy figures on the bank.

'Let's get 'em aboard. Sea boats away!'

'We're moving!' PO Davies called. 'Now we're buggered!'

'Phalanx – Port TDS, enemy coming through the trees. Target bearing 157 degrees. Range two hundred yards.'

'How far?' Jenny called.

'Its no good—'

'How far did he say!' she snapped 'Tell me!'

'Two hundred.'

She worked it in her head, flat out. 'Set Phalanx, eight degrees down, on 153 degrees! Fire!' she snatched up a head-set. 'TDS, Phalanx. Call the shot.'

'Do it!' Selby said. Davies entered the numbers, said, Please, God, and hit the fire-control button. Outside the hutch the Phalanx burped, ninety rounds leaving the barrels in a heart-beat.

'Left fifty!' from the TDS.

'Same elevation, bearing 148!'

The Gatling gun fired again, and the bush along the riverbank erupted in fire and explosions.

'Got 'em!' from the TDS.

Davies punched the air with a closed fist, a euphoric grin on his face. Behind him Jenny smiled, her eyes alive.

'Outstanding, Teller!' Selby, lying on the floor, said with a grin. 'Keep it up!' and with that he slithered out over the coaming.

On the bridge, Marston and Channing were behind pillow-case sandbags, but crouched high enough to see the shoreline out of the bridge windscreens. Everyone else was on the floor, except the quartermaster on the helm. This was Clubs, the ship's physical education instructor. Further across on the starboard side, Sally Wallace, the Officer of the Watch, sneaked a look out at the river and then dropped down again. Hang on, she thought. Something didn't look right. What was that? She popped up again. 'Captain, boats approaching!' she yelled. 'Upriver, dead ahead!'

They pounded in through the last few yards, the ground burning under their feet, the once-verdant riverbank now a smoking, churned, muddy, blackened charnel house. At the base of the sangar was a defilade, a natural depression which offered almost complete protection, and they dropped into it.

McLean, his heart pounding, drew great draughts of air into his lungs, and looked out behind them as the last of them came in. The depression was full of people, exhausted, muddy, wet, filthy, many wounded, moaning, some crying – relief, pain – finally giving up to it. Sloth was one of the last, carrying Sister Jo, followed by Furby as tail-end Charlie, the Padre over his shoulder. He was moving slower, his legs going, but then he was up again, finally putting the Padre carefully down. He fell into the cover of the sangar.

To the right, Lowry's 3 Troop were already positioning their guns to defend that flank.

McLean looked out over the hundred yards of brown, swirling water at HMS *Winchester*. Her upper decks were wreathed in cordite smoke, her small, close-in weapon systems pouring out suppression fire. Christ, she's big! he thought. Big and beautiful, and I have never been so pleased to see anything in my life!

'Sea boats approaching, sir!' Willis yelled.

A face appeared in the entrance hole to the sangar and a cheery voice called, ''Allo, lads!' But he was pulled bodily back and another marine slithered out of the hole.

'Major McLean? Connors, sir. Zulu. Four Five. Nice to see you all. Sir, this is a clusterfuck. If your people are ready, let's get them aboard and get the fuck out of here.'

'Right,' McLean said, taking it all in. There had been a hell of a fight here. Bodies littered the bush, and he could see the spent ammo casings in the base of the sangar and the tired state of the marines who had defended the staging post.

'You have done well, Sergeant Connors. You and your men. Sergeant Willis?' Willis slithered over. 'Your gimmpy and one 3-Troop gun to Connors. Your lads relieve the sangar. Sergeant Connors, your lads away first. Get yourselves back in the stern, up high somewhere and set up your guns to give suppression fire. Once you're ready and we can keep everyone's heads down, the civvies away. Then my blokes, OK? That Clansman working?'

Connors had seen himself and his men there till the end, and he rankled slightly, but knew better than to argue with a company commander. He nodded through bloodshot eyes. 'Yes, it's OK.'

'Boats, sir!' someone called. The noise was incredible – a cacophony of gunfire, explosions, and acrid smoke wreathed through the air. The civvies were lying low, huddled down, arms covering faces and heads, terrified as the gunfire tore over their heads. Sloth looked over at the Padre. Still deaf and concussed, he was kneeling over someone on the ground. Furby. Sloth crawled over.

Furby had been hit several times, his shirt and trousers wet with blood and he was gasping for breath. 'Fuck no! No! Gubby! Gubby!' He pulled his shell dressing out and tried to get at the wounds in Furby's chest. 'Please, no?' he called out appealing to anyone who would listen. 'He's my mate. Jesus!' The Padre was trying to do something lower down, and he looked up at Sloth, who was crying with frustration and anger as emotions tore through him. Through his dulled senses, he understood one man's love for another in its truest sense, that between brothers-in-arms. Woven through it, the futility of war, the horror of it, the nobility of sacrifice, the selfless courage of this young man, who had been mortally wounded carrying him to safety. Gubby pulled them both back and went to it.

'Let's do it!' McLean snapped. 'I'll let 'em know what we are doing.'

The 2-Troop marines scrambled into the sangar to relieve

Connors' men, who slithered down through the mud in the depression towards the water and the incoming seaboat.

The 2- and 3-Troop men poured out fire at a tremendous rate, caring nothing for conserving ammunition now. Even the mortarmen got into the action, their tubes pointed almost straight up to drop the bombs in close, sixty yards out in the bush, as their colleagues swept Furby up, piled into the two boats and raced way. The boats were drawing fire, but they were the ultimate moving target, accelerating away very quickly and ducking in behind the *Winchester*'s stern.

'Take it with the gun, sir?'

'No!' Channing snapped, watching the heavy, steel barge chug up the river towards them, thinking that its old engine must have been going flat out to give her enough speed over the ground in the seven-knot current to make any headway at all. It was still half a mile away.

'It's too close to the channel. The current will carry it as it is sinking, and if it goes down in there, we'll never get out of here. Maybe that's his intent. If he moves any closer to the bank we can take it.' Rounds hit the bridge again, this time shattering windows weakened by previous strikes. Everyone ignored the falling perspex.

'First boat's coming inboard, sir.'

'Very well. Mr Marston, how close is that barge to the channel?'

Marston looked away from the sightlines he was using on the bank 'Very, sir. Another fifty feet to port and he's smack in it.' Back to the job of keeping *Winchester* stable in the current, looking through the gyrocompass, taking bearings on the shoreline. 'Thirty-five on both.'

'Aye aye, thirty-five on both.'

'OOW, keep an eye on it. The other two could be line astern.'

'Sir.'

'First marines are aboard, sir. Boats are standing by to go back once they are in position.'

'Thirty on both,' Marston called to the QM.

'Very well.' From the Captain.

The boats could take eight people each, but they crammed them in, each boat with civilians and marines – ten in total – the marines returning fire at the shoreline over the inflatable walls. Sister Jo had Shagger beside her. As they turned round in *Winchester*'s shadow, da Silva grinned like a pirate.

On the ship, Connors had the two machine guns set up high where they could dominate the fight as they raked the shoreline. There was far more fire coming from the marines and the ship now. It was almost as if the Unita men in the jungle knew they had lost their prize. The second trip six minutes later was almost uneventful, and as the boats ran back into the beach for the last sixteen men, Kevin pointed out at the water where the big, steel barge was now only two hundred yards from the ship. Armed men were aboard, standing round the wheelhouse.

McLean nodded, understanding immediately why Channing hadn't engaged it.

'Popeye, your gun in this boat. You two' – he pointed at Sloth and Dave Hobson – 'with me.' Where's Furby? he was thinking. 'Sergeant Willis, on the helm. Mr Harvey, LAWs. Everyone else in the other boat and back to the ship. Let's go!'

The *Winchester*'s coxswain was unceremoniously bundled into the second boat and both boats pushed off together, Willis immediately turning his boat downriver and opening the throttle flat out, Kevin already lying in the bow, his GPMG set up, pointing at the barge. He opened fire in measured bursts. Sloth and Hobson dropped either side of him, while aft the CSM opened out an LAW tube. They had humped them the better part of fifty miles and now they would at last be useful. Someone on the barge began to shoot back at them.

'The big one. Hit 'em,' McLean snapped to the CSM. 'When we get there, everyone board and fire at will. Do not let them scuttle it!'

CSM Harvey stood up, leant on Willis's shoulders, and sighted the LAW.

'Steady the boat!'

Willis corrected his weaving approach, and he resighted and fired. The rocket seared away over the heads of the men in the bows, and sixty metres away slammed into the wheelhouse of the barge with a massive blast. They seemed to cover the last yards in seconds, because Willis was suddenly pulling the power off, and they were nudging the rusty sides of the barge. Sloth and Hobson were up and firing over the top, spraying bullets everywhere till Kevin could get the gimmpy up.

McLean was over first, followed by Willis. Unita men – deafened, dazed or hurt by the LAW missile strike – failed to see them in time and went down as the two marines opened fire. Sloth and Hobson followed, racing back to the wheelhouse.

The two smaller boats were bearing away now, but Sloth's eyes were on the last of the Unita men, and he took them down with four sighted shots. 'Secure forward!' Harvey bellowed. He was up in the bows, still holding the painter from the sea boat.

'Secure midships!' from Willis.

'Secure aft!' Sloth yelled.

'Well done! Sergeant Willis, steer this thing into the bank over there. Rest of you, engage those other boats. Keep them moving away.'

Sloth looked out at the retreating boats. There in the stern looking back was a man – huge, colossal, with presence. That's him. That's – He swung his rifle up and, controlling his breathing, fired a single shot, but the man was gone. The huge frame had just dropped from sight.

As the sea boat was hoisted inboard, an officer looked at McLean.

'I'm Selby, Exec. Captain's compliments. He is on the bridge.' McLean nodded.

'My people?'

'Civvies and wounded all below. Your other blokes are in the hangar winding down. We're getting clean kit and showers organised for them, and the galley will be open in about an hour,' he said, and looked at the CSM. 'Don't worry. I'll get them properly fed and watered later, but there's egg-and-bacon sarnies and hot chai coming up, and later the Supply Officer will allocate a bunk on a mess deck.'

'Thanks. Do me a favour?' McLean asked.

'Name it,' Selby responded.

McLean spoke to Captain Lowry, Willis and the CSM, then moved forward to find his way up to the bridge, while down below two men were already opening the big fridges in the PO's mess, and cases of cold beer were being pulled out for delivery to the hangar.

McLean moved up the steep stairs, cleared the coaming at the top of the hatch and stepped on to the bridge. It seemed busy. Four officers, a yeoman, .two ratings, and a quartermaster were all there. The shattered plexiglass had been cleared away, but the pillowcase sandbags were still in place, and a stocky figure was sitting in the Captain's chair facing the other way.

'Permission to enter the bridge?' McLean called.

'Yes, please,' from Sally Wallace.

Channing turned to face the unfamiliar voice. The man he saw was in filthy green camouflage trousers, wet, red-mud-splattered boots and a green T-shirt underneath belt order. His stubbly face was still covered in the remnants of cam cream, the blond hair beneath his Royal Marines green beret matted and full of grass and dirt. His eyes were red-rimmed with fatigue, and dried blood crusted his T-shirt. His suntanned arms were bare and he was lean, with no thin layer of fat under the skin, so every vein stood out. He was still carrying a rifle, an AK47, and everyone turned to look at him for a second or two, even the quartermaster on the little wheel. He looked like shit, he knew, but their look wasn't seeing that. The looks were seeing someone back from the dead, someone who had no right to be there at all, someone given up for lost by many of them. It was curious, appraising, real interest – fascination almost.

Channing grinned and stood up, offering his hand. 'Dr Livingstone, I presume?'

They walked out on to the bridge wing, Matadi passing away to their left, and McLean looked back towards the pool. Smoke rose up. The bush was burning, plumes of smoke spiralling into the sky, and out behind that – he knew – bodies littering the bush after a forty-five-mile ongoing contact.

He pointed back. 'The Ambassador in Kinshasa. He told the Minister of whatever that we would be twenty-four hours there and back. No one would ever know we were there.'

'Ha!' Channing barked. 'No one would ever know you were there? Christ!' he said with a grin, looking back at the smoke. 'You could hardly miss it!'

There was a pause and McLean took the offered cigarette. 'Thanks,' he said. 'For coming to get us.'

'Pleasure.' He pulled out a lighter. 'I need to report,' Channing said, flicking his Zippo. 'We have your wounded below, but how many of them are back there?'

'Seventeen.'

'Jesus!' Channing said softly. 'I've two dead, six wounded. Why? Do you know why?'

'Diamonds,' McLean replied. 'Makuma thinks we had diamonds.'

'You been having a lovely walkies then?' A female rating was bent over, rubbing Shagger's ear. 'What's his name?' she asked one of the marines – still filthy, but now beaming from ear to ear, lolling back with his second cold can of beer in his hand. 'Shagger,' he replied. 'Be careful or you'll soon see why.'

'Nonsense. He's a lovely boy,' she retorted.

'Bollocks,' he replied. 'That is a hard-core, salty Royal Marine.'

'He is that,' a woman's voice said. 'Real Gucci kit.' They looked around. It was Sister Jo, now carrying a huge tray of food, her cup of tea perched on one end of the tray. 'Can't sleep. Can I join you?' she asked, her eyes on Sloth for a full second. He looked at her as she dropped down beside him.

By 0900 *Winchester* was well below Matadi and powering

her way towards the coast. The marines had been billeted below, the port and starboard watches now hot bunking to free up space for them. The nuns were in the women's mess. Doctor Carter had grabbed a couple of hours sleep and was now scrubbed up and with Gubby, the ship's LMA and the Australian dentist. The four of them were going to work, about to perform surgery on patients now stabilised. The list was long, and they would work on two tables – Penny and the dentist on the operating theatre table in the wardroom, assisted by Sister Jo, and the other two down in the sickbay, working on less serious cases. Furby was dead. His body had given up the fight before he made it below. He had been hit six times, and how he had managed to run the last few yards carrying another man, no one knew.

Nellie Tusker, on the critical list, was up first. Delivered up to them, he was in the passage outside the wardroom, where Penny came out to get him. As she stepped out, she saw a female rating lean over the pale form.

Jenny Teller looked down at him. 'Oi, you,' she said softly. 'Wake up, you soft git.' He opened his eyes, and even heavily sedated, he took her in and smiled.

'You fancy me, don't you? I know you do. Go on. Admit it,' she teased.

He nodded. 'Guilty,' he whispered.

'Well, if you don't get well, how you gonna take me out, then?' He smiled weakly and nodded and closed his eyes.

'That was sweet of you,' Penny said, aware of the non-fraternisation rules, but also aware of the effect that positive attitude could have on survival rates.

'I meant it,' Jenny said with a smile and walked away. She was riding high. The Captain had already spoken to her. He would use every contact he could, every influence he had, to see her accepted into a Navy-funded university degree programme to prepare her for training as a Weapons Engineering Officer.

That evening, the ship now in the open Atlantic, McLean was doing the rounds of his wounded, and Dalton, lying in a

bunk with his legs bandaged, called him over. 'That little –
ah – incident at the mission with your radio chap. I won't be
filing a complaint against him. I feel a bit of a prick, to tell
you the truth.' McLean just nodded. He was miles way.

'You OK?' Dalton asked.

'Yeah. Just wondering if Maneru got home OK. He was –
he was great.'

'I hope so,' Dalton relied. 'It was something he needed to
do. He was down in Katanga in the sixties. He was a Simba.
He needed to work it off. Pay back somehow.'

'Well, he did that.'

One deck up, Sloth was cleaning Furby's kit before he
handed it over to Company admin, and found the woman's
watch he had seen Furby pull from the dead Unita man's wrist.
It was still encrusted with dried blood and needed a wash.

Three minutes later, Sloth knocked on the wardroom door.
It was now back to its original purpose, and there were a dozen
officers in there, waiting for the first sitting at the table. Doctor
Carter was there, a glass of wine in her hand, and she was called
to the door where the marine waited.

'The LMA thought this might be yours, marm.' He held up
the watch, now clean.

'It is,' she said, one hand to her mouth. 'Where did you—?'
She looked up at him.

'Best not ask,' he replied. She was so pleased to see it again,
she wanted to cry.

The following day, the Padre, his ears still ringing, held
a drumhead service on the landing deck. During the night a
rating, one of the wounded, had died, and the service was
a funeral – a remembrance for each of those who had died,
starting with Sister Mary Stuanides of the mission at Tenta, and
finishing with Furby. It was also a thanksgiving for those who
had survived. As people filed away, Chops Roberts, ever one
to take his responsibilities seriously, cornered the marines.

'Now, come on, fellas. Who wants a raffle ticket, then?
Draw tonight. Great prizes.'

An hour later, McLean was walking the weather deck and

came across Sister Marie-Claire. She looked at him as he took a place at the rail beside her.

'So, Sister. What now for you?'

'Oh, I'll be going back,' she said with a smile, turning to look at him.

'To Tenta?'

'Yes,' she replied. 'To Tenta. It wasn't the local people that did it, and even if it had been, then if it was good enough for Christ to die doing his work, then it is good enough for me. Besides, if every missionary ran away every time there was trouble, where would our faith be? There's a time for everything, Major McLean. A time to move on, to heal' – she looked at him again – 'and a time to forgive.'

'Some things are difficult to forgive.'

'Then it will have value when you do.'

The civilians and marines were put ashore in Freetown, Sierra Leone. The civvies were booked on an Air France flight to Charles de Gaulle and an RAF C130 was waiting to take the marines home. On the dock where people were boarding buses for the airport, Sister Jo sought out the man she was looking for.

They had seen little of each other on the ship. On different mess decks, and with little reason to spend time together, their differing lives had dawn them apart.

'I wanted to thank you,' she said.

'Can't we—' he began, but she cut him off. 'No. No, we can't.' But her eyes said, if I ever did, it would be you. She took something from her pocket and pushed it into his hands, closing them around it with her own. His heart pounded at her touch. It was warm, soft, gentle, silky. 'Take care of yourself. I'll remember you. Always.' She turned and walked way.

It was ten days later that da Silva arrived back at his site. Most of the canvas camp was still there, and the men were back, working slowly under their local foreman, and eagerly hoping for da Silva's return, since he still had their last pay packets in his pocket. The machinery was back too. He said his hellos and caught up on progress, and half an hour later, he went to his tent, the first time he had seen it in daylight since he had originally left for Kinshasa over two weeks before. Some of his stuff had been taken, but his servant had remade the camp bed, washed his clothes, and tidied up. There on the bedside table was an envelope. It hadn't been there when he had looked in through the flap on his last, fleeting visit. He looked at the servant, an old man, who pointed at the floor beneath the table where he had found it.

In the envelope was a letter in English, in small, neat, familiar writing. It was from André, the young Swiss miner whose body had been recovered from the mine the week before.

> Darling,
> I missed you! By an hour or so, I missed you. I wanted some of your loving tonight, you big, hairy beast, you! Anyway. You are up in K, and so I shall go back to Tenta. Ooh, look after something for me, will you? There's a rumour among the staff that we are going to be robbed, and I don't want to lose my share of what we have won from the river. It's in the hollow in the tree where you first had me! I'll collect it next week from you. Be good, or if not, be impressive!
>> Lots of love
>> Andre

He put the letter in his pocket, pushed thoughts of the lithe, young, blond man from his mind and walked back into the bush behind the camp, to the place where he and André had stopped during their walk the first day he had visited the camp.

It was where he said it would be, in the hollow in the tree's root structure. A small package wrapped in newspaper. He took it and hefted it. Heavy. His heart pounded and he went pale. Oh no. Jesus, no. He unrolled the newspaper and then opened the simple, muslin, drawstring bag. It was full of mostly industrial quality rough diamonds, but in among them were half a dozen of what looked to him like large, good, clear jeweller's quality stones. He didn't know what they were worth, but it was a lot.

Oh, André, what did you do to us? You weren't to know, but you – he tailed off then, realising he was only talking to himself and a dead man.

Dalton took leave and spent the next week relaxing, recuperating, getting round on crutches, and at times picking up Sister Mary's journal and reading it. The most recent addition to the little bits and pieces of memorabilia was a page from a magazine. Only a month or so old, written in Greek, it was obviously a light interview piece looking at a day in the life of the interviewee, with each hour in bold and some text below. There was a photograph of Sister Mary at the mission, surrounded by smiling children. He put it back and began to concentrate on the handwritten entries, but struggled. He begged the services of a translator from the paper's list and it took her four days, but she translated the Greek pieces, putting a typed translation into each section of the journal.

'Look, usually I just translate, you know, but this – Where did it come from?'

'The Congo,' he replied.

'It's not yours?'

Dalton shook his head.

'Take care of it,' she said. 'It's all to the same person. It's – it's love letters,' she said. 'Quite beautiful in places. Made me cry. The rest of it – it's like, like nothing I ever read before. It's quite beautiful – simple, humbling, like you are seeing into her soul. Such honesty, such faith. I'd like to meet her.' Then she got all businesslike again. 'I work for publishers, simpatico people. This, they would love. If your people – I – Just it would be so easy to cock this up, you know? It should go to Virago, or—'

'You won't meet her,' Dalton interrupted. 'She's dead. And

this' – he had made his decision, no one was seeing the journal, it was too personal, too private – 'this isn't for publication.'

He took it home, and with a pot of coffee on the warmer and a bottle of Scotch on the side table, he began to read. The last entry was on the morning of the attack.

Vous,

It's been some weeks since I wrote, but as usual, you have been in my thoughts daily. Once, as I have said so often, I worried about this, about all this thinking about you, this obsession, this love I feel for you – it is not as it should be for one with my vocation. But as the time has gone by, it has concerned me less, for my love of my Lord is no less. If anything, it's stronger, because now I understand how He loves us, loves us all.

I think sometimes that it was His will that brought us together, that fleeting moment all those years ago. It certainly gave me balance, gave me something warm, something decent, a nice feeling when I thought about you, all these years hence. I hope it did for you.

I am fearful, *vous*. We received word last night, a warning to us that armed men are coming, that we will be attacked. I am the only one here who remembers last time, so perhaps I understand the implications better than the others. I sometimes think that that memory is a curse, but then remember you from the same time, clear like it was yesterday, and I would part with that memory for nothing but the Lord himself, for that would mean parting with you, and I would rather bear the scars of that which brought us together, and still have *vous*.

If they come, they will come. You will not be here this time, and the Lord's will be done.

My time is over soon, anyway, my darling. I know he wants me back with him and I take strength from that. But what of *vous*? Who with mortal flesh and blood will love you then? For we all need that. I shall be with you, watching over you as you sleep, there for you as you were for me. I hope you are happy, Henri. I hope your life has been as good as mine. You will never know the pleasure of knowing you, the way your eyes light up when you smile, the decency, the strength that lies within you.

You will never know how just knowing you, knowing you were out there somewhere, perhaps looking at the same moon as I, just how much strength that gave me when times were hard. I would think of you, the way you look when you smile, and I would smile too. So, for me, you were not in conflict with my faith, you were part of it. You were from God as much as the bees and the flowers and the rains.

Maybe I will write again, maybe not. If not, then this is a parting well made. Sleep sweetly, my prince. I shall love you forever. *Toujours vous, toujours.*

Three days later there was a knock on his door. A man stood there – iron-grey hair, his back ramrod straight.

'Mr Perrin Dalton?'

'Yes.'

'I am 'Enri Lefage.'

Dalton was stunned. All efforts at the paper to track him down had failed, and he was despairing of finding any trace of the man so loved, so quietly, for so long by Mary Stuanides.

Lefage stayed there for two hours, and as he was leaving, Dalton stood up, went into the study of the borrowed flat and came out with the journal.

'This,' he said, 'was Sister Mary's.' He held it out. 'It's for – it's for *vous*.'

'Anyway, if there is anything I can do . . .' Lefage noticed the French, but didn't comment, and left with the journal in a Harrods shopping bag. At the door he turned and looked at Dalton.

'There is a small service,' Lefage replied, thinking, Your people failed to find me but maybe they weren't trying very hard. 'Perhaps you, with your experience in Africa, you can 'elp. How do I go about finding someone in Africa?'

'Who?'

Lefage told him.

He had been there when the aircraft landed. Standing away to one side, away from the throng of press and relatives, a lonely-looking man in a light coat, defence against the evening chill. It took him just three hours to find McLean's address, but after the visit with Dalton he spent time with the journal reading and rereading it, understanding Dalton's use of the word *vous*, the link with Mary stronger by the day – seeing, delighting, taking great comfort in her feelings for him, however unconsummated.

One day, while out driving, he found himself drawn up a tiny single-lane track in Sussex. At the top was a tiny, ancient church that nestled at the foot of the South Downs. He stopped the car and walked through the churchyard. The church, at Didling, was a fair distance from any house and was normally locked to prevent vandalism and theft, but that morning there had been a Christening and the man with the key had yet to come back and lock up, so when Lefage tried the door, it opened and he went inside, went into a church for the first time in nearly forty years.

He found himself sitting in a pew, one of only a dozen or so. Sitting thinking about his life, about Mary, something odd began to happen, and he found himself in prayer for the first time in his life. He found faith.

Three weeks later, after a doctor's appointment, he drove down to Taunton and knocked on McLean's door.

It was answered by a woman, the doctor who was with them, he recognised her immediately.

'I am sorry to disturb you. Major McLean. He is in?'

'No. Sorry. He's at work. Back at about eight, he said.'

'You are Doctor Carter?'

'Yes.'

'I think you may have known a friend of mine, Sister Mary, at the mission at Tenta.'

She was a woman, and had been a doctor long enough to know when someone wanted to talk, wanted to reach out. 'Please come in,' she said.

'You were at the mission. You knew her? Worked with her?'

'Yes. Yes, I did.'

They talked, Lefage mostly, Penny skilfully drawing it out of him. He seemed in pain at times, and not just emotional pain. Talked of another time long ago in another country, of a beautiful, Greek girl with huge, dark eyes, and a heart full of compassion and love for her fellow man, and a young soldier who met her on a riverbank and fell instantly in love with her. An hour later they were sitting with wine at the kitchen table. At one point he looked at his watch and took some tablets out of his pocket, two little bottles. As he took one from each, she looked at him.

'May I?'

He nodded and she looked at the labels and then gave them back to him.

'When I left, I thought we would meet again, as you do when you are young. Have you ever lost someone you loved?'

'Yes.' She looked at him. 'Yes, I have,' she replied. 'But I was lucky. I found him again.'

'It is precious, is it not?'

'It is.'

He smiled. 'You were lucky. I was once. The cross she gave me. It protected me, guarded me. I had an angel after that. I worked as a soldier for another twenty-four years, on and off. Some things you would have heard about, others no one ever knew were going on – going into places, going into trouble that should have seen me dead. I worked with Hoare, Dennard, Schramme. I was charmed. The others called me Lucky.' He smiled, looking at her. 'And always I thought about her. I bought a business in Corsica, a Renault garage. Then others, there, here in England. Always thought that one day we would meet again. Now she is dead.'

'But you are not. You must go on,' Penny said. 'Put this behind you.'

'No,' he said. 'It is not that easy.'

'Henri, you need to know this. Maybe it will help. She didn't have long. She had a melanoma and was very ill by the time Makuma's men came.'

He smiled bleakly. A fleeting grimace. The reference in the letter, the last entry. They talked for a while longer and then he looked at her and lifted his glass.

'*C'est la vie, c'est la guerre,*' and drank the contents in one slug. 'I must go.'

He took her hand and kissed it, in an old-fashioned, gallant kind of way, 'Thank you, Doctor.'

When McLean got home, Penny told him about their visitor. 'He wants to talk to you.'

'Why? There's nothing I can tell him that hasn't been documented in the press.'

'Just call him. It's important,' Penny said. Why? he was thinking. Christ, I just want to forget the whole thing ever happened. 'Call him, OK?' she continued. 'It won't take long and it's important to him.' She looked at him. 'Look, Doug, he's dying. He's got cancer. He's like an old bull elephant going back in time, back over his journeys. Just phone him, OK?'

McLean phoned him the next day, but Lefage didn't want to talk about Sister Mary or 1964. He wanted to know about Makuma.

McLean told him what he could and finished by saying, 'In all honesty, I know I shouldn't say this, but if I saw him walking down the street, I'd kill him – and I would feel nothing but satisfaction.'

Later that evening Lefage found Sloth and Kevin at the White Horse. He recognised them immediately – the haircuts, the way they stood. Soldiers. He walked over and stood by them, bought them a drink and began to talk about the Congo, two generations of soldiers blooded on the same red soil.

'We got Ndube,' Sloth said. 'He was the second-in-command. Nasty little shit. Furby slotted him. But Makuma got away.' Sloth paused, and then added pointedly, 'The pisser is that he's going to get away with it.'

'I'd slot the cunt,' Kevin said. ''E's a fucking nutter.'

Lefage smiled fleetingly like he knew something they didn't. 'Can you tell me about it? Makuma. I want to know all you can tell me about him.'

'We're going into a club in town now, but tomorrow?' Kevin looked at Sloth, who nodded. 'Lunch time, maybe? Here?'

Lefage nodded.

Sloth and Kevin left and went to the Ace of Spades, where all the 2-Troop survivors were gathered. Furby's little brother had come down, and many of 3 Troop were there as well, and guys from 1 and Support who had known Grandad and the Love Machine. They had waited till now for those in hospital to rejoin the unit, and just before midnight the DJ played the Verve's 'Bitter Sweet Symphony'. No one danced, badly or otherwise. No one. People knew.

When the song finished, a nineteen-year-old bootie from Support saw a girl he fancied and talked to her and danced with her and bought her a drink with an umbrella, and Sloth smiled. But it was a sad, wistful smile, that of a man remembering another girl in another place, and he sometimes touched the cross he now wore round his neck, the gift she had given him. She was back there now, with Shagger, who would never have liked cold, wet England. He was an African dog.

Angola

Four months later a rumour moved around Luanda. A story about a white man who, with two others, had walked into a small shanty beer seller in Lubango, a place knocked up from old corrugated iron, hammered-out kerosene tins and plywood car crates. It would have been called a shebeen anywhere else, full of men drinking, some drunk already – blowsy, fly-blown women who would service their needs for a few coins moving around them. The place went quiet as he entered. This was unusual. There had never been a white man in this place let alone three, not down this end of Lubango.

The old one looked around, found the man he wanted, pulled out a gun and shot him six times, the last two into his head as he lay dying in the spit, snot, spilt beer and cigarette ends on the filthy dirt floor. The other two had pulled out guns and stood facing the room, ready to kill also.

With the final shot the killer spat in the dead man's face, and if any of the drinkers were better travelled, they might have known it to be a particularly Corsican thing to do. The dead man's name was Makuma.

The man who shot him escaped with his friends, some said like a chimera. He was just gone, never seen again. Lucky, others said, for this was a Unita stronghold, and although the man who died was out of favour, nevertheless he was a lifelong Unita supporter, and a once-senior commander with the military wing, who would have had many comrades never very far away who would have avenged him. Or so they thought.

No one missed him. No one cared. If anything, many, upon hearing of his death, celebrated.

It was about this time, mid-August, that Kevin and Sloth returned to Taunton from a three-week holiday, taking in, they said, Botswana and Zimbabwe.

Henri Lefage, one of the last of the Wild Geese, died seven months later of cancer of the colon. He chose not to die in England, where he had lived for the last ten years, or Corsica, his home, but in Greece, in a place called Heraklion, where he had become friendly with the two sisters and brother of a woman who they barely knew. She had joined the Dominicans and gone off to Africa. They exchanged stories, the Frenchman always interested in hearing of their childhood and what Mary was like as a teenager before she went away. Beautiful, her sister said. She had many men of the village who came courting, but she saw none of them. Her life was chosen for her. When she died they had a plot prepared for her, as they did for all of them, but the body never came home, so there was just a headstone.

He worked with the Dominicans and the Greek Embassy in Kinshasa, and had her body exhumed from its grave in the red

earth at the mission at Tenta and flown back to Greece, back
to Heraklion, where she was buried in the family plot.

They would sit and play chess, talk, eat olives and bread
and drink local wine – and when the sun dropped he would
walk up to the small cemetery and sit by her grave.

In no time he became known to all the villagers, a familiar
sight, always wearing a faded red bandanna round his neck.

He died in the front bedroom of her younger sister's house,
the house they had all been born in. Just never woke up. The
family, with the deep understanding and wisdom of old people,
knew that for the Frenchman their sister had been more than a
nun in a mission, for round his neck he wore the crucifix their
mother and father had given her the day she left the village.
They had grown to know him and like him, and knew he had
no one. So when he died they called the priest and buried him
in their family plot next to Mary.

Lefage's estate, substantial by any standards, was split. One
third went to the Sisters of the Dominican order for their work
in Africa. One third went to a Royal Marines widows and
orphans benevolent fund set up in the name of Mary Stuanides,
in its first five years to be administered jointly by the 3rd
Commando Brigade and the Padre of 40 Commando. Also
to be included in that covenant were the families of the three
French aircrew who had died in their helicopter. The last third
went to the church in Heraklion, because the roof leaked.

Perrin Dalton, who for decency's sake waited till Lefage had
died, wrote a book which was condensed into a compelling,
serialised feature piece for the Saturday edition. It was a retrospective on the incident at Tenta, a retrospective drawn around
the lives of two of the people involved, and finished with
pictures of the two graves in Heraklion. Widely syndicated,
it won acclaim for its sensitive investigative journalism.

After that story went out, it could be said that there was
sufficient in the fund so that the roof would never leak again,
and yet within six months, another very substantial amount
of money was put into the three funds, this time from an
anonymous but generous benefactor in Portugal.